Collision of Evil

Collision of Evil

A NOVEL

John J. Le Beau

Oceanview Publishing

IPSWICH, MASSACHUSETTS

Copyright © 2009 by John J. Le Beau

FIRST EDITION

ISBN: 978-1-933515-54-0

Published in the United States of America by Oceanview Publishing, Ipswich, Massachusetts
www.oceanviewpub.com

2 4 6 8 10 9 7 5 3 1

PRINTED IN THE UNITED STATES OF AMERICA

To my mother, Edith, my aunt Jane, and my late father, Lawrence, all of whom have provided a ceaseless fountain of affectionate support and wise counsel.

Acknowledgments

It goes without saying that any faults of fact or fiction in this novel are the author's alone, but its measure of accuracy owes much to the wise counsel of a number of others. The development of this book was greatly enhanced by frequent and wide-ranging conversations with a number of terrorism specialists in the academic field, most notably Professors Nick Pratt and Christopher Harmon, both active in the counterterrorism program of the George C. Marshall Center for International and Security Studies, located in Garmisch-Partenkirchen, Germany. Both of them have decades of counterterrorism experience to draw on, and both were entirely generous in sacrificing their time and offering their thoughts as valuable background for this enterprise. In Nick's case, collegiality extended to sharing a windblown tent in the frigid temperatures of winter in Afghanistan. As well, John Sawicki, a fine friend and confidant, was instrumental in helping me move this work along from a series of rough thoughts to its present form.

I salute as well the many necessarily anonymous counterterrorism practitioners with whom I have had the privilege to engage with over the years. Their commitment, energy, and deeds largely play out in the shadows of an invisible landscape, and the accolades they merit are all the greater for that.

Finally, I am indebted to the team at Oceanview Publishing for their professionalism, interest in this book, and genuine helpfulness throughout the publication process. Their friendly and inclusive attitude is surely the binding mortar of teamwork, and is, by my lights, no small virtue.

Collision of Evil

SALZBURG, AUSTRIA, JUNE 2003

Judged by the discriminating standards of Salzburg, Austria, the neighborhood was without charm and of slightly shabby appearance, with three-story concrete apartment buildings of no distinction facing onto an unremarkable street. It was late on a July afternoon in 2003, a day when brief bursts of sunlight competed with sudden passing showers, when a bomb weighing five hundred pounds was discovered by construction workers laboring on a building site. The deadly cargo was not the creation of Islamic terrorists and had, in fact, been manufactured in the United States.

This explosive device was of venerable pedigree, one of hundreds of bombs dropped over Salzburg by the U.S. Army Air Force in 1944, as World War II wound down in its last convulsions. The other bombs dropped on that long-ago summer afternoon had exploded on impact, leveling entire apartment blocks, railroad facilities, and warehouses of Wehrmacht military stores while at the same time ending scores of lives, young and aged, military and civilian.

This particular bomb, however, had not exploded with its siblings due to the vagaries of its construction and the soil conditions at the spot where it landed. Instead, the heavy metal, finned cylinder had burrowed deep into a muddy lot where it slept, the path of its travel and its subterranean lair concealed by earth and debris.

The bomb continued its marathon sleep through the end of the war in 1945, the reconstruction of Salzburg in the early 1950s, the filming of *The Sound of Music* in the 1960s, and decades of concerts at the Salzburg Music Festival. Over time, most of the combatants who had fought in the war, for which the bomb was intended, died of natural causes. Year after year, hundreds of tourists visiting this handsome Austrian city strolled along a sidewalk only yards away from the concealed explosive, oblivious to its lethargic but lethal presence.

The explosive package, its frame rusted and matted with deep brown earth, was only uncovered in 2003 as a backhoe dug a cellar hole for a new, architecturally prosaic building. Three bomb disposal specialists from the Austrian Department of the Interior were called and set about defusing the bomb. Something in the procedure went unaccountably wrong, however, and the antique device was shaken from its half century of slumber, exploding with a massive flash and accompanying roar sufficient to destroy nearby automobiles, damage apartments on the street, and shatter windows a kilometer away.

The low, growling report of the explosion was heard by tourists at the Salzburg Fortress on a hill above the city. Many of the tourists were American, like the bomb itself, and were unaware of the provenance of the sound, imagining it to be alpine thunder. Of the three Austrians working to defuse the device, two were instantly killed, indeed atomized, and the third suffered severe wounds. Although none of these men had been alive in 1944, they were, in a very real sense, victims of the Second World War.

The American crew that had dropped the bomb in the mid-twentieth century would never have believed their air raid would reap victims unborn at the time of their combat flight, in a future too distant and alien to be imagined. It is even likely that some member of the crew had visited Salzburg years after the war, both to listen to some Mozart and to contemplate once again those small, invariably personal events of wartime— "See that steeple, Ethel? I remember it. We came in low from the west, and Jimmy was trying to follow the river to guide in on the train station. We took flak from over that way—"

The explosion of the bomb on an otherwise quiet afternoon might suggest something more than the much-uttered truism that actions produce unanticipated consequences and that the past can reach out and grasp the present in an embrace not always benign.

Chapter 1

Charles Hirter felt a surge of freshness after his long morning shower and he studied himself in the mirror as he toweled his thick hair. Although not vain by nature, he concluded that he looked as well as he felt. The long days of backpacking through the mountainous Bavarian countryside had left him taut and tanned and with a reserve of energy that had become depleted prior to this much-anticipated vacation. Had someone been able to inform him that he would be dead before the day was done, his body a wreck of blood, shattered bone, and ripped tissue, Hirter would have branded the person insane as well as tasteless. Dressing quickly into casual clothes, he collected his wallet and room key and took the stairs down to the hotel breakfast room on the ground floor, looking forward to the continental buffet that would constitute his last meal.

He lingered over a cup of strong Tchibo coffee, toyed with the remains of a sunflower seed roll, and leafed idly through the sports section of the *International Herald Tribune*, grateful for the comfortable familiarity of letters strung together to form his mother tongue. A few minutes later, he continued his vacation ritual by rising from his table and wandering into the broad hotel lobby.

The Hotel Alpenhof was decorated in faux Old Bavarian style, not surprising in view of the hotel's location in the Upper Bavarian Alps a few miles from the Austrian border. In addition to an oversized fireplace, with logs burning day and night, the lobby contained much dark wood, a beamed ceiling, and terra cotta floor replete with handwoven country rugs. The walls were outfitted with early twentieth century romantic oil paintings depicting hunting scenes and rural landscapes. The rustic effect was enhanced by a row of antlers above the front desk and the folkloric *Trachten* outfits for the staff, male and female. Although some guests might have considered the overall effect too studied, a sort of Disney-does-Germany, Charles found the decorative embrace quite cozy.

A glance out the lobby picture window confirmed that the morning weather was sunny, although rainstorms had been predicted for late afternoon. Charles stretched, smiled at an attractive passing waitress, and decided he had better strike out while the weather held. He returned to his room for his hiking boots, backpack, and map and emerged from the hotel minutes later, rejoicing in the feel of the sun and the alpine landscape.

During the past two days Charles had explored the narrow valley, walking several kilometers a day, returning to his lodgings in the evening. The terrain consisted of grassy mountain meadows called *alm* by the Germans, interspersed with brooding expanses of dark pine forest, all of it crisscrossed by clear mountain streams, winding down from the summits above in serpentine patterns.

It was the mountains that interested Charles, and he consulted his creased topographical map for a sense of where to strike out. He traced his finger along a prospective route where the ground rose gradually. The map revealed a footpath that would take him through high meadows and eventually into a large stand of woods, which should then fall away to reveal dramatic dolomite peaks. Charles moved his eyes to the alpine massif above and formed an impression of where he was headed. "Okay," he muttered out loud, "up and back by nightfall." He noted he had left his rain poncho back in the room, but the skies were intensely blue with no hint of clouds and he decided to chance it. He cinched his nylon backpack straps tightly about his shoulders and started on his way.

At mid-morning it was warm, but not uncomfortable, in the direct sun; the afternoon promised to be warmer still, but Charles reasoned that he should reach the wooded heights by that time and the temperature would be cooler in the shade. He kept a steady pace, aware that once he had reached the peaks he would have to return as well. He still had another week of vacation ahead of him and intended to enjoy all of it, and had plans to visit nearby Salzburg if the weather turned inclement.

It was true that his vacation had not developed as originally planned. The trip had been the idea of Jeanette, his girlfriend of four years. The two of them had planned the details, sitting on the floor of his Newton, Massachusetts, apartment with glasses of wine and tourist brochures spread out before them. They had purchased two round-trip tickets from Boston to Munich at an excellent price six months in advance. Charles and Jeanette's enthusiasm for the trip had been intense, but in the intervening six months their enthusiasm for one another had waned.

Thinking about it as his boots dug into the rugged path, Charles concluded that there had been no single event that had ended their relationship. It was as if they were both positive magnets; they had come as close to one another as they could but could not bridge some final gap. By degree they had distanced until the time came for them to travel together. It had been Jeannette who had the courage to say that she had decided to forego the trip, using the pretext of needing to spend time with her aging parents. And so, he now found himself exploring the Alps alone.

Charles stopped for a moment to check his bearings. The hotel was out of sight and the path had taken him higher, into rocky meadowland flush with high grass. A herd of cows grazed nearby, noting his presence in their bovine way, but otherwise paying him no heed. Charles unclipped his water bottle and indulged in a long drink while observing that the sky had now darkened. Purple cloud banks were moving in silently, as if hoping to cover the sun by stealth. For a second Charles considered cutting short his trek and returning to the hotel, but he reasoned that the clouds might pass, and he did not want to spend the afternoon sipping beer in the hotel bar. Even if it rained, he concluded, that wouldn't kill him.

By one in the afternoon, it was obvious that the ascent was taking longer than anticipated due to the rough, untraveled route. Although the terrain remained open ground with a scattering of boulders, the grade was steep enough that his calves and ankles ached. More troubling was that the blue skies of morning had now been entirely vanquished and the clouds were of a brooding gun metal hue. Still, Charles thought, there might be a hut up ahead where he could wait out the storm. He moved on.

An hour later the first drops of rain pelted down with force. Within minutes the storm intensified, the water turning to hail, driven by a sudden wind and accompanied by a drop in temperature. "Shit" Charles muttered as he pulled a crumpled Boston Red Sox baseball cap from his backpack. He noted through waves of hail that the meadows gave way to a tree line up ahead, offering a prospect of protection. Breathing in deeply, he broke into a trot, skidding from time to time on the slick grass beneath his feet. He passed through the first row of pine trees and felt the cushioning carpet of needles under his boots. The assault of hail and rain diminished, absorbed by the tangle of branches above him.

It was dark in the woods. The sky, stripped of sun by the storm, and the thick forest filtered away most of the remaining light, and color was reduced to somber greens and browns. Leaning against the bark of a large tree, Charles pulled a Corny energy bar from his jeans and consumed it in slow bites while considering what to do. Before he finished with the snack, the first flash of lightning and the jolting report of thunder nearly threw him to the ground. The blast had struck somewhere very close, and he heard the unmistakable sound of shearing timber. It occurred to him that he was now in exactly the wrong place during a thunderstorm, and he felt a knot tighten in his stomach.

Searching for better shelter, Charles saw an outcropping of gray stone up ahead through the sentinel ranks of the trees. He forced his aching legs into motion and moved toward the rocks, slipped, and fell hard into the pine needles below, the contents of his backpack slamming into his spine. With effort, he raised himself from the dank surface and launched again toward the gray mass in front of him. Three minutes later he was at the outcropping and saw that its rough surface was the exposed base of the massif itself, thrusting up from the earth and forming an alpine peak high above. The stone was slick, rivulets of water cascading down from the torrent.

Another flash seared his eyes, the tear of a thunderclap reverberating off the rock before him. Charles pitched forward, cutting his cheek against the jagged stone. He was aware of his heart pumping heavily in his chest. The sting of the cold water in his eyes blurred his vision, and he grasped at the wall of stone with both hands, edging along it in a crab walk, hoping to find a crevice in its surface affording better shelter. An angry gust of wind stripped off his cap, but he did not try to retrieve it and continued following the stone outcropping like a blind man, his palms starting to bleed as they ran across the sharp, uneven surface.

He was suddenly aware that there was no longer a surface under his hands; the massif sheared away from him at a sharp angle. He moved to follow its contour again, crashing loudly through a maze of brush and fallen branches. A crevice he thought, just as he had hoped. He stumbled over loose slate and fell forward with enough force to drive the air from his lungs. Charles pulled himself up to a kneeling position. It was then that he was aware that it was no longer raining. At least, not raining on him. The sound of the storm was behind him but he was protected from its assault. Glancing up he saw darkness and understood that he had found a cave, as if a hole had been punched into the expanse of dolomite.

As his eyes focused, he was able to make out that his refuge was narrow but appeared deep. He twisted around and saw the forest and the cave entrance a foot or so behind him. He felt the talons of fear loosen their grip and he knew that he was safe from the elements; he could wait out the storm and return to the hotel after it had passed. He pulled the backpack off his shoulders and settled it at his knees, digging at it until he located the small plastic flashlight. Flicking it on, he played the beam of light around him.

He was in a rock arch, the natural ceiling perhaps seven feet above his head. The cave floor consisted of a scattering of pine needles blown in over time from the forest and a surface of pungent earth, its primordial smell filling his nostrils. Edging the light ahead of him he saw that the cave was indeed narrow but deep, disappearing into the distance. He left his backpack where it had dropped and decided to see how far the cave went; he might as well explore his find while the storm raged on. The walls were not uniform, at intervals bulging and receding from his path, but the passage remained sufficiently broad to permit him to navigate its length. He was surprised that after five minutes of walking the cave debouched into a rough chamber perhaps twenty feet across and fifty feet deep. But the pale, steady glare of his flashlight revealed more. At first, he was not certain what he was looking at.

A series of cubic shapes, perfect squares, were stacked across the chamber. Charles finally realized that the forms he was staring at were crates, their wooden planks heavy with dust. On some of the crates Charles could distinguish black stenciled numbers beneath the veneer of grime. *What have we here, deep in an alpine fastness*, he wondered as he moved forward to investigate, the recent perils of the storm forgotten.

Like a temper tantrum that had spent itself, the mountain thunderstorm hurled down the last of its fury before sputtering into a soft shower, the mass of clouds gradually thinning and drifting off. It was nearly dusk and such vestigial light as there was promised to be fleeting. The pine trees cast long shadows across the grasses and the rich greens of the alpine meadows were rendered richer still, enhanced by the magical, deep golden light of a summer's afternoon in noble decline. Somewhere, far below the craggy dolomite peaks, a cowbell rang as its charge meandered to a rude hut in the valley to spend its night.

Pushing aside the chaos of fallen branches and brush that had concealed the mouth of the cave, Charles emerged from his shelter, breathed deeply of the cold post-storm mountain air, and retraced his path back through the somber stand of pines, the woods alive with the sound of falling drops of water. The scent of spruce was overwhelming and Charles found it pleasant after the stale, claustrophobic air of the cavern. He stopped and noted his surroundings carefully, consulting his map. He would need to come back here to what he had discovered, and did not want to risk losing the location. Satisfied that he could find the cave again, Charles moved ahead, picking his way through the woods in the fading light. After twenty minutes of hiking, he could detect the brighter green of the meadow in the distance. He breathed easier and concluded that even if darkness descended before he reached the hotel, he should have no trouble navigating through the fields with the aid of his flashlight. The worst was behind him.

He continued to walk downward, the incline steep enough to cause him to shift his weight backward to avoid pitching forward. The nocturnal panorama of the valley spread out around him now and the first stars crept into a sky still not entirely surrendered to darkness. He found the path that had lead him from the valley floor and knew that he had simply to follow it down until he arrived at the hotel. Just a matter of one step at a time. A crudely erected timber fence embraced the meadow near the path and he moved to it, leaning his weight against the wood for a moment of rest before continuing on. He slipped off his backpack and indulgently stretched his taut muscles.

The force of the first blow was massive, sufficient to drive him to his knees. The blow caught him hard at the back of the head and he was strangely conscious of a resounding crack as his skull lost integrity. He was in the process of trying to turn and understand what was happening when the second assault caught him full between the shoulder blades, slamming him forward into the fence, the rough wood tearing his cheeks and lips. He felt a sticky tide of warmth cover his back and extend over his ribcage and he knew that it was his own blood. He felt oddly detached but fought to remain conscious and to understand. His limbs were shaking uncontrollably now, but he struggled to push himself up to see his attacker. The third blow ended that attempt with shattering finality, a sharpened edge of metal cleaving through Charles's thick dark hair, ripping scalp tissue and sundering his skull. A mist of blood sprayed from the head wound, a strip of pulsing brain tissue revealed and steaming in the cold alpine air. His final feeling, no longer fully sentient as his mind shut down, was of overwhelming confusion. That he was experiencing his own death he did comprehend, the terror of its breathtaking suddenness combining with an equal amount of wonder as to why it was happening at all.

That a guest had not returned to his lodgings that night was not noted by the hotel staff that, in the European fashion, treated customers with both discretion and distance. The corpse might have gone undiscovered for days given its solitary location, had it not been for the passing of a *Bergwacht* climber who had decided to check the high meadows to see if lightning strikes from the storm had hit any cows.

Indeed, the man at first thought that Charles's body, seen initially from a distance, was a calf, but wondered at the adjacent blue splash of color from what later was discovered to be a backpack. Proximity having clarified his initial error, the *Bergwacht* worker vomited into the tall grass near where the body lay. After some minutes of heavy breathing, he pulled a cell phone from his windbreaker and had the operator connect him with the Bavarian police. The police responded with celerity, their four-wheel-drive Mercedes wagon climbing into the meadow twenty minutes later, flashing blue lights dwarfed against the majestic background of the mountains.

After several paper cups of coffee at the scene offered by the policemen, the *Bergwacht* volunteer was permitted to return home, having told his tale many times, and now free to deliver its morbid details yet again to a circle of fascinated friends who would buy him rounds of beer in exchange. Charles's wallet was in a pocket of his jeans and made identification a simple affair. It was short work to determine that he had been a guest at the nearby Hotel Alpenhof and his plane ticket was soon after found in the room. A list of scrawled telephone numbers in his pocket organizer, also found in the room, made next of kin notification a minor task. At the top of Charles Hirter's telephone list was the name of one Robert Hirter.

As the deceased was an American, the local police decided to have one of their men with high-school-level English make the call to Robert Hirter and to the nearest U.S. consulate, which was in Munich. The "death of a U.S. citizen" notification to a consular official was concluded with cool dispatch on both ends, but the policeman knew that notifying a relative of such an unanticipated loss was trickier. The six-hour difference in time zones between Bavaria and the East Coast meant that Robert Hirter was awakened from sleep at four in the morning.

For a moment, it was apparent to the policeman that Robert Hirter did not understand the phrase "We have find your brother Charles who it is sorry for us to say now is dead." The policeman's efforts were quickly simplified when Robert Hirter began asking questions in very passable German. The policeman gently, politely provided what details he thought appropriate, determined that his interlocutor was the older brother of the murder victim, and advised him how best to journey to Gamsdorf to claim the remains and arrange for their transport to the United States. When, after a few minutes, Robert Hirter stopped asking questions and began to sob, the policeman understood that the conversation was at an end.

Chapter 2

Dulles Airport and the Virginia suburbs surrounding Washington, D.C., fell away rapidly, the distinctive patterns of housing developments and other visual details framed by the small double-paned window of the passenger plane. In a few minutes there was no trace of solid land at all, only the soundless expanse of the Atlantic, shimmering dull silver in the subdued light of an overcast afternoon. The ocean, too, lost detail as the aircraft gained elevation until there was nothing but clouds pressing close and gray against the gently humming fuselage.

The time-zone difference meant that Robert Hirter would fly to Munich through the night, arriving in early morning, the unseen crossing of the sea rendered banal by bad films and worse food, plastic knives that could not cut and plastic forks that could not stab. The events of 2001 had made air travel safer by placing passengers in the position of self-destructive patients in a mental asylum. *A necessary response to brutal times*, Robert thought. The nature of brutality had occupied him considerably in the day it had taken to find his passport and arrange his flight. The Bavarian policeman had been quite clear on the point that his brother Charles had been murdered.

The policeman had explained that someone had purposefully ended Charles's life with a series of blows from a sharp object. It made no sense; Charles knew no one in Europe, had never before visited there, and had hardly been killed in an area known as a cesspit of violence. Yet, Robert did not doubt that it had happened just that way; a vicious, primitive attack at dusk in a cow pasture in the mountains.

At least he had some time to try to make sense of things. Robert had used no leave this year and bought a ticket permitting him a full three weeks in Bavaria. He would bring Charles's body back with him; it mattered little if the funeral was delayed, there were no other siblings and their parents had died years ago. More important was being present for the hunt for the murderer. An arrest would bring some degree of comprehension, some sense of why his brother had been killed. Robert shifted in the narrow economy-class seat and listened to the subdued hum of the engines.

The police had offered to meet him at Strauss Airport in Munich but he had declined and reserved a rental car, intending to drive to Gamsdorf. He wanted time alone after arrival to sort out his thoughts before confronting foreign officials. He had reserved a room at the same hotel where his brother had lodged. With a final glance at the gray skies, Robert pressed a button on the arm of his seat and eased it back, intent on trying to sleep to limit his raggedness upon arrival in Munich.

Police *Kommissar* Franz Waldbaer stood alone in the high meadow and gazed down the slope of grassy green toward the valley floor far below. It was nearly dusk and he permitted himself his third and final cigarette of the day, cupping his hand around it in a protective gesture against the slight summer breeze. He had parked his unmarked police car near the Alpenhof and arrived at this place by foot, alone. It had taken him longer than expected, the unaccustomed climb straining his legs, racing his heart, and causing him to gulp in prodigious amounts of air. It occurred to him that he had stopped routine walks in the mountains a decade ago. This unhappy realization lead to depressing thoughts about age, mortality, and the decline of the human body; he shook the unwelcome theme resolutely from his head. At fifty-five, he had decided that it was best not to contemplate such topics.

He glanced again at the rough-hewn fence before him and the area surrounding it, but the image revealed nothing. There was nothing apparent to suggest what had happened here a few days ago. The young, clever technical boys had gone over everything with commendable thoroughness. They'd found nothing of interest secreted in their grass samples, slivers of wood or dabs of dried blood. But he had anticipated nothing and was not disappointed. He was, he thought, almost pleased about this in a perverse sense; the lack of antiseptically produced evidence crying out that there was yet a role for outmoded, old-fashioned police work. His cigarette down to the filter, he let it drop to the moist vegetation and pressed it into the dirt with his shoe.

Franz Waldbaer had no doubt that the act that had played out here, transforming this pastoral meadow into a brief theatre of remorseless violence, had been a cold and pitiless act. And he felt with unshakable certitude that the killer knew no remorse and was incapable of reasoning in terms of right and wrong, *Tugend und untugend:* virtue and vice. What was it an old Benedictine monk had said to him years ago? Evil is merely the absence of good. Yes.

The commissioner pushed the thoughts away and studied the terrain once again, staring for a full minute at the dark and silent line of forest from which Charles Hirter had emerged and arrived at his death scene. Had the American gone deeply into the woods? All the way to the dolomite peaks? For protection against the elements? There was no way to know, at least not yet. The storm with its driving rain and merciless hail had erased any trace of Charles's movements. He noted that the landscape was darkening by degree, mirroring the deepening hue of the cloudless sky above. He felt the air cooling and rubbed his hands together. Unlike southern Italy, the Alps did not permit waning warmth to linger after the sun departed the visible world. Like a jealous God, the sun removed warmth with it, content to let night reign over its domain in frosty coolness. The mountain peaks high above would be bitingly cold tonight.

Waldbaer watched as a serpentine line of street lamps flickered into life in the valley below, a necklace of pale light against the rapidly obscuring land. Waldbaer permitted himself a tired sigh as he began the slow descent to his automobile. The scene around him appeared tranquil, but he knew this to be a deceit. Somewhere nearby, at least one author of an evil act remained undetected. A chill hit him suddenly, not caused by the drop in temperature alone. A terrible thing had recently transpired here, but he sensed that more malevolent things were set to happen still, were perhaps beginning to happen already. Authored by what unseen hand or agency he did not know.

Chapter 3

German roadmaps being clear and detailed, Robert had no difficulty driving from Munich south to Upper Bavaria, taking the A-8 autobahn. An hour underway, he crested a hill and was presented with a spectacular view of the Chiemsee Lake spread out below him, the perfection of its deep blue waters and surrounding hilly shore looking like a postcard.

He felt guilty for even noticing the scenery. He was here because someone had killed his brother and because he intended to have it solved. He set his jaw and edged the speed higher, recalling that there was no speed limit on the autobahn. Seconds later, with a straight stretch of road in front of him he was doing a hundred miles an hour. He eased back on the gas pedal, but felt exhilarated at the feeling of movement after the passivity of sitting in an airplane.

The broad expanse of lake now behind him, Robert began to look for the exit marked Gamsdorf, knowing that it could not be far ahead. He felt grimy from the flight and had decided to go directly to the hotel for a shower, something to eat, and sleep. He also intended a brief walk around the hotel environs to get a sense of what his brother had seen during his time there. He would call the police from his room and make an appointment to see them in the morning, and later visit the morgue. He pulled a crumpled slip of paper from the pocket of his tweed blazer, checking to ensure that the police telephone number was legible. He read again the name of the officer in charge of the homicide investigation. *Kommissar* Franz Waldbaer.

* * *

In the morning light, Robert found the police station in the middle of town. It was not a separate structure but occupied space in the city hall, an elegant nineteenth-century building painted a giddy pale blue and sporting two decorative towers. An ancient coat of arms was emblazoned above the main entrance with the designation "Gamsdorf City Hall" etched underneath it in gold leaf. A more prosaic marker off to the side of the main portal carried the simple notation *Polizei*, printed in white against a navy blue background.

Robert parked his vehicle nearby, checked his appearance in the rearview mirror, adjusted his travel-rumpled tie, and stepped out into the brilliance of a late summer morning in the Alps. Crossing the street to the police station, he pushed open the heavy oak door and found himself in a foyer with arched ceilings. A cardboard sign with an arrow directed him to the basement. The walls along the stairwell were decorated with wanted posters for an assortment of heavy-browed, grim-visaged thieves and terrorists. There was a general dinginess to the paint and a faintly musty institutional smell to the air. It occurred to him that there existed an international police station motif of which this was a sterling example. Police offices from Buffalo to Berlin shared the same look.

The bottom of the stairs opened onto a large bay area with a long, high reception desk and several office cubicles. Half a dozen green-uniformed policemen were engaged at their computers or in conversation over cups of coffee. One of them, a thin, balding man in his thirties, approached the reception desk upon seeing Robert.

"How can I help you?" the policeman asked in German, a combination of courtesy and mild concern detectable in his voice.

"I have an appointment with Kommissar Waldbaer" Robert replied in the same language.

"Are you Herr Hirter?"

When Robert answered affirmatively, the policeman offered him his hand. "I am sorry about your brother, Herr Hirter. We will do everything we can to be of assistance. The Kommissar is expecting you. Please follow me."

The police officer led him past the reception desk and through a maze of metal cubicles. At the back of the bay area, a door led on to a private office, which the policeman signaled for Robert to enter before he himself returned to his colleagues. Robert knocked once and opened the door.

"*Gruess Gott*," a voice intoned deeply from behind a desk. Robert returned the traditional, ancient Catholic greeting, recalling that it was the common invocation used in Bavaria rather than the simple *guten tag* employed in northern Germany.

The man behind the greeting was slumped casually in a cracked leather chair and rose to his feet with an audible grunt. He was shorter than his visitor by a few inches, and broader, not so much fat as solidly built, his excess pounds having the lived-in look of comfortable permanence. Graying hair was cut short above a slightly rounded face complete with the unmistakable signs of incipient jowls. The Kommissar was outfitted in a blue linen jacket, horn-buttoned and of Bavarian cut. The jacket, while of good quality, displayed a network of creases and had undoubtedly not seen the inside of a dry cleaner's in a long time.

"My name is Waldbaer, Herr Hirter," the police official stated, shaking hands with a firm grip and looking Robert in the eye. He offered his guest a chair and leaned back again in his own oversized one, issuing a contented sigh as his weight settled. Waldbaer offered his condolences, then moved the conversation into more substantive waters.

"You no doubt have questions. I can give you some answers, but there is much that we still don't know. I'm glad to see you speak German, that will make things a lot easier. My English is, unfortunately, not very strong. By the way, how is it that you speak German so well? Most Americans I've encountered don't bother much with foreign languages."

Hirter laughed at this truth about his countrymen. "My grandparents were immigrants from Germany. They left for Massachusetts from Bremen before the First World War. They ensured that their son, my father, kept the language and he passed it along to my brother and me. It's rusty, but I expect it will get better in the next few days."

Waldbaer nodded. He placed his hands squarely on the desk in front of him and leaned forward. "The hotel staff recollected that your brother spoke German to them. That puzzled me; now I understand. Maybe the best procedure is for me to tell you what we have come up with to date."

Robert signaled agreement and the Kommissar continued, locking eyes with his visitor.

"Your brother was at the hotel alone. As far as we can tell from hotel staff testimony, he knew no one there. He dined alone and would sometimes read a paper by himself in the lobby. He might have exchanged a few words with other guests, but didn't strike up any real acquaintances. Your brother seemed mainly interested in hiking and was most of the time out on the country paths. He had walking shoes and gear on him at the time of his death. He was athletic your brother?"

"Yes. More than me. He's — was — younger and always took to sports."

The policeman nodded and continued. "Your brother had purchased terrain maps of the area, so he had a sense of where to go. Some of the other Alpenhof guests recalled having seen him on some of the paths on the valley floor where the hotel is located."

"I'm staying at the same hotel," Robert interjected.

"I know," his host replied with a thin trace of smile.

"On the day of his death your brother decided to hike in a different direction; up the slopes rather than traversing the valley. He set out rather late though, at least a waiter recalled him leaving the hotel in mid-morning. I think your brother underestimated how long it would take to reach the peaks and return; it's a common mistake for tourists. Anyway, he took a path that isn't heavily traveled due to its steep incline. The path is on the map he had in his possession when he died, and there's a pencil mark next to it. The path he chose goes through a series of meadows, some fairly high, and then winds through heavily wooded areas before opening up to the rock face of the mountain summits. But I don't think he ever got to the peaks." Waldbaer leaned back in his chair, eyes still on Robert.

"Why don't you think he got that far?"

The official ran a hand through the patch of hair above his broad forehead. "I don't think he reached the summit because it's a rough go once you clear the woods. He had no climbing equipment, just hiking gear. There are places where you can make it to the top without ropes, but I don't believe your brother would have known where. And the soles of his shoes were covered with mud and pine needles, not traces of stone. He also had no minor leg abrasions, which we would expect to see if he had made a strenuous climb without mountain gear. So, he never got where he intended to go."

"Which means he was killed before then," Robert concluded.

"No," came the unexpected reply.

"I'm sorry, Kommissar, I don't follow you," Robert said, a trace of stiffness in his voice.

The detective shook his head knowingly and clasped his hands under his chin. "Your brother, I am certain, on his ascent went safely past the place where he was later killed. He went higher, into the woods. He probably meant to get to the mountaintop initially, but gave up on this when the weather turned bad. There was a fierce thunderstorm that afternoon, bad enough in the valley, but it would have been especially forceful up high. He would have left the open meadow and headed for cover. Not always the wisest thing to do with lightning strikes, but he probably figured he'd find someplace reasonably safe in the forest. I think your brother was killed after the storm subsided. He left the woods behind and was on his *return* to the hotel when he was attacked." Waldbaer waited for a reaction.

Robert was trying to envision the scene, but knew that a central question was not being addressed. "I'm sure you know what you're talking about. But nothing I've heard so far tells me why Charles was killed or who could have done it. I'm glad you're telling me what probably happened beforehand, but why did he die in that meadow?"

Waldbaer regarded him steadily. "I don't know why; not yet. But we can rule some things out. There haven't been other attacks like this in the area, so it's not a serial killer or similar. There's nothing to suggest that drugs were involved; your brother's system was clean. There's nothing to suggest that your brother irritated anyone at the hotel, had a fight over a girl, or anything like that. All of which leads me to believe that your brother was, as the saying goes, in absolutely the wrong place at exactly the wrong time. I'm not trying to be flippant, but I think your brother would be alive now if he had taken a different path that day. Something he saw up there, something he stumbled upon caused him to be killed."

"That doesn't take us very far," Robert said, aware that his tone was curt, but not really caring. It was apparent to him that the police did not have a lead and he knew that the longer it took to develop a lead, the greater the likelihood that a killer would never be found.

"I understand your disappointment. But something like this can be very complicated. There are no witnesses, none. The place where the murder took place is entirely unpopulated. No weapon has been recovered. We have no motive. But I think we'll get somewhere. I have a feeling that we will get someone for this. I've been around crime a while and I give these feelings their due."

Robert nodded without actually agreeing. He had a heavy feeling in his stomach that he might end up flying home with his brother's cold remains in the cargo hold of a United Airlines flight and without any answers. He pushed the thought away. "How did he die? I want to know whatever you can tell me, and please don't pretty it up for me."

Waldbaer looked up at the ceiling and pursed his lips. "Fair enough. I will tell you as accurately as I can, *Ja?* First, we did have a bit of luck, insofar as the body was discovered within twenty-four hours of death. The crime scene is remote and it could have easily been a week or more before someone happened upon your brother. There was no attempt to conceal the body. I find that interesting."

Waldbaer ran a hand slowly over the back of his neck before continuing. "A number of possible reasons come to mind. Perhaps the attacker was scared and wanted to get out of the area quickly after the crime. That would suggest the killer is not a professional. It could also be that it was getting dark and the killer didn't have the visibility to find a place to put the body and needed to concentrate on getting away. Or maybe the killer didn't have the strength to move the body, although the force of the blows he — or she — delivered would seem to indicate otherwise. But who knows, weak heart, asthma? Just as possible, the killer could have left the body where it fell because he was sure that the crime could never be traced to him. Why go through the effort of moving a body if its discovery won't reveal anything?"

Waldbaer paused, but his visitor interjected neither comment nor question.

"When we arrived at the scene, the body was still wet from the thunderstorm the previous afternoon. There was no water collected in the nostrils or oral cavity, which suggests that your brother was killed after the storm had abated. That means early evening sometime, around dusk, at the latest. Your brother was struck from behind, three times. Two of the three blows were to the head and either one alone would have been fatal. One blow was delivered between the shoulder blades and taken by itself might not have been killing, but I personally believe that the loss of blood and damage to the spinal column from even this wound would have made it impossible for your brother to have gotten out of that meadow. Even with that one blow, I think he would have died up there, just more slowly. The killer was leaving nothing to chance however."

The Kommissar paused. The American's breathing had become audible.

"Do you want some water? Or should we stop for today?"

"No, it's okay," Robert replied. "Keep going."

Waldbaer nodded and resumed his narrative. "All right. We don't have a murder weapon, and we aren't certain exactly what it is. An axe or hatchet or something similar. The weapon was swung with significant force. This is surely not pleasant for you, but it needs to be said: Your brother's head was cleaved open to and through the brain by one of the blows, probably the last one. The other head blow was severe too, but the one that penetrated the cerebral cavity was devastating. It would have been apparent to the killer that this blow had been fatal. This was not a struggle in which your brother happened to be killed. There was no struggle. Your brother was very deliberately murdered."

The detective must have noticed a slight tic in Hirter's cheek, and decided that the man was fighting to control his emotions. "I think that suffices for today. We can meet tomorrow."

His guest cut him off. "How painful do you think it was? Did Charles suffer a lot? Would he have lost consciousness from that first blow to the head?"

The Kommissar released a breath slowly, contemplating the top of his scarred desk.

"I can't answer that," he said. "I don't know. When the first blow hit him it was enough to drive him to his knees, we can tell by the way the mud clotted on his trousers. If you want my speculative view, he was conscious after that first blow hit, but probably wasn't sure what was happening. Remember, he couldn't see his attacker, who was standing behind him. The second strike propelled him forward into a fence. But I'm certain that all sensation and consciousness stopped the instant that third blow penetrated his skull. My suspicion is that the pain was not overwhelming; I think the body opiates against that. But who knows? You would like to think it was a quick death, Herr Hirter; so would I, but I can't give you a real answer. Not what you would prefer to hear, I expect, but you asked for a truthful rendition of things."

"Right," Robert uttered the word barely audible. "What's next?"

"Go back to your hotel. Take a walk in this gorgeous weather; not every day here is this desirable. Try to relax. I'll meet you at the Alpenhof tomorrow morning for coffee, and we can talk about identifying your brother."

Robert nodded, rose, and shook hands with the tired-looking Bavarian. Moments later he found himself standing by his car and wondering how he had gotten there. The sun was shining with almost painful intensity against a pale blue sky, but the incontestable beauty of the day failed to rescue him from a feeling of emptiness.

It was to the meadows and woods that he felt inexorably drawn. After an hour in his hotel room and a ham sandwich lunch, Robert knew that he had no choice; he had to see where his brother's life had come to its unanticipated halt. He donned worn jeans, a thin sweater, and track shoes. Leaving the hotel behind, hearing the creak of the double doors swinging shut, Robert wondered what sense it really made to visit the scene of the crime. The German detective had told him graphically enough what had happened. Still, one foot stepped ahead of the other and Robert knew that he had to make the journey. He had his own map and experienced no difficulty in finding the path his brother had taken.

Robert paused at intervals during his climb, rested his hands on his hips, and surveyed the scenery. He had passed some hikers near the hotel but none up higher; most of the tourists preferred the lighter athletic diversion provided by the valley floor. When he arrived at the high meadows, he quickly found the spot where Charles had been killed. The tall grass bore traces of the disturbance caused by the recent comings and goings there, and orange tape stenciled with the word *Polizei* was strewn haphazardly around the area it had once, briefly, corralled. A small herd of milk cows nearby observed him with bovine indifference. Robert knelt on one knee at the meadow fence and touched it where he imagined his brother's head had slammed into the rails, but there was no distinguishing sign of this, no trace, no electric current emanating from the weathered wood announcing *it was exactly here*.

But he did feel something. A sensation teasing and opaque. He felt with certainty that he was being watched. There was nothing in his field of vision save the cows and it was not their dumb gaze that he felt crawl along his skin. The conviction that some being both sentient and malevolent was studying him would not fade. He rose, slowly, and turned to take in the terrain behind him. Higher still, but close enough to be reached with a ten minutes walk, the dark line of fir trees that marked the forest's edge fixed his gaze. There was no hint of motion, no betraying movement of branches or flash of color. But Robert knew that his watcher was there, concealed in the mottled shadows of black and brown.

This feeling of surveillance was unexpected, and he was unprepared for it. He wanted to go to the woods and find whoever it was who was there. But he felt embraced by the cold grip of fear, and began his descent back toward the hotel far below. As he walked with steps careful enough to prevent a stumble, he continued to look back at the brooding dark forest and the secrets locked within.

Chapter 4

Kill him too perhaps; it might be the most prudent course, the figure reasoned. As with the first one taken down, there was no other party in the area to interfere. This new intruder could be killed like the other, quickly, efficiently. But this time it would be judicious to move the body into the woods and bury it. He followed the steady retreat of the figure intently from his refuge in the deep and embracing forest shadows. He felt the heft of the edged weapon in his hand and flexed his toned biceps, savoring the feel of rushing adrenaline. If it is to be done, it must be done soon; the target was steadily moving away.

Perhaps it would not be so easy this time. For one thing, the intruder did not take his eyes from the tree line as he headed back toward the valley floor. The man was suspicious, as if he sensed he was being watched. A headlong rush toward him from the woods would be detected and the man would run downhill at top speed, maybe bellowing for help. If the fellow was a good runner, he might be difficult to catch or, infinitely worse, might not be caught at all. There was no darkness to conceal an attack this time. And if the assault succeeded, even if the corpse were buried, the end result might still be a redoubling of police activity.

The matter of what was secreted in the cave was far too important to endanger. It would, in theory, be a fine thing to kill this intruder, but there was considerable risk involved and he dared not wager such enormously high stakes in a game of chance.

He watched the figure recede into the pastoral distance until he disappeared below the slope of the hill. You will live for now, the watcher thought, but events yet unseen will in the end determine your destiny, and, for that matter, my own.

Chapter 5

"Gruess Gott," Waldbaer intoned as Robert stepped from the elevator into the deeply veneered comfort of the hotel lobby. After a perfunctory handshake, the detective guided the American to a small corner table in the high-ceilinged breakfast room. A teenage waitress wearing a puffy-shouldered green dirndl served them coffee. With her departure, Robert leaned across the table and half-whispered, "I think someone was watching me yesterday."

Waldbaer looked steadily at his table partner and waited for more.

"I went up to where my brother was killed. I found the meadow. While I was standing there, I had this feeling that I was being watched."

"A feeling," Waldbaer repeated evenly. Hirter raised his hands in protest. "I know what you're going to say. I don't have proof. That's right. And I didn't actually *see* anything. But I'm certain someone was there behind me, in the woods, watching."

The police official still said nothing, and Robert's voice took on an injured tone. "I'm not saying you need to believe it, but I want to tell you what I felt. Take it or leave it."

"I'll take it, Herr Hirter, but on my own terms if you don't mind. You are correct that your feelings, no matter how compelling to you, are not evidence. Any investigation relies on facts. A feeling is not a fact. A feeling is not rational." He paused and placed both hands around his ceramic coffee cup. "But I've been around long enough to conclude that there's always a bit of room on the margins of an investigation for the irrational. So, I don't dismiss it, even if I can't *do* much with it. At the very least, I have to consider the possibility that whoever killed your brother might still be in the area. Which logically opens up the possibility that you might have been followed. I can assign an officer to watch over you during your stay."

Robert considered, furrowed his brow while reaching for his own cup of black Dahlmeier coffee. "No. Thanks, I don't want that. I'd feel funny. Anyway, I'm not saying someone is out to kill me, just that I think someone was watching me there."

A silence crept across the table as both parties reflected on what to say. The Kommissar was the first to articulate his thought. "You should think about going home soon," he said. "I'll take you to the morgue to view the body. Then fly home with your brother. The U.S. consulate in Munich will help you with the paperwork needed for the airline. There's nothing more for you to do here. You've seen where your brother was killed. You have met me and established that we are conducting an investigation. It's good that you've done those things, but what you can accomplish is ended. I'll advise you personally about how our investigation progresses."

Robert gripped the white cotton tablecloth in his hands as if preparing to snap it away in a magician's trick. "I'm not going anywhere yet. You haven't told me much that I couldn't have figured out myself. I owe it to Charles to stay until his killer is found. You might not be comfortable with that, but I don't care. Am I a nuisance? Probably. Am I a complication? Fine. But I'll be on Bavarian soil for a while yet, Herr Waldbaer." Robert's face was flush, and his voice had turned brittle.

"Stay if you want. That's your decision. But there is only so much we can do for you. Like it or not, this investigation will go ahead at its own pace."

"I have time."

The detective pushed his chair away from the table, the wooden legs scratching the varnished wooden floor. "That leaves your visit to see your brother. We don't have a morgue here; his body is in Rosenheim. If you drive to the police station this afternoon, you can follow me there. After that, you will be on your own. *Guten tag.*"

The detective departed with a nod of his head but without shaking hands.

It was the coolness of the room and the cloying antiseptic scent of the air that Robert noticed. A morgue, he thought distantly, is the anteroom to the grave, a brief pause before the finality of being placed in the indifferent earth. The room was cavernous and bare of furnishings except for metal gurneys and tables, lit by bright tubular lamps overhead that glared off the white-tiled walls. Waldbaer had ushered the American into the chamber without comment, his silence not betraying whether it stemmed from respect for the dead or annoyance with the living.

There was only one other man in the room. He was balding and middle aged, with a thin frame wrapped in light blue, disposable surgical attire. The man's complexion was sallow and the cut of his face severe, the sum effect suggesting that he had been predestined for this solemn work. Waldbaer introduced the man with the title of doctor, but Robert did not catch the long German name. The doctor nodded his head as he was introduced, muttered, "I'm sorry for your loss," and gestured with his arm to a bundle on a wheeled gurney behind him.

The bundle, shrouded in a white cotton sheet, was, Robert knew, the sum of his brother's existence. He felt his stomach do a turn and wished he were somewhere else, anywhere but in this stainless place of corruption. The thought passed quickly, and Robert found himself standing ramrod straight and tense, inches away from the remains of his brother, whose countenance he had last encountered over Chinese food in a seedy restaurant in Boston's Chinatown. The doctor stepped to the other side of the metal gurney and deftly pulled at the cloth covering.

In a way, the form and face confronting Robert did not look much like his brother, though his brother it unmistakably was. It was not so much the awful intrusion of injuries to the head that accounted for this as the odd passivity of the features. He had, Hirter realized, probably never seen his brother in repose since they were children. Robbed of animation, his brother seemed almost surreal to him. This was what death meant; everything rendered quiet and motionless.

"This is my brother. No question about it". He looked first at the doctor and then at the Kommissar as he spoke. Both men nodded. The doctor moved to replace the covering over the body.

"Wait," Robert said. He studied his brother one final time, his attention drawn to the invasive and disfiguring attack wounds. It was clear that the skull had been literally caved in, the top of the head a distorted mélange of matted hair, bone, and congealed blood. His brother's nose had been broken and flattened by being driven into the fence post; it remained dark purple even now.

"You haven't autopsied?" Robert inquired.

The doctor answered. "We've conducted preliminary examinations sufficient to confirm cause of death and provide my police colleagues with whatever information could be gathered. A full autopsy was awaiting your identifying the deceased."

Robert nodded.

Waldbaer spoke softly. "If there's nothing else, Herr Hirter, we can leave and permit the doctor to resume his duties." Robert shook the doctor's hand and followed the detective from the chamber.

Outside the temperature was notably warmer, but the sky had turned steel gray, perfectly suiting Robert's mood. The two men stood together, both with hands in pockets as if they might find some object within to assist in conversation.

"I take it from your comments earlier that you will be remaining in the hotel a while?"

"Right, Kommissar. You can reach me there if you need me."

The detective sighed loudly, his chin inclined toward the sky as if searching for something. "That's the problem, Herr Hirter. There's no need for you here. Unless you want to try to enjoy Bavaria, visit the castles of King Ludwig or something. But have it your way." He turned to leave, stopped, and added with a puzzled tone in his voice. "One last detail. This morning the lab boys called me, the ones who examined the murder scene; the meadow that you visited. It's probably not important but they've found a piece of wood wedged into your brother's shoes. Not a twig. A sliver of wood from a crate more than likely. Not part of the natural surroundings. It's probably not important, but I thought I'd pass it along to show that we *are* checking every shred of evidence, literally."

Robert muttered his thanks, still not sure how to judge the policeman. As an unexpected aside Waldbaer added, "At the hotel bar you might want to try the dark wheat beer, it's *Weihenstephan*, one of the better examples of that style. *Auf wiedersehen*, Herr Hirter."

Driving the autobahn south from Rosenheim, Waldbaer distracted himself by reconsidering the oddities that defined *Fall Hirter*; the Hirter case. First fact: a young American tourist with no known contacts in Bavaria arrives in the region for a vacation alone. Fair enough; Bavaria plays host to millions of tourists every summer. Second fact: the American has no criminal record and it is unlikely that he can be considered a "dubious person" in any sense. Third fact: interviews with hotel staff established that the young man fit the hiker profile and had not been involved in any scenes at the hotel bar, with the cleaning staff, or so forth. All very well.

But things started to fall apart with the fourth fact. The young hiker was murdered in a postcard-perfect alpine meadow after a thunderstorm early one evening. Fifth fact: as far as could be determined, nothing was stolen from the deceased nor was there any other suggestion of motive for the crime. Sixth fact: there were no witnesses — no wonder, given the isolated location of the murder, inclement weather, and time of day. Seventh fact: the police had no suspect.

Random murder. The words had always filled Waldbaer with professional skepticism. How many people in the world were actually murdered at random? Some, doubtless, but not many. It was statistically unlikely that the notion of "a random murder" had any application to *Fall Hirter*. Eighth fact: the victim's brother arrived in Bavaria not only to identify and claim the body, but to watchdog the investigation. Waldbaer had briefly entertained Robert Hirter as a potential suspect or someone with special knowledge about what happened, but quickly dismissed the notion. Robert Hirter was becoming an irritant, like a small pebble lodged in a shoe, but was neither murderer nor conspirator.

But where did this assembly of facts lead? Nowhere, Waldbaer concluded, braking expertly as a museum-vintage truck with faded Turkish license plates pulled out in front of him. "*Scheisskopf*," he muttered unheard at the lorry driver. If no other information developed over the coming days, it would become a mathematical certainty that the murder would not be solved. This irritated him; murder offended his sense of order and he viscerally wanted the murderer found and made to pay. He felt himself beginning the descent into a foul mood and wanted to arrest it; ill-temper jibed poorly with a criminal investigation. A beer, perhaps a few beers, would certainly help, he concluded.

Robert Hirter swung his car into the hedge-trimmed Alpenhof parking lot and sat for a while before locking it and walking into the building. The air in the lobby was colder than outside, the air conditioner a concession to tourists who insisted that seasonal temperatures be steadily arrested at around mid-April.

As he picked up his room key at the main desk, the young dirndl-clad desk girl passed him an envelope that had his name broadly scrawled in blue ink across the front.

"What's this?" he mumbled.

The girl raised her eyebrows and shrugged her strong country shoulders. "I don't know, sir. It was dropped off by a gentleman who said to give it to you as soon as possible."

Waldbaer again, Hirter thought automatically.

"Was he about fifty, rumpled, a bit heavy?"

The girl shook her head sideways with the conviction of the just. "Oh no, sir, I took the letter from him myself and I'd guess that he must be in his late seventies with white hair. And the gentleman is not heavy, quite trim in fact." She smiled and Robert returned the courtesy, knowing there was nothing more to be clarified with her.

He decided to read the unexpected missive in the lobby. The envelope was unsealed and the slip of paper slid out easily. Robert unfolded it, translating the broad, jerky handwritten scrawl into English as he went along.

Herr Hirter,

It has come to my attention that you are staying at this hotel and are engaged with the circumstances surrounding the death of your brother nearby, an event covered in some detail in the local newspaper. It could be that I can add something to the limited information that the police have likely provided you. Let me ensure that there is no misunderstanding: I have nothing to do with the murder nor do I know who the murderer is. But I do perhaps possess some historical background that might prove of interest to you.

This is strictly a private initiative of my own. If you choose to involve the police or show them this note I will — as is my right — decline to speak to you since, as I have noted, I have no knowledge of the crime itself. If you choose to meet with me, you should be at the Alte Post restaurant this evening at seven. If you are not present by seven fifteen, I will conclude that you have no interest in conversing and my offer will be from that point void.

August Sedlmeyer

Robert read the message again. The letter was odd. It was an offer to provide information, but only vaguely suggestive of relevance to his brother's death. Historical background. The tone was odd as well. The phrasing in native German was imperious, as if from someone accustomed to giving orders. The handwriting was unsteady, supporting the hotel desk girl's observation that the person who delivered the note, presumably Sedlmeyer himself, was an older man.

Perhaps Sedlmeyer was a crank who had simply read newspaper articles about his brother's death and wanted to rant.

Meeting with Sedlmeyer could prove a waste of time. Still, Robert considered, it was hard to envision that meeting with the old man could be a real *mistake*. Other than time, there was little to lose. The proposed meeting was in a public place and Robert hardly felt physically threatened by someone who might be a deranged septuagenarian. So why not? He would need to eat somewhere at any rate. He returned to the still-smiling desk girl and inquired as to how to get to a restaurant called the Alte Post.

Chapter 6

The ancient slash in the mountain dolomite that comprised the cave had always been a cold place; had been that way for millions of years. Day or night caused little difference in the temperature of the cave and there was dampness in the mildly fetid air. He had placed a lamp on the floor of the cavern and the light it cast was spectral against the creviced stone. Glancing around, he noted that nothing appeared amiss, the rows of dusty wooden crates lying undisturbed as they had for so long. Still, there had been an intruder, an unfortunate and potentially disastrous turn of events. Danger had been averted only due to the sheerest luck, that most fickle of commodities.

It was close to a mathematical impossibility that he, the protector of this place, had been in the woods near the cave when the intruder found his way here. Waiting outside in the slapping rain and darkness, he had watched the pale flicker of a flashlight within the stone chamber. And he had waited, not patiently, but angrily, but he had waited nonetheless. It would not have been prudent to rush in. What if the intruder had been armed? He had kept his head and thought the situation through with dispassion. Kill him when he leaves, when he isn't expecting anything. Then think about next steps.

It would have been preferable if the body had never been discovered. He had thought of that at the time, but there were no other solutions. With the crime committed, with blood and other DNA traces on his clothing, he did not want to risk dragging the body somewhere. Killing was the main thing. Death brought with it one virtue: silence, pure and chaste.

He had believed that with the intruder dispatched, he would

have a few days to figure out what to do with the body before anyone stumbled upon it in that remote meadow. He had been wrong, but again, luck, this time bad, had to be held accountable for the rescue worker appearing in the area so unexpectedly. The discovery of the body had ensured predictable consequences: police and forensic experts wandering around, news broadcasts, and requests for potential witnesses to come forward. He allowed himself a thin smile. There were no witnesses other than him and no evidence that would lead anywhere. This meant that the crates and their cargo were safe. The cave was well concealed and far enough from the murder scene to remain secure.

Still, the episode carried a warning. Perhaps the contents of the cave should be moved to another location, possibly to a warehouse in Rosenheim. The items would have to be moved sometime soon anyway if they were to be put to use. The mountain recess, this primordial fissure, had served well for decades. But there had now been a total of three murders in the vicinity. Best not to tempt fate indefinitely.

The first two bodies had never been discovered and now lay, not far removed from the stone chamber, in improvised graves dug into the moist, pungent earth of the pine forest. He recalled how the victims had looked; mouths open in stupefied amazement, as he had slashed the life out of them in wide-arced gouging strokes. In their late teens, both of them, male and female looking so much alike; studies in pale skin, long, oily hair, and dilated pupils. Drug addicts with nothing on them but their narcotic and some needles, the clothes on their back, and a handful of soiled Deutsche marks. That had been almost a decade ago. This meant that nature and its attendant court of insects had doubtless done their work. The corpses would be nothing more than shreds of denim and fabric, and a collection of bones.

The couple had been camping under a tarpaulin in the woods, no doubt retreating from the society that they thought they had rejected but that had, in fact, cast them out. Their great misfortune was to have seen him as he made his way one late afternoon to the cave.

"Hi, man," the male had said with a total lack of cognition.

It had been instantly clear that the two had to die. He could not risk any chance that they might follow him to his destination.

The rest had been simple, over in a couple of brutal, screaming minutes. He had walked wordlessly up to the two, pulled from his backpack the machete he used to cut through the brush, and started to slash. The male went first. The first slash was straight to the neck and delivered swiftly before the boy could raise his arms to ward off the blow. He went down, blowing a mist of blood with a gurgling wheeze. The female just whimpered during the seconds it took to kill her mate and didn't even attempt to run. He swung his blade with full force into her dirty black sweater and she let out a loud, surprisingly baritone "Ooohh," as she crumpled to her knees.

He had gone to the cave, taking the pairs' tarpaulin with him, fished out a rusting shovel from a crate of tools, and returned to bury the sacks of dirty flesh. He had been careful to cover the site with generous mounds of pine needles, fir cones, and twigs. He had done this in such an accomplished manner that the area seemed undisturbed and he had difficulty finding the spot a week later. With trepidation he had read the newspapers for weeks after the murders and listened to the hourly radio news on *Bayern Funf*. But there had been no mention of a twin disappearance. He had concluded that the victims were such societal detritus that they enjoyed no family ties and were missed by no one. And so the circle of life and death for the two dropouts had closed seamlessly and quietly.

But all of that had been long ago, his memories of those moments less vivid, as if the color had drained from his recollections, leaving only a sepia trace. He now had to focus on the future and on moving the crates. He might be required to kill again, but he was content to let fate arbitrate that particular matter.

Chapter 7

Gamsdorf slumbered in the waning sun of a long-shadowed late afternoon, its buildings looking much as they had for decades. The village was arranged in typical Bavarian form; a centuries-old church at its center, a whitewashed stone steeple rising high above it. The steeple was topped with a green-patina copper dome, shaped like a gigantic onion. A cemetery surrounded the church on all sides, braced by a low wall designed either to keep undesired visitors out or restless spirits in. The permanent residents of the churchyard comprised a democratic selection of the recently deceased and those who had lain in their graves for centuries. Some gravestones were so old that time and the elements had rendered them nearly blank stone slates, with only a gothic letter or two still discernible.

In one corner of the cemetery stood a large granite rectangle, relentlessly polished, topped with a gilded crucifix and a German soldier's steel helmet. The monument memorialized the villagers, mostly young men with last names still common to the village, who had fallen in battle during the lost World Wars of 1914–1918 and 1939–1945. Their remains were not here, but scattered on battlefields from Tannenberg to Kiev, from Normandy to Tobruk.

Most of the graves, and the war memorial, too, were well tended and graced with bright flowers. The community of the dead was a full partner of the community of the living and often visited by the villagers, if mostly by the elderly, as if they were carefully inspecting their next residence.

A narrow street passed by the front of the church, lined by linden trees, thick leaves shading the pavement below. Across from the church stood a three-hundred-year-old tavern, a painted shingle above the door identifying it as *"Zum Alte Post"*; The Old Post Office. Which it had once been, but that was long ago when Bavaria had been ruled by the whims of kings, both mad and enlightened. In those days, the tavern keeper had tended the mail and it was here that the royal mail wagons delivered packets, bills of lading, notices of births and deaths. Now bored federal postal employees in every-day garb delivered letters and advertising flyers in VW vans. The Old Post no longer kept the mail, but remained a tavern.

A dog yapped in the distance as Robert parked his car under the linden trees and made his way to the restaurant. The village was somnolent with no noise of traffic to mar the gradual descent of a summer's evening. There was a trace of fertilizer and mown grass in the air, a reminder of the rolling farm meadows flanking the place.

The front double-door was made of rude, battered wooden planks decorated with a carved star at waist level. One of the doors was propped open with a crumbling brick to allow the outside air into thick-walled chambers. The doors faced into a broad hallway with a high-arched ceiling and red tile floor. A heavy oak country chest was placed against one wall; an equally heavy framed mirror hung above it. Robert checked his image briefly in the glass and noted dark rings under his eyes. He ran a hand across his hair to make his appearance a bit more orderly.

The hallway opened onto two large rooms, to the right and left. Robert peeked into the room to his left and found it festively deco-rated in rural Bavarian style with framed lithographs of alpine scenes, a few pieces of antique furniture bearing heavy vases of fresh moun-tain flowers. The dozen or so tables were covered with crisp blue and white linen tablecloths, and the places were set with matching nap-kins, wineglasses, and utensils. But there were no guests to be seen. The carefully prepared room was empty of life, looking a bit like a museum piece.

Animated conversation and muffled laughter drifted across the floor from behind, and Robert knew that the opposite room was oc-cupied. Robert turned and entered the space that was the same size as the room he had just vacated. Other than the similarity of size, everything was different.

This chamber was full of people dining and talking. A portly and expressionless waitress of indeterminate age clad in a green and red dirndl circulated among the tables distributing half-liter glasses of foaming beer. The unornamented tables here were bare wood with paper napkins. A large crucifix stared down from one corner, the pained grimace on the visage of Jesus presiding over a universe of gossip, humor, and malice.

No one looked up as Robert entered. The American surveyed the room for someone who might be August Sedlmeyer. The task took only a second. Nearly all of the guests in the room were seated in groups. Only one man sat alone. He was, as Robert had expected, quite old, his general appearance announcing someone in his early eighties. The man's face and hands were burnished bronze and his hair startlingly white, with just a streak of muted black remaining.

August Sedlmeyer sat ramrod straight in his hard-backed chair, hands spread protectively around a glass of beer on the table before him, looking rather like a priest about to lift his chalice. The old man wore a well-brushed, if threadbare, collarless charcoal Bavarian jacket, the sleeves and pockets trimmed in forest green. He stared straight ahead as if lost in thought.

Robert walked to the old man's table. "Excuse me sir, are you Herr Sedlmeyer? I'm Robert Hirter."

The old man nodded an acknowledgment with a quick up-down wag of the chin and gestured to the empty chair opposite him. "Please have a seat Herr Hirter. I expected that you might show up. Order something if you wish; the food here is acceptable. Or just a beer perhaps? I will not detain you long. I intend to make my points succinctly." The old man spoke in clipped sentences in a voice that was steady but betrayed the inflections of advanced age. Robert had the mildly discomforting feeling that Sedlmeyer was somehow in charge and accustomed to issuing directives.

The thickly built waitress suddenly loomed over the table, contemplating Robert with sullen eyes, as so many waitresses had regarded their customers in so many guesthouses over the centuries. Robert ordered a Spaten ale and the woman disappeared, trundling away with a clumping, horsey gait.

"I got the note you left at the hotel," Robert said, not quite knowing where to go conversationally. "I'm a bit confused by it, but I gather that you have something to say about my brother's murder."

The old man surveyed the American without blinking, his deep brown eyes conveying no humor. "My note was not clear, I suppose. It was meant to be an invitation that you could take or leave, Herr Hirter. Before we go further, let me ensure that you understand one thing: I do not know who killed your brother. What I am offering you is background that might be relevant — no more, no less. You must decide whether what I have to say is worth hearing." The old man paused to see if his visitor would interject a comment. The waitress appeared from behind them and deposited a mug of pale beer on the table in front of Robert. She departed as wordlessly as she had arrived.

"One other thing," Sedlmeyer rasped. "This story that you are about to hear is meant for you, not for the police. If you repeat what I say to the police and they make inquiries of me, I'll deny that I said anything, *Klar?* Consider this conversation purely personal. Those are my rules. You can, of course, decide to just drink your *Helles* and leave without listening to me." Sedlmeyer reached for his own beer but did not take his dark, deep-set eyes off of Robert.

Robert took a long draw of his Spaten. *In for a dime, in for a dollar*, he thought. "I'll stay. I want to hear about this history. And you can be certain, Herr Sedlmeyer, that I won't bring the police in if, as you say, there is no relevance to my brother's murder. Fair enough?"

Sedlmeyer gave a sharp, martial nod and leaned his spare frame back in his chair, its legs issuing a protesting creak. The old man's gaze found a place to rest somewhere over Robert's right shoulder and did not wander. With his weathered, liver-spotted hands folded on the table, he began to relate what Robert would always remember as "*The SS Man's Tale.*"

.   .   .

The color gray, sullen and suffocating, seemed the predominant, reigning hue of that season and year. It was mid-March by the calendar, but the wet, sickly wind, perpetually low sky, and chilling temperatures rendered it more like deep winter than the onset of spring. I do not recall seeing a single crocus or emerging blade of grass to add color and life to the world; it was as if any signal of joy or optimism or renewal had been banned by wartime decree. There was no promise in the air, unless it was the promise of hardships yet to come. Our temperament was hugely gray as well, as deeply impregnated with that color as our field uniforms. It was 1945, and bleakly clear where the fortunes of the German Reich were headed.

Berlin had once been vibrant, imperiously proud, a true world city. I had reveled in the monumentality and hubris of the place during treasured weeks of leave from the insanity of the Eastern Front in 1942, and again in 1943. Now, an extraordinary conspiracy of fate and ironic circumstance had transformed Berlin *into* the Eastern Front, or more accurately, was about to. Who would have believed it even a year earlier, even six months earlier? Berlin had wholly lost its worldly and charmingly haughty look, like a terminal cancer patient whose wasted shell has little in common with the healthy being who inhabited the same skin before the disease took its final, implacable hold.

The city was a ruin; whole sections gutted and uninhabited wrecks due to the cumulative, daily attentions of the Allied air forces. Hours after the raids, you could still smell phosphorous in the air. The Reich chancellery was a discolored shell, most of the other ministries abandoned. By 1945, it was a novelty to discover a building that had not been damaged in the air raids. Concrete dust mixed with ash was everywhere; this was the brutalized soil from which a New Germany would have to emerge after the war, but that is another story for another time.

We were gathered at the *Reichsbank* on that raw morning just after dawn, the first light of day an anemic yellow against our

rumpled and abused field uniforms. We were "swine of the front" as
we used to say, and we looked it. My comrades and I had been
stripped of any parade-ground finery long ago, save perhaps the runic
double S flash on our tunic collars. Some of us had a heavy *Stahlhelm*
jammed over our heads, but most favored gray rough wool foraging
caps. Every boot was thick with mud and dirt; it didn't seem worth
the effort to clean them anymore.

You might think from this remark that our morale was kaput, but
it wasn't, not really. We were in no mood to surrender to the first
Ivan who appeared. There was an unspoken communal understanding that the war had been lost with finality many months ago somewhere in the Slavic east, and a sure sense that any chance of victory
had slipped through our fingers forever. We were still sitting at the
poker table but with an irredeemably losing hand.

We didn't think much about the war ending; it was a theme best
left unreflected upon. We had our orders, which were to assemble in
front of the Berlin Reichsbank at daybreak, take breakfast standing
up from a mobile field kitchen, and await instructions. There were
about fifty of us, a detachment from our father unit the *Leibstandarte
Adolf Hitler*, the fuehrer's own name division. Our longtime commander Sepp Dietrich was no longer leading us by this chapter of
the war; he was in Hungary with the remnants of the Sixth Panzer
Army, preparing for a hopeless offensive there to stop the Russian advance against Vienna.

As we stood before the National Socialist bulk of the Reichsbank in that penetrating cold, a young *Hauptsturmfuehrer* new to the
unit gave permission to smoke and most of us shoved into our maws
that garbage that passed for cigarettes back then. Uwe Dering stood
next to me on the street in front of the massive Reichsbank building, its once impressive edifice streaked black with soot, windows
missing from the concussion of bombs. The British had conducted an
air raid the night before in Berlin North, and the Americans would
doubtless appear later in the morning. That was the routine: Brits at
night, Amis by day. Our big eighty-eights roared back at the fleets of

planes and brought some down, but nothing could stop this relent-less assault from the air.

Uwe and I had served together for years in the East, sharing long stretches of boredom, minor skirmishes, and major battles. We had both been slightly wounded by a Russian mortar shell that exploded near our trench in the Ukraine. There were others who had been part of our circle but they had fallen victim to time, transfers, or casualty lists.

In this Berlin detachment, only Uwe and I were "Old Fighters," although we were hardly old. We were physical opposites, the two of us. I was tall and lanky, while Uwe was squat and powerfully built. Uwe was from a Hamburg family of minor Protestant Hanseatic mer-chants and I was from the rural Catholic Bavarian south, but the war and the designation SS had long ago transcended any differences of outlook between us.

Uwe stamped his feet against the cobblestones and rubbed his hands together in a vain ritual to offset the biting cold. "Shit weather: *Scheiss Wetter*. I'd rather be back in the Crimea, at least the air is drier there."

"You wouldn't want to be in the Crimea now, Uwe," I told him. "It's full of Ivans. They tossed us out smartly the other year if you recall."

"You know what I mean. If we stay around here, we'll all end up in the tubercular ward. But from what I hear, we aren't staying. We move out today."

There were always rumors that made the rounds, about moving out, changes of commanders, new conscripts, who had been put in for the Iron Cross. In my experience, rumors were true about half the time. Still, I hadn't heard this one and had presumed that our de-tachment would be told to dig in to protect the Reichsbank during what was shaping up to be the pending battle of Berlin.

"We aren't moving out, Uwe," I said, "there's no transport here. Anyway, most of our vehicles have been sent off with Dietrich to Hungary."

Uwe sniffled and rubbed a coated sleeve across his nose and broad red cheeks. "Transport's in the courtyard behind the bank. It's not SS, the trucks are Wehrmacht. I heard two officers talking when I went to take a piss in the bank."

I mumbled some noncommittal response and looked around.

The troops loitered in small clusters, and every now and then someone eyed the sky nervously in what had come to be called the "German glance." But the skies remained mercifully empty. Just then the oversized bronze doors of the Reichsbank burst open and a phalanx of leather-coated officers issued onto the granite steps. They moved smartly and with purpose, the nature of which we could not divine. This procession of peaked caps adorned with the Death's Head insignia was set off here and there by a wide-brimmed fedora or Borsalino, a sprinkling of civilians with silk cravats and worried expressions.

"Something's up," I muttered to Uwe.

"I told you," he said. The other SS men had taken notice too and, as if answering to some primeval instinct, assumed more military postures.

One of the officers emerging from the bank wore the insignia of a *Stuermbannfuehrer*, and had one arm in a white sling, the hand of which was heavily bandaged, with a dried blood stain showing through like a badge of honor. He clutched a black leather attaché case with his good hand and had what appeared to be a map rolled up under his arm. I had never seen this officer before. He was thin-lipped, chiseled in an athletic way, and looked like a front soldier who had left his sense of humor in another jacket.

The wounded officer moved toward Uwe and me and said, "Line up for the trucks. You two up front with the driver. You there," he gestured to three soldiers just behind us, "get in the back with the cargo."

He marched down the sidewalk waving at the scattered soldiers, directing them where to stand. This done, he pulled himself into a camouflaged Volkswagen tactical car. Sitting next to a silent driver, he unrolled the map, pushed his cap far up on his forehead, and fixed his vision on the parchment. From the end of the block came a wheezing rumble of engines, announcing the arrival of a caravan of old military trucks with Wehrmacht registration plates.

"Only the best transportation for the Fatherland's elite," I said to Uwe.

"Right. Something to ease our journey to the site of the final victory." He snorted again, spit into the air and looked for a moment like a great dray horse incongruous against the ruined urban landscape.

The trucks coughed their way to the front of the bank, avoiding the potholes filled with fetid water and the enormous hills of debris, the detritus of destroyed apartment blocks. Noncommissioned officers busied themselves up and down the line once the trucks pulled to a stop.

"*Mach Schnell, Mach Schnell,*" they intoned, directing the enlisted men to their vehicles. It was clear that they wanted to get underway quickly to avoid any allied air raid.

Uwe followed me into the cab of the truck, our rifles banging into the dented door emblazoned with a painted Iron Cross. I moved in next to the grimacing, hatless driver. Uwe slammed in next to me. "Morning," we both uttered to the driver, who looked straight ahead out the windshield. He told us that his name was Ruediger, he was SS from the *Das Reich* division, had been in a hospital near Spandau recovering from shrapnel wounds until two days ago. The trucks had been picked up last night at an assembly area near Wilhelmstrasse and driven to the Reichsbank in darkness.

Organizing a unit of troops, even experienced ones, can take longer than you think, and I estimate it was fifteen minutes before our convoy groaned to life and began its plodding trajectory down the ruined street, past sentinel rows of silent, yawning facades framing spilled slagheaps of rubble and plumbing. The field car bearing the officer with the sling pulled ahead and led the column. I noticed that a large wooden crate lay heavy in the backseat, another SS officer beside it armed with a machine pistol and a *Panzer Faust* against tanks. The cabin of our truck was warm and full of fuel fumes and for a while no one spoke.

Our herd of metal beasts headed west, avoiding the network of autobahn. There were two reasons for this, even though the auto-bahn should have provided the quickest egress from the city. First, months of intense bombing had rendered the highways treacherous, removing their advantage as high-speed avenues of travel. Second, the bombings were increasingly frequent. Any convoy spotted from the air along these wide ribbons of asphalt would fall prey to enemy machines. Accordingly, the officer with the sling directed us through a maze of back streets until we left the Berlin suburbs and then took a series of country roads with the overall direction of southwest. After leaving Berlin by midday, we continued through the flat coun-tryside without pause until evening.

We garrisoned in a small farming village. It was a spectral and boarded-up place, the menfolk off to war and the women doing their best to raise the children and work the land. It was a losing proposi-tion and the faces we encountered were bitter. There was a *gasthof*, which we commandeered, and we enjoined the owner, a woman in her seventies, to break out some bottles of potato schnapps. We paid, of course, but she knew that the currency of the Reich wouldn't be worth a toss in a month or two.

There was a parish hall in the village and we slept there, our threadbare, coarse military blankets spread on the pinewood floors. It was infinitely better than those times of retreat in Russia when there was no sleep for days. In the morning the noncoms came round and told us where the field kitchen had been set up. Ersatz coffee was provided and we shoved down great gouts of the stuff to release our heads from the final, grasping talons of the previous night's schnapps.

As we drank our artificial coffee, a gray-haired *Scharrfuehrer* made the rounds and advised us that we could go back to bed or wander around the village as long as we stayed nearby. We would move out at dusk, he said, and added that from now on we would travel only during the hours of darkness until we reached our destination.

"Which is where?" Uwe asked.

"I don't know where we're headed anymore than you do," the *Scharrfuehrer* replied. "My bet is Munich to join with other *Waffen-SS* units to form a Southern Front. But who knows?" He contemplated the ground at his feet for an instant and wandered off.

Uwe and I had noticed the civilians the evening before in the village. There were perhaps a half dozen of them, swathed in expensive cashmere or loden greatcoats. They had been at the bank in Berlin. The clutch of civilians were a quiet lot and they didn't mingle with the troops or make conversation. Which was fine with me. Years of combat had given me a preference for the company of soldiers.

"I think they're golden pheasants," Uwe had pronounced when a trio of the civilians walked taciturnly by near the *gasthof*. Golden pheasants meant Nazi Party functionaries, derided for their handsome brown uniforms with gold insignia on a red field at their collars and on their caps. The Party officials were never popular with the troops; they wore uniforms without having earned the honor by fire.

"They aren't pheasants," I chastised Uwe, "they're wearing suits."

Uwe snickered and lowered his voice. "How many of the dainty Party boys do you figure are strutting around in uniforms and high boots these days with the Russian bear pawing at the door? They've probably burned anything with a swastika on it and have managed to get a ride south where they can fall on their knees to the Amis instead of the Ivans. Worthless louts."

I shrugged my shoulders. It wasn't worth arguing. Still, I doubted that the Waffen-SS would just agree to provide escort to Party hacks trying to dodge the Russians. This wasn't a delegation at the level of Goebbels or the Bormann brothers. And there was something else. These people looked intelligent in the way that professors and Jews often do. These weren't politicians.

As our second evening in the village approached and the first strain of darkness insinuated itself, we packed our kits and prepared to move out. A noncom insisted that we check our weapons and keep a round in the chamber; we would have done it anyway, like breathing. We tossed our sleeping bags into the truck bed and that was when I thought about the crates. Our truck, like all of the others, had three or four large wooden crates tied down with rope. There were numbers stamped in black ink across them, but nothing to betray the nature of the contents. We wedged our belongings in next to the crates, and I began to think about what sort of cargo we were carrying south. It occurred to me that it was the cargo — not us — that was important.

I was curious enough to seek out the weary but decent *Scharrfuehrer* we had encountered the previous evening. I found him smoking a pipe across the rutted lane from the *gasthof*, in the shadows of an old oak. He looked up with cavernous eyes as I approached. I asked what was in the crates and a thin smile traced itself across his lined visage.

"You don't really think a *Scharrfuehrer* would be privy to that kind of information, do you?"

"Maybe not, but you might have heard something from the officers."

He pulled the pipe from his mouth and studied it. "I don't have a clue what's in those boxes. Not munitions, the boxes aren't marked that way and it wouldn't make sense to transport explosives south. Could be documents. Don't forget we were in Berlin, which is getting the hell blasted out of it. Documents would make sense, from the *Reichskanzlei* or OKW Headquarters. Maybe historical items written by the Fuehrer. Who knows? Get the stuff to safekeeping in Bavaria, in some alpine fortress maybe."

I nodded and dragged a boot through the viscous, clutching mud. He was right, documents made sense.

The *Scharrfuehrer* replaced the pipe in his mouth, shifted his position and added a few sentences. "There's another possibility, but I wouldn't mention it too loudly if I were you. Where did we leave from? The Reichsbank. You know, keepers of the imperial gold among other things. The reichsmark isn't worth a damn anymore, but gold is always valuable. And if the war is to continue in some mountain redoubt in the south, money will be needed. Put two and two together. Enough said."

He looked at me again with an expression that was either indifferent or fatalistic. Then he wandered off toward the column of trucks.

Gold made more sense than documents. Why would we have otherwise gathered at the bank? To protect the transfer of gold bars from the vaults to the convoy. And to send it south to Munich or Upper Bavaria, the first home of the Party and now it's last bastion. As I walked back to the truck, the implications of the *Scharrfuehrer's* remarks took root.

This little group of armed, desperate men was sitting on top of the treasure of the entire Third Reich. The gold didn't alter the fact that the war was irretrievably lost. And who would it be delivered to? Party hacks in Munich who had enough common sense to realize that the ride was over. And who would find a way to vanish with the gold in their own pockets to secure a plush postwar life in Switzerland or South America?

Even more perversely, my comrades and I were supposed to protect this shipment with our lives. It's funny, I suppose, but men are willing to die for an ideal, a nation, a race, or a leader. They are considerably less willing to have their lifeblood drained out to protect somebody's economic well-being.

By the time I reached our truck, I had resolved not to say a word about my chat with the Scharrfuehrer, not even to Uwe. Under the circumstances, a rumor that gold was our cargo could be explosively corrosive. And so I kept my mouth shut, but the thought was planted and roiled around in my head.

Minutes later darkness held the terrain, and the gaunt officer with the sling told us to mount our vehicles and move out. A freezing, wind-driven rain had begun, adding to our prevailing depression. Our column of trucks ground through the grasping mire, leaving the village and striking out south. Through the cracked and mud-flecked windshield we saw the local residents observing our departure through doorways and weakly illuminated kitchen windows. They were our countrymen. And yet not even one of those solemn faces betrayed a look that wished us well.

We made poor headway that night due to the unrelenting downpour. As a result, the officers decided to keep pushing forward even after dawn broke, violating their own *Verbot* on daytime movement. This proved unwise. It was about seven thirty that morning when we spotted the American Mustang fighters, three of them in tight formation, not too high above the tree line. More to the point, the fighters spotted us, and the resonance of their engines turned angry as they banked for a strafing run.

"Deep fliers! Get off the damned road," someone yelled. The convoy disintegrated, individual trucks slamming hard across the terrain seeking out cover in the treeline edging the rural road.

Our driver kept muttering "shit" beneath his breath like some mystical incantation, and careened the old vehicle into a maze of scrub pines and brush. A sapling whipped by on my side and decapitated the rearview mirror. Uwe and I were half-under the heavy dashboard, trying to ready our rifles, but they were unwieldy in the confined space of the cab.

I heard the first, long baritone burst of machine gun fire behind us; the fighter planes had found a target and opened up. A few Mauser rifle shots rang out ineffectively in reply. There was the unmistakable sound of metal hitting metal and the chaotic, high-pitched scream of a vehicle crashing on its side and sliding.

Our driver cajoled the truck deeper into the undergrowth and we banged roughly along, rocks and brush slamming the belly of our transport. Still, the driver was good and had found a deer trace and moved along this path of least resistance. We were all breathing hard. Then the truck jolted to a stop, and I noticed that Ruediger, the driver, had pushed down on the foot brake.

"Here is okay," he mumbled. I looked through the side window and saw only high, yellow reeds and thin birch trunks, like the Pripet marshes we had encountered in Russia during that first exhilarating advance in 1941.

We heard the fighters swoop away overhead, engines singing. The sound faded and then seconds later intensified as the machines approached again for a second attack. There were panicked shouts and then the thudding impact of more airborne machine-gun rounds. Return fire sounded less ragged this time. And then the aircraft were gone. I caught a fleeting glimpse of them gaining altitude and soaring over a brown ridgeline in the distance, the burnished metal of their wings dully reflecting the muddy sunlight. It was as if they had lost interest in us and had decided to hunt for more worthy game. More likely, they had hit the limit of their fuel capacity and had to return to their airfield, somewhere along the Rhine.

We spilled out of the truck and, as one, stretched like cats after an extended nap. Behind us we could hear the voices of our comrades, plaintive requests for medical attention, orders bellowed out by the officers. There was a thick plume of oily black smoke issuing from the trees near the road and the crackle of flames from brush that had caught fire. After taking enough time to empty our bladders, Uwe, Ruediger, and I picked our way through the undergrowth back to the rest of the column.

Things were not as bad as they could have been. A line of SS men stood sentinel around the chaos, scanning the sky for any return of the American planes. One truck was on its side nestled among some austere-looking saplings. Two bodies had been pulled from the vehicle and lay alongside it.

I noted that both corpses had been spared disfigurement. Internal injuries, I concluded.

A second truck was burning madly still; its paint already devoured. A sort of charred sweet scent in the air, like a whore's cheap perfume gone bad, instructed us that the passengers of this vehicle were part of the pyre. Not a good death, I thought, hoping that, if my time came on this trip, it would be a bullet to the back of the head. One second you're here, the next second you're not.

"You there, help those fellows move the crates into the other trucks." It was the officer with the sling, clearly in command, two noncoms at his side. He gestured to the overturned vehicle where four or five solders were grunting and wrestling the heavy wooden containers from the canvas-covered bed.

"*Jawohl,*" Uwe said and we added ourselves without complaint to the little troop. As we maneuvered the first container to the ground, we heard the unmistakable tinkle of broken glass issue from inside.

"You need to be careful," a voice intoned from behind us.

Uwe and I turned and saw that it was one of the civilians, a thin, dour-looking man with a crushed hat and long, cadaverous face. He was wearing pince-nez glasses, which gave him a professorial cast.

"We're doing what we can," I said, evenly. "Whatever's broken in here broke when the truck slid over, not because we're manhandling it."

The civilian nodded and adjusted his glasses with a finicky motion. "I know, I know. It's just that we want as little damage as possible."

I was about to ask the fellow what sort of breakable stuff there was inside the crate, but before I could get the words out, he had touched the brim of his hat in a salute and turned away. It occurred to me that gold does not break or tinkle like glass. Was there also precious crystal or Dresden porcelain among the cargo? I returned to the ancient human task of lifting and pulling.

Within the hour we were underway again, leaving the wreckage behind. We buried the two comrades from the overturned truck in a gully by the road and an officer had recited a prayer and we had given the National Socialist salute. Their stahlhelm were placed atop crude crosses fashioned of branches from nearby trees and we inscribed their names on scraps of cardboard. It was the same ceremony I had witnessed a hundred times during the years in Russia. But now this feral, rushed ceremony preceding another retreat was being conducted on the soil of the Fatherland. What could speak more clearly of defeat?

We had to leave the charred and twisted remains of the four soldiers inside the burning truck. The truck was still too hot to approach, and we had to get moving, the little Scharrfuehrer said,
before the Americans returned. We moved to a small farm a few kilometers away, concealing our trucks in the barns and flush along the
sides of the outbuildings. We waited for the return of dusk, the time
that had now become our friend and steadfast protector.

So it went. Uneventful days huddled in villages, eating hardtack
and thin soup from the field kitchen and radishes and last year's
potatoes or whatever could be scrounged from the local inhabitants.
Underway by night, south, southwest. On a few occasions we heard
a radio broadcast of the latest war news in a gasthof. Even with
the best efforts of Goebbel's Reich Propaganda Ministry, the news
was bad.

Fronts collapsing east and west, entire Wehrmacht divisions
erased or overwhelmed by force majeure, the Rhine breached by
the Americans, panicked refugees from the east clogging the autobahn network, massive air raids incinerating Berlin, Dresden, and
Hamburg.

Of course, the commentary was peppered with references to Final
Victory, secret miracle weapons that would turn the tide, and odes
to the heroic individuals who were forcing the foe to "pay a heavy
price." But it didn't take a genius to know where things were going,
and Dante had described those surroundings rather well.

We heard Allied airplanes often over the next few days, but they
were at high altitude and on their way to or from somewhere else.
We crossed into Bavaria one night, traversing a winding one-lane
road surrounded by vineyards near Wuerzburg. We avoided the city
itself as it represented a bombing target. Here and there we encountered the corpses of Wehrmacht conscripts who had been
hanged by order of a flying court for desertion. Most of them looked
either too young or too old to be soldiers. Their crimes were written
on placards hung around their necks.

We passed the outskirts of Munich in moonlit semidarkness the next night, and I could see the shattered towers of the *Frauenkirche* like spectral giants brooding over the carcass of that ancient city. We did not pause; Munich was not our destination.

And then the next evening we found ourselves deep in the towering, protective folds of the Bavarian Alps, with lines of fir trees marching from the valley floor to heights far above us. My comrades and I were not far removed from where the two of us are sitting now. When dawn broke, it was as if we had entered a different world, as if the last months, even the last years, had been a bad dream.

Even at this stage of the war, the region had been largely spared the malevolent, consuming grasp of the conflict. There was no major city nearby, which meant that Allied bombers focused their attentions elsewhere. The battlefronts were getting closer by the day, but the countryside still remained unmolested and perversely peaceful.

We were able to dine on fresh milk and eggs and smoked ham. The locals had enough of these things and provided for us. We parked our convoy under the shelter of trees along the bank of a valley stream. The mountain water was pristine, and we drank huge, gulping mouthfuls and used it to wash the accumulated filth and sweat and stink of fear from our uniforms.

For two days we did nothing else; ate, drank, slept, and wandered around that patch of countryside, reveling in the scenery and stillness. No one spoke of the war. It was as if the topic — the center of our lives for the past six years — had suddenly become taboo.

On the third day, around ten in the morning, we were told to prepare for a short journey. Uwe, Ruediger, and I mounted our vehicle without enthusiasm, content to forget military duties altogether and await the conclusion of hostilities, whatever that might bring. But we did as we were ordered.

"What do you think is up?" Ruediger asked.

Uwe grumbled out a laugh and slapped his meaty hands together. "It's one of two things. Either we are all going to some field where we will be instructed to shoot ourselves as exemplary heroes for the Fatherland in its last hours, or we're going to unload these crates."

"The Fuehrer Headquarters in Obersalzburg," Ruediger mused. "That might be where we're headed. Its not far from here; thirty kilometers maybe. It's bound to have bunkers and tunnels, exactly what's needed to store whatever the hell is in these crates."

Uwe and I shrugged, judging that the next few hours would resolve the issue.

Our column wheezed to life in a cloud of exhaust fumes. The Volkswagen with its Waffen-SS officer was in the lead. One of the civilians was seated next to the Stuermbannfuehrer with the arm sling. The wounded officer had his well-creased topographical map out and communicated the route to his driver.

We moved from the valley road to a well-paved but serpentine way that took us into the mountains. When the asphalt ended, we found ourselves jostling along a rough earthen path, the valley floor from which we had issued now a distant emerald vision far below us.

There was a dissonant cacophony of engines grinding away, and I wondered how high the abused vehicles could manage to go before they overheated. The Stuermbannfuehrer turned in his seat every now and then, checking the halting progress of his troop. His expression seemed as granitic as the jagged peaks rising above us. Despite the protesting motors, the trucks doggedly moved higher into the terrain, untended meadows to the right and left. The sweep of tall grass was dotted with mountain wildflowers, an iridescent aquarelle of white, yellow, and blue. The rough road curved to the left and the meadows slipped away behind us. Deep shadows from rows of fir trees rolled protectively over the hoods of our vehicles. We entered high forest, and the ground was transformed from green to burnished gold from a thick carpet of needles.

Up ahead of the column, I saw a trio of men standing motionless at the base of a towering pine tree. One of the men wore a brown Nazi Party uniform set off with a swastika armband; a *kreisleiter* perhaps. His two companions were more humbly dressed in Bavarian country attire, with battered loden hats and worn workmen's boots.

The Stuermbannfuehrer raised his arm and the column eased to a stop, the engines of our vehicles winding down to a low grumble.

The trio of men approached the Volkswagen and the Party official stretched out his arm in the Hitler salute, which was casually returned by the SS officer. The men huddled together in conference, occasionally glancing back at the column of lorries. It occurred to me that the conclave could involve a discussion of surrender arrangements. Perhaps the golden pheasant represented the local *gauleiter* and was empowered to come up with the best way for German forces in the area to give up to the Americans, whose arrival was expected any day. I was mistaken.

The Stuerbannfuehrer gestured for some of the other officers to join him, and after the exchange of a few words, they moved along the line of trucks issuing orders in curt, staccato style.

"Engines off. Everyone out of the vehicles, *Mach Schnell*. Five minute pause. We'll be unloading the cargo after that and returning to the valley. Under no circumstances are the crates to be opened."

Doors groaned against bent hinges, and we issued forth to the pine needle-coated earth that was like a sponge beneath our boots. Everyone spent their first minute stretching, coaxing away the small hurts caused by our rough journey. The crates would be heavy and unwieldy, and we knew that there was heavy lifting in our immediate future.

Uwe stood next to me and fished a small, unlabeled bottle of schnapps from the voluminous pocket of his greatcoat. He took a swig, and passed the glass container to me. I took a sip without much enthusiasm but enjoyed the burst of warmth as the crude alcohol attacked my throat. We strode into the rows of fir trees.

"I expect this is our last mission, comrade. The rest should be a matter of waiting for the hordes of Negroes and Red Indians to sweep us up." Uwe's tone was fatalistic.

"Most GIs look like we do, Uwe, just different uniforms. But you're right, I guess this is the end of the road. We unload this stuff, whatever it is, and head back down the valley and wait. If the Americans come in a few days they'll ship us off to some prisoner-of-war camp. If they are delayed, some of our younger recruits will slip away; try to make it home on their own. Not me. I'm waiting. We've made it through six years of war without getting killed, and I don't intend to take a bullet now. I'm content to sit on my ass and wait."

Uwe breathed out a laugh. "Smart man. I'll tell you one thing, though. I thank God that we got these orders to head south. I couldn't have surrendered to the Ivans. I'd shove my Mauser in my mouth before being shipped off in a cattle car to Siberia." Uwe was smiling, but there was a hardness around his eyes that I had seen before during combat. He was earnest.

I craned my head up toward the dark and tangled tree tops and saw swaths of brilliant blue sky through the branches. It occurred to me that I wanted to see lots of blue skies.

The unmistakable report of a pistol cast all further thought into hiding. "What the hell—" I heard Uwe exclaim and then we were both running toward the trucks, our rifles held chest high, fingers near the trigger guards. We scrambled loudly through the chaos of pine branches. There had been only a single shot, a subsequent protest of irate ravens forced from their arboreal perch, and then silence. A knot of soldiers was gathered round one of the vehicles near the end of the column. Uwe and I joined the gray-uniformed mass. We edged through the crowd for a look.

I recognized the soldier on the ground and knew that his last name was Fehlmann. He had been with us for maybe eight months and spoke with a Swabian accent. There was little more that I knew about him. Except that he was now dead. A dark, still expanding circular blotch of blood at the hairline just above the nape of his neck marked the entrance wound. The exit wound had caused catastrophic damage. Fehlmann's lower jaw had been separated from the rest of his face and hung grotesquely low. His upper palate was mostly gone. Fehlmann had been hit by a bullet fired close-up.

"Scharrfuehrer, when they get their fill of gaping, have a couple of men bury this trash under the trees. Then we unload the trucks." It was the Stuermbannfuehrer, an officer's Luger automatic clutched in a black-gloved hand, the one not supported by the sling.

"Jawohl, Stuermbannfuehrer," roared the noncom, his parade-ground voice betraying no emotion.

The officer nodded, seemingly soothed by the noncom's compliance and the familiar tone of obedience. Glancing around at the gathered soldiers, the SS officer pointed his pistol at the body lying in the porridge of sludge near the rear tires of the truck. He used the weapon to gesture, the metal-blue barrel holding our attention as a conductor's baton holds together an orchestra.

"There are a few lessons that bear mentioning, *Soldaten*. One, follow orders. Two, do the job assigned. Three, never do what is not permitted. Our disgraced comrade here violated all of these principles. I discovered him rifling open a crate at the back of this truck. That was a very poor decision."

The officer holstered his weapon and took a few steps toward the corpse. He nudged the body with the toe of his high boots.

"You will recall that I ordered that no one opens the crates. I will brook no disobedience. Our mission, the mission we began in Berlin, is too important."

I glanced around and noted that the Party official and the civilians were nodding agreement.

After this deadly illustration, our group was not about to split up without an explicit command, something that the Sturembannfuehrer sensed.

"All right. Lesson over. Get ready to move the cargo. Four men to each crate and put your shoulders into it. Bring the crates to the civilians up the hill for final disposition; they know what to do. After that, we leave." He paused a second and invoked the SS motto, "*Unsere ehre ist treue*." Our honor is loyalty.

We did put our shoulders into it and our backs too, hands chafing against the roughly planed wood. Some crates were heavier than others, but four men to each made the burden bearable. Still, there were a considerable number of containers and we had to make multiple trips. We moved slowly up the hill and the rude road became a path and then a deer trace and finally nothing at all.

As we staggered upward, the flush-faced Party official worried himself around us, flitting here and there, ceremonial dagger like a miniature Roman broadsword clanging against his belt. Now and then he would intone "Slow but sure," "That's the way boys," and other moronic utterances, but we said nothing in reproach.

As instructed, we deposited the freight high up on a spit of ground where the civilians had gathered. The two workmen were there, and I noticed that their shoulders held thick coils of rope. They would be dragging the crates to some final place, presumably close by.

Indifferent to our exertions, the afternoon waned, shifting the forest latticework of sunlight and shadow into new and changing designs. By the time we finished, it was that strangely quiet interval before dusk, that bundle of moments when all living things seem to pause and await the onset of darkness.

As promised by our SS commander, we loaded back onto our trucks, the lot of us bone-tired and thirsty, and began the slow, jogging return to the valley from which we had set out that morning. Our group now numbered one less. As our truck groaned its way downhill, Uwe, Ruediger, and I glanced over at the raised mound of earth near the roadside. Fehlmann's final resting place was unmarked. I do not recall that we engaged in conversation during the return journey, content to cede pride of place to silence, that fearsome but respected companion of soldiers everywhere.

As events developed, we were not to wait out the remaining days of the war idling by the rushing valley stream. Two days after we rid ourselves of the crates, a Wehrmacht motorcycle appeared from the direction of Bad Reichenhall, its grim-visaged rider sporting the distinctive metal breastplate of a courier. He passed a sheet of paper to our commander, who read it slowly. He tucked the message into his tunic and told the other officers to prepare us to move out.

Upon hearing this news, Uwe began his litany of "damn" and "shit," interspersed with an equestrian stamping of his feet.

Off we rode, crossing the former border of Austria, currently *Ostmark*, a province of the Greater German Reich. The weather remained fine, improving our mood, and the scenery was no less

breathtaking than in the alpine valley. We drove across the broad
Salzach plain, the line of mountains pulling farther away. The proud
fortress of the former Prince-Archbishop Paris Lodron of Salzburg
was to our left, still imperiously presiding over the city below it after
all those long centuries.

And then the plain and Salzburg slipped away and we were again
moving along narrow slips of road between mountain peaks. Place
names rolled by in large black, block letters on white road signs.
Bischofshofen, Sankt Johann, other towns now forgotten. And then
we entered Zell am See, an isolated lake resort with its high meadows, stone farmhouses, and country folk with angular Albrecht Dürer
faces.

The commander led the column in his Volkswagen. He signaled
for us to leave the main road and we pulled onto a lane flanked by
sweeping meadows, violently green and inviting. Scattered throughout the meadows were small wooden huts used to store hay, their
dark edifices like shadows against the shining land. Raising his one
good arm, the commander signaled the column to pull off to the side
of the road. Our commander dismounted, hopped a rail fence, strode
into the meadow, and yelled for us to follow. We did, weapons slung
barrel down over our shoulders.

The officer strode deep into the meadow, long, curved blades of
grass extending to his waist. "All right. Gather round. I expect you'll
want to hear what I have to say." He tugged his peaked cap from his
head and ran his good hand through his short-cropped blond and
gray hair. We formed a circle around him and listened.

"Tonight we billet in these sheds," he gestured vaguely at the
rude structures peppered through the meadows. "Leave the vehicles
where they stand. We won't be needing them anymore. I am advised
that the war is officially ending soon and not in a German victory.
The Fuehrer is dead; fallen in the battle for Berlin. As far as I can figure out from the communiqués, Grand Admiral Doenitz is now
reichskanzler. He's with the remains of the *Kriegsmarine* in Kiel.
Serious fighting seems to have stopped in the west, but there are
sharp delaying actions in the east, where our troops are trying to

protect German civilians from that Mongol garbage and get them safely to the American and British areas. An official cease-fire will happen soon, but as far as I'm concerned, we have a cease-fire here and now for all of us."

He looked from soldier to soldier now, as if seeking out a personal connection with us. "Remember, *SS-Maenner*, there is no dishonor in surrendering to overwhelmingly superior forces. We've done our duty for *fuehrer, volk, und vaterland*. Remain proud."

The commander kicked at a clod of earth with a booted heel. We all remained still, mesmerized not just by what we were hearing, but by what it meant. We had come to the end of the war. Its end was here, incongruously, in this green meadow with snow-capped peaks serving as a backdrop. We who remained, who stood in this nameless farmer's field, were the survivors. The moving hand of Providence had spared us.

The commander breathed a great sigh, like a man who has just surfaced from a long time under water. "We'll stack our weapons here. I ask the noncommissioned officers to go to the nearest farmhouses and find sheets or white cloth to hang on the trucks and for armbands. I don't want any mistakes when the Amis arrive. We have sufficient rations for a few days so all we have to do is sit tight and wait; it won't be long before we are gathered up. No doubt, we'll be in prison camps for a while, but I don't expect it to be too bad; the entire German Army will be prisoner for God's sake. After a while, they'll tell us to go home and rebuild the country that they bombed all to hell. And I expect that we will.

"One final thing. This last mission that we conducted after leaving Berlin is something to forget. I appeal to your SS honor. Say nothing about the cargo, for the sake of the old Germany and the new one that will emerge. Forget about it. As far as the Amis are concerned, we're just one more convoy that was fleeing from east to west when everything collapsed. All right. Smoke and drink if you want, but don't get carried away. Keep discipline. When we surrender, we do so as front soldiers. Dismissed."

And that was all. At first we just stood there, uncertain of what to do. The commander moved first, slowly walking away from us deeper into the meadows. Our company of dirty, gray-clad men then broke up, fanning out aimlessly through the grass or back toward the vehicles. And there is, it seems to me, nothing more to say about that time long ago or about those comrades, now mostly gone down into that silent, dark place from which no word ever issues.

A cascade of foam glided down the side of Sedlmeyer's beer glass and pooled on the cardboard coaster beneath it. The waitress had just delivered another round and swept up the four empty glasses the two had drained during the course of the old man's monologue. Sedlmeyer raised the glass with a hand like ancient paper, nodded his head in a little salute, and took a long drink. Placing the glass back on its coaster, he muttered softly "So then, that's it," and settled back into his chair, looking his table companion in the eye.

Hirter had found the story engrossing but could not detect its relevance to his brother's death. He wondered why Sedlmeyer had called him here to listen to this panegyric to long-dead Teutonic warriors. But he knew that he had to tread cautiously with the old man.

"That's a powerful story, Herr Sedlmeyer," he began. "I guess you should count yourself lucky to have lived through those times."

Sedlmeyer displayed no reaction.

"What happened to your friend Uwe and the SS officer with the sling?"

The old man shrugged his narrow shoulders. "Uwe and I stayed in touch for years, a letter here, a phone call there. He eventually got a job as a bartender, saved his money, and opened up his own *kneipe*, or pub, in Hamburg. A heart attack took him seven years ago. The Stuermbannfuehrer I'm less sure about; I can't even recall his name anymore. It's odd; he was gone by the time the Amis showed up in our Austrian meadow. Vanished during the night. I heard years later from some of the other unit veterans that he escaped on foot to northern Italy, and managed to cross into Switzerland. It was years later before he was able to get back to Germany, with a new identity of course. It was easier to arrange those things back then. But who knows, maybe he never made it back at all."

Hirter suspected that his host was not being transparent in every respect but judged that it didn't matter.

"You didn't ask, but our driver, Ruediger, got to put his skills to good use. He begged the Americans to be allowed to keep the Wehrmacht truck he had been driving. They let him. He drove it back to his home town and started the local transport service, hauling stuff back and forth in exchange for a dozen eggs or a bottle of schnapps. He eventually bought a second truck and another and today owns one of the largest transportation companies in Germany."

"Herr Sedlmeyer, don't get me wrong or think me ungrateful but —"

The white-maned man stopped him with the curt wave of a hand.

"Herr Hirter, you're wondering what my story could possibly have to do with your brother's death, *nicht wahr?* As I said earlier, I have only history to offer you; I don't know about the murder. I understand that you want facts; what I offer you is just background."

"I understand," Robert intoned, careful to keep annoyance from his voice, "but I don't see how anything you've told me has the slightest connection to my brother's death."

Sedlmeyer leaned forward on his elbows, clasped hands forming an arch above his beer glass, perching like an old bird of prey. "Just this. The place where Fehlmann was killed is close to where your brother was found. Our convoy drove right through the high meadow where your brother died. So, two acts of violence in nearly the same location over the course of half a century. Coincidence? Maybe. But I wonder. Our mysterious cargo is probably still up there somewhere, forgotten. Or maybe someone spirited it off after we left. But for what it's worth, I have a feeling it's still hidden up there. Ruined by the years and the elements perhaps, but up there still."

Robert Hirter nodded slowly. "You're saying that my brother's death could be connected to that Nazi gold or whatever it was. You think that maybe he found it?"

Sedlmeyer shook his head. "I did not say that. I have no idea what your brother did or didn't do, what he did or did not find. I only provide you something to consider. Maybe it means nothing, maybe it means everything. That is for you to explore, not me. But I wonder why some tourist would be murdered up there for no apparent reason."

"Herr Sedlmeyer, why are you telling me this? You might be right; this history could be relevant to Charles's murder. But why did you seek me out? And why haven't you gone to the police?"

The veteran's eyes narrowed, which gave him an almost reptilian appearance. "The police? No. It's unwise for a former SS man to go to the police and relate tales of violence, no matter how ancient. You say in English 'let sleeping dogs lie.' That is a sensible phrase. Why did I relate my story to you? For closure, I suppose. I read about the murder, and it got me wondering about those events from long ago. It was an impulse. I feel now that I have settled an account. If I had said nothing to you, it would have seemed like unfinished business. At my age, I don't much care for unfinished business; I want to wrap up loose ends. The violence from the war was sufficient for a lifetime. But I sometimes think that Fehlmann's ghost wanders around up there. For a soldier to die just before a war ends is a wretched fate. Does your brother's spirit now roam those meadows and woods as well? You decide." The old man paused and lowered his voice to a sibilant whisper. "There is one other reason that I'm here."

"Which is?"

"Because you, Herr Hirter, are buying the beer. *Auf wiedersehen.*" And with that he rose and slipped away, moving with the careful grace of a hunter and so silently that Hirter wondered for a moment whether the old man had really been there at all.

Chapter 8

Hirter departed the Alte Post without ever having noted that Wald-baer had been sitting in the establishment the entire time, obscured from view by a broad stone column. Waldbaer, sitting with his usual cluster of companions, had been surprised to see the American enter the place. He had been more surprised to watch him share a table with old Sedlmeyer and engage in a long conversation with the octogenarian. On the surface of it, the convergence of these two very different men made little sense. Was this incident relevant to the murder of Hirter's brother?

Waldbaer could not imagine how Sedlmeyer, a long-retired villager, could have any connection to the murder. But if not, why was Hirter so earnestly conversing with him?

"Franz, what's on your mind? Not drifting back to police work tonight are we?" It was the voice of Markus, once a school chum of the Kommissar and, for the last twenty years, a teacher at the local high school. Markus had his usual cynical smile affixed to his fea-tures, small, dark eyes rendered obscure behind thick granny glasses. His gray hair was long in the back, touching the collar of a worn, burgundy wool sweater.

"Not police work exactly. Just connecting some thoughts."

Markus feigned a grimace. "Sounds like we're getting very close to breaking the rules, Franz. You need to guard against that tendency, you know."

The third party at the table snickered into a half-full glass of Spaten. Hans Lechner, who had just eased into his seventies, was a retired general practitioner who now spent his leisure time painting alpine landscapes.

As a riposte to the older man's snicker and the teacher's chastisement, Waldbaer raised both hands as if to ward off a blow. "I know the rules. I won't violate them. Not tonight anyway."

The Kommissar's reference was to the rules governing the *stammtisch*, the little social circle that met with weekly regularity at the same table at Zum Alte Post. When the group of friends had decided to form a stammtisch a decade ago, it had been made a condition that members would not carry their work into the establishment, but would pursue enlightenment through exploring other themes. Politics, economics, the arts, all were accepted fare. But the details of daily employ were to be left at the door.

"I pose a question," Waldbaer said portentously.

His two companions nodded acceptance.

"It is in the way of a puzzle. We live in a small, self-contained village."

More nods.

"Sometimes there are visitors. Usually friends or relatives of someone who lives here. But sometimes there are other visitors — tourists or foreigners who don't have connections here, who don't know anyone locally. Maybe they're here for the scenery and the isolation. Bearing that in mind, here's the question: Why would a visitor with no ties here hold a long conversation with a villager? What would be the purpose? Responses from this august audience are eagerly awaited."

Markus, the teacher, rubbed his chin, as if to determine whether there was any stubble there. "This has to do with something real, doesn't it, not something theoretical?"

Hans, the doctor, raised a finger in the air as if to test wind direction inside the room. "Not just that, Markus. Our detective friend is trying to move us into his professional domain through the back door. Not as cleverly as he thinks. This question is connected to vile police affairs, rely on it. But let's permit him his conceit. What we need are more details. For example, are we talking about a brief conversation between two people, a few minutes? Are they male and female, same age? A few more scraps of information, please, Herr Kommissar."

Waldbaer took a sip of his warming beer. "Perceptive as always,"
he remarked. "More details. The two people I mention are not the
same age by a long shot and both are male. The foreigner is fairly
young; early forties. The villager is twice that age. They confer for
about an hour. So, what would the two people I have just described
have to discuss?"

Markus rapped the table lightly with a fist. "My first guess follows the Law of Simplicity — always look for the least torturous explanation. I say they were talking about something touristy. You
know — some local point of interest. An old villager would know
that stuff and a foreigner, a hiker say, would be interested in those
sorts of details."

Waldbaer shook his head. "It's too simple. Why wouldn't the foreigner just go to the tourist bureau or buy a guidebook? The local
fellow, by the way, isn't one of these old mountain goats who can
describe every trail and rock between Chiemsee and Kufstein. You'll
have to do better, Markus."

The school teacher shrugged and looked over at Hans. "Your
turn."

Hans steepled his fingers. "There has to be a reason why this
tourist held a long conversation with this *particular* villager. What
that connection is might be unknowable at present. But, you want
possibilities. What you describe could be a chance meeting — two
people find themselves in the same place and just start talking and
the conversation sustains itself for a while. Not all that farfetched because a foreigner and a local would each have completely different
life experiences to relate. But, if we want to rule out chance encounter, one of the two would have had to initiate the contact. Either the foreigner contacted the villager or the villager contacted
the foreigner."

Waldbaer thought about this and released a slow sigh. "You
might be right. But I don't think the foreigner knows anybody

around here. Which would mean that the villager contacted this visitor. For reasons unknown."

The school teacher spoke up, one hand idly playing at the sleeve of his sweater. "You know something that you aren't telling us. Any additional tidbit to cough up, Franz?"

The Kommissar smiled. "Maybe. But telling you anything more would make you accomplices to police work."

His companions emitted a chorus of protestations. "Well," said Markus, "we're this far already, let's finish it. What do you know, Franz?" The detective knew that he had successfully hooked them, as intended. He had only to keep an eye to police propriety and not reveal privileged information.

"All right, gentlemen. The foreigner is no tourist. He's here for a reason. He is a close relation to someone murdered here recently; the case is active with no solid leads. He's lodging in the area and intent on staying until we uncover the murderer."

The doctor seemed newly energized and his eyes betrayed passion for the first time that evening. "This meeting with a villager has to do with the murder. It's a lead the visitor turned up, or someone has offered him information. Does this foreigner speak German?"

"Yes. Speaks it well."

"That clinches it," the retired doctor continued with assurance, "something to do with information about the murder."

Waldbaer turned the beer glass slowly around between his palms and wondered. Perhaps it was after all just coincidence that brought Hirter and Sedlmeyer together. But his nature rebelled at this facile explanation. Coincidences occurred in life, but rarely, like miracles. Waldbaer did not feel disposed to base the plinth of his investigation on such uncertain ground. Odd as it might be, his table companions were probably right; the murder was the key. Hirter was focused solely on his brother's death. The American would not be interested in chatting to some wizened local about the origins of Bavarian wood carving.

But what could Sedlmeyer know that could even vaguely be associated with the murder of Hirter's brother? There was only one way to find out. He would have to confront Hirter or Sedlmeyer, or both, and ask directly what they had discussed. This conclusion reached, Waldbaer felt better and permitted himself a long swallow of beer.

"All right," he said to his two friends. "You've convinced me. The meeting must have had to do with the murder. I'll pursue matters accordingly."

The two others at table beamed with self-satisfaction bordering on smugness. The detective raised his glass and invoked the Germanic equivalent of "cheers." *Zum Wohl*.

Chapter 9

It was a tactic designed to underline his authority. Waldbaer had called Hirter at the hotel and curtly requested that the American meet him at the police station. He had toyed with driving out to meet Hirter at the Hotel Alpenhof, but rejected the notion as overly deferential. After all, he was the Kommissar charged with the investigation and Hirter was merely a next of kin to the victim. Waldbaer intended to do some direct talking to Hirter about Sedlmeyer, and the hotel lobby was hardly the most conducive setting for such a dialogue. Much better the spartan ambience of police offices exuding unalloyed seriousness of purpose.

Waldbaer flipped through the front section of the *Sueddeutsche Zeitung* as he drank his second cup of morning coffee, but found nothing meriting more than a quick glance. He had asked Hirter to meet him at eleven and the clock on the wall informed him that it was now a quarter past that assigned hour. The lack of punctuality annoyed Waldbaer, who had purposely given Hirter a civilized appointment time.

With its usual squeak of protest, the wooden door to Waldbaer's office groaned and an orange-sweatered girl from the secretarial pool with equally orange hair peeked in.

"There's a Herr Hirter to see you. If you're busy, he can wait by the main desk."

Waldbaer shook his head from side to side, noting that his neck felt slightly stiff.

"No. Have him come in. Any coffee out there?"

"Not anymore. Except from the machine upstairs. Want me to get you a cup of that?"

"Let the motor vehicle boys drink that swill. I'll get something across the street later."

With a nod, the orange apparition disappeared, replaced seconds later by the lanky, unsmiling form of Robert Hirter.

"Guten morgen, Herr Hirter," the Kommissar beckoned his visitor to a chair in front of his desk.

Waldbaer noted with mild annoyance that his guest had dressed for the occasion in a striped polo shirt, blue jeans, and Nikes. In an act of silent sartorial censure, the police officer adjusted his tie. Waldbaer folded the newspaper on his desk with a fastidious motion. He sighed, something he found himself doing often these days.

"Some development in my brother's case, I hope, is why you asked me to come here?" The American was leaning forward, both hands grasping the overstuffed arms of the chair.

Waldbaer held a hand up in the universal gesture for "stop" and drilled his eyes into Hirter's.

"Herr Hirter, today you will answer questions, not pose them. But since you've asked, the answer is no, there is not a stitch of anything new in your brother's murder case. But maybe you have something for me."

The police officer stopped to gauge Hirter's reaction, but the American just gave him a puzzled look.

"Herr Hirter, I've tried to be as open with you as the law permits. I try to make allowances for the pain you feel. But one thing I cannot have is a person like yourself starting his own parallel investigation."

"I'm doing no such thing. Although I think I have every right—"

The Kommissar reinvoked the "stop" gesture to arrest the comment.

"Herr Hirter, let me get to the point. You held a lengthy conversation with one August Sedlmeyer last night in Zum Alte Post."

He paused again, letting his eyes hunt across Hirter's face. It was clear that Hirter was surprised the police were so well informed about his activities. *He will suspect he is under surveillance,* Waldbaer thought, *an illusion which need not be dispelled.*

He continued, his voice neutral, the way he wanted it. *The voice,* he remembered from the Academy, *is the interrogator's paramount tool.* "You spent considerable time with Sedlmeyer and paid for his drinks. I'd like to have your version of the conversation, please."

Right, your version, *suggesting without explicitly stating that Sedlmeyer had already talked about the episode.*

Hirter looked unhappy and brushed a hand through his hair. He looked away from the detective and his eyes rested for a moment on the two topographical maps affixed to one office wall, one of Bavaria, the other of *Bundesrepublik Deutschland*.

"I'm over here, Herr Hirter," the policeman intoned without inflection.

Hirter sighed. "As far as I'm aware, I can talk to whomever I want. The Third Reich is over, I understand."

Waldbaer decided to ignore the barb and let his silence carry the conversation along.

"The man you mentioned — Sedlmeyer — contacted me. I met at his request. He left a note at the hotel saying he wanted to talk. That he had background that might indirectly have relevance to my brother's death. So naturally I went to hear him out."

My two friends were exactly right, Waldbaer noted to himself. He waited to see if Hirter would offer any elaboration without prompting.

"This fellow Sedlmeyer didn't have any information about the murder. It was an interesting evening, but I can't believe it was important."

"Well, Herr Hirter, that's one possible conclusion. But permit me to make my own judgment. I'd like to hear how the conversation went."

"Kommissar, I told Sedlmeyer that our conversation would remain private. That's the way he wanted it and I agreed."

"What is it you Americans are so fond of saying? 'That was then, this is now.' I'm investigating a murder and I will judge whether or not Sedlmeyer's remarks are relevant. Not you. Not him. Me. I'm waiting."

Hirter threw Waldbaer a reproachful look. "All right," he said flatly. "He told me about the end of the war and what he had seen. He told me that he witnessed a murder back then not far from where my brother was killed. An SS officer shot a soldier. Back in 1945, according to Sedlmeyer, a convoy brought secret cargo up through that high meadow and into the woods. I suppose you want details."

Waldbaer nodded affirmatively. Things were moving somewhere. Relevance to the murder was hardly certain, but Waldbaer had a feeling that here was a trace to be followed.

"Tell me the details, and take your time," the policeman said.

Ninety minutes later Waldbaer placed his Mont Blanc ballpoint on his desk and pushed aside the sheets of paper on which he had scribed notes in a rippling, jagged script.

Hirter had been right in his initial remark; this was ancient history. It was hard to imagine that the events described could help resolve the murder. Still, Waldbaer knew from long investigative experience, it was best to consider the facts described, to roll them over, rather than dismiss them with undue haste.

"Are you hungry?" he asked his guest.

"I could use a sandwich, I guess," Hirter replied.

"Or a sandwich and a beer," Waldbaer mused aloud. He pushed his chair back from the desk, grimacing at the shriek of wooden legs against the tile floor. "There's a cafe across the street which hasn't poisoned me yet. Let's go there. Any further questions I have I can ask while we eat. After that, feel free to head back to the hotel. Or back to the States, though I expect you are still resisting that sensible idea."

"Right," Hirter replied.

Waldbaer nodded, buttoned his rumpled forest green loden jacket, and led the way from the police station, feeling unaccountably weary.

The cafe was closed, a cardboard sign hung on the glass door announcing the reason as an unexpected death in the family. The detective turned toward his guest. "How about a Doener kebab?"

"A what?" Hirter replied, puzzled.

"Turkish sandwich in pita bread. More popular in Germany than your cheeseburgers. They're spicy and hearty. Try one."

Hirter nodded agreement, and the two men wandered down the street to a shop front with a take-out window. An olive-skinned, black-bearded man was cutting sizzling strips of lamb from a slowly turning rotisserie. Waldbaer walked up to the metal counter and ordered two kebabs and two bottles of pilsner. The Turk nodded, expertly slicing the bread and stuffing the pocket with meat, yoghurt, lettuce, diced tomatoes, and onions. The policeman paid, moved to a bistro table on the sidewalk, and offered a Doener and a bottle of beer to Hirter. The two chewed slowly as they surveyed the street.

"Good?" Waldbaer inquired between gulps.

"Good," Hirter affirmed.

"So, Herr Kommissar, maybe you can tell me off the record what you think happened to my brother. Just between us. I know there aren't many facts, but what do your instincts tell you?"

Waldbaer weighed the question and decided that it was fair enough. "Instinct is for animals. It's nature's compensation for beasts that can't think properly. But I know what you mean. Every investigator develops a feeling for things, even before all the evidence is available to examine. My feeling is that your brother wasn't randomly killed. I have a sense that whoever killed your brother is still around. And that the killer had a reason to murder, or thought he did." Waldbaer brought the pilsner bottle to his lips.

"What reason?" Hirter asked.

The detective shrugged. "Don't know. Not yet. But in general it would make sense that your brother saw something he shouldn't have. And to that extent, the murder was defensive. By which I mean, it wasn't robbery, sex thrills, or political assault. Someone has something to hide. That's what I think, but cannot at the moment prove. But this, too, might change."

Hirter nodded. Maybe this rumpled, overweight heap of a small-town detective is the right man after all, he conceded.

Chapter 10

August Sedlmeyer slept deeply and dreamt of death. This happened invariably on those occasions when he had stirred up the embers of his past and permitted memories to give life to long, somber columns of ghosts. He turned onto his side to ease the chronic ache of old bones, stretching slowly in the wide bed that was his alone since the passing of his wife, Anna, ten years ago. His spouse of more than thirty years was a ghost too; a spirit, but she did not populate his dreams this night.

Sedlmeyer dreamt now of German ghosts, spectral ranks wearing the SS camouflage pattern. The German phantoms were comrades; death did not sever those bonds. The ghosts that visited Sedlmeyer this night did not display the twisted rictus of violent death, but looked at him with visages entirely alive. Why were they visiting him this night? Was his time finally here? No, not quite yet, he felt certain.

He had remained loyal to them, *treu*. He considered again his conversation with the young American. Had he said too much? No. He had related events from long ago that could neither jeopardize nor dishonor his comrades. He had felt impelled to do this, but didn't know why exactly. Perhaps there *was* some obscure connection between the events of long ago and the death of the American's brother.

Sedlmeyer turned again in his uneasy slumber. He had not told Hirter everything. Some postwar events had found no place in his tale. Sedlmeyer would say nothing further about the SS officer with the sling. He sank deeper into the caressing embrace of sleep and saw again the long, taciturn line of phantoms, faces expressionless, patiently waiting for him across an expanse of field in the gloaming. And he thought again with fascinated dread of that dark and silent land from which no courier ever returns.

Waldbaer parked on the side of the narrow valley road, turning off in sequence the *Bayern Funf* classical music station from Munich and the ignition. Even with the radio off, the gentle, bittersweet musical sentiment of Bruckner's String Quintet in F Major played on in his head. He nudged open the car door with his shoulder and climbed out, releasing a sigh more from habit than from any burst of exertion. He found that he sighed often these days and worried about what it meant. He stretched and was mildly concerned about the brittle snapping sound that his elbows seemed to make lately.

The detective took a few steps into the rich grass lining the road, his sturdy loafers, unpolished and neglected, sinking into the sea of soft blades. He noted how verdant the valley looked in the lush late afternoon sunlight. It was, he thought, like one of those eighteenth-century landscape paintings on display at the Lembach gallery in Munich, with their arresting contrasts of vivid color and deep shadow. The scenes of paint and canvas had long outlived their creators. We are ephemerons, he mused, but a few leave something behind for others to reflect upon. He turned his mind to more pressing directions.

He could not shake the sense that the recent murder might be connected to old Sedlmeyer's story. Two events separated by half a century, but both transpiring in roughly the same patch of terrain. Both events were violent; an SS man had been shot at war's end by one of his own, according to Sedlmeyer's tale.

And there was something else that Waldbaer recalled from several years ago. Two young campers had gone missing. The couple had been seen in this valley before their disappearance. The episode was never resolved and the police eventually lost interest. But now Waldbaer was unsure about what might have transpired and wondered if there was not a pattern forming. Over a long time span, there had been a series of deaths and disappearances in the same tract of mountainous terrain.

Waldbaer's thoughts were broken by the noisy passing of a flock of wild geese high above. He followed their trajectory for a moment, concluding that they were headed for the broad waters of the Chiemsee, miles away. Waldbaer returned his gaze to the mountain massif in the distance. If there were answers, they were there, concealed amidst the dense tangle of pine and ragged peaks of unforgiving dolomite. The answers would not reveal themselves without effort. He would have to pry them from this alpine terrain, at once so seductive and so forbidding.

Chapter 11

Perhaps it had been a vision, a revelation. He sat up in the bed in the small, undecorated room and felt the sheen of sweat cooling against his skin. He reflected on what he had seen before waking. The dream had been remarkable for its clarity. The new interloper, following where the other had gone. In his dream, the man moved through meadows and woods and into the cavern. The interloper moved as if he knew where to go, as if he knew where the secrets were hidden. And then other men followed him into the cave and the secret was secret no more, and the things hidden there were discovered. All of his efforts were laid waste. So much planning destroyed. It made him feel ill.

He pushed a hand through sleep-matted hair to ascertain that he was fully awake and he thought some more about the dream, which might have been a vision, that metaphysical borderland where the terrestrial is touched by the invisible.

At least he knew that the cave had not *yet* been discovered, there was no cause for despair, only a message of warning. The earlier intruder had entered the cave and paid with his life. The new intruder would have to be killed, too; that was the advice of the dream. He frowned, uncertain at this interpretation of the nocturnal images.

There were others in the dream. Surely he couldn't kill them all? He suspected that the dream was meant to convey another message: it was time to move the contents of the cave. The place that had provided decades of safe haven was no longer secure.

And, once the evacuation of the objects had been accomplished, it would be time for action, for the justified and implacable violence that had lain dormant too long. He smiled at the thought of doling out death; the idea was like a stimulant.

He knew that he would have to contact the others. Emptying the cave was not something he could accomplish alone. The man resolved to gather his associates. Even this was no simple act, it demanded discretion.

Dressing quickly, he locked his one-bedroom apartment behind him and took the stairs to the street below. Fresh air and the sights and sounds of vehicles and pedestrians greeted him. He walked three blocks to a small grocery, went inside, and purchased an apple. Emerging again onto the street, he checked his surroundings to ensure that no one was following him. All seemed normal. He continued his stroll, entered a *tabak*, studied the wares, and bought a pack of cigarettes. He stood outside the store and lit one, again employing the half-minute of time to check for surveillance. There was none.

More relaxed now, he continued his journey to the post office and the row of yellow telephone booths in front of it. Of the six public phones, three were equipped to take phone cards and three for change. He chose a booth that accepted change, knowing it would leave no trail that could be traced back to him. The glass of the booth was smudged but provided sufficient clarity to view the surrounding area. He glanced around furtively and determined again that the world was indifferent to his presence. Removing a battered wallet from his jeans, he searched for a carefully folded slip of paper containing scrawled phone numbers. He found the first one that he required. There were six digits. The first two digits written on the paper were in reality the last two digits of the telephone number. The last two digits were in fact the third and fourth in the sequence. The middle digits written on the strip of paper were to be dialed first. He dialed and waited for the voice on the other end.

"Hello," said a tinny, suspicious voice.

"Hello, my friend. You recognize me? I think we should try to go bowling tomorrow night." There was a brief pause as the individual who had been called let the covert meaning of the words sink in.

"Yes. I'm sure I can make it; there's nothing else going on that I need attend to. I'll get in touch with our other friend, but I have no doubt it will be fine with him too. I presume you are well?"

"I am entirely well."

"Good. See you at the usual time."

"Yes. Okay. Good-bye till then."

He hung the phone back on its metal hook, pushed open the door, and left the booth. He let the images run through his mind like a film. The associate he had spoken to would now also go to a pay phone. The associate would dial up a third man and pass the same bowling information. The third man would go to a pay phone not directly in his neighborhood and dial a fourth colleague, re-peating the message. Through an arrangement made at their last per-sonal meeting nearly a year ago, they already knew where and when to meet. His interlocutor had inquired if he was well. That was the code to establish that the call had not been initiated under duress, at police direction.

The brief conversation was anonymous, simple, and entirely se-cure. Even in the highly unlikely event that they were overheard by the authorities, the dialogue would provide no clues as to what was going on, or when or where. He smiled at the elegance of it.

The conspirative machinery set in motion, he took his time re-turning to the apartment, enjoying the cascade of sunlight that had broken through the early morning blanket of clouds. The street had picked up more bustle as rush hour approached. He had time to enjoy his usual strong coffee and fresh rolls with sunflower seeds. After that, he would open up his little business below the apartment and prepare for the day. He would have time to consider the issues to be addressed tomorrow night at the bowling alley. He would make no notes; the agenda was secure in his head.

The undertaking at hand would be difficult, but this did not deter him. What he and his comrades were undertaking was of supreme importance, this was his unshakeable conviction. The everyday

slights and resentments of his life counted for nothing when measured against his mission. He felt exhilarated, wanted to laugh aloud.
It did not occur to him that he was considerably more than a little
mad, and that his brain had for years been a haven for malign
thoughts.

Chapter 12

Waldbaer had decided on a dark Franziskaner wheat beer and so informed the dour waitress, who marched off to the tap to draw it. It was early evening in the middle of the week and Zum Alte Post was nearly empty. A steady rain had come in from Baden-Wuerttenburg and moved over the Alps, promising to remain until the following morning. The temperature had dropped, and it was understandable that few people had ventured out. Other than the inspector, only Hans, the doctor, was present from the regular stammtisch.

"As I was saying, it could be that something from the end of the war is hidden up there. On the other hand, the war ended over half a century ago, and whatever was secreted could have been removed in the intervening years."

The doctor held a hand up to signal a pause. "Who do you think would have removed whatever was hidden away?"

"My guess would be the people who brought it there in the first place."

The doctor plucked at his multiplicity of chins. "You mean the SS troops?"

"Well, the SS officers anyway, or maybe just one of them. It could just as easily be the case that the stuff was never removed. Maybe the officers who concealed the items were killed or didn't care about it once the war ended. Who knows?"

The doctor snorted out a guttural laugh. "I imagine that depends entirely on what was hidden. If it was Nazi gold, and someone knew it, I expect it's no longer in the neighborhood. I tell you one thing, it wouldn't be if I knew about it."

The waitress appeared, indifferently tossed a beer coaster on the table in front of Waldbaer and placed a foaming glass on top of it with a thud. The glass bore the image of a smiling, corpulent Franciscan monk drinking a beer and rubbing his belly contentedly. Waldbaer thought the image bore a disturbing likeness to Hans, seated across from him.

"Hans, the problem with this lead is its vagueness. What was the SS hiding? Gold bars? Plundered art from France? Items belonging to Hitler? Secret documents? The cargo came out of Berlin, the heart of the Reich. But there's no way to know what was in those crates, presuming that Sedlmeyer's story is true, and I think it is."

The doctor rapped his knuckles on the table. "We can speculate all day and it won't bring anything. I presume that your criminologist's mind has determined what to do?"

Waldbaer nodded and took a sip of the tart beer. "I know what I have to do. Call for a search. Get enough police together and search the meadows and the woods all the way up to the peaks. But how far to look, for what, how big, these are all unknowns."

"And the alternatives?"

"There aren't any. We're at a dead end. My betters in the police department are not going to like this recommendation one bit. It's expensive, requires lots of manpower, and isn't much better than working a hunch. Maybe we'll get lucky."

"Good," the doctor remarked, satisfied. "You're wrong about one thing, though."

"What might that be?" the inspector inquired with a note of suspicion.

"You said you don't know how big it is — whatever you're searching for. But you do. The cargo required a convoy of trucks as transport. That means that you aren't looking for something small. This means that a lot of space would be required for storage. That makes your search easier. Big things are more difficult to conceal than small items. If something massive is up there somewhere, I think you'll find it."

Waldbaer nodded in uncertain agreement. Perhaps Hans was right, perhaps developments in the case were about to improve. He felt like having another beer and raised his arm to attract the attention of the grimacing, put-upon waitress.

Chapter 13

The deep, hollow sound of a bowling ball rolling with angry force toward its targets was only half-heard by the men huddled around an orange vinyl-topped table near the pizza counter. In contrast to the actual bowling area nearby, the overhead lights here were dim and the conclave sat half-concealed amid a conspiracy of shadows. The man who had initiated the phone call chain led the conversation with his three colleagues.

"We need to get this done quickly. Let's look at everything we'll need. Two rental trucks. We should probably try to get everything out of the cavern in one night, taking any longer than that is tempting fate. Two trucks, two trips each, should do it. We go to Sixt car rental in Bad Reichenhall for the vehicles."

The other men nodded.

"I'll help with the logistics," one of the men across the table intoned. "But we need to know where we're bringing the crates. How far from the cave are we going to travel?"

The leader of the group pursed his lips and nodded. "I rented warehouse space not far from here a year ago, when we started to think that a move might be required. I'm glad I did, it makes everything easier." The others seemed impressed at his prescience.

"Anyway, since we have to drive slowly, especially with the trucks loaded, I estimate about ninety minutes from cave to the warehouse. We'll need more time unloading the stuff at the end destination, of course, but the critical period is the time at the cave and the drive to the valley road. It could seem strange for trucks to be driving around up there, and I want to avoid attention."

"You didn't say where this warehouse is located," said one of the men.

The leader smiled coolly. "I know where it is; that's what's important. You will all know once we arrive there. It's best for now that we each carry in our heads only those details requiring our immediate attention. I think you understand, yes?"

The trio issued a collective low murmur of assent.

"We have to be careful moving these items; we don't want breakage. I bought some battery-operated lamps at the home maintenance store. We'll place them in the cave before we start moving things to ensure good visibility. We need to do this right the first time." The group leader rubbed a hand absently against his cheek. "Okay. Anybody want coffee? I'll buy. Any questions?"

"No," one of the men said. "I'm happy that we're finally getting underway after years of waiting."

"Right," the organizer agreed. "We mustn't forget what we are doing. Remember our goal. Our lives up to now have only been the process of waiting for this moment. In a matter of days, everything changes. Everything."

A cavernous boom reverberated from behind them, another bowling ball striking against wooden pins. The leader smiled. "It will be like that. What we are going to do will be a lot like that. A hard hit, a smashing. It will change everything."

The others smiled with anticipatory satisfaction. And had there been anyone there to judge such a thing, it would have been noted that despite the smiles there was not a trace of humor on their faces or, for that matter, in their souls.

Chapter 14

Waldbaer had established the uncomfortable conviction that he was not merely out of shape, but was, in fact, in bad shape. He reflected on the droll aphorism muttered regularly by his friend Hans: strong mind, strong body, take your choice.

He stopped his plodding ascent through the forest and slumped forward, resting his arms on his knees. He tried to breathe in deeply from the pure mountain air but could not, his lungs only able to ingest shallow, teasing wisps of oxygen. His hammering heart seemed intent on boring a way out of his chest and the racetrack tempo of its beat filled his ears. He concluded that his decision to make a survey of the mountainous terrain on foot had been a misjudgment. The related decision to make the survey alone held potential as a very grave misjudgment. No one knew he was here, and even if he raised someone on his cell phone, how to communicate with any precision where he was? Somewhere in the woods above the valley? Recognition of this error caused his fear to mix with self-reproach.

Not moving, forcing himself to concentrate on the task of breathing, he willed himself to focus on something other than his physical condition. Glancing around, he took in his Arcadian surroundings. Pines, silent and thick, stretched out on all sides. He was standing in old forest, dark and damp, the air earthy with a trace of the fetid, a plush carpet of pine needles underfoot. After what seemed an interminable time, the protestations of his heart lessened and he breathed more steadily. He leaned for a moment against the bark of a broad tree and felt measurably better.

He debated turning back, but expected that the worst part of the ascent was behind him. He was high above the place where the meadows surrendered to the woods, and the degree of incline ahead seemed less severe. He would try to venture to where the trees stopped at the dolomite outcroppings. He could go no farther than that without mountain climbing gear, which, in his condition, was no more than a theoretical possibility. Still, he might find *something* by then. But what? He did not know, he admitted to himself. Some sign, perhaps, of where Hirter had passed before his death, some disrupted area of earth suggestive of struggle or flight. He would just have to see. But he retained the sense that this piece of terrain was key to Hirter's murder.

Pushing away from the tree with some effort, Waldbaer propelled himself forward. He found a slow stride and kept to it, intent on maintaining regular breathing and heartbeat. He surveyed the ground as he moved, looking for any suggestion of something out of the ordinary. But all seemed undisturbed, an early autumn pastoral scene, summer having slipped away only day's ago, the subtle shading of chestnut trees in the valley whispering of Father Winter's impending, unwelcome approach.

Fifteen minutes later he noticed a dark slash in the rolling swell of the forest floor. A shadow? No, something more substantial. He walked toward it. As he neared, it became evident that he was looking at tire tracks. The tracks traced the line of least resistance heading toward the cliffs above. The spoor had deely rutted the soft, damp earth. Waldbaer paused and thought. Was this something unusual or not? He considered that there were no meadows up above, thus no agricultural reason for a tractor or farm vehicle to travel this far into the woods. He also knew that this stand of forest was not being worked for lumber. Which left open the question, why did someone bother to drive up here?

Waldbaer bent slowly to his knees and let his hands trace over the track marks. How recent? The sides of the impression were crisp and rough, and there was no veneer of forest debris over the tracks to suggest that they were old. It had rained heavily four days ago; he was certain the tracks were more recent than that. Examining the tire marks carefully, Waldbaer noticed that this path had been used in both directions; the vehicle had come back down the hill via the same route. He followed the trajectory of the tire marks with his eyes and saw that they zigzagged through the trees in the direction of the cliffs above. With a groan he hoisted himself erect again and followed the track upward, careful to stand off to one side.

Twenty minutes later Waldbaer stood at the imposing face of the rock outcropping, a mass that rose above him like a fortress. He could see where the vehicle had moved back and forth near the cliff, as if seeking a good position. A good position for what, he wondered. Moving closer, he gingerly pushed at some of the brush along the rock face near where the vehicle had parked. Surprisingly, the brush fell away. He pulled at the branches with more earnestness and soon uncovered a yawning black recess in the stone. He stepped hesitantly into the mouth of the cavern and found himself enveloped in blackness.

Using his hands to guide him along the rough cave wall, he moved a few yards forward. He felt smooth, hard-packed dirt beneath his feet and knew that this place had been used by men for some covert purpose. His temple connected sharply with rock and he realized that it would be pointless and dangerous to venture farther without light. Turning on his heels, he made his way back out of the cave.

Once out, he did not pause but began his descent toward the valley, following the route of the tire tracks once again. When he returned here, he knew, it would be with an array of lamps and the full paraphernalia of a police investigation, which he intended to conduct with exacting German thoroughness.

A half dozen green and white police Volkswagen SUVs were positioned wherever space allowed in the vicinity of the uncovered cave. The vehicles had their blue lights flashing, although Waldbaer could not understand the point of it, as they were far from any trace of humanity. At least the sirens were not whining. Procedures, no doubt, he allowed, aware that abiding by procedures, sensible or not, was tonic to the Germanic soul. The usually bucolic stand of forest was awash with flashes of motion; in addition to the detective, there were nearly twenty uniformed police and white-clad forensic offi-cers on site.

Earlier that morning, Waldbaer had ranged around the terrain near the cavern, looking for anything out of place. He had been lucky. Largely hidden in the ebony shadows of an old spruce tree, he had detected a hint of navy blue. Moving there, he used a twig to carefully lift a baseball cap from its bed of needles and cones. Blue cotton fabric, stylized red letter logo on the front. Boston Red Sox. The headgear was not old; there was no sign of the decay that time and exposure would have wrought. This must have belonged to Hirter, the Massachusetts native. He carried the cap on his stick like a totem, depositing it in a plastic bag at one of the police cars, where it was tagged as evidence.

Two policemen were taking a resin cast of the tire tracks that had lead Waldbaer to this place. Two others were wandering around apparently photographing at random. Trees, cave walls, rocks, all seemed of sufficient merit for a photograph. Although he did not dispute the need to record the scene, Waldbaer was skeptical about the investigatory value.

Eventually tiring of surveying the scene, Waldbaer walked back into the cavern, which was now brightly illuminated by portable lamps. The shadows were gone, the aura of mystery the cave once possessed banished as well. The stone walls told him nothing, re-vealed nothing; the cave was empty. The information he sought was elsewhere. Turning this unhappy fact over in his mind, Waldbaer di-rected his vision to the items that had attracted his attention when they had first lit the cavern earlier that morning. Wood splinters, not large, but a number of them scattered on the ground. The splin-ters were smooth, planed wood, and the detective was certain that they issued from crates. Probably heavy crates that had been moved toward the cave entrance with difficulty. He contemplated this and a small flag waved in his mind.

Hirter's body. A wood shaving caught in the tread of his hiking shoes. Yes. Which meant that — in all likelihood — Hirter had been inside this place prior to his death. More than likely *just* prior to his death, or else the shaving would have worked its way out of the shoe. Waldbaer felt elated at making the connection, and a satisfied smile lightened his normally brooding countenance.

This covert place was connected to the murder; of this Waldbaer was certain. Something had been stored here in wooden crates. Whatever had been warehoused in this stony surround had been sufficiently valuable to drive someone to murder. And possibly more than one murder, he mused, recalling the two hikers who had gone missing all those years ago. What dark and damning thing had been secreted here?

Surely this cavern and its undefined contents were related to Sedlmeyer's tale of the *Kriegsende*, the end of the war. The old man claimed to have been an eyewitness to a delivery of mysterious goods — in *wooden crates* — to precisely this part of the mountain. How many caves concealing hidden goods could there be up here? This had been the storage venue for crates dating back to 1945. But what mute prize was contained within the National Socialist packaging?

"At least it's a start," Waldbaer muttered, ignoring the glance and raised eyebrow of a nearby police officer. He balled his fists and shoved them deep into the pockets of his sports coat. The problem was, the trail discovered now seemed to end. Whatever had rested here for decades had been moved. To where? The tracks to and from the cave could be traced only as far as the asphalt of the valley road below. To find the killers of Charles Hirter, they needed to determine the new location of the crates. At exactly that location, Waldbaer was convinced, all would fall together and the deadly sequence of events would be resolved. The detective's love of clarity would be fulfilled.

Waldbaer exited the cavern and stood under the pines, their sentinel stillness broken by the creaking of a branch high above. Perhaps someone had seen the truck or trucks that had been up here. It wasn't impossible and represented the only real hope that the investigation could progress further. True, the mountains here were uninhabited and only sporadically invaded by hunters and hikers. But farther down toward the valley, where the meadows were located, there were a few farm dwellings. A long shot, perhaps, but one of the farmers might have noticed a vehicle moving up into the hilly terrain.

Farmers. An interesting archetype. He ran through the qualities he assigned them: stubborn, narrow, loud, complaining. But at the same time: generally honest, hard-working, straightforward. Perhaps not bad on balance. Still, Waldbaer did not want to invest his time in visiting the three or four farmhouses within observing distance of the meadows. It would entail sitting in their rustic kitchens trying to pry out information word by word.

"Colleague Eibel," he said, and a bulky policeman nearby turned at the name. His complexion was like raw ground beef.

"Yes, Herr Kommissar, what can I do for you?" The voice rumbled as if from some watery subterranean depth, thick with Upper Bavarian accent and a long intimacy with alcohol.

"I want you to do something for me when you're finished here. On the way back to the main road, you'll see a few farmhouses. Pay them a visit. I'm hoping one of the farmers or their wives, distrustful, nosy creatures that they are, noticed the vehicle that traveled up here. If one of them has seen anything, let me know immediately."

"Jawohl, Herr Kommissar," the policeman intoned, hitching his trousers a centimeter higher over his generous, beer-built abdomen.

Waldbaer walked over to the all-terrain vehicle he had driven up in, opened the door, and permitted gravity to assist him into the seat. There was nothing more to be gained here he concluded. Better to head back to the office and reflect. Maybe he should check on Hirter at the Alpenhof and give him the courtesy of an update. At least there had been some progress, however modest. Finding the baseball cap had been a good piece of luck; he was certain that a DNA test would definitively establish its provenance.

Still, despite the day's successes, he could not rid himself of an unsettling sense that some rapacious malignancy was let loose, larger in its dimensions than the brutal murder of Charles Hirter taken alone. There was no evidence for this sentiment, no facts to sustain it. It was an inchoate and primordial feeling only, but it weighed on him like a stone. A whisper that the evils recently unveiled were about to procreate explosively. He worried that he needed to do something to intervene against pending events but felt as helpless as a weak swimmer amid the waves of the North Sea. He heard fleetingly from inside his head the somber chords of Rachmaninov's *Isle of the Dead*. He would have preferred to summon the vestigial strains of Mozart or perhaps Haydn, but the joyous notes would not come.

Chapter 15

Forty kilometers from the cavern, the crates lay in neat, military rows upon a concrete floor. The clandestine transfer of the items had gone without incident. The rented vehicles had been emptied quietly at their destination. The man who had organized these events gazed out over the cargo, his eyes squinting against the glare of neon lighting in the warehouse. He felt satisfied and the sensation coursed through him like blood. He was aware that a new stage in the operation had been achieved after years of waiting. Now the tempo of events would quicken and move along a trajectory toward violent completion. He wondered for a moment at the zeitgeist, a fine word from the German. The Spirit of the Age. Exactingly precise, he thought. Events were moving as they must, impelled by some invisible force toward an ordained conclusion. Destiny.

It was not as if he himself had no part to play in the unfolding events; his personal fate was bound up with the cargo. The purpose of his life was contained in those wooden boxes. He was aware that the American he had killed had served as a catalyst for the movement of the cargo and its pending employment. In his own way, then, the American had served as a tool of the Spirit of the Age, and why not. They all had their role to play; whether wittingly or not was beside the point.

The weekend would be busy. There was assembly to be finished, carefully, professionally. And phone calls to be made. It was critical that their activities be conducted clandestinely, but this should not prove difficult. He felt certain that the police, that herd of otherwise unemployable dullards, could not prevent them from fulfilling their destiny. Even if the police managed to find the cavern where the goods had lain for so long, it would bring them nothing. Too late, friends, too late. It will lead you no farther, so go back to your liters of beer and your low-stakes card games. You will have more than enough to occupy you before long. He smiled broadly and broke into laughter, its resonance filling the otherwise silent warehouse.

Chapter 16

Waldbaer sat across the kitchen table from the couple, his back uncomfortable on the hard and unforgiving wooden bench. He felt the warmth of the steaming coffee cup between his hands. The farm kitchen was as he expected it to be — down to the last detail. Whitewashed walls and rustic, unvarnished pine cabinets. A collection of ceramic beer mugs with pewter lids arranged in a neat row under a window sill. The round, rude hardwood table before him was worn and scarred. It was impossible to tell whether it was twenty years old or two hundred. A large, hand-carved crucifix hung in one corner, its age equally a mystery. A calendar was thumbtacked to one wall, each month decorated with a color photograph of alpine flora. Edelweiss this month, prosaic but inoffensive. There was no chaos in this kitchen; this domain was ruled by an orderly housewife with an iron hand.

The iron housewife sat silently across from Waldbaer, her farmer husband next to her, equally quiet, waiting for the detective to initiate the conversation now that the required pleasantries had been concluded. Waldbaer had been summoned here by the policeman he had dispatched to inquire at the farmhouses bordering the mountain access road. Herr Andreas and Frau Gisela Schneider, both in their late sixties, had advised the uniformed policeman that, indeed, they had seen vehicles underway to the forest above. They had additionally advised that they had some details about the vehicles. This information having been relayed to Waldbaer, he decided it best to conduct the interview himself.

"Ja, Herr and Frau Schneider, I'm interested in what you can tell me. My colleague says that you recall having seen vehicles underway above. I'm interested in your recollections."

The couple glanced quickly, almost furtively, at one another. The eternally suspicious nature of the farmer, Waldbaer thought unkindly. Herr Schneider pursed his lips and ran the palms of his meaty hands along the surface of the table. His heavyset spouse feigned disinterest, but covertly eyed the police official. Bovine eyes, Waldbaer thought, unable, or at least unwilling to stem his instinctive lack of sympathy for the couple. You are being unfair, he chastised himself, give them a chance.

After some seconds, the broad-shouldered farmer offered a response. "*Naja,* I saw something. Why does this interest you, Herr Kommissar? Does it have to do with the murder of the American?"

Waldbaer did nothing to conceal his sigh. He had expected that these country people would feel free to pose more questions than they willingly answered. Let's get this out of the way he thought. "As I'm sure you'll both appreciate, I'm not at liberty to discuss the murder investigation. But I can tell you that the reason I'm here is not unrelated to the murder of Charles Hirter. That's as far as I can go for the moment. Now, back to my question if you don't mind, Herr Schneider."

The farmer shifted in his chair and nodded as if considering whether he minded or not. His wife stared at her well-scrubbed, folded hands. Her husband looked Waldbaer in the eyes as he spoke.

"It was just luck that we noticed anything at all. Often we aren't here. On a farm there's always something to do, deliveries to town, finance things with the bank, the farmers market." The farmer paused and Waldbaer arranged his features in the requisite look of sympathy for daily tasks.

"Anyway, we were here one evening when two trucks drove up the meadow road. It was just after dusk, and we noticed the headlights through the window." He turned his head a notch and indicated the square panes of glass. "Cars go up there sometimes, just looking around most of them, following a dirt road; tourists. Now and then we see someone from the forestry office from Munich or climbers. But they go up during the day. After dark, well, seldom. But going up at night? Why?"

"A fair observation, Herr Schneider," the policeman interjected, oiling the track for more conversation. "I can't imagine that there would be much reason for traveling up there at night."

Frau Schneider released a dismissive snort. Waldbaer was reminded uncomfortably of a mare. "Maybe a local Casanova with a girl, but even they don't have to travel that far. Whoever drives up to the mountains at night is up to no good, count on it." The woman darted a hand over her thick bun of pinned-up gray hair, glanced knowingly at the police official, and then returned her gaze to the tabletop.

"So," Waldbaer resumed after a gulp of coffee, "perhaps you can tell me what precisely you saw after you noticed the headlights through the window?"

The farmer made a noise in his throat as if to acknowledge the gravity of the information he had to impart. "Like I said, when I noticed headlights at that hour, I thought it was funny. That made me curious. I was here in the kitchen, so I opened the front door and walked outside to get a good look, Ja? That's when I noticed that there were two trucks, traveling together. They seemed to know where they were headed, they were moving fast enough. Not like they weren't sure whether they should turn around or not. They went right by the field in front here, then up past the high meadows and into the trees. I could see their lights in the forest for a few moments. And I heard the motors even longer; sound travels pretty well downhill in this area. And then they were gone."

"Andreas is right," Frau Schneider added, half-turning to her spouse. "I saw the same thing from the window. Two trucks, small ones. Not like those big lorries on the autobahn with all the extra wheels."

Waldbaer considered. "You're sure these were trucks, not those jeep-like things — SUVs like the Americans say?"

"No, trucks," Herr Schneider confirmed with a trace of irritation. "With this type of ground it would make more sense if they were all-terrain vehicles, but they weren't. They were trucks. The kind businesses use to make deliveries."

"Delivery trucks," Waldbaer muttered. "Used not just to drop things off, but to pick things up."

Frau Gisela Schneider issued another equestrian snort. "Nothing to pick up in the forest. Except wood. And there's lots of that in the valley. More likely dumping garbage or hazardous chemicals or something."

"What else can you tell me about the trucks?" Waldbaer had determined that Herr Schneider was the more factual interlocutor, his wife more prone to opinion.

The farmer scratched at his ear. "Two trucks. Both the same size. It was dark, but they were white or beige, light-toned anyway. They were well past me before I could see more."

Waldbaer nodded affirmatively but felt defeated. The couple was cooperative, but they offered a limited array of facts. At least he knew now that two trucks had traveled up to the cavern, the existence of which was clearly not known to the Schneiders. But this information was insufficient to bring the investigation further. Waldbaer realized with a sinking feeling that his investigation in any serious sense was quite possibly over.

"Thank you for your time," the police officer said, intent on hiding his disappointment. "I'll be going now."

The farmer swiped a large hand in the air indicating that his guest should sit back down. "Why go now? I told you about what I saw when the trucks went up. Don't you want to hear what I saw when they came back down?"

Waldbaer slipped back onto the kitchen bench and eyed the man intently.

"I told you earlier, the trucks traveled up and later on traveled back to the valley. The return trip was a lot later. Three hours anyway. It was late because I was about to head up to bed. Close to midnight maybe. I heard the engines first; that gave me some time. I put on a jacket and went out front. I stood under that oak tree near the road. There's a bit of brush there, and I didn't want them to see me watching. It pays to be careful. They drove out of the tree line and down past the meadows. Slower this time than before. I could tell that there were two people in the cab of each truck; four people in all. I noticed something else. The cars had BGL license plates. I can't remember the numbers."

"BGL," Waldbaer interrupted, "Berchestgardner Land."

"Right. But not just that. On the back bumper of both trucks there was a decal. There was enough moonlight for me to read it. Sixt."

Waldbaer leaned forward. "Sixt? The rental car company? Are you certain?"

The farmer gave a self-satisfied smile. "One hundred percent. Sixt rental cars. And the decal also read 'Bad Reichenhall.' That was smaller, but I could make it out."

Waldbaer felt his depression evaporate. The trucks were rented, and from the Bad Reichenhall affiliate of the German firm Sixt, not forty kilometers distant. Easy enough to trace and determine who had rented delivery trucks over the last several days. For a criminal investigator, it was like winning the lottery.

The elated detective reached across the table and slapped Herr Schneider on the shoulder. "Well done, Herr Schneider. If you ever run into me in the Alte Post, I'll buy you a beer. This has been a splendid afternoon."

"You really do want to get out of here don't you, Herr Kommissar?" Schneider's rustic visage broke into a smile. "You see, there's one other detail that I didn't mention yet. There were four people in those two trucks. I couldn't make out much naturally, under those light conditions. But the passenger in the second truck, the fellow closest to where I was standing, I got a decent look at him. Not like I could identify him if I saw him again. But enough to see one thing for certain. He wasn't German. His truck might have originated from Bad Reichenhall, but you can trust me that he didn't."

Frau Schneider whinnied in unrestrained amusement.

Chapter 17

Two trucks. Rented by two men who arrived together and were acquainted with one another. Yes, Waldbaer thought, that was the advantage of small cities like Bad Reichenhall; the businesses did not have so much to do that the employees were incapable of remembering customers.

The twenty-year-old, bleached-blonde girl who worked the Sixt rental car counter evidenced an eye for detail and her recollections hit the right note, neither too vague nor implausibly detailed. She advised that someone had dropped the two men off and driven away. The two men who rented the trucks were taciturn. Although they arrived together, they went out of their way not to communicate in the rental office, as if to promote the fiction that they were unacquainted. Both men were polite but not conversational; responses to questions about extra insurance and fuel-refill policy were simply negative or affirmative, no banter, no requests for elaboration.

"You are most helpful. I'm sorry, your name again was?"

"Sieglinde Reuth, Herr Kommissar." The girl smiled self-consciously, and in a true anachronism almost curtsied, a bit nervous but intrigued by her first brush with the exotic world of police work. She brushed at a stray strand of hair. She still has pimples, Waldbaer noticed.

For a second he was transported back to his youth, that distant epoch upon which he reflected so little, and to a lost sense of unrelenting yearning, and the face of another girl, grown misty with time but not erased. In those days, of course, girls did not wear studs in their nose, an affectation to which Sieglinde had succumbed. A shame he thought, then chided himself for his antique sentiments.

"Frau Reuth, tell me what these men looked like, in your own words. I want you to think of the first man that rented one of the trucks. Think of his appearance. His features, how he was dressed, short or tall. It would be of great help." He left it there, not wanting to get too theatrical.

The girl nodded, a look of concentration on her face. She touched a finger momentarily to the stud in her nose. "The first man was shorter than his comrade. Solid too. Not fat like our beer hall guys, but heavy. He had black hair, and it was really thick." She giggled. "His hairline was halfway down his forehead. I remember that when he talked he showed bad teeth and smelled of garlic. Funny, that I would remember that."

"How old?" the detective prompted, having allowed a conversational pause, not wanting to interrupt the flow of recollection, a mystic stream that should be permitted to run its course.

"Older. Maybe forty. It's hard for me to tell age after about forty. He could be fifty, maybe, but I think more toward forty."

Waldbaer nodded sagaciously, feeling certain that the girl regarded him as likely on his last assignment before being pensioned. "Any more details?"

"Yes. He was dark. I don't mean that he was a black guy, but dark like a Turk. He was wearing an acrylic sweater, but I can't recall the color. It was cheap though, like something you find at C and A, not Izod or Ralph Lauren boutique stuff. You know what I mean, Herr Kommissar?"

"Of course," Waldbaer replied. He pictured a foreigner, and not a prosperous one. "Any accent detectable?"

Young Frau Reuth frowned. "I guess so. But he really only gave yes and no answers. We didn't have a normal conversation. But I don't think he was born in Germany." Her frown transformed into a smile. "At least he didn't speak Bavarian, you know." she added in country dialect.

Waldbaer smiled in kind, sharing the bond of a common local language, a vestige of ancient tribes and peoples.

"The second man had a beard, too, and lots of black hair, but his was matted, like he hadn't showered for a while. Taller, he was, and thin."

"Was he also a foreigner?"

The girl nodded without hesitation. "Yes, like the first man."

Waldbaer considered. Non-Germans. The girl's comment had been corroborated previously by the farmer, Herr Schneider. Progress was being made. Still, he could not rid himself of the sense that he had little time left to find these anonymous foreigners, men who were presently no more substantial than shadows.

"Frau Reuth, is there anything else that you recall? Anything to help identify these fellows?"

Frau Reuth wrinkled her forehead before responding. "No, I think that's everything, Herr Kommissar. One was tall and thin, the other one was shorter and stockier. Both had black hair, and the tall one had a beard. They were dressed in cheap clothes. They were Turks or Pakistanis or something. One more thing: I didn't like them; I found them strange. That might sound prejudiced, but a lot of people come in here, and I like most of them. There was something about these two that I didn't like."

Waldbaer nodded sympathetically. "I've learned in this profession to dismiss neither intuition nor feelings, Frau Reuth. Now, perhaps we can have a look at the forms these two men filled out and signed?"

Frau Reuth smiled slightly, like a woman in a Botticelli painting, Waldbaer thought with a fleeting sense of delight. The girl moved to a computer, an invention for which Waldbaer felt only loathing, and busied herself with the keyboard. Waldbaer had purposely not asked for the rental forms until now, wanting to hear the girl's commentary untainted by what he might read. It was an established habit with him, if an idiosyncratic atavism. The room filled with a low grinding noise and a printer behind the counter produced two sheets of paper.

Frau Reuth offered him the sheets. Most of the material was numerical — license plates, vehicle identification number, credit card information. It was valuable for the investigation, but it reminded Waldbaer once again to what degree mankind was in thralldom to the cold rule of digits. He turned his attention to the name on the forms. Al-Assad. Not a name he was familiar with. The same with the second form; the name Baran meant nothing to him.

"*Sehr gut,*" he intoned to the Sixt girl, "very good, just what I was hoping for."

Frau Reuth beamed. She pointed to the sheets Waldbaer was holding. "I always check forms carefully. It's easy to get sloppy, but I don't get rushed, even when there are customers lined up. It has to be done correctly."

Waldbaer smiled at this perfect expression of the Teutonic desire for order in things large and small. "You are to be commended," he said, wanting to make her day a bit memorable and to buttress her fledgling sense of individual responsibility. He hoped that at some point in the future her world would broaden beyond the rental car counter.

Waldbaer drove to work with more speed than usual the next morning, his sense of urgency enticing him to pass cars that he might normally have coasted behind. The asphalt of the autobahn rolled noiselessly under his wheels, and he drank in the sounds of Christian Thielemann conducting *Carmina Burana* on his CD player. He now had substantial threads in hand and needed to weave them together to produce a tapestry of the murder. He was anxious to see what hits might have surfaced on the identities on the rental car forms. Still, he could not shake the feeling that he was dealing not only with a crime committed but with crimes yet to transpire. He eased the gas pedal farther to the floor.

Once inside the familiar confines of the police station, Waldbaer braced the young sergeant responsible for assembling background information on suspects. "Karger, what do you have on my rental car driver, al-Assad?"

Julius Karger had the lean and pallid features of an ascetic, and was regarded by his law enforcement colleagues as proficient but humorless. Nothing in his demeanor on this morning contradicted that assessment.

"There are a few indisputable facts at present, Herr Kommissar. First, the name Mohammed al-Assad is real, not fictitious. Second, Herr al-Assad was born in Cologne of a Turkish mother and a Syrian father, both deceased. Third, he is a German citizen. Fourth, he is unmarried and without children. Fifth, his registered place of residence is Gamsdorf. And finally, al-Assad is the proprietor of the Doener kebab snack shop down the street from here." Having delivered this information, Karger sat back in his desk chair and gazed at Waldbaer without evident emotion.

Waldbaer stared back at the twenty-something sergeant whose unremarkable features were framed by wire-rimmed glasses and close-cropped dark hair. "You mean the Turkish carryout? He's the owner? I must have seen him a dozen times in the past year." Waldbaer tried but could not summon up a face, an image. Such are the penalties of our anonymous society, he concluded. "Photo?"

"Yes, sir," the sergeant replied, passing over a sheet of paper from his desktop. "This is a copy of his driver's license photo. The quality isn't award winning, but it's all we have."

The Kommissar held the image at half-arm's length and let his imperfect eyes consider it. Yes, he recalled the man, in a vague way. Frau Reuthe at the Sixt counter had described him accurately. Thick black hair, trimmed beard absent a trace of gray. The face staring back from the photo was sullen, the lips thin, the eyes too close together. It was an Ottoman rather than a European face, but otherwise unremarkable.

"One more thing that might interest you, Herr Kommissar." Waldbaer moved his eyes from the photo back to Sergeant Karger. "And that might be?"

"I checked the carryout this morning. Closed. No sign in the window, but the place is locked and dark. Maybe al-Assad's on vacation."

This news made Waldbaer uncomfortable. Perhaps Assad had

gone to ground. Did he sense that he was a murder suspect? Or was it something less sinister? Weighing the possibilities, Waldbaer quizzed Karger again. "The second fellow who rented a truck, what do we have on him?"

Karger shuffled through his papers. "The name is Ibrahim Baran. He has a residency permit for Bavaria, but not German citizenship. He's half-Egyptian, born in Cairo in 1971. His mother is Turkish. He's single, and his parents are in Egypt. He's been in Germany for four years, initially got a student visa, completed only one year of technical school in Hamburg, apparently dropped out, and headed south. His current visa status seems uncertain. He's unemployed. There isn't much else. No outstanding Interpol warrants."

Waldbaer mumbled his acknowledgment and turned toward his office.

He slipped into the plushness of his leather chair and was preparing to assemble his case notes when his eyes rested on a yellow note fixed to the center of his desk. He picked it up, squinted, and brought it into focus. The note, written in his secretary's precise hand read, "You received a call from Mr. Hirter. He wants an appointment. You can call him at his hotel or he will come by the station this afternoon." Waldbaer rubbed at his forehead and emitted a long, resigned sigh.

Chapter 18

The few narrow, heavily grimed windows of the warehouse were built high into the walls and had been covered over with black masking tape so no sliver of light would escape to the outside world. To any casual passerby on the little-traveled street outside, the warehouse would appear unoccupied and lifeless, just another unexceptional and inelegant structure in a district of dull and indifferently constructed buildings. Inside the warehouse, life surged and pulsed. Four men were present and each was a vessel of purposeful activity, focused on some assigned task in the dim illumination of the low-wattage bulbs installed to lessen the chances of inadvertent discovery.

Mohammed al-Assad was contemplating a row of metal antiseptic-looking cylinders on the table before him. The polished vessels looked much like thermos bottles. Ah, but the contents are much different than Eduscho coffee, al-Assad noted with a smile. He was reaching for one of the cylinders when his Nokia cell phone rang, the tinny refrain of Mozart's *Eine Kliene Nachtmusik* echoing incongruously through the cavernous space. Al-Assad activated the phone and listened to the voice on the other end.

"This is Ibrahim. Can you hear me?"

"I can hear you just fine, Ibrahim. How are you?" Assad felt a frisson of excitement course through him but willed himself to speak naturally, calmly.

"I'm great. The cold that I had earlier is gone, and I couldn't be feeling better." Al-Assad relaxed. Ibrahim had just delivered the agreed-to code; the reference to not having a cold meant that he was not calling under duress, and "couldn't be better" meant that Ibrahim believed himself free of surveillance.

"I've been busy. I was talking to the father of the bride. He thinks that the wedding should take place soon. He sees no reason to delay it, since his daughter is excited about the ceremony he feels the wedding should go ahead. He's looking forward to it and hopes many guests will attend."

Al-Assad kept his voice casual, trying to convey the illusion of boredom. "Wonderful. Pass along my congratulations to the bridal party. I'm certain it will be a wedding to remember. I've got things to take care of, so I'll ring off now, Ibrahim. See you soon and thanks for the call."

"Okay," Ibrahim replied. "I have a few chores to do here, but I expect to be back in a few days. See you then, my friend."

Al-Assad punched the off button on the Nokia and considered what he had learned. Ibrahim Baran had apparently done well on his trip to Ankara. He had departed on a Lufthansa flight from Munich two days ago and was already reporting back. It was obvious that Ibrahim had, as planned, contacted Abdul Al-Masri, who had traveled to Turkey from Pakistan expressly to pass instructions to Ibrahim. The details, of course, would have to await Ibrahim's return to Bavaria.

Nonetheless, Ibrahim had communicated the most important piece of information. The operation should proceed. Al-Assad smiled broadly. Excellent. This was the message that he had awaited, had longed for, had dared to pray for. Now things would happen as they should. He noticed that his three associates were arrayed in front of him, alerted to the prospect of news from his telephone conversation. Nodding solemnly, he stretched out his arms as if to envelop the men.

"Brothers. I have wonderful news. The time has come to purify our hearts and put aside daily concerns. Make yourself ready for what awaits, that which will honor us and our families for generations."

As one, the trio responded with hands raised toward the sky as they intoned the venerable chant "*Allahu Akbar,*" the triumphant syllables reverberating against the solid brick walls of what had become a temple of implacable and murderous sentiment and purpose.

Chapter 19

Waldbaer stared at Hirter. Perhaps he had misheard. The subdued background sounds of the police station, voices, and coffee machines went on around them, unheard.

"I can help with names. I can help a lot with names. Herr Kommissar, you just need to provide me whatever information you have on these people — full identification, date and place of birth, criminal record, known relatives, and known aliases."

Waldbaer half-rose from the embracing richness of his leather chair. "Aliases? Aliases? What are you talking about, Hirter? And, why in God's name do you think you can acquire information that a police officer can't? Do you think we're untutored buffoons?" Waldbaer sank back into his chair. "I know that since you arrived here you've wanted to play a role in solving your brother's murder. But you need to understand that, despite your best intentions, no untrained amateur —"

"I am a CIA officer."

Waldbaer found himself momentarily speechless. He wondered whether he was experiencing a sudden hearing disorder.

"You have some sort of badge, an ID?" Waldbaer's question was intended to give him a few seconds to get over his shock.

"As you might understand, Kommissar, we don't usually carry compromising official identification in countries where we aren't declared. At least not those of us in the Clandestine Service, which is the CIA directorate where I work. If you don't believe me, I can give you an official phone number to call, and someone will confirm my affiliation, someone can even meet you if you insist."

Waldbaer rubbed a hand against his temple. "Herr Hirter, enlighten me, why didn't you tell me this earlier?"

"I would have told you earlier, but I only received permission to break cover last night. These things take time. I received a phone call from Langley last night, due to the different time zones. There are details of a secrecy agreement that we'll have to talk about, but we can leave that for later. The salient point for you is that I — and the CIA — can conduct international name traces and background checks."

Waldbaer continued to stare at Hirter. The Kommissar was aware that his plans for the day had suddenly, irrevocably changed.

"Hirter," he said at last, not without a trace of wonder in his graveled voice, "you're right. We need to talk. We need to talk a lot. But not without beer, Hirter, not without some beer. You still have that rental car? You drive, I provide directions; it's not far to where we're going."

Zum Hirschen was as quiet as a monastery refectory given the early hour. Waldbaer and Hirter sat at a small square table on which two tall glasses of dark Wieninger wheat beer were placed. Waldbaer slowly drummed his thick fingers on the creviced tabletop.

"You are aware, Herr Hirter, that there is an official side to international cooperation on criminal cases in Germany. If you're representing American Intelligence and offering to assist the police, this has to go through channels. There is a procedure. I believe you are who you say you are — why would you lie about it? But I have to coordinate this with my superiors. I can't even guarantee that liaison with the CIA will be approved in a case like this."

Hirter swept some unruly hair from his face and nodded. "Well, that's one way to do things."

"You are suggesting that there are other ways?" Waldbaer suppressed a frown, reached for the glass in front of him, and took a swallow.

"Sure. There's always an informal alternative for things like this. Nothing officially declared, no memo, just conversation that no one needs to acknowledge. It's often the more efficient way to conduct business, in my experience."

Waldbaer's face creased in a slight smile. "Ah yes, you mean *Der kleine Dienstweg*; the little path of the services, as the phrase goes. Not exactly a legal alternative, you understand."

Hirter leaned in toward the table, his chair scrapping against the terra cotta floor. "Right. Not the sort of thing a bureaucrat would warm to. But you're a Kommissar and I'm an intelligence case officer. My logical partner would be the German Foreign Intelligence Service, the BND. And you would be more comfortable dealing with an FBI legal attaché. True, but that's not the situation we find ourselves in. If we try to do this with official coordination and memos back and forth, this could turn into a shipwreck. You want this case solved as much as I do. Not just to clear up a murder. We both feel that something else is going on here, something sinister. Something we need to prevent."

Waldbaer heard himself sigh. He worried again that he was sighing too often these days and wondered if it was a signal of incipient depression. "All right. Maybe we can work offline. I'm probably making a mistake. I have an unpleasant feeling that I'll get in trouble for this, but okay. We can at least start on an informal basis and see how it functions. But, Herr Hirter, there is one thing you need to agree to up front. It is this: I am the lead agency and I make the decisions, period, full stop, no discussion. I am willing to let you into the investigation in what is a highly irregular arrangement. I'm willing to let you have privileged information. You can accompany me on investigative matters — when I decree. In return, I expect you to provide me with anything and everything that your organization turns up relevant to this investigation. No games. I don't have the temperament for games. Those are the unshakable rules of the road if you want to do things outside of channels."

Hirter considered the proposal, moving his beer glass across the table. Eventually he nodded and looked the police detective in the eyes. "Agreed. You're in charge. I play a subordinate role on the side.

I'll pass you any and all information the CIA clears for passage. I'll also provide you my professional views for you to accept or ignore. When you say go, I go, and when you say stop, I stop. I can live with that. We are in agreement?"

Waldbaer stared across the table and clasped his hands underneath his chin. "Yes. For the time being anyway."

Hirter smiled and raised his glass in a toast to Waldbaer. "Herr Kommissar, it occurs to me that our little agreement means that we're partners of sorts. Am I right?"

The police detective pulled down on the knot of his ancient cravat and undid the button of his frayed collar before raising his beer glass in a riposte. "I fear that you are correct, Herr Hirter, I do fear that you are correct."

Chapter 20

Security was infinitely important now. Every minor activity, every seemingly inconsequential move would have to be considered. They could not afford discovery so close to achieving the goal they had worked toward for years. The goal they had killed to protect. The quartet had pulled up metal stools alongside a workbench that served as a table. The shadows from the dim lighting emphasized their cheekbones and brows. Al-Assad raised a finger in the air in the traditional Arabic gesture of emphasis.

"Our rules must change, brothers, as our behavior must change. I remind you that you have sworn loyalty to me and promised to follow my orders. We are in a strong position to implement our plan but things could still go wrong, something that we must prevent at any cost. Whatever trials we go through are done to fulfill Allah's will. So, from now on, there will be no more contact with our families. We have disappeared to them. We are dead to them. They will understand later. Allah will inscribe a message on their hearts."

The trio around the leader nodded without comment, eyes lowered contemplatively. Satisfied, al-Assad continued. "From this moment there will be no more contact with anyone outside of this room. We are our own self-contained universe. This means that you don't need your cell phones anymore. We are as the dead, and the dead do not talk. I want you all to take out your cell phones and crush them underfoot. Crush them as you would crush the skull of Satan's serpent."

The men shuffled to their feet, searching for the telephones. Three black plastic Siemens phones hit the floor. A moment later they had been splintered into unrecognizable heaps of component parts. This accomplished, al-Assad motioned the men to sit back down.

"Good. We are now safe from the outside world. I have my cell phone to receive calls from our other brothers, including Ibrahim, may Allah protect him and guide his return. But the number of this phone is known only to a few, only to those who support our mission. Still, we must do more to avoid detection. We cannot take the chance of being seen or risk an encounter with the police for any reason, like a traffic accident or passport check. So, it's best if we remain here in this place, and make it our home as well as our workplace for the remaining time."

The tallest of the trio replied. "You mean eat and sleep here? We don't have beds. We don't have anything to cook with."

Al-Assad smiled thinly and looked across the expanse of the warehouse as he replied. "Yes, Sayyid, we sleep and dine here. It is not a perfect setting, but it will do. These are small sacrifices, surely."

The others murmured agreement.

"I will drive out later and purchase sleeping bags. I will bring a portable stove and food and utensils. We already have water here for tea and for cleaning. The important thing is to reduce our profile to the world to almost nothing. Whatever errands are required, I will do. We are blessed with much space in this warehouse, so staying here should not be unbearable. Remember, if we would be caught for some reason, we would all occupy a small cell in very short order."

"Yes," Sayyid interjected, "a cell in Guantanamo." The men laughed in unison.

Al-Assad continued. "As you know, we turned the rental trucks in at Munich, after we delivered the equipment here. It was purposely not the nearest place; we use distance as a means of security. With these procedures we should be safe. Do nothing to alter that. We would all be disgraced if we fail to carry out our holy duty, our noble task."

It was at precisely that moment that they heard the unmistakable sound of cartons falling to the concrete floor in the storage room at the far end of the warehouse.

Chapter 21

The morning after he had discovered the names of the suspects, Hirter drove down the autobahn to Salzburg, Austria. Alpine landscape flew by like a living postcard; rustic villages, lush meadows, and the indigo of Bavarian lakes presented themselves in a panorama. Salzburg itself was on display to best advantage that morning, canopied by a cloudless sky, the triumphant sunlight emphasizing the Italianate architecture of the buildings lining the Salzach River. The high, crenellated walls of Salzburg castle crowned a cliff above the city, presiding with sovereign majesty.

The old city was crowded full with Americans, Japanese, and Europeans. Wealthy Russians of suspicious means were the latest addition. They turned the winding length of the Getreidegasse, replete with fashion boutiques, into a battle zone of jostling, sweating, and gesturing figures, inappropriately dressed and girded with cameras and videocams.

Salzburg residents regarded the occupation of their city with stoic fatalism. Tourism, after all, kept Salzburg wealthy and famous. Salzburg profited mightily from the sale of outrageously priced concert tickets and every manner of good emblazoned with the name Mozart or Amadeus. The enigmatic image of young, white-wigged Mozart stared at passersby from rows of coffee mugs and boxes of candy. Like the Lord God of the Salzburg archbishops, Mozart was omnipresent.

Hirter, however, was not wandering the cobblestone passages of Salzburg to take in the sights. He was to meet a CIA officer from the Clandestine Service who would transmit the identities of the murder suspects back to agency headquarters in Virginia for name tracing. The venue, Hirter had been advised in a brief, cryptic phone call, was the coffee house Tomaseli, located in the old town, not far from the magnificent, twin-steepled façade of the cathedral. The CIA officer would be wearing a yellow polo shirt and prominently reading a copy of the *International Herald Tribune*. Hirter did not need to know anything else.

As it was mid-morning, Hirter found the usually well-visited coffee house only partially filled. The outside tables facing the plaza betrayed no one of the proper description, and Hirter ventured into the cool and dark interior, its gravitas enhanced by heavy oil portraits lining the walls. The air was redolent with the scents of strongly brewed coffee, exotic teas, and rich chocolate. Hirter spotted his quarry, lounging at a corner table with a view of the door and the plaza beyond.

The man in canary yellow appeared to be glancing at the English-language paper, but Hirter knew that his entry had been spotted and that his CIA colleague was checking to see if any activity in the plaza suggested that he had been followed. Through years of surveillance training, Hirter knew the answer to that question was no. He permitted himself the pleasure of deeply inhaling the inviting Tomaseli aromas and moved to his counterpart, taking an empty seat opposite him.

"You're clean," the man in Tommy Hilfiger yellow mumbled, putting the paper aside. He looked about forty, ruddy, athletic, and with thinning hair.

Hirter nodded in confirmation, adding, "I didn't see anyone suspicious behind me during the trip. I'm sure we're okay."

This established, the CIA officer in yellow folded his paper with studied care and regarded Hirter with a smile, sizing him up.

"I'm Andrew. Coffee is on me."

Hirter shook his head. "Coffee would be great." His interlocutor summoned a harried-looking waitress who, without remark, brought a steaming white porcelain cup of dark coffee, accompanied by a glass of water in the Austrian custom.

Hirter extracted a thin manila envelope from his sports coat and inserted it into the officer's folded newspaper. "Here's everything the police have pulled together. Names, car rental agreement, photos, last known legal addresses, that kind of thing."

Andrew nodded, satisfied. "Date and place of birth?"

"Yeah. Everything is there."

The other officer smiled again and took a sip from his mug of hot chocolate. "Great. I'll get this stuff transmitted and it should be at headquarters by close of business today. I don't expect it to take more than a day or two to get a response."

"Okay. Should I wait for another call from you at the hotel?"

The man in yellow cotton shook his head. "No, that would just tie you down. I presume you're bird-dogging the police and will be out and about."

Hirter laughed quietly. "A Kommissar, actually. There's a Kommissar running the case, and I guess I'm getting more into his shadow than he's comfortable with. So what do you suggest, Andrew?"

Andrew extracted a Nokia cell phone from the pocket of his Dockers khaki slacks and passed it to Hirter. "This is for you. It's got a prepaid card. It also has robust commercial encryption. I and the station are the only ones that know the number. I'll use it exclusively to call you, and you can reach me the same way. Check the address book and you'll find a number listed for Andrew. It all looks perfectly innocent to the casual observer. Don't lose it, though, it's an accountable item."

"Isn't everything these days?" Hirter replied. "Thanks, Andrew. We'll be talking."

Hirter gulped the remains of his coffee and started to leave when Andrew touched his arm lightly. "If we need to have another personal meeting, it should be in Munich; it's bigger than Salzburg and easier to get lost in. There's a little restaurant called Torbraeu; you can find the address in the phone book. We can meet there."

"Fine, Andrew. Torbraeu it is. Do they serve good food there?"

The CIA officer wrinkled his brow. "No, not especially. But it's located up one story and has a great view of the street in both directions."

Chapter 22

The information on Mohammed al-Assad and Ibrahim Baran was transmitted electronically to CIA Headquarters in Langley, Virginia, from an agency communications facility in Austria. There it waited in queue for someone to read it on a secure PC. The message was one of thousands that inundated the CIA building on that day, as on any day, from scores of undercover locations around the globe.

Caroline O'Kendell had gotten to the CIA compound early that morning in an attempt to beat the choking beltway traffic. Finding an empty space for her Audi in the west parking lot, she walked to the New Headquarters Building, constructed during the Reagan presidency, and entered a personal recognition code and ID card pin number at security. She smiled a good morning to the three armed guards and took the escalator down to the coffee shop where she picked up a large Starbuck's and a cinnamon roll. She would work the calories off in the gym later, she assured herself. Her heels clicked against the polished marble tiles as she made her way back to the atrium, past the potted trees and under the black, large-scale model of a U-2 CIA spy plane. Sipping the hot coffee, she took an elevator to her office in the north tower.

Caroline liked arriving early. She would be one of the first in the vault, aside from a secretary or two. She entered the cipher code on the door and stepped in. As expected, the spaces were nearly empty. Fluorescent lights glowed from the ceiling overhead, and she made her way past fabric-sided cubicles to her office with its view of the agency loading docks. At least she had a window, unlike many of her colleagues, allowing a glimpse of the Virginia countryside. The

site had been rural once, having originally been acquired when avun-
cular, pipe-smoking Allen Dulles was director of Central Intelligence
all those decades ago. Eisenhower had been president, and on his
behalf, Dulles and the agency had sought to penetrate what had been
called the "Iron Curtain" over Eastern Europe. Back then, McLean
had been a perfectly isolated spot for an espionage agency that val-
ued privacy — its own, not that of others. Now, past the treeline,
the agency buildings were surrounded by mansions.

After a sip of coffee, its temperature now tolerable, Caroline entered her password into a secure computer and began to troll the
classified traffic that had arrived overnight. It was the morning ritual, as there might be an operational message from overseas requiring quick response. This morning's traffic appeared staid. There were
reports of meetings with foreign counterterrorist specialists in several
countries, a request for funds to enlarge a surveillance team in Asia,
an account of a meeting in Cyprus between a case officer and a
Lebanese who claimed to have access to Hezbollah. Might be real,
but he was probably a fabricator looking to pry cash or a green card
from the Americans. She did not fancy herself a cynic, but had seen
enough of human nature to make her suspicious of motives and skeptical about altruism.

Another message caught her eye, from Austria. It was a name
trace request, a query for information on individuals with Arabic
names. She vaguely recalled the case. A fellow Clandestine Service
officer whom she had met on a few occasions was involved — Robert
Hirter. The circumstances were depressing. Hirter's brother had been
murdered while on vacation in Germany. No suspect had been identified. Robert had taken leave and traveled to Germany. She knew
that he had been out of touch for a while before making contact
with another field officer a day or so ago. That field officer had authored the cable she was reading.

Caroline let her gaze move down the screen to the Arabic names.
The information seemed sufficiently complete to permit a trace. An
attachment contained photographs of the individuals. In the photos,
both of the dark-haired, bearded suspects stared sullenly into the

camera, their eyes no more expressive than those of a shark, their faces ciphers.

"Let's see who they might be," she whispered to herself, punching a button on her keyboard and sending the cable to a printer at the far end of the vault. There were other things she could be doing this morning, she reasoned. Still, she knew Robert Hirter a bit, and found the task of aiding a murder investigation worthy of her attention. True, a police investigation was a law enforcement matter, not really something for an intelligence agency's resources. Nonetheless, she had an intuitive sense that the massive CIA database might harbor useful information on the two severe-looking faces staring at her from the computer screen.

The Clandestine Service database was a vast and venerable repository of information, Caroline knew. Once, the holdings comprised paper files. Retired agency officers had told her how, decades removed, they had journeyed to the headquarters basement, a windowless and dim expanse, and returned with arms straining under bursting manila folders, to sort the contents at their desks. How archaic that seemed now, when a trace request could be processed via desktop computer. Still, she thought, there was a loss of atmosphere; the tactile sense of hunting through rustling paper documents was gone.

Even devoid of atmosphere, the database was impressive. It contained information dating back to World War II and the CIA predecessor organization, the Office of Strategic Services, OSS. Most of the information had been covertly collected — stolen, purchased, elicited from the unwitting or extracted during interrogation. The ranks of subjects included legions of dubious characters from every country on the globe. The files held details on thousands of criminals, narcotics traffickers, information peddlers, arms dealers, terrorists, mercenaries, and extremists of every stripe.

All of which meant that it was possible that CIA headquarters might possess some threads of information on the Arabic subjects living in the alpine fastness of Bavaria. She hoped the trace would turn up something of use to her colleague.

Chapter 23

Andreas Niedermeier had stumbled, as he often stumbled after finishing off a bottle of discount schnapps. An avalanche of the boxes and cartons that filled the poorly lit storage room had tumbled noisily to the concrete floor, upending him in the process. "Shit," he muttered as he eased himself up, sore from the unexpected fall. He exhaled sour breath into his rampant, graying beard and stood upright, surveying the damage. Most of the boxes seemed empty and there had been no sound of breakage; for that he was grateful. He would rearrange the crates in a semblance of order and leave well enough alone. Nothing would betray his little accident.

He had used the warehouse often in the past as a dry place to sleep off the effects of binge drinking and he did not want to foul the nest. Although Niedermeier did not engage in anything approaching future planning, he knew that he would continue to drink heavily whenever he could put together enough change for a bottle and would, accordingly, require these gratis accommodations in the future. Having discovered the weakness of the rusty door lock years ago, he did not want to be forced to find an alternate warehouse to protect him from the elements. There were always the wooden benches at the train station as a last resort, but the police showed up unpredictably and demonstrated little tolerance for his situation. He burped wetly and set about stacking the boxes with tremulous hands.

Mohammed al-Assad had drawn the compact Walther pistol from his waistband and slipped off the safety, placing a finger carefully inside the trigger guard. Sayyid was behind him, a large, serrated-blade kitchen knife gripped in his fist. Soundlessly, Mohammed eased open the door to the storage area, just sufficient to permit a view into the room.

He saw a man. Mohammed noted with satisfaction that he was facing the intruder's back. The man swayed slightly as he replaced the fallen boxes, clearly oblivious to the presence of others. Al-Assad's mind assessed the situation. The uninvited visitor was no police official. Even at a distance it was evident that his thick hair was matted and uncombed, betraying the greasy veneer of the long-term unwashed. The man appeared to be in his fifties and was dressed in a shapeless, stained cotton long coat torn at the collar and missing some buttons.

Al-Assad nodded in comprehension. A common drunk. The type of inveterate alcoholic to be found throughout Germany, al-Assad reflected with a shiver of disgust at life in the Western world. He knew the type, had sometimes been forced to serve them a Doener kebab at his shop when they showed up with a handful of smeared euros. Al-Assad judged that he was observing a homeless drinker who had broken into the warehouse for some fitful sleep before another foray with the bottle.

But there would be no future foray, al-Assad knew. The drunkard might decide to explore farther in the warehouse and discover them. That could not be permitted. With this type of human flotsam it was unlikely that a missing person notice would even be filed.

Al-Assad signaled his partner to hold the door open as he silently approached the distracted man from behind. From a step away and with adrenalin-driven force he slammed the metal stock of his pistol into the back of the man's head, feeling the shivering connection of metal with bone.

Andreas Niedermeier dropped wordlessly to his knees, which cracked loudly against the concrete. He lurched forward full on his face, once again upsetting the boxes he had moments ago so carefully arranged.

Al-Assad turned and signaled his compatriot to enter the room. Sayyid, kitchen knife at the ready, stood above Niedermeier's prostrate form and pushed at it roughly with his foot. There was no response. "He's dead. Now what?"

Al-Assad had already worked it out like a mathematical problem. "I'll tell the others what happened and clarify that there is nothing to be concerned about."

Al-Assad noted uncertainty in his comrade's eyes. "Don't worry, brother, this changes nothing. For him maybe," he wagged his chin at Niedermeier, "but not for us. We just have to do some cleanup work."

"Cleanup work?" Al-Assad noted the slight tremor in Sayyid's voice.

"Yes, Sayyid. You have a knife, and we'll put it to good use. Slaughter him as infidels should be slaughtered, in the manner that Al-Zarqawi, peace be upon him, slaughtered many of our enemies. Then pack him up and toss his filthy remains into the empty freezer at the other end of the building."

Sayyid nodded and tugged at his beard. He seemed uneasy, but al-Assad decided that such a reaction to an unexpected situation was permissible.

"The manner of al-Zarqawi. You mean the head?"

"Yes. A proper slaughter; cut off his filthy, canine head. If he's still alive, he won't be when you've finished. If his neck sprays, it means he's still pumping blood. When everything is done, find some garbage bags and fit him into the freezer. Make him fit, I don't care how. When you're done, we can get back to our work."

He stopped and considered. "It's almost like this is a message for us. To demonstrate that we live surrounded by danger but are nonetheless protected. This worthless type could have discovered us and reported us to the police. But that was not permitted to happen. What you will do to him now is ordained. Rejoice, Sayyid, rejoice, and send him off to hell."

Sayyid nodded firmly, with renewed determination in his eyes.

After al-Assad left the storage room, he grabbed a handful of Niedermeier's greasy hair and pulled the man's head back, exposing the neck. Niedermeier's features were slack, eyes closed. The man was either dead already or unconscious and uncomprehending of what was about to happen. Sayyid placed the metal blade along the curve of neck, directly against a visible artery. He began to carve at the flesh as he would at a thick piece of meat. Immediately a spray of blood shot forth like a geyser followed by a strong convulsion of Niedermeier's torso. Sayyid kept working the blade the way he had studied in Internet videos of al-Zarqawi in Iraq.

Niedermeier made no sound other than a wheezing rush of air from his windpipe as it was severed. A moment later the head of the alcoholic had been separated from the body and Sayyid lifted it triumphantly like a trophy. He let the knife fall from his grip, the blade a thick, viscous blanket of red, flecked with dangling pieces of tissue.

"*Allah Akbar,*" he cried out, as the severed head secreted thick streams of dark blood onto the bare concrete floor.

Chapter 24

The trace results had been assembled into a cable classified "secret" and sent to Caroline O'Kendell for transmission overseas. Since the contents were intended to be shared with German authorities, the details in the message were presented in a manner to protect the sources of the information.

Caroline read the cable one last time, one hand absently toying with the collar of her business suit. She found the substance of the message troubling. It was five p.m. by the time she had edited the cable into final shape. The radio on her desk announced that afternoon rush hour traffic was building on the beltway. The sky was slate gray and rain was expected, guaranteed to make the traffic worse.

After a final review of the text, Caroline clicked the "release" box on the cable template that sent the message across the building to the communications center where it would be encrypted and transmitted in unbreakable form to a CIA facility in Vienna. Given the time difference, Caroline knew — it was now eleven p.m. in Vienna — there would be no one present at this hour to read the message. The CIA cable would be automatically decrypted and sit in the Vienna inbox, waiting for the case officer named Andrew when he arrived the following morning.

At seven in the evening August Sedlmeyer sat on a wrought-iron park bench and thought of something he had not recalled in decades. The thought had come unsummoned, as thoughts seemed to do increasingly as he aged. Perhaps, he mused, it had to do with not having many opportunities for conversation. Most of his friends had died in the last several years; those who had survived the war. It seemed as if the last years had been one long marathon funeral attendance. The ranks of the living known to him diminished relentlessly.

Sedlmeyer understood that he had outlived not only his companions, but his time. How long remained to him he did not know. A few years perhaps? A few weeks? He nodded at the wisdom of the biblical injunction about not knowing the day or the hour. After a long journey, there was rightness about death. Sedlmeyer pushed away these reflections and concentrated on what had occurred to him moments before. He did not know why he remembered this thing now, after so many years.

Kaltenberg. That was the name he now recalled, the name he had for so long forgotten. The first name he did not know, had never known. He had known the man only by his last name and his rank, the rank by which Kaltenberg had been addressed. *Stuermbannfuehrer* Kaltenberg. The Waffen-SS officer who had commanded that convoy on its harried sojourn from ruined Berlin to the unwounded Austrian meadows. Kaltenberg — the stern officer who had unflinchingly gunned down Fehlmann. Stuermbannfuehrer Kaltenberg, the SS officer with one arm in a sling who had vanished into the Austrian night just before the Americans in their jeeps arrived to take them prisoner.

Sedlmeyer recalled a few other snippets of information as well. Rumors really, postwar gossip from old comrades, whispered furtively during rare, quiet SS reunions in smoky Bavarian beer halls. Talk that Kaltenberg had fled to Switzerland and adopted a new identity. A remark made in the 1960s that Kaltenberg had established himself as an international salesman with lucrative connections in the Middle East. Maybe all of it was true. Or perhaps some of it was true, or possibly none of it at all. Old soldiers liked to talk as much as old women; the veracity of what was said was a secondary consideration. If Kaltenberg were still alive, he would be a few years older than Sedlmeyer. Dead or alive, Kaltenberg inhabited the past.

Still, perhaps the SS officer was not entirely a creature of the past; perhaps he had one booted foot solidly in the present. Perhaps Kaltenberg — or more precisely what Kaltenberg knew — would be of interest to Robert Hirter. Kaltenberg surely knew the contents of the convoy consignment; he knew the provenance of the sealed crates that had been so carefully transported to a remote corner of the Alps.

Sedlmeyer considered, observing the sun descend behind distant peaks. Should he let the past slumber? Wasn't it prudent to forget that he had recalled Kaltenberg's name? Or should he pass along this detail to the young American? He was unsure. The matter unresolved, he watched a flock of mallards cross the darkening sky, calling confidently to one another on their way to some tranquil lake and the promise of nocturnal rest.

Chapter 25

The center of Munich was vibrant, the streets of the city filled with throngs of tourists and businessmen. A parking space proving difficult to locate, Hirter left his car in the underground garage below the Bavarian opera, a ten minute walk from the restaurant where he was to meet his clandestine colleague, Andrew. The weather was overcast, but there was a fresh breeze in the air, edged with a distinct scent of hops from the nearby Paulaner Brewery.

Hirter moved with the crowds, taking in the displays in the storefronts of the street called Im Tal. He made use of the show windows of various shops. Feigning an interest in the products displayed, he checked the reflections in the glass to unobtrusively determine whether he was under surveillance. He noted nothing alerting. Another three minutes walk and Hirter found himself at the Torbraeu Hotel and Café, located across from one of the ancient city gates of Munich, its mass of stone painted rich ochre.

With a final glance for surveillance, Hirter entered the small, tasteful lobby of the hotel and followed a sign to the coffee shop located up the stairs on the second floor. He quickly spotted Andrew. By design, Andrew had seated himself at a table on the balcony permitting an unobstructed view of the street below.

"Greetings, Robert," Andrew intoned jovially, the remains of a cappuccino and a largely devoured chocolate croissant on the table in front of him. As Hirter pulled up a chair, his host whispered, "No one on your tail. I'd have been surprised if there were."

Hirter nodded agreement. "I haven't seen a thing, and I had a good countersurveillance route." Hirter took in the surroundings.

The restaurant was airy and bright; a few pastel oil scenes decorated the walls. There were few customers, mostly elderly women klatching over coffee, all of them out of earshot.

"I have something from our friends back home," Andrew interjected. From the folds of the *Muenchner Merkur* newspaper he withdrew a manila envelope and slid it across the table.

Hirter tucked the envelope into the inside pocket of his cotton windbreaker. "It's nice to have something to read."

Andrew sipped his cappuccino. "Yes, for your reading pleasure. And for your police friend, the content has been cleared for passage. It was waiting in the office for me yesterday. I knew you'd want it as soon as possible."

"I appreciate your traveling here. I know you must have other stuff on the front burner. Anything interesting in your view?"

Andrew leaned back in his chair and looked down at the bustling street below, the ebb and flow of Teutons and tourists. "You don't want me to spoil your reading, do you? I'm sure you'll find the contents interesting."

"Good. I'll read it before I hand it over. What's the gist?" A young waitress appeared, and Hirter ordered a latte.

Andrew considered, a shadow of concentration settling in his features. "The trace results are positive for those guys. There's enough stuff there to suggest that you folks have stumbled onto some bad characters. Two names turned up a connection to a third name, also living in Germany; it's all in there. One of them is a Turk and one an Egyptian. The Turk is ethnically half-Lebanese, it would appear."

"Criminal backgrounds?" Hirter asked.

"Yes. One with garden-variety petty crime and a case of assault in Istanbul; you'll see the details. Still, it's the other stuff headquarters found that worries me."

Hirter said nothing, waiting for his companion to continue. The waitress returned like an apparition, and Hirter's latte appeared on the table in front of him.

"The link analysis turned up something. These guys have nasty connections. The information suggests that they might be more into extremism than run-of-the-mill offenses. I know this is a murder investigation, but I have to tell you, these gents strike me as pursuing other interests."

Hirter nodded and placed his hands around the warm café latte cup. "Thanks. I don't know what to think at this stage. But I have a feeling that Waldbaer is onto something with these suspects."

"What's he like?" Andrew asked.

Hirter's features creased with a half-smile. "Well, he can be a stubborn pain in the ass. But then, you can understand that he probably didn't need me turning up to complicate his investigation. As far as I can tell, Waldbaer is an experienced investigator even if he's stuck out in the Bavarian pastures. He really wants to solve my brother's murder. Waldbaer intends to get the guys that did it and put them away, period. I like that kind of commitment."

"Of course you do," Andrew said. "How do you think it will go between you two now that he knows you're CIA? Will that make it easier or more difficult?"

Hirter shrugged his shoulders and drank some latte. "Hard to tell. A lot rides on chemistry. I think I can read him a bit, and I'll try to avoid doing anything to raise his hackles. Even though the agency is involved now, it's Waldbaer who's in charge. I think we can make this work. We both have the same goal — finding the murderer."

It was Andrew's turn to nod. He swiped a hand through thinning hair and leaned into the table. "Oh, before I forget, I got an e-mail from headquarters along with the cable. I'm supposed to pass along greetings and wish you luck."

"Thanks. Who sent the e-mail?"

"Someone I met once back home on a temporary duty assignment. Her name is Caroline O'Kendell. She works on the European Terrorism desk and she released the cable. I seem to recall that she's pretty cute. You must know her if she asked me to pass you her regards."

There was a loud report from the street and both of the Americans glanced out, alert. They heard the high-pitched whine of a small engine and quickly determined that a Vespa motor scooter had backfired.

Hirter returned to the conversation. "Caroline O'Kendell. I know her, but slightly. She trained at The Farm a year after I did. She's been doing European terrorism for a while. We were in some staff meetings together and at the same dinner party once in Alexandria. If you get a moment, drop her a line from me and say thanks for the thought."

"No problem," said Andrew with a smile.

"And Andrew, you're right, as I recall she is cute. She would also kill us if she heard us talking this way about her."

Waldbaer and Hirter each had a copy of the CIA memo and sat reviewing it in the detective's unadorned office. Waldbaer took notes on yellow sheets of paper, the tops of which were emblazoned with the stylized shield of the German police. Waldbaer wrote in slashing strokes, his beefy hand clutched near the nib of the pen.

"Quite interesting," Waldbaer said, snorting loudly. "I'd love to know where you got some of these details." He gave Hirter a fatalistic glance.

"Even I don't know the sourcing, Kommissar. You can believe that or not, but I don't have any details additional to the trace report."

Waldbaer's eyes communicated skepticism along with the usual world-weariness. "As you say, Herr Hirter. If we ever go to a court trial, it could get sticky if we can't identify sources of information, but it's premature to worry about that yet."

Exhaling a breath, the detective smoothed the pad in front of him, the move suggesting reverence for the written word. "Here's what we have. A group of immigrants to Germany, all young males, all with some sort of undesirable record. One of them," Waldbaer consulted his notes, "that would be Mohammed al-Assad, has at least one episode of violent assault to his credit. That is not unimportant, considering that this is a murder investigation. In my experience, except with crimes of passion, murderers often have a trail of

violence in their past. This is the one I want to focus on. I have a
feeling that if we can locate him, we probably will have the man
who killed your brother."

"I have the same intuition, Kommissar. I don't know why he
would have killed Charles, but I share your feeling that this is the guy
we're looking for. What's more, I think my headquarters turned up
things worth examining beyond his criminal record."

He watched Waldbaer scan the CIA information again, the detective's finger moving down the page as he read.

"You mean al-Assad's associations? I agree they're intriguing, but
might be unrelated to the murder." Waldbaer looked up from his
notes to see what the American might add.

"Al-Assad has a track record of contacts that I find disturbing.
He's more than a criminal. He's been in direct contact with several
individuals internationally who are known figures in the jihadist
movement. For example, he met in Istanbul with two fundamental-
ist Turks, one of whom later detonated himself in a suicide-bombing
attack on the British Consulate. He also assisted two Egyptian members of the Muslim Brotherhood in entering Europe via Austria."

Waldbaer nodded. "Right. Al-Assad is also believed, according
to CIA, to have visited Pakistan on three occasions in the last few
years. Your colleagues suggest that the purpose of the trips was not
tourism; he was sighted in North Waziristan, in the company of
Taliban operatives. Your side believes that al-Assad has terrorist
friends. My reply is that this is interesting, but perhaps not relevant
to your brother's death. It doesn't matter in the end. Until we get
al-Assad in our clutches, all we can do is speculate."

A telephone rang in an office nearby as Hirter spoke. "Kommissar, I don't think al-Assad just has terrorist friends. I think he's a terrorist himself, and since he's a resident in Bavaria that should
concern you. These people don't change their stripes and they don't
leave the jihad. Intelligence information is always partial, but there's
enough here to suggest that you and I have stumbled onto a terrorist cell. Al-Assad and his buddies are involved in some current activity. My brother's murder might be the least troubling thing you

have to worry about." Hirter lifted himself from his chair and began to pace the threadbare carpeting of Waldbaer's office. "These guys are an operational unit."

Waldbaer remained behind his desk. "Why do you say that solving your brother's murder is the least of my problems?"

"Because Charles is dead. His murder is a crime committed; it's in the past. I suspect that al-Assad and his compatriots have plans for future activities. They were using that cave as a clandestine storage place. They recently cleared it out and moved the goods to an unknown location. Why? All of these guys have gone to ground; they disappeared and even their relatives don't know where they are. I put these facts together with what I know about terrorist modus operandi, and it fits a pattern. In my view, Herr Kommissar, these guys are planning an attack, probably soon. And although we know who they are, we don't have a clue as to where they are. That should worry you."

Waldbaer crossed his arms and gazed at Hirter. "What you're saying is that I don't just have a crime to solve, I have one to prevent. If your suspicions are correct, and they could be, I need to call in help. The German federal internal service, the BFV, for example. Maybe other agencies. That will put things on a whole new level. The problem with such a big circus is that too much coordination could reduce our chances of getting al-Assad and his friends. I have a sense they are still in Bavaria. Here's what I'm going to do. For the moment, I'll put aside the need to coordinate with my superiors. Let's concentrate on getting lucky."

Hirter looked puzzled. "How do you do that, Kommissar?"

Waldbaer's features creased with a wry smile. "We get lucky, Herr Hirter, through you. You should be happy; you've wanted a role in this investigation all along. Here's your opportunity. The background information your Langley friends have provided has been helpful. Now, get your agency actively — but unofficially — involved. Increase our chance of getting lucky, Herr Hirter, and I will be obliged."

Chapter 26

The vast black-paved parking lots surrounding CIA headquarters in Langley were mostly empty. It was late and the night shift enjoyed dominion. At this hour, most of the personnel present were analysts pulling together the latest classified items for the PDB, the Presidential Daily Brief, the intelligence assessment of world events presented every morning to the commander in chief. Cleaning crews were present as well, machine waxing and buffing the immense gray vinyl floors. Also present was the legion of uniformed, Glock-armed CIA security guards manning posts at all of the entrances to the building. They held night-shift boredom at bay with cardboard cups of coffee, cans of Coca-Cola, and packages of potato chips and Twinkies.

A small gathering of Clandestine Service officers was also huddled in the headquarters building on this evening. They had been grouped together in a small, windowless conference room on the sixth floor since four in the afternoon and were together still, trying to reach closure. The issue was not without contention and sharp exchanges of view. Caroline O'Kendell was one of the more junior officers present, but had not hesitated to make her position clear. Randolph Warren Stockbridge, the senior officer, recapitulated the issue. His hands toyed with a thick, black Pelikan fountain pen as he spoke.

"Okay. Let's wrap this up. We have two questions to resolve. The first is how much to cooperate with the Germans in this investigation. Do we continue unofficially and informally, or do we establish a formal bilateral operation, bringing in the German intelligence service? The other question, which impacts the first: what have we stumbled onto here? These Middle Easterners are bad actors. It's clear that we happened onto a terrorist cell, not just a collection of criminals. What are they up to? Are they a support network for an action cell located somewhere else or are they themselves an action cell? What do we do about them? So, gents," he inclined his head toward Caroline and a female analyst from the Terrorism Center, "and, of course, ladies, what are your thoughts?"

Caroline wanted to get home too and plunged in, sure of her position. "I don't see where there's a need to go for a formal relationship. Maybe later, but there's nothing yet that screams at us to bring in the BND and go formally to the German authorities. We all know that will take time to arrange, and the Germans, being Germans, will start setting rules on how we do things, and whether our methods are legal in Germany and other nonsense. Let's not go there. We can use Robert Hirter as the go-between with the police like we are now. He's a trained case officer and directly in touch with a Kommissar, that should suffice. A formal arrangement will take time, and we might not have lots of time at our disposal."

A sleek-haired whippet of a man with the drawn look of a marathon runner objected. "That won't work. We'd be better off making this an orderly joint investigation. We can get an MOU, a memorandum of understanding, signed by both sides. That's also the thinking of our people in Berlin who are, frankly, uncomfortable with the whole Hirter arrangement. They don't feel they have sufficient control over this."

"Control?" Caroline shot back with undisguised exasperation. "Control? They don't need control. They're in the loop, they're advised what's going on, aren't they? Frankly, there isn't a lot that Berlin can do for this case, the action element is back here and if we dispatch people to the field it won't be to Berlin. Gamsdorf is hundreds of miles from Berlin."

The whippet looked sullen but said nothing more, masking his retreat by soberly doodling on his notepad.

Stockbridge, silver-haired, well-dressed in a black summer-weight suit and with wire-rimmed spectacles magnifying his gray eyes, placed his fountain pen on the tabletop with a precise touch. "I'm persuaded that Caroline is right. We have a functional situation and I'm not sure what happens if we make a formal approach to the Germans. They can be complicated, like their cars. Don't forget, the Germans could turn down a cooperative effort and tell us to mind our own business. They don't like Guantanamo, they don't like renditions, and they don't like our interrogation methods. My preference is not to open a can of worms when we have a reasonable arrangement. Let's stay with the Hirter connection; apologies to Berlin. Caroline, take responsibility for communicating with Hirter. Handle this personally."

Caroline tried unsuccessfully to subdue a smile.

"We aren't done yet," Stockbridge continued, adjusting his striped silk tie. "What are we going to do about this cell other than unofficially provide the Germans background? What's our plan of action?"

A middle-aged, overweight officer from the Central Europe desk shifted in his chair and spoke in a gravelly voice. "Well, we don't know where these terrorists are holed up, that's the main problem, otherwise the Germans could bag them. Like the realtors say, its location, location, location. I think we should put any technical surveillance means we have available in Germany on this. See if we come up with a suspicious phone call, fax, or e-mail. I know we have technical limitations, but its worth trying."

The whippet interjected. "You're right, we should try technical means. My suspicion, though, is that this cell is security conscious. They know that phone calls can be intercepted. If they communicate, they'll speak in code and if they're using throwaway cell phones — the Germans call those "handies" I think — it'll be hard to get a fix on them."

Stockbridge considered, his flinty eyes focusing on the tabletop. "Let's start with what we have. Have we picked up anything suspicious with a Bavarian connection in the last few days that might suggest a terrorist operation? Has anything come across our screen that could be a piece of this puzzle?"

Caroline arched her eyebrows and flipped through the folder in front of her. "Maybe," she said, her voice barely audible. She located the piece of paper that she sought. "This is an intercept from a technical site near Bad Toelz. It's cryptic and it might have nothing to do with this case."

"Go on," Stockbridge said. "You must find it interesting or you wouldn't have raised it."

"All right," Caroline said. "Some guy in Ankara makes a phone call to a cell phone in Bavaria. Ostensibly, the conversation is about a pending wedding. There's talk about the father of the bride and not postponing the wedding and everything being fine."

"Sounds innocuous, Caroline," Stockbridge said.

"Right. The thing is, our voice analysis guys think the topic is a cover. The conversation is stilted, unnatural. Now this doesn't have to be terrorism, it could be narcotics trafficking. The call is from a male who identifies himself as Ibrahim. The male in Bavaria obviously knows him. One of the guys who rented a vehicle from Sixt is named Ibrahim Baran."

"Phone numbers?" Stockbridge prodded, his hands gently working the smooth surface of his ebony pen.

"On the Bavarian end, a cell phone number that we have nothing on. On the Ankara end, the call originated from a public phone."

There was an audible, collective sigh of resignation.

Caroline waved a hand to subdue the murmuring. "Just a second, here's the interesting part. We show a trace on that public phone number in Ankara. The same phone has been used by an identified jihadist terrorist at least twice. Someone named Abdul al-Masri. Wanted in Pakistan since 2003, but never caught."

"Wanted for what?" the gravelly voiced man asked.

Caroline drew in her breath. "Al-Masri was an associate of KSM, an experienced operator and a combat veteran of Afghanistan."

The initials were shorthand for Khalid Sheikh Mohammed, the architect of 9/11 and operations chief for Osama bin Laden. KSM had been captured in Afghanistan, rendered into CIA custody, and interrogated at a secret location to the edge of the law for information that might prevent additional terrorist attacks. Initially arrogant and uncooperative, KSM had eventually offered up much of value to his persistent captors. He ultimately ended up at Guantanamo.

"Holy shit," someone muttered.

Caroline did not want the tidbit to seem more meaningful than it might be and sought to dampen unreasonable expectations. "I know, it's interesting. Still, it could be coincidence that al-Masri and this Ibrahim used the same public phone. How many people use public phones in Ankara on any given day? Ankara has a population of about four million, and a few hundred thousand people a day must be making calls. We need to keep perspective; it's interesting information, but that's all it is."

Stockbridge rubbed a hand against his neck. "It might be all we have at the moment, Caroline, so let's try to flesh it out. Talk tomorrow to the guys who listen to the tapes. I want to know what their wonderfully technical minds suspect. The number in Bavaria, you say we have nothing other than that it's a cell phone?"

"Right," Caroline affirmed.

"Pass the number to Hirter and have him give it to his German detective. Our informal cooperative effort should be a two-way street. Maybe that phone in Bavaria has history."

Caroline made a note on a yellow sticky attached to her folder.

Stockbridge shook his silver mane. "And, Caroline, not now. Tomorrow. Tonight we are all leaving this conference room and going home. Even spies need sleep." They rose to depart to the dispersed suburbs of McLean, Alexandria, and Reston.

Caroline felt the accumulated hours of the day weigh on her shoulders, but the weariness was subordinate to a growing sense that a major intelligence operation was underway.

Chapter 27

Ibrahim Baran drank the steaming hot, unsweetened tea from a small glass, holding it gingerly by the rim so as not to burn his fingers. He closed his eyes and savored the taste. He heard in the distance the bustling traffic of Ankara; aging and abused city buses, diesel auto engines, the soprano whine of underpowered motorbikes. Western machines, he thought, western inventions. Why did the faithful have to be transported to their daily chores in infidel devices? He frowned, having no answer to the question. Ibrahim breathed deeply of the pungent, urban Turkish air and opened his deep brown eyes again.

He was in an apartment on the fourth floor of a nondescript, concrete apartment building, its exterior a dull yellow faded by time and solar rays, the cheap paint layered with accretions of traffic soot. It was cool inside the thick walls, though, and comfortable to sit protected from the harsh sun reigning outside. The apartment was located downtown, not far from the heights of Anitkabir, the imposing, solemn stone mausoleum of Mustapha Kemal Attaturk, the relentlessly secular founder of modern Turkey. Attaturk, a man who stirred, even in death, passionate hatred in Ibrahim. The day will come, Ibrahim thought fleetingly, when the decaying bones of that scotch-swilling dog will be disinterred and scattered to the winds sweeping over this arid landscape. He shook the satisfying vision of vengeance away; there were more pressing concerns that required his attention.

Ibrahim glanced across the table to the serious, thickly bearded man who regarded him silently. Abdul al-Masri was a personage of importance, someone who possessed a reputation as a man both resolute and ruthless in the performance of the jihad against the far enemy, against the inhabitants of the *dar al-harb*, the house of war.

"Brother, what are you thinking?" al-Masri asked after what seemed a full minute of silence.

Ibrahim looked the bronze-skinned man in the eyes. "I was just letting thoughts run through my mind. I couldn't help thinking of that heap of stones on the hill, the monument to the apostate who betrayed Islam and ended the caliphate."

Al-Masri's lined visage acquired a small, knowing smile, hard and humorless. "Don't worry about him. His heresy has doubtless been given justice by Allah. If you want to worry about something, worry about his misguided children." He inclined his bearded head toward the window opening onto the street below. "Worry about these Turks who want to be like the crusaders, who reject the veiling of women and every other form of modesty. Worry about these Turks who call themselves Moslems but drink Effis beer and spend their nights in clubs dancing to western music. Worry about them, not about that rotting sack of garbage in a decaying suit, Attaturk. What we will do, Ibrahim, will bring many of these lost ones back on the right path, to the true meaning of the Koran and the Prophet. Peace be upon him."

Ibrahim muttered agreement into his tea glass, impressed, as always with al-Masri's pronouncements. They were, he knew, uttered with authority.

"We must talk about the business at hand, Ibrahim." Al-Masri stood up slowly, moved aside a faded polyester orange curtain and glanced out the window, observing the street for any sign of a police presence. He detected nothing other than clutches of pedestrians crossing an intersection to the jeering beep of car horns and old women lined up at a take-out pastry shop across the street. He let his hand touch the butt of the Walther automatic pistol tucked into his belt, a ritual unconsciously performed a hundred times a day. He turned his attention back to the room and his seated companion.

"Ibrahim, let's to go over the details of your return to Germany.

Get your ticket tomorrow at a travel agency. Pay by credit card, it looks natural; cash payments arouse suspicion these days. Book the flight for a few days from now. It can attract the wrong kind of attention to get a ticket at the last moment."

Ibrahim smiled at his superior. "Yes, profiling. I know about air traveler profiling."

Al-Masri nodded. They all understood the requirements of operational security in international travel. "I don't want you to carry a written message. Memorize what I have told you and will tell you. Put some gifts in your luggage — Turkish Delight candy, trinkets, pistachios — just in case customs in Germany inspects your stuff. You need to look like every other Turk returning to Germany after a vacation in the home country. And don't be nervous, there is nothing to be nervous about. You will be carrying no physical object, nothing to jeopardize the mission. Stay cool, that's the most important piece of advice I can offer you."

Ibrahim nodded to al-Masri, confidant that there would be no problem, not in Ankara, not in Munich.

"Once you clear customs in Munich, take the S-Bahn to the city and spend the night. Find a hotel. This is a precaution. Frankly, if there is any compromise of our operation, I would rather that the Germans got you alone rather than you and the group together. We will let al-Assad know when you should arrive. If your arrival is delayed without explanation they will know to go ahead on their own."

Ibrahim became more somber. "Don't worry, Abdul al-Masri, I will do my duty. I am prepared to sacrifice all for this task. Even if I must become a martyr, a *Shahid*."

He means it, al-Masri thought. "I know your quality, Ibrahim, may you be blessed for it. I expect nothing to happen; this has been a most secure operation. You and your friends are professionals and have been discrete in your activities. All of you have earned my unqualified trust."

That was not exactly the truth, he knew. Al-Masri was somewhat troubled by al-Assad, the group leader in Germany. Dedicated, undoubtedly; clever, yes. But impulsive, maybe too thirsty for infidel blood, as demonstrated with the hiker. Such emotions were understandable, but emotions had to be controlled, individual personalities had to submit to the needs of the cause. One bad choice, one hot-headed moment could compromise the careful work of years.

Still, al-Masri knew that he had to work with those in place and hope for the best. And, indeed, there had, to date, not been a hint of compromise, now that the special material had been removed from the cave.

"All right, Ibrahim. Now is a good time for us to review the message for your friends. We will go over this several times until you are comfortable with having it down. We have as much time as you need, so don't be anxious. Relax and listen. I will relate the orders to you and then repeat them, until you are able to repeat the message back to me easily and accurately. Sit comfortably, Ibrahim, and listen."

Outside, the traffic sounds of Ankara droned on.

Chapter 28

Sayyid forced the green garbage bag containing Niedermeyer's torso deep into the recesses of the freezer. It was a tight fit; the dead man had broad shoulders underneath his soiled shirt. Still, after a few minutes struggle with the segmented corpse, Sayyid was satisfied; the body was jammed tight in the depths of the copious freezer. Niedermeyer's head was concealed in a smaller plastic bag that Sayyid had located. The freezer was very cold and no scent of corruption should betray the presence of the dead man. Relieved that his disagreeable task had been accomplished, Sayyid washed the clotting blood of his victim from his hands in the tiny downstairs bathroom and rejoined his comrades on the floor above.

Al-Assad greeted Sayyid and slapped him on the back in approval. "Well done, brother," he said. The others were leaning against the stained walls, listening. Al-Assad moved to the center of the room and addressed them, arms folded across his white shirt.

"Everything is fine, my friends. The intruder is dead and no one will miss a worthless type like that. We are free to continue as planned. Ibrahim will be returning to us soon with final instructions from al-Masri. It is for us now to put the devices into their final configuration. All of the equipment seems to be functioning perfectly, the move damaged nothing." Al-Assad's features became more solemn, his voice lower.

"Before we get to work again, there is something I ask of you. Each of you should write a farewell letter. I will do the same. On the day we leave to conduct the operation, we'll post the letters to our families. Let them know that you died a Shahid—a martyr for the faith. Let them know that you will await them in paradise. Write that you have worked in Allah's holy cause against the arrogant infidel. We will be an inspiration to generations of Moslems in the *dar al-islam*. Our names will be spoken with reverence and captured in poetry. As you write these letters, do not be sad. Be full of pride and the strength of your faith." He did not doubt that all of what he said was true, every word, he did not doubt it for an instant.

Robert walked into the cool, shadowed lobby of the Alpenhof. He paused in the nearly empty expanse of lobby, contemplating the dark, nineteenth-century hunting scenes for a moment and debating whether to duck into the alluring shadows of the hotel bar for a glass of red Franconian wine, to end the day on a civilized note. Before he could move, he heard his name spoken in a young girl's voice.

"Herr Hirter? Excuse me, but I have a letter for you. A gentleman left it at the front desk earlier and asked that we give it to you as soon as you returned." The pretty flaxen-haired receptionist in a stylish burgundy and gold dirndl handed the envelope to him, smiled with a flash of perfect teeth, and returned to the reception desk.

Hirter looked at the envelope with his name written across the front in large but shaky block letters. He turned the letter over and saw the name scrawled on the reverse. August Sedlmeyer. What did the old man have now, he wondered, easing open the flap. Extracting the single piece of vanilla stationary he read the German script. "Kaltenberg" was the sole word that he whispered to himself.

Chapter 29

"Kaltenberg," Caroline read aloud from the message on her computer screen, "SS-Stuermbannfuehrer." She raised her eyebrows and tapped her nails on the desktop. The name had been sent in by Robert Hirter for tracing. Some World War II Nazi? She couldn't imagine how it could be relevant to the pursuit of the terrorists or to the murder of Charles Hirter. Still, headquarters should support field requests and not second-guess operational matters. She decided to take the trace request personally to the German desk; her friend Laura Castleman worked there and could offer advice. Laura was steeped in German history, spoke the language fluently, and had completed two tours in the country under diplomatic cover.

Caroline walked at a brisk pace down the wide corridor opposite the main courtyard. On the wall opposite the courtyard, the portraits of past directors of Central Intelligence gazed down on passersby. Some of the portraits smiled, others were fixed with solemn expressions. The wall of paintings captured the exotic and often controversial history of the CIA. There was Allen Dulles, master spy, Cold-War architect, and the man forced to leave office by JFK following the Bay of Pigs debacle. Nearby was flinty-featured Admiral Stansfield Turner, widely despised within the service as a dilettante. He had instituted a reduction in CIA personnel, which had damaged morale and from which it had taken years to recover. Under Turner, nonetheless, CIA had performed some of its most daring operations in Iran in unsuccessful attempts to get American Embassy hostages released. Farther up the corridor of large oil portraits, Bill Casey stared down, looking as rumpled in art as he had in life. Casey had been Ronald Reagan's aggressive DCI, launching covert action in countries as dispersed as El Salvador and Nicaragua, Angola and Afghanistan. Like a number of DCIs before and after him, Casey was utterly consumed by the craft of intelligence. Caroline reflected that she did not aspire to such career greatness. It was the fabric of the work that she enjoyed, the shadow world of espionage and secrets; management responsibility was something that failed to excite her.

Caroline located Laura Castleman's cubicle. Laura, red-haired, short-necked and overweight, was gazing at photographs spilled across her battlefield of a desk, sharing space with a coffee thermos, a gnawed blueberry donut on a paper plate, and stacks of papers.

Glancing up at her visitor she said, "Hey Caroline, welcome to my world." Sweeping thick fingers through hair that had not been washed that morning, Laura raised her eyebrows and sighed theatrically. "The new German intelligence chief assigned to Washington is visiting headquarters tomorrow for lunch with the DCIA in the executive dining room. I'm trying to work the details with protocol. What time do the Germans arrive at the front gate? Who meets them at the visitor's center and issues the "escort required" badges? Are briefings in German or English? Do we have talking points for the DCIA? Will there be an exchange of gifts? I'd rather be running a surveillance operation in the rain in Hamburg than wasting my time with this crap." Laura surveyed her desktop, spotted the donut remnant and took another bite. "Anyway," she continued, her jaws working slowly, "what can I do for you, Caroline?"

Caroline found a chair and cleared it of a stack of documents. "The last thing I want to do is drop more work on you, but I was wondering if you could run a priority trace on a German name for me. The name is Kaltenberg; written like this." Caroline slipped a piece of paper across the desk to her friend. "He could be dead. Kaltenberg was apparently an SS officer during the war. If we have anything on him, it's probably archived. And, not to be pushy, close of business today would be nice." Caroline flashed a smile.

Laura finished with the donut and nodded. "Yeah, I can run a trace and get it to you soon — providing we have anything on him. But since when have you terrorism folks started chasing geriatric Nazis?"

"We don't. The name came up in the course of a terrorism case. It's bizarre, but I need to chase down every lead. Anyway Laura, you just earned breakfast at a time and date of your choosing."

Laura smiled, contemplating the eventual culinary reward.

Good to her word, Laura electronically forwarded trace information on Kaltenberg to Caroline by late afternoon. There was more than Caroline had expected. She scrolled through the material, much of it of wartime vintage.

Last name: Kaltenberg, First name: Horst. Date of birth: 12 October 1908. Place of birth: Potsdam, Prussia. Father's profession: apothecary, killed on the Western Front during the Easter offensive, 1918. Mother: Siegrid Kaltenberg nee Mueller. Died in Potsdam, 1943 of cancer. Horst Kaltenberg had no siblings.

Career: Educated at the University of Berlin, diploma in chemistry. Joined the National Socialist German Workers Party (NSDAP — Nazi Party) in 1928. Selected for the SS in 1931 by high-ranking SS officer Sepp Dietrich, who would later command the division *Leibstandarte Adolf Hitler*. Kaltenberg served in Berlin, Bad Toelz, and fought with the Waffen-SS on the Eastern Front. Kaltenberg's name was connected with war crime allegations in the Ukraine, but the charges were never substantiated. According to a postwar debriefing of another SS officer, Kaltenberg's Berlin assignment was related to a top secret (*Streng Geheim*) scientific project. According to the same source, Kaltenberg had been selected for this assignment based on his chemistry expertise, NFI (no further information).

Captured German military records indicated that Kaltenberg had been wounded in the arm by shrapnel on the Eastern Front in mid-1944 and returned to Berlin to convalesce. His wounds were serious but not life-threatening. He was sufficiently recovered by November 1944 to be assigned to a place called Dyernfurth-am-Oder, east of Berlin, but no details of that assignment existed. German tactical orders acquired in Berlin after the war suggested that Kaltenberg led a Waffen-SS unit from Berlin into Bavaria in 1945, possibly to reinforce a last-ditch "alpine redoubt" in the mountains.

At that point, Kaltenberg vanished from official German records, a not uncommon development in the last weeks of the war. U.S. military intelligence officers reviewing the files of mid-level SS officers in 1947 concluded that Kaltenberg had probably been killed in action somewhere in Bavaria. Nonetheless, his death could not be confirmed, and there was a possibility that, like other wanted SS officers, Kaltenberg had gone to ground and established a new, clean identity. There was no record of Kaltenberg from 1945 until 1962.

In 1962, a human source of undetermined reliability volunteered information to a CIA officer in what was at the time West Germany that Kaltenberg had in the immediate postwar period assumed the identity of Dr. Johann Bergdorfer, using false documents manufactured by the SS prior to the collapse of the Third Reich.

According to the German source, himself a former SS soldier, "Bergdorfer" worked as a chemical broker in the Middle East in the 1950s and into the early 1960s. He maintained a residence in Freilassing, Bavaria, across the border from Salzburg, Austria. Bergdorfer allegedly conducted business in Egypt, Turkey, and Syria.

The German, who provided this information to the CIA in exchange for a small, one-time cash payment, added that Bergdorfer had converted to Islam at some point, not out of any real belief, but as a cynical device to buttress Middle East business prospects. Whether his Moslem business partners believed in the sincerity of the conversion was impossible to say.

There were no additional trace results. The Kaltenberg/Bergdorfer file ended with the information from 1962. This was hardly astounding, Caroline thought. In 1962, Nazi Germany was an episode from the past, and the Cold War was in full swing. The Soviets, not the Nazis, were the focus of allied intelligence attentions. No one cared whether some former SS officer had reinvented himself as a salesman. There were other fish to fry, Slavic not Aryan.

Caroline considered the information. There was one element that she found interesting, the link between Kaltenberg and the Middle East. That would seem to be the only remote connection to the Hirter case. The suspects in Bavaria were Middle Easterners, some of them originating from the countries where Kaltenberg had apparently been engaged in his business pursuits. Kaltenberg's chemical background was also unusual, but she was unsure whether it meant anything. It would be up to Robert Hirter and the Germans to weigh the merits of the information on the SS officer. She prepared the trace results in cable format marked "immediate."

Hirter and Waldbaer stared at the name Horst Kaltenberg, which Waldbaer had written with black magic marker on a whiteboard in his office.

"What are you thinking, Kommissar?" Hirter asked.

Waldbaer cupped his hands under his chin and narrowed his eyes. "I think we can find out more about this apparently fictitious Herr Bergdorfer. Although he had false documents and a new identity, Bergdorfer would nonetheless have had to register in Germany. You can't just live here anonymously. If he lives in Freilassing, which is about an hour ride from here, we can find him. If Kaltenberg/ Bergdorfer was responsible for putting stuff in the cave, this could be a great lead. He would have to know what was stored up there in the rocks for all of these years."

The Kommissar picked up the phone on his desk. "Sergeant? I want the address and any other information we have on an individual located in or near Freilassing. Name: Dr. Johann Bergdorfer. Quickly, please." Waldbaer hung up the phone and gave Hirter a smile. "I'm driving to Freilassing once we get the address. Want to come along?" The query was purely pro forma.

The names of the cell members had been watch-listed for electronic intercept in a memo from CIA Headquarters. Four days later, Caroline received an e-mail from a technical collection unit advising that an Ibrahim Baran had purchased a ticket in Ankara for a flight to Munich in three days time. A first call to the travel agency had been placed from the pay phone that had been previously intercepted. Ibrahim was traveling alone, as best as could be determined.

An hour after having received these details, Caroline found herself in the office of Randolph Stockbridge, on the sixth floor of the CIA building. The office was spacious, respectably appointed with government-issued Drexel furniture, but bare of personal touches of any sort. The space was entirely utilitarian, providing no clue on the makeup of the current occupant. It confirmed Caroline's sense of Stockbridge as a private person, aloof and professional, though invariably courteous.

As was often the case, Stockbridge on this occasion provided an example of studied elegance. His French blue Brooks Brothers shirt was exactly the right match for his well-tailored gray suit, and his red and gold silk tie matched the gold cufflinks surmounted with a red crest. Stockbridge gave a brief tug to his cravat as he took in Caroline's report.

"Interesting, isn't it?" he said quietly. "You know what to do with this, right?"

"Not really," Caroline replied guilelessly, "That's why I'm here. What do you think we should do? Ask the Germans to scoop him once he lands in Munich?"

Stockbridge shook his head. "No. That won't do. In fact, I'm not sure the Germans even have sufficient legal grounds to detain him. Let's avoid Germany for now. Put the focus on Turkey, that's where Ibrahim is, and things are more rough-and-tumble over there, which is good for us. We have Ibrahim's full name and flight information. Have our people in Ankara contact the Turks, read them in, and see if they want to grab the guy for joint interrogation."

"Anything else?" Caroline inquired.

Stockbridge gave her a look suggesting that she shouldn't require further elaboration. "The Turks are pretty cooperative on terrorism matters these days. They haven't forgotten the assist we gave them in operations against their Kurdish extremists. Let's see how they want to play it, but we need to debrief this guy, with or without the Turks. Let's not waste time — draft a message now to our people in Ankara, so that we have an action plan before Ibrahim gets on that flight."

Chapter 30

"Perhaps it would be best if you were to explain exactly what you would like us to do, Mr. Peters." The voice spoke in English, the words accented with a Turkish lilt. Ahmet Saygun paused to take a sip of sweetened tea.

Peters, the blond and sunburned CIA officer across from him, smiled thinly and glanced at his surroundings, the unremarkable spartan office space of the Turkish intelligence bureau in Ankara. The sole window was closed against the noonday sun and the un-air-conditioned room was close and dank. Peters, too, sipped at the tea that had been provided him by his host. "Well, I can only recommend some possibilities for your consideration, this is your country and you can decide your operational preferences."

Peters noted his host's acknowledgment of this deference to Turkish sovereignty, always a delicate issue with the proud Ottomans.

"As I mentioned, Ibrahim Baran is tied to a dubious group of people in Europe. We believe they're engaged in planning terrorist activity, but we lack evidence and details at the moment. Ibrahim can provide those details. We judge that he's here in Turkey on terrorism-related business, making him, no doubt, of interest to your service as well as ours."

The Turk nodded agreement, his dark countenance displaying no emotion.

"We propose a joint interrogation. We get this guy off the street, unsettle him, and see how he sings. He has information we can exploit in Europe, and he may have leads in Turkey of interest to you."

"Yes," said the Turkish officer, sipping again at the cup of tea, collecting his thoughts. "He certainly has operational contacts here and we want to know who they are. We'll work with you on this case. We need to consider the mechanics of it. We don't know exactly where Ibrahim is residing, other than that he is in Ankara, along with millions of other people." He offered a fleeting smile. "But we don't need to find him. We know that he will be in the airport in three days, we know his name, and we know he is going to Munich. So, we let him come to us. I'll have my people at the check-in counter. When he presents his ticket to the airline clerk, we move in and grab him. You follow so far?"

"Sounds good," Peters allowed. "A simple plan is always best. What happens next?"

The Turk clasped his hands in front of him and pursed his lips. "It stays simple, really. We toss him in a car. Being accosted like that will unnerve him. We don't identify ourselves. We blindfold him and drive him to a safe house not far from the airport. Then we start the psychological games. Your people can participate in the interrogation. Acceptable?"

"Acceptable, good in fact. I can have a Turkish-speaking officer available. Ibrahim will know from the accent that he isn't Turkish, but he won't be able to tell more than that. He might think our man is German, or Israeli for that matter."

The Turk gave a quick burst of laughter, revealing perfectly white teeth that contrasted with his swarthy features. "I'm sure he would be happy thinking he is in the tender hands of the Mossad. That deception might pay dividends."

"Exactly," replied Peters, smiling as well.

"One other point," the Turk said, his demeanor more serious. "We need to clarify something beforehand. In the interrogation, the techniques we employ to elicit Ibrahim's cooperation. How far are we prepared to go?"

Peters squirmed in his seat. He hated this aspect of joint interrogation discussions, not least because saying the wrong thing could be a career-ender. "Well, no torture. I know that there are competing definitions of what constitutes torture, but we should keep this as clean of physical coercion as possible. Especially as this case might result in legal indictments in Europe. We both know how supercilious the Europeans can be."

The Turk nodded agreement. "Our European friends can indeed be complicated. They whine about how we deal with the PKK insurgents, although they have no idea what it means to have civil war waged in a part of your country. But we will keep it clean, as you put it. No torture. Still, I think you understand that we might need to get a little unorthodox. This Ibrahim is certain to be a tough character, and he's not about to cooperate just because we cuff him. What else do we need to consider?"

Peters thought a moment before answering. "We have to keep our eye on actionable intelligence. We can't let the cell members in Germany suspect that their buddy in Ankara has a problem. That means we might have to get Ibrahim's cooperation to call them or send them a parole that he's all right. We'll need to think about this once we get Ibrahim talking."

"*If* we can get him talking," said the Turk.

"I don't even want to consider that alternative, not for a second," Peters replied. "This guy is our best bet to stop a likely terrorist attack in Germany before it happens. If we get him in our hands, we've got to break him. First things first; that means grabbing Ibrahim at the airport. Right now I'm just hoping that he actually shows up and doesn't change his mind at the last minute."

The Turk finished his tea with a last swallow and smiled at the American. "Relax. It will be okay. I can feel it — they say that Turks have good instincts."

The morning broke clear and hot with the prospect of getting hotter. Ibrahim took a taxi from downtown Ankara to the airport. His single, battered suitcase was in the trunk; the carry-on was on his lap. The bored taxi driver was playing Turkish pop music at high volume on his tinny-sounding radio, which was fine with Ibrahim as it made conversation impossible. Ibrahim detested conversation with strangers. It made him nervous.

The taxi, which clearly needed shock absorbers, bolted down the broad highway through a nearly treeless countryside. The terrain was a succession of mauve hills, barren and unattractive. Every now and then they would pass the ruined detritus of shantytowns that the government had forcibly removed, evicting the tenants. The only remaining structures in these devastated, illegal settlements were the mosques, holy places that government officials were reluctant to raze lest it stir the violent enmity of the fundamentalists.

Rise up, Ibrahim thought as he surveyed silent minarets, rise up and slay the unbelievers. The apostates are surely even worse than the Crusaders and Jews, those sons of pigs and descendants of apes.

The taxi continued through the countryside toward the airport. There was little traffic on this early morning. Ibrahim wanted to be there in plenty of time for the 8:30 a.m. Turkish Air flight to Munich. The taxi slowed momentarily to permit passage across the highway to a scrawny-looking herd of half-wild goats, the outlines of their ribs clearly visible. Accelerating again, the driver pointed ahead and muttered a few words that were half-consumed by the whining music. Sunlight reflected on glass and stone. The Attaturk Airport loomed ahead, its modern terminal testimony to the expansive aspirations of this antique former empire.

The taxi deposited Ibrahim in front of a set of tinted, automatic doors. He paid the driver, collected his luggage, and entered the refreshing, machine-induced coolness of the spotless terminal. He passed a shop whose sole product seemed to be portraits of Mustapha Kermil Attaturk. The former Young Turk glowered sternly from the pictures, communicating well the look of the "Historic Man," and one with a taste for the sartorial fashions of the day. In most of the portraits Attaturk sported a tailored western suit. Ibrahim gritted his teeth and moved past the display, his eyes searching for the sign indicating the Turkish Air check-in desk. The airport was newly constructed, and polished marble seemed to be everywhere, the vast spaces broken by atriums and fountains. They are aping the airports of the Infidel, Ibrahim concluded. One day they will pay for their apostasy.

He found the Turkish Air counter and was pleased to see that there was almost no line, even for economy class. He touched his shirt pocket to ensure himself that his passport and plane ticket were there. His piece of ersatz black leather hand luggage contained candy and small gifts, to provide the appearance of a typical Turkish resident of Germany returning to his exile home. He had written some cryptic phrases into a small, blue spiral notebook. He had tried hard to memorize al-Masri's instructions, but found that he had no talent for that sort of thing. As a precaution, he had committed the remarks to paper in his own personal code so that it would appear innocuous if examined. The elderly woman passenger at the counter before him gathered up her carry-on bag and trundled away.

It was his turn to check in.

Ibrahim forced a false smile at the young, smartly dressed and unveiled check-in attendant and produced his passport and ticket, laying both out on the counter. Westernized whore, he thought, as he continued to smile vaguely, brushing aside an incipient, unsummoned strain of desire.

The young woman regarded the passport briefly and held the ticket in her manicured hand. "Ibrahim Baran, traveling economy class to Josef Strauss Airport, Munich?" Her inquiry sounded pro forma.

"Yes. I'm returning to Munich. My German residency permit is in the passport."

The attendant smiled in a plastic way and began to use the keyboard of the computer in front of her.

The passenger could not see the computer screen but presumed she was entering the usual sequence of flight confirmation data. In fact, as instructed early that morning by a Turkish intelligence officer, she had clicked on another icon and entered a secure messaging area unrelated to the airline's booking system. She typed simply: It is him. Ibrahim Baran is at the counter in front of me.

Ibrahim noticed nothing out of the ordinary. Not until he felt himself being raised off of the polished floor and thrown backward. For a few seconds he could not imagine what was happening. An earthquake? He felt himself crash back onto the floor, his shoulder blades throbbing suddenly with the jolting, hard contact. There were hands on him, holding him down. He looked frantically about and saw that two large men in dark suits were pinning him to the floor.

The young woman at the counter had vanished. There was no one else around. He tried to push the men away without success. They were strong and determined.

"Let me go," he began to scream at the top of his voice.

A fist slammed into his nose, breaking it. He felt numbness around his nostrils and became aware of a warm sensation passing his lips and working into his beard. He was bleeding. Wide-eyed, he noted that one of his assailants had a chrome-plated revolver clipped to his belt. Police, Ibrahim thought, or maybe worse. Why were they doing this? he thought in a blur of confusion. What did they suspect?

He was lifted to his feet like a rag doll and was aware that he was being half-carried, half-dragged across the smooth tile surface of the terminal toward the exit. The automatic glass doors opened, and he felt again for a fleeting moment a blast of brutally searing Turkish heat.

A second later he was shoved into the back of an idling black BMW sedan. A large man was seated to his left, his features obscured by reflecting sunglasses. This man, as taciturn as the officers who had wrestled Ibrahim to the ground, smiled coldly. A large ham of a hand pinned Ibrahim's head to the back of the plush seat. The man deftly inserted a long syringe needle into the bulging vein in Ibrahim's neck and withdrew it an instant later. Ibrahim moaned softly, his brown eyes wide with rampant fear. The sound of the smooth car engine and its whispering air conditioner drifted far away and Ibrahim slumped forward, aware of absolutely nothing at all.

He did not awaken at once; rather, regaining consciousness was a process, a series of stages taking the better part of an hour. He rose up slowly from the void, like a deep-sea diver trying to reach a distant surface while avoiding the bends. Ibrahim determined eventually that he was seated in a rude wooden chair, his hands shackled to its sides. His feet were manacled to the cold concrete floor. His vision was not entirely clear yet; he wanted to rub his eyes, but could not because of the metal restraints. He saw that he was in a small, windowless room, its neglected walls damp and stained with moisture; a basement perhaps. Two metal chairs and a folding table were set up at a remove from him. There was no other furniture. His face felt odd and he determined that it was tightly bandaged at the bridge of his nose. His mouth felt very dry and he wanted water.

He considered his situation and was overwhelmed with feelings of shame, self-reproach, and fear. He could not envision how things might possibly turn out well for him.

The single door entering into the room opened. Two men entered, surveying Ibrahim as if he were prey. Both men were middle-aged but otherwise very different. The one who entered first was obviously a Turk, his ethnicity betrayed by his visage. He was wearing a suit and tie, but the refined clothes did not cloak the brutal earnestness of his expression. The Turk might have been one of the men who had accosted Ibrahim at the airport; he could not tell for sure. The second man was obviously not from the region. He was blond, with short, thinning hair and he carried himself with assertive cockiness. An American perhaps, Ibrahim wondered, or perhaps German. Were the Bavarians somehow onto them?

The two visitors pulled up the metal chairs and sat in them, the legs scraping the raw floor. Communicating not at all, they stared at their captive for minutes, as if contemplating what species he might represent. Seizing the moments of silence, Ibrahim whispered "water."

"What's that?" the Turk inquired, his eyebrows raised.

"Water. I need water. I am very dry."

The Turk in the charcoal suit, whose first name was Ahmet, snorted. "You think this is a hotel? You make requests and we scurry around to carry out your wishes? Not likely, friend. But then, maybe water will loosen your lips. We're looking forward to enjoying a nice, informative chat with you. Okay, I'll get you a glass of water, just so you don't think that I'm a monster. But in the meantime, I want you to listen to my friend. He has been so interested in meeting you that he traveled here from far away. I wouldn't disappoint him if I were you. I'll be back with your glass of water."

With a quick surge of movement, the Turk rose and was gone. Ibrahim regarded the blond man, just as the blond man regarded him. The interrogator drummed his fingers on the tabletop for a moment and then stopped. He began to speak a slightly accented but fluent Turkish. "My colleague is right. I have questions for you. Quite a few questions, in fact. But first, I should say a few words about myself, just to provide perspective. You don't know who I am or where I'm from, do you, Ibrahim?"

Ibrahim did not respond, his silent gaze fluently communicating loathing.

"Okay, have it your way. You can stay quiet for now if you want — for now. Let me tell you a few things you should know. I'm not a Turk, as you have doubtless figured out, smart fellow that you are. Would you care to guess where I'm from?"

Again Ibrahim did not react.

"Okay. I am not from Europe and not from the Germany that you were intending to return to on the flight you unfortunately missed. I'm also not from the United States. As it transpires, I'm from Israel, a small state in the Middle East you may have heard of. I work for the Israeli government. My work for Israel involves protecting its citizens from harm. The agency that employs me is called Mossad. You've perhaps heard of it. My colleagues and I travel the world to uncover threats to our country. This brings me to you, my friend, and why I am here."

The blond man stopped and tried to discern a reaction. Detecting no change of demeanor, the man cleared his throat and continued his monologue.

"As it develops, the organization I represent is quite certain you keep bad company. You'll probably want to deny this, but that would be, frankly speaking, a waste of time for us all. We know for a fact that you are a terrorist — from an Israeli perspective — and I believe from the perspective of the Turkish government as well. So, what do you think we should do about this situation that we find ourselves in, with me sitting here and you in those unfashionable chains? Doesn't look too promising for you, does it, Ibrahim?"

This time the prisoner did react. Extending his neck he hurled spittle at his interrogator and muttered a guttural curse.

The blond man, sitting out of range, frowned disapprovingly and adjusted his magenta tie.

At that moment the door to the room opened and Ahmed entered, bearing a glass of water. He noted the baleful stare of the shackled man and the tension in the room. "Something wrong?" he inquired.

The blond official shrugged, his jacket bunching slightly at his shoulders. "It seems that our friend here is unhappy, not to mention ill-mannered. He doesn't want to cooperate, sadly enough."

Ahmet nodded and smiled slightly. "Well, no water for him then." He raised the glass to his own lips and drank.

The blond man gave a soft laugh and addressed the chained prisoner. "Let's give it one more chance, shall we, Ibrahim?"

There was no response.

"All right. We have your notes, the ones you took to the airport with you. The writing is in your hand, we have established that from the signature on your passport. The notes have to do with preparation to commit a terrorist act in Germany. This would make you a terrorist courier, Ibrahim. Do you recall these sentences from your notes? 'Target location will be left up to you. It is vital that locations be selected for mass casualties. Confined spaces are essential for success.' That strikes me as incriminating stuff, Ibrahim. In fact, it's astounding that you choose to carry such notes with you."

Ibrahim could not prevent a trace of surprise from crossing his features.

The interrogator named Ahmed detected it immediately. "Didn't expect that, did you? You wrote your notes in a code you made up.

The problem, Ibrahim, is that you did it so poorly. You're an amateur. Our decryption officers turned your sophomoric code into plain text in record time. The only thing the code did was to establish your role as a terrorist. Or perhaps, as an untutored associate of real terrorists."

The prisoner strained at his restraints and barked curses at the Turk, who, in return, only smiled, further infuriating the shackled man.

The blond man interjected. "Here's the deal, Ibrahim. If you cooperate, your incompetence as a terrorist will be considered in your sentencing, meaning you might actually go free some day, presuming you renounce your past associations."

"Never," the prisoner shouted hoarsely, "*Allah Akhbar.*"

"Have it your way," the blond man breathed, his voice trailing off. "Our alternative plan you will find exceedingly unpleasant." At precisely that moment a falsetto scream pierced the thick walls of the cell, the notes held in the air for several seconds before fading into electric silence.

The two suited men acted as if they had heard nothing.

The Turkish official looked at his manicured fingernails. "Ibrahim, we have the goods on you. You belong to us. I can assure you that you will talk. The easiest way is to talk voluntarily, but we're prepared to employ some persuasive techniques to defeat your intransigence. I'll let you think about this. I'll even have someone bring you water, as you requested earlier. Sorry I drank yours down. Sleep on it, to the extent that you can sleep in here. Tomorrow morning you will talk, one way or another."

In an instant the two intelligence officers were gone, leaving Ibrahim alone with his thoughts, which were infinitely dark.

The restless half-sleep into which Ibrahim drifted ended abruptly at ten minutes past six the next morning. The door to the cell swung open noisily. Two large men used keys to open the shackles on his arms and the manacles on his legs. The devices fell to the floor with an angry metal clang. Ibrahim was torn unceremoniously from his seat and dragged from the cell into a narrow, poorly illuminated corridor, its air stale and moist. He felt fear and could taste it.

He was fast-walked down the length of the corridor to a door at its end. His captors opened the green-painted metal door forcefully, causing it to groan on parched hinges. The room he was dragged into was brilliant with light, like a surgery. The two men pushed Ibrahim toward a wall where, he saw, he was to be manacled. His arms were yanked up and away from his torso and secured to the rusting wall restraints. His feet touched the floor but just; he was almost on his toes to secure adequate purchase. It was over in a moment, and then the two men were gone, the metal door reverberating shut.

Ibrahim surveyed his new accommodations. He was alone. There were other manacles attached to the wall, absent occupants. He winced at the intense illumination and noted that the ceiling hosted batteries of strong rectangular lamps that emitted a slight but steady hum. A metal workbench occupied the center of the room, its surface reflecting the glare of the lights above. There was a folding chair behind the workbench, its beige paint heavily chipped. Ibrahim noticed that the bench top was strewn with various objects. Closer inspection revealed that they were tools; he made out a screwdriver, a wrench, and electric drills. On one of the drills, he could make out the name Black and Decker. Shifting his gaze, Ibrahim saw there was a gurney in one corner of the room. It was equipped with what appeared to be restraining straps. Ibrahim felt confused; he did not understand the purpose of the room, but he very much disliked being in its confines. He wondered why he had been moved here from his cell. The apostates could just as easily talk to him there, as they had the day before.

His lamentations were cut short by a prolonged scream that penetrated the thick, spotted walls. The scream was deeper that the one he had heard the previous day. It seemed to go on for a full minute. When the sound faded, it was followed by a series of lower, but audible moans, redolent with exhaustion and despair. Ibrahim felt nausea play at his stomach and felt an acrid taste of copper take up residence in his mouth. Allah give me strength, he said to himself.

The door to the room banged open. The pale-skinned, blond-haired foreigner who had questioned Ibrahim the previous day appeared, his countenance suggesting an unhappy state of mind. The man glanced at the prisoner fleetingly, moving with deliberation to the table at the center of the room. He opened a drawer underneath the tabletop and withdrew a folded white smock, which he shook open and put on over his neatly pressed olive-colored summer suit. The man surveyed the items on the table while buttoning the smock, and then addressed his manacled guest.

"So, how are we this morning? Well rested? Probably not, I expect, under the circumstances. Let's try one more time shall we, starting from where we left off yesterday. I want you to talk to me, to answer my questions. It's that simple. If you comply, presuming I'm satisfied with your answers, life here will become more pleasant for you. I can arrange for you to have decent accommodations, no handcuffs, freedom to walk around your cell, edible food, a Koran, maybe a television. And no abuse from the guards. Given the position you find yourself in, I'd say that isn't a bad deal. In fact, if you start answering my queries now, I can have you enjoying these privileges by tonight. So, consider carefully, Ibrahim. Will you provide me the information I need?"

Ibrahim did consider the offer, in silence. He wanted a comfortable cell and a bed to collapse in. Still, he knew that he was part of a mission, a member of a company of the just, fighting on the path of Allah. How could he betray them? There would be no forgiveness in this world or the next for such disgraceful behavior.

"I will never help you, Mossad filth," he heard himself say. "The Jew is never to be trusted. The Prophet himself, peace be upon him, instructed us so."

"Whatever," replied the blond man without emotion, his voice barely audible. "Have it your way. But you will talk in the end, it's a scientific certainty. The gentleman in the next room was stubborn too, regrettably. He forced me to employ technical methods that I find personally distasteful, degrading even. But that was his choice, as it is yours. He's talking now by the way. You will be talking at some point today, Ibrahim, I assure you. I'll make you talk, it's my profession. Of course, your lack of cooperation, and forcing me to do things I prefer not to do, means that you will get no privileges. Once I'm done, your time here will be an unbroken episode of humiliation and pain. But that's clearly your preference."

The foreigner's words, uttered with detachment, cut at Ibrahim's psyche like a blade, drawing not blood but fear. He sensed with awful fatalism that very bad things were about to transpire. "Allah strengthen me, be my shield against the infidels," he muttered.

The blond officer heard Ibrahim's invocations and smiled without humor. "Too late for that," he said. "Now where to start?"

The man grasped a pair of pliers in one hand, checking the tool's heft. He nodded to himself. "Sometimes the best thing is to stick to the old tried-and-true methods. We'll go with the textbook Mossad employs for occasions like this. We'll begin with the fingers of your left hand and proceed from there. I presume that you are right handed? You see, in the event that you decide to cooperate after I've destroyed your left hand, you'd still retain use of your right hand. I am not inconsiderate. I am a practical interrogator, not some sadist. Left hand, yes?" He gripped the pliers tightly.

Ibrahim was barely aware that he had begun to sob. His eyes were riveted to the implement held by the Mossad officer. He felt overwhelmed by helplessness. There was nothing he could do to defend himself. He was chained to a wall, facing a determined foe who was about to use carpentry tools against his flesh. He would lose use of one of his hands. "Please —" he heard himself implore.

"No," the Israeli replied.

"Please don't," Ibrahim breathed.

"Talk to me."

"I can't, you must understand, I can't."

"But you will, eventually. Now, I'm afraid we must start the procedure without further delay."

The man in the white smock crossed to the wall where the prisoner was shackled. Ibrahim thought he detected a hint of sadness in the man's visage. The foreigner placed the pliers loosely around Ibrahim's thumb and very slowly began to apply incremental pressure. "We'll attain what in my service is called the 'threshold of pain' momentarily. That point will be reached precisely when your thumb will be of no future use to you for the rest of your life. We will then proceed to the next digit, and so on, until you talk." The pliers were now exerting tolerable, but increasing pressure against the prisoner's thumb.

"Stop! I beg you! I am part of a secret group, a group in Germany. I admit it, just stop!" Ibrahim Baran seemed in awe that it was his own voice uttering this confessional.

The blond man ceased exerting pressure and removed the pliers from the shackled man's hand. With an affirmative nod he walked back to the shining metal table. "All right, perhaps we're getting somewhere. It's a bit early to tell, but we'll see. If I become disappointed with your level of cooperation, we can always return to coercive methods. I'm sure you agree that simple, candid conversation is preferable to the uncivilized but effective methods of the twelfth century."

The sound of the prisoner's labored breathing filled the room.

The blond man stroked his square chin and considered. "You admit to belonging to a group, a secret group you called it. Where is the group located?"

Ibrahim looked at the dirty floor beneath his feet, still shocked that he had given in to the infidel, but terrified at the prospect of becoming a disfigured cripple. "The group is in Bavaria, Germany." Perhaps torture could be avoided, Ibrahim reasoned, by parceling out generalities that would not endanger his brothers. He would try to satisfy his interrogator while revealing little.

The Mossad man nodded slowly. "All right. Your group is in Bavaria. Where exactly"?

"We come from around Gamsdorf, about an hour from Munich."

The questioner removed a small pad of paper from underneath his smock and made a note with a ballpoint pen. "Good. Where are your friends now? At what address can they be found?"

Ibrahim swallowed bile. "I don't know. I would tell you if I knew, but I don't know where they are."

The blond man grimaced. "Bad answer. Not the type of cooperation I had in mind, Ibrahim. But let's see if we can't still do business. Answer this for me: What is the name of the leader of your group? You certainly would have to know that, wouldn't you?"

Ibrahim's eyes darted around the room. "He uses many names. Aliases. He calls himself Omar mostly. Due to secrecy, the rest of us don't know his real name." Ibrahim tried to breathe evenly, hoping that the deceit worked.

The interrogator smiled. "A plausible answer, suggesting concern for security. Nonetheless, you're lying to me, which is unfortunate. I *know* that you know the name of the cell leader. You've decided not to tell me. So, rather than waste time with fantasy, we'll return to more corporeal pursuits."

Without a glance to determine how the prisoner reacted, the officer picked up an electric drill. A second later he located a long drill bit and inserted it into the device with an audible click. After ensuring that the orange electric cable was connected to a wall socket, the Mossad officer pressed down on the trigger.

The drill emitted a high-pitched whine that jolted Ibrahim in his shackles. His mind fought unsuccessfully to block out contemplation of what might happen next.

"This, Ibrahim, is a Black and Decker drill, housing a very solid bit. It can bore quite nicely through a concrete wall. Have you ever seen what a drill does to human flesh? You are about to. Consider it a learning experience."

The Israeli again moved to the prisoner's side, the drill cord following in his wake. "We'll begin by drilling a hole in your thigh; I anticipate hitting bone. At that point, you'll most likely pass out from the pain, which is a common, involuntary physical response. I will revive you, however, and we'll continue. I recall one particularly stubborn gentleman that I worked on this way. By the time he finally decided to talk, his legs and arms looked like a wool coat that had been hit by a cloud of moths. He required a wheelchair after that, of course. Let's see how many holes we need to punch into you. Right about here would be fine, I expect."

Ibrahim heard and felt the drill shred through his denim trousers. At precisely that moment his bladder gave way and his legs were swept by a warm, damp wave.

"His name is Mohammed al-Assad! Our leader is Mohammed al-Assad, Allah forgive me! He lives in Germany. He's registered there, you can check! Please don't use the drill, not the drill." The prisoner breathed in the stench of his own urine and began to sob.

The intelligence officer observed him carefully. Yes, he concluded, the clinical point of humiliation and self-loathing has been achieved. He can't go back; he will answer any question now. The man let the prisoner continue to weep and returned the drill to the table.

He was pleased with how the ploy had gone. The American was certain that posing as a Mossad officer had been a propitious start. Terrorists feared the Israelis even more than they did the Americans. Still, the interrogation could have failed. If Ibrahim had been a man of more fortitude, the game would have been up soon enough. There was never any question of actually applying crude physical torture. The screams from the adjoining room were the result of acting at its finest; a Turkish guard had supplied the voice. And other than a light squeeze with the pliers and the theater with the drill tearing the prisoner's trousers, all of the methods employed had been psychological.

Still, the CIA track record with such practices was positive; most suspects ending up babbling away, frightened to death by their own imaginings. The reason was simple. The terrorists themselves would not have hesitated to employ the most vicious methods to an "infidel" prisoner and automatically assumed the same techniques would apply to them.

The interrogation for actionable intelligence could continue. The CIA officer left the room and its weeping prisoner behind, advising his Turkish colleague Ahmet that they could begin with their list of questions.

Chapter 31

Kommissar Waldbaer and Robert Hirter stood silently, contemplating the rectangular granite gravestone before them. The name of the man who lay in the Bavarian earth beneath the stone was engraved in gold leaf. DR. JOHANN ANTON BERGDORFER. A smaller line of script beneath the name provided the bookends of his life: *12 October 1908–22 January 2003*. Affixed to the polished granite surface was a small, framed oval photograph from which the face of the deceased peered out at visitors. The face was long and angular, eyes deeply set. The visage beneath the swept-back gray hairline spoke of earnestness; the portrait selected to greet the ages betrayed no smile on the thin lips of the deceased. The man in the photograph appeared to be in his sixties. Whoever had chosen the image had decided to forego a *memento mori* recording the remorseless decrepitude of advanced old age that a more recent picture would have betrayed.

"We're too late," Hirter said, breaking the silence.

"So it would seem, but perhaps not entirely," the detective responded softly, almost reverentially. "He's beyond our reach. But our information indicates that his widow survives and lives here in Freilassing. It would make sense to have a few words with Frau Bergdorfer, don't you agree?"

Hirter shrugged, signaling skepticism. "I suppose. It's funny, isn't it? That's Kaltenberg buried there, under an assumed name. He carried a lie with him to the grave. Did his wife know that? How much help do you think some ninety-year-old woman, probably half-senile, can really provide?"

Waldbaer raised a finger in mock admonition. "You didn't read the information at the police station thoroughly, Herr Hirter. The widow Bergdorfer is not the same age as her husband. She is nineteen years younger. This means that the chances of her being firm of mind are statistically rather high. Whether she's willing to be cooperative is a separate matter. But let's determine that ourselves."

The two men turned from the grave, Waldbaer giving the glass-encased photograph a last fleeting look. Their shoes crunching on the white gravel of the pathway, they left the tree-shaded cemetery behind. Waldbaer had noticed that there were fresh-cut red roses carefully placed on the burial plot.

Frau Sieglinde Bergdorfer was tall and thin, her back unyieldingly straight, her face still handsome, if severe. She betrayed no evident sign of encroaching decline. Neither did she try to mimic vanished youth; her cheeks were bare of rouge and her mouth bore no trace of lipstick. She wore a traditional Bavarian dirndl, a conservative pattern of black and deep red, and a high-collared white blouse with puffed sleeves.

Frau Bergdorfer had not invited the two men into her home, but had led them into the garden behind the rustic Bavarian house, complete with its carved wooden balcony. The garden was walled and private, with a small bronze fountain as a centerpiece, the metal long since concealed beneath a green patina. A gray fieldstone walkway traversed the garden, which was half-wild, by design or neglect. Herbs cascaded from a small knoll in thick bundles, roses and tiger lilies had staked out their own separate spaces, and low-lying heather fought with the grass for dominion.

"Thank you for permitting us to take some of your time, Frau Bergdorfer," Waldbaer intoned.

"I have lots of time, Herr Kommissar," the gray-haired woman replied, absent discernable emotion.

The Kommissar noted that the woman had been nonplussed at the arrival of the police at her door. Even the comment that they wanted to discuss her late husband had not prompted any apparent anxiety. She is hard to read, Waldbaer judged, but she might respond to direct questioning, no games required.

The trio walked slowly through the garden, taking in its sights. Hirter remained silent, and the elderly woman seemed to presume that he was Waldbaer's assistant.

"What did your husband die of, if I might inquire, Frau Bergdorfer?"

The tall form of the woman stopped in its tracks, and she lifted her chin a degree, as if to sniff the air. "You may inquire. My husband died of advanced stomach cancer. He never knew that he was ill until a few weeks before his death. By the time it was discovered, there was nothing to do, except limit the pain. He was old and had enjoyed a very long life. Right up until that final illness he had been quite fit. He walked everywhere — and didn't need a cane."

Waldbaer nodded sympathetically. The trio resumed their stroll through the garden. "Let me speak frankly, Frau Bergdorfer. You are aware, I presume, that your husband was in fact named Kaltenberg and changed his identity after 1945. As far as I am informed, your husband achieved high rank in the *Schutz Staffel* during the war. I must assume that activities he engaged in during his SS career motivated his later change of identity. Did he speak of these things?"

Frau Berdorfer reached out a slender arm and inspected a tiger lily. "He didn't speak much about the war. Perhaps he might have, had I expressed interest in it. But I didn't. Those were difficult times for everyone of my generation. My husband and I tried to focus on more joyful things. The reasons for his name change didn't interest me either; he was escaping from things past, I suppose, and I never wanted to know the details. Why should I? But you are speaking imprecisely, Herr Kommissar. What exactly is your interest? Not history, surely. You are a policeman, which means you deal with those who break the law. Are you here to resolve old, alleged SS crimes involving my husband? Crimes from over half a century ago? I would think that whatever he did during the war was buried with him. My husband was a front soldier and he spent years fighting in the east, in the most inhuman of circumstances. For me, he was a German hero, and will remain so, especially in this age of German self-absorption and cowardice — these days everyone has angst about everything. Whatever my husband did, under whatever name, he did for Germany. What are your true interests, Herr Kommissar?"

"A fair question deserves a fair answer, Frau Bergdorfer." Waldbaer pushed a hand through his hair and frowned. "My colleague and I don't care about whatever transgressions Herr Kaltenberg might have engaged in with the SS. You're quite right — it's too late for any settling of accounts. My interests are not war crimes. I am interested in solving a recent murder, and your late husband's final mission of the war, odd as it might seem, could help shed light on that murder. I need to explore your husband's activities in 1945 to the extent that I can. That is, to the extent that you will permit."

The old woman shook her head in disbelief. "I can't imagine that anything that happened in 1945 could have relevance to a contemporary crime. That doesn't make sense. Still, I don't mind talking to you, Herr Kommissar, but it's unlikely that I can tell you much. Horst seldom discussed those times."

Waldbaer kicked his scuffed shoe at a large pebble. "I understand, Frau Bergdorfer. But let's see what you might recall." He employed his most solicitous tone, aware that the woman could at any time decide to say nothing, and he would be powerless to force her cooperation.

"You are aware perhaps that Herr Kaltenberg was in Berlin in early 1945. He was ordered to lead a convoy to southern Germany. That much is documented. The convoy made it to Austria. Did your husband mention that episode to you?" Waldbaer had toyed with revealing a few more details, but decided to hold off. No sense displaying your cards too soon, he had long ago learned.

Frau Bergdorfer sighed, with a sound like dry leaves propelled by a breeze. "Yes, I know something about that journey. It was, after all, his last experience in uniform, something anyone would remember." She turned and looked Waldbaer full in the eyes, assessing him with her sharp orbs. "He told me the journey had been hugely risky, he wasn't sure they would make it south, things were collapsing so rapidly along the Berlin front. The Red Army was moving westward, and American and British planes ruled the skies day and night.

Everything in Germany was falling apart." She stopped, mute for a moment in the dark recollections of a much younger girl.

"Yes, so I understand," Waldbaer added, his words a device to move the woman's narrative along.

"Yes," she said at length, pushing back the unwelcome image of flaming buildings and wailing air raid sirens. "Horst was lucky to avoid the Russians. But they were experienced fighters, and they made it south, despite everything. Horst was proud of having completed his mission. He told me that."

Go gently, Waldbaer commanded himself. "It was certainly an accomplishment against great odds. Did your husband mention what his mission had been? Did he ever say what the convoy was supposed to accomplish? It's ancient history, I know, but it might help me, Frau Bergdorfer."

"His assignment, you mean? It was secret. Quite secret. *Streng Geheim.*"

Waldbaer felt his heart sink and noted, from the corner of his eye, a downcast look cross Hirter's face as well. A secret mission; they knew that much from Sedlmeyer. Did she not know, or was it that she would not tell, would not betray the memory of the honored loved and lost?

"A secret mission. Yes. Like so much in that war, I suppose. Of course, those secrets don't need to remain secrets anymore. The secrets of a regime that no longer exists can't count for much. But, if your husband never related these secrets to you, there's little else to say."

A smile creased Frau Bergdorfer's thin lips without communicating warmth. She looked again at Waldbaer with eyes that struck him as uncomfortably predatory. "You're not as subtle as you think, Herr Kommissar. I didn't say that I knew nothing, only that my husband was on a secret assignment for the Reich when the war ended. That assignment was successfully completed. That much I know, even though Horst was circumspect about it. He felt that he'd done his duty one last time."

Waldbaer nodded. "I won't treat you like a child, Frau Bergdorfer. Since we're being honest with one another, let me ask the obvious question. Your husband's mission involved delivering cargo somewhere. What was the consignment? What did the convoy transport all the way from Berlin? Did your husband reveal that to you? To be frank, it's the key for which I am looking, perhaps it will unlock the door to a recent murder."

"Remember what I said, Herr Kommissar, my husband was not one of those aging, beer-swilling men who regaled one and all in the *gasthaus* with war stories. He was taciturn by nature and silent on these matters by discipline. I never pushed, why should I have? My life with him was in the present, not the past. I don't know exactly what was inside those military trucks."

The detective considered the formulation of her words. "I believe you, it goes without saying. It's too bad, for me that is. Why don't we do this: tell me whatever your husband did say about this mysterious freight."

"All right, Herr Kommissar, I can do that. But the garden grows chilly for my old bones. Perhaps you and your assistant would care to invite me for a cup of tea? There's a little café in Freilassing center, five minutes by car."

"It would be an honor, *gnadige frau*," Waldbaer replied, using the ancient formulation for "honored woman." Frau Bergdorfer responded with a smile that, for once, was not at all predatory.

Chapter 32

Peters was pleased with how the interrogation had progressed but troubled by the results. He was certain that Ibrahim had been truly broken and was revealing whatever he knew with as much accuracy as he could muster. Ahmet agreed; the information Ibrahim was providing was valid. That was the problem. The details that Ibrahim provided were alarming.

Peters glanced around his office in the Ankara CIA facility. The off-white walls were decorated only with a government-issue calendar and two framed United Airlines travel posters, one of the Grand Canyon and one of cherry tree blossoms in Washington, DC. They were an inheritance, having been there when he took over the office from his predecessor. After a few moments, Peters put his pen to a pad of paper and wrote rapidly in large block letters:

SECRET

TO: COUNTER TERRORISM CENTER. RESTRICTED HANDLING

IBRAHIM BARAN (SUBJECT) OFFERED FOLLOWING INFORMATION TO JOINT INTERVIEW TEAM DURING THREE-HOUR SESSION TODAY. ALTHOUGH NERVOUS, SUBJECT RESPONDED OPENLY TO QUERIES. FULL INTERRORGATION TRANSCRIPT IS BEING SUBMITTED SEPARATELY. SALIENT AND TIME-SENSITIVE POINTS ARE NOTED BELOW.

1. SUBJECT IS ACTIVE MEMBER OF JIHADIST CELL LOCATED IN SOUTHERN GERMANY AND CONTINUES TO IDENTIFY MOHAMMED AL-ASSAD AS CHIEF OPERATIVE OF THIS CELL.

2. SUBJECT TRAVELED TO ANKARA ON AL-ASSAD'S INSTRUCTION TO MEET WITH ABDUL AL-MASRI, A MIDDLEMAN TO AL QAEDA LEADERSHIP IN WAZIRISTAN. SUBJECT CONTACTED AL-MASRI AND RECEIVED PERMISSION TO INITIATE A TERRORIST ACT IN GERMANY.

3. SUBJECT PROVIDED ADDRESS OF SAFE HOUSE WHERE HE MET AL-MASRI ON MULTIPLE OCCASIONS. TURKISH INTELLIGENCE IS PREPARING TO RAID THE APARTMENT; ONE OF OUR OFFICERS WILL ACCOMPANY AND REPORT RESULTS UPON COMPLETION OF RAID.

4. ACCORDING TO SUBJECT, JIHADIST CELL IN GERMANY IS PREPARING "SOMETHING BIG" IN NEAR TERM. SUBJECT CONFIRMED THAT THIS REFERS TO A TERRORIST ATTACK IN GERMANY. AL-ASSAD HAS NOT TOLD CELL MEMBERS SPECIFIC TARGET. IN CONVERSATIONS WITH AL-MASRI, SUBJECT LEARNED THAT TARGET SELECTION IS BEING LEFT TO AL-ASSAD'S DISCRETION. CODED NOTES CAPTURED WITH SUBJECT CONFIRM THIS. SUBJECT SURMISES THE ATTACK WILL TAKE PLACE WITHIN GERMANY AND NOT INVOLVE A CROSS-BORDER OPERATION TO ANOTHER EUROPEAN COUNTRY DUE TO SECURITY CONSIDERATIONS.

5. SUBJECT ADVISED INTERROGATORS THAT THE ATTACK WILL BE LAUNCHED EMPLOYING MATERIAL HIDDEN FOR LONG PERIOD OF TIME IN A CAVERN IN THE BAVARIAN ALPS AND RECENTLY RELOCATED TO A WAREHOUSE IN ROSENHEIM AREA (NO FURTHER INFORMATION). SUBJECT DOES NOT KNOW THE NATURE OF THE STORED MATERIAL. HE DESCRIBED THE MATERIAL AS "SCIENTIFIC DEVICES" WITH WHICH HE IS UNFAMILIAR. AT ONE POINT SUBJECT SAID HE UNDERSTANDS THAT THE EQUIPMENT IS "LABORATORY EQUIPMENT" BUT CANNOT ADD DETAILS.

Peters rubbed his chin and considered the last sentences he had scribed. He had a case officer's intuition and decided to note it for the record.

FIELD COMMENT: CASE OFFICER BELIEVES SUBJECT MAY BE REFERING TO EQUIPMENT REQUIRED TO PRODUCE UNCONVENTIONAL WEAPON OF SOME SORT. NOTATION OF LABORATORY EQUIPMENT AND "SCIENTIFIC" MATERIAL

WOULD NOT SEEM TO FIT WITH PRODUCTION OF CONVENTIONAL EXPLO-
SIVES WHICH COULD BE READILY PRODUCED IN AN APARTMENT, EMPLOYING
HOUSEHOLD OR COMMERCIAL ITEMS. JIHADIST CELL MAY BE PLANNING AN AT-
TACK USING A RADIOLOGICAL, CHEMICAL OR BIOLOGICAL WEAPON. CASE
OFFICER VIEW ON THIS POSSIBILITY IS REINFORCED BY SUBJECT'S DECRYPTED
NOTES WHICH QUOTE AL-MASRI AS CLAIMING THE ATTACK WILL BE "DEVAS-
TATING" AND REPRESENTS NEW LEVEL OF TERROR AGAINST WESTERN
INTERESTS.

Peters had a queasy sensation that he and his associates had uncovered enough information to provide warning of a pending attack,
but had failed to garner sufficient detail to prevent it. He ran through
the unknowns. Where would the attack take place? No information.
When was the attack scheduled? No information. What type of attack would it be? No information. Still, he consoled himself, we have
something. The material for the attack is in a warehouse in the
Rosenheim area. That was a lead that could be pursued. In addition,
a raid on al-Masri's safe house in Ankara was even now unfolding. If
they bagged al-Masri, they would acquire more information that
could be exploited to stop the attack. Things could work out posi-
tively, Peters concluded. He put the chances of preventing a terrorist event in Germany at fifty-fifty. Not good math, he thought to
himself, not nearly good enough.

Chapter 33

The coffee tasted bitter to Waldbaer, so he dropped in another cube of sugar. Frau Bergdorfer was contentedly sipping her Ceylon tea from a fragile-looking porcelain cup, and Hirter was idly moving a spoon in his steaming mug of hot chocolate. The small café across from the Freilassing church was nearly empty. Two young, bored waitresses engaged in desultory conversation by the front door. Waldbaer found the chairs far too dainty and unstable and worried that his own might, with the wrong move, collapse unceremoniously beneath him. Glancing about, he noted that the décor was entirely feminine. There was garish wallpaper exuberant with pink roses, and prints of nineteenth-century Parisian scenes were placed at precise intervals. He preferred the honest rusticity of Zum Alte Post.

Frau Bergdorfer was comfortable in these surroundings. The waitresses had smiled at her in recognition. The old woman pointed a long, thin finger at the street outside the window. "Freilassing isn't much to look at these days. When my husband and I first settled here in the 1950s, things were different. The German border with Austria is at the bridge over the Saalach River less than a kilometer away. Freilassing was a border town. Salzburg residents traveled here for German products not available in Austria. All of that business made Freilassing a lively place. But that's gone now. The European Union put an end to the border. All of a sudden, Freilassing was nothing special and went into decline. Businesses closed up, people moved to Munich to find work. Still, this is my home. My husband is buried in the cemetery, and I will join him there one of these days."

"There are red roses on his grave," Waldbaer said softly.

The woman regarded him. "Yes, Herr Kommissar. From me. Once a week I visit his resting place and leave roses for him. False name or not, he was my husband for many years. I knew him better than anyone. If he can be judged on this earth, I can judge him best."

"Exactly," Waldbaer replied. "Now perhaps we can discuss his final mission of the war?"

Frau Bergdorfer's eyes narrowed and she knew that the conversation had been maneuvered to where the detective wanted it. She took another sip of tea, holding the cup in both hands before replacing it on the saucer.

"Horst told me this much, years ago. He said he was ordered to transport valuable scientific items to Bavaria and hide them. Some of the cargo originated from the fortress Zitadelle in Spandau. Some scientists from Berlin accompanied the convoy to ensure things were properly stored. They found a location that was suitable and placed the items there. That's about all I can tell you."

Waldbaer considered the information. "Why would they want to store these items, for what purpose?"

Frau Bergdorfer nodded almost imperceptibly. "They thought it might be of military use to a German resistance to the occupation. That's why Nazi Party functionaries accompanied my husband. They needed to know the location to be able to access the items in the future. Of course, a resistance never developed. Almost everyone welcomed the end of the war; they didn't want to go back to fighting. They wanted to get on with their lives. This meant that the cargo remained hidden. No one wanted to make use of it. In the end, my husband's last mission was for nothing."

"Frau Bergorfer, let me tell you this. Somebody discovered these hidden items and recently moved them away. I'm troubled by that. Did your husband know what was in that consignment?"

"Yes, he knew. He never told me though, not that I would have understood anything technical."

"Is there anything else, Frau Bergdorfer, any detail that might help me?"

"One thing perhaps. Horst said he had not been chosen to lead

the mission at random. It was because of his background, his educa-
tion before the war. Horst had been a well-respected young chemist;
he went into the chemical export business after the war, perhaps you
know that. Anyway, I suppose that means that the material in the
convoy had something to do with chemicals."

Waldbaer locked eyes with Hirter who lowered his cup of hot
chocolate to the table with a discernable thud. Yet still, despite her
seeming openness, the detective could not shake the feeling that the
graceful old woman was concealing something.

Chapter 34

Ahmet Saygun chambered a hollow-point round in his 9-millimeter automatic pistol and glanced up at the apartment with rustling orange curtains flowing from an open window. There were three other officers with him in the sedan, and another sedan parked across the street contained three more Turkish intelligence operatives as well as a dark-complexioned CIA case officer. Ahmet was aware that two of the officers in the other car carried compact Ingram submachine guns under their jackets for added firepower. A radio crackled; the men in the other vehicle wanted to know how long before they entered the apartment block. "Tell them it will be a few minutes," Ahmet said to the driver who was monitoring the scrambled communications. "We go first; they follow thirty seconds after we enter the front door. I don't want us bunching up on the street. We take the elevator, they work the stairs."

Ahmet flexed his thick fingers and returned his pistol to the holster under his left arm, the safety off. He wanted to get his hands on al-Masri. That would be good for his career, of course, but he had other motivations. He had a visceral dislike for jihadists and their smug conviction that their acts were divinely sanctioned. Ahmet Saygun was the product of secular Turkey and he worried mightily about Islamist fundamentalists gaining power and destroying Attaturk's imperfect, but functional, legacy. That little bastard al-Masri isn't even a Turk, Ahmet reasoned, what the hell right did he think he had operating in Ankara? He glanced at the ticking hands on his Swatch and exhaled a breath.

"Let's move," he said and all four doors of the sedan opened simultaneously.

The men spilled from the street to the sidewalk, weapons concealed, eliciting no attention from passersby. The door into the apartment building was unlocked, as Ahmet knew it would be. A surreptitious entry specialist from his unit had disabled the lock discreetly before dawn.

Once inside the door, the four men found themselves in a narrow, empty lobby devoid of decoration save for a dust-shrouded plastic palm tree and an undistinguished painting of an Anatolian village. Dulled street noise seeped through the door behind them, its glass panes bathing the lobby in diffuse, gray light. "Mustapha, get the elevator."

In response, one of the men punched a green button on the wall next to the lift. A bell rang and the metal doors to the elevator opened. The men piled in, drawing their weapons. As Ahmet pushed his square frame into the elevator's narrow confines, he noted with satisfaction that the second team of officers was just entering the lobby and heading toward the stairwell. Good, he thought, everything is moving as it should.

The polished metal elevator traveled up to the fourth floor, vibrating slightly before shuddering to a halt at its destination. The doors opened with a clang, and the officer named Mustapha was first into the hallway, his pistol preceding him, barrel toward the ceiling. Ahmet and the others followed. He could hear the muffled approach of his other men as they mounted the stairs.

All knew where to go; they moved in unison toward the door at the end of the corridor, number 421. The apartment of Abdul al-Masri. Ahmet knew they required no battering ram; a covert inspection some days earlier had revealed that the apartments had been built with cheap particleboard doors. The group moved down the hall with quiet celerity. Ahmet glanced at the brown hallway carpet and the bare light bulbs illuminating the scene. They closed in on the apartment just as the second quartet of men debouched from the stairwell, brandishing their weapons. The pungent smell of frying garlic permeated the narrow hallway.

"Let's do it, gentlemen," Ahmet intoned.

The two men in front launched at the door shoulders first. There was the sharp report of cracking wood as the door emblazoned with the number 421 gave way and separated from its frame. The four men squeezed through the entrance and stood in a sparsely furnished living room. There was no one there.

"Kitchen next," Mustapha said, concealing his disappointment that he had not immediately confronted a quivering, bug-eyed al-Masri. Mustapha entered the narrow kitchen, his automatic pistol held at shoulder height.

Simultaneously, the second unit of four men was moving in file through the apartment door when an intense flash illuminated the apartment followed a second later by the explosion that slammed through their ear drums.

Ahmet felt himself thrown backward by the searing blast; he felt its angry heat flow over him as he slammed into the linoleum floor tiles. A bomb, he judged instantly, that scum al-Masri had rigged his own apartment with explosives. Ahmet rolled onto his side and pushed himself to a kneeling posture. He felt blood in his mouth and knew from a burning sting that his face was lacerated. His weapon had been blown from his grip by the blast.

With effort, Ahmet forced his eyes open. Although his vision was milky, he knew with relief that he had not lost his eyes. He took inventory of the scene. Mustapha lay nearby and was clearly dead; his head hung grotesquely from his solid shoulders by a thread of tissue; a pool of blood spreading out from the shattered corpse. All of the other men were lying on the floor, their bodies in flailing animation like worms after a rain storm. Visibility was poor as the lights had been destroyed by the blast, and the air was thick with smoke and floating particles of debris. Ahmet heard voices whispering feverishly. With a start he realized that they were not, in fact, whispering. His comrades were moaning and screaming for assistance. The sound of the detonation had temporarily ruined his hearing.

Pulling himself to his feet, Ahmet slid his hands over his body searching for major wounds. He found none, but worried about possible internal injuries.

"I can't move my arms," he heard one of his men say.

Ahmet reached into his tattered trouser pocket and gripped his encrypted cell phone in a tremulous hand, punching in the number for the operations control vehicle parked a few blocks away. He could not hear whether someone answered on the other end, but presumed they had. "We've got an emergency in the apartment. A bomb has gone off. Everybody is wounded. We have one confirmed dead, and some of the others are in bad straits. Get ambulances here and make sure they have trauma doctors onboard, not just medics. Al-Masri isn't here. The place was empty. Alert border control, but it's probably too late. That bastard knew we were on to him some-how. Just get the ambulances and have them bring blood. My people are losing lots of blood."

Ahmet was just able to punch off his cell phone before passing out and falling to the floor where the fibers of his tailored charcoal suit soaked in the arterial blood of his companions.

Chapter 35

There was a breeze issuing from the south, sufficient to stir small waves upon the placid surface of the broad Chiemsee Lake. The waves lapped at the long, wooden wharf near the ancient convent on the Island of Ladies, *Fraueninsel,* the name a reference to the nuns who had tended the place for centuries, and continued to do so. The sky was iridescent blue laced with milk white clouds, and the distant mountains were starkly visible in the crisp autumn air. Waldbaer and Hirter sat outside at a small table on a leafy terrace of the Cloister Inn.

The two men had identical meals in front of them; *renke,* a mild fish netted from the depths of the lake, and fried potatoes garnished with onion. Also gracing the table were two glasses of beer from a brewery in nearby Traunstein. Waldbaer had invited the American to the island so that they might speak with more privacy than at the police station and because the detective had a weakness for dining al fresco on sunny days. He enjoyed the atmosphere of the island and the boat ride from the nearby village of Prien.

Waldbaer took a long swallow of beer and pointed to the sky. "*Himmel der Bayer,*" he said to his counterpart. "The heaven of the Bavarians. That refers to a blue sky with white clouds — the colors of the Bavarian flag. This kind of wonderful weather occurs mostly in the fall. Summer is often rainy or humid; autumn is the time for beer gardens."

"Not to mention the Munich Oktoberfest," Hirter added as he stared out at the lakefront and a passing sleek white sailboat.

"Right. The Oktoberfest usually enjoys good weather. Have you ever visited it? Two weeks long every year and millions of visitors. And even though it's called the Oktoberfest, most of it takes place in September. The festival ends on the first weekend of October."

Hirter took a forkful of white fish. "No, I never went to the Oktoberfest. Some of my CIA buddies who've been stationed in Germany have told me about it. They think it's a lot of fun, but it sounds like a mob scene to me. Giant tents full of thousands of sweating, singing drunks doesn't strike me as a must."

Waldbaer laughed and lifted his face to the warming sunlight. "You're a cynic, Herr Hirter, perhaps a snob. You're right about the mob scene. All of the Munich breweries maintain elaborately decorated tents that hold several thousand people each. Low class? Absolutely. Fun? Let's say I enjoy going once every year."

Waldbaer moved the conversation back to the investigation. "Regarding the case: the next step is to find the warehouse that Ibrahim Baran mentioned. He said it's in Rosenheim, not far from here. Rosenheim is a fair-sized city, and finding the right warehouse won't be easy. We're putting together a plan to check warehouses systematically. I expect the first checks to start this afternoon, beginning near the train station and radiating outward. We might get lucky early on. I hope so."

Hirter nodded agreement. "This is a solid lead. As for what we're searching for, I think we have an idea, and it doesn't make me happy. Chemicals, laboratory equipment. I have a feeling that Kaltenberg's background as a chemist is no coincidence. His widow says that's one reason he was selected to move the goods. So we have a trained chemist and trusted SS officer in charge of the stuff that made its way to that cavern. Now, somehow, the Nazi cargo is in the hands of known terrorists. And, according to what Ibrahim admitted under interrogation, an attack is being planned. When I add it all up with my operational math, the answer I end up with is a chemical weapon."

Waldbaer thought for a moment and his eyes followed a bee's flight until it disappeared into a bush of wild roses. "Kaltenberg having been a chemist makes me nervous too, especially with the press writing about weapons of mass destruction. Still, I just don't know enough about the subject to judge what al-Assad is planning. Maybe it's all coincidence."

Hirter shook his head. "My case officer instincts tell me otherwise. Kaltenberg is key to all of this, I'm sure of it. If we find the Rosenheim warehouse, all will become clear. I just hope that we find it before these guys blow something up."

"That's another point," the detective said. "We don't know the intended target for the attack. The prisoner in Turkey doesn't know himself. This means that we can't put security on a specific location. If we knew the target, I'd feel a lot better than I do right now."

Hirter nodded. "I know. Let me tell you something, Kommissar. I've learned about terrorist modus operandi over the years. The real professionals know how to keep a secret and restrict information even in their own circle. The plans for nine eleven weren't widely known within Al-Qaeda. Even some of Mohammed Atta's people aboard the aircraft weren't sure what was going to happen until the last moment. Baran is telling the truth. He doesn't know the target because he doesn't need to know it. My suspicion is that the cell leader alone—al-Assad—knows where they're going to strike. I think the terrorists are exercising good operational security. That doesn't mean they can't slip up, but I don't count on identifying the target until we can scoop up these guys."

Waldbaer gazed out over the sparkling water of the Chiemsee and focused on a pair of gulls hovering over the wharf. Gulls are perpetually hungry, he thought, never content, never satisfied. "They might slip up. We might get lucky. But all in all, Herr Hirter, I'd prefer better odds. Let's eat up, catch the boat to Prien, and drive to Rosenheim to check some warehouses. That, at least, will give us the illusion of progress."

Chapter 36

He stood in a vast sea of blood that stretched off to a distant horizon. A soft, warm breeze caressed his face and the sun reflected like thousands of twinkling diamonds on the brilliant red surface of the sea. The sky above was indigo blue and shorn of clouds. There was no sound, only perfect silence, ineffably pure and soothing. He had never in his life felt so at peace.

His feet and ankles were immersed in warm blood, washed by it. He was garbed in a robe of spotless white that moved slightly with the gentle touch of the diffident breeze. Even when the hem touched the red sea it remained unsullied. His hands were at his side, palms up, and he could feel the persistent warmth of the sun embrace his skin. He stood like this for a long time and no longer cared about minutes or hours or days.

After a while, how long he could not say, he noticed another object in the sky aside from the orb of the sun. This object reflected the sun with such intensity that he could not readily determine its shape. Without worry, he watched the object and determined that it was growing in size and brilliance. No, he concluded, it is not growing in size, it approaches. The reflection was moving toward him and it cast a black shadow upon the blood of the sea. It is meant for me, he knew. He was not surprised when the object, moving with stately deliberation, came to rest in the air directly in front of him at a distance of a few feet. He looked upon the shining object, but his eyes were not troubled by its intensity, and he knew that the thing was enchanted. By stages, the reflection on the surface of the object dulled until he could perceive its form.

It was, he saw, a sword, a curved scimitar, its burnished blade engraved with script, its hilt ornately crafted from solid gold. He began to weep with the unrestrained happiness of the saved because he knew that the sword was a gift for him. He reached out his hands until they closed on the warm metal hilt gently and reverently. This was no dead thing; the weapon's energy pulsed into his palms. He brought the blade to his lips and kissed it. I will be worthy, I will not dishonor you. The weapon, he knew, was intended for use and he had been selected as the warrior who would wield it.

He looked again at the extraordinary scene before him, the expanse of burgundy blood merging on the horizon with the flawless blue sky. He intuited that there was something else yet, and waited. Eventually, he noted a change in the distance. The deep blue of the sky deepened further still until it became a wall of black cloud, its surface billowing and angry. At intervals he could detect a jagged flash of silent lightning, there and gone. The storm was at a great remove from him and did not threaten. Still, he felt tendrils of concern. The storm blemished the perfection of the scene. And provided a warning.

Mohammad al-Assad awoke with a start and was, for a moment, unsure of where he was. In a few seconds, he could make out the dark confines of the warehouse walls and the stained ceiling above his sleeping bag. He released a deep breath and heard one of the other men turn in his sleep, seeking a more comfortable position on the concrete floor. He closed his eyes again and considered the dream. No, he corrected himself, not a dream. It was a vision, doubtless similar to the mystic episodes that the Prophet, peace be upon him, had himself experienced. He did not doubt that what he had witnessed was real, that the blood red sea physically existed in some other place. It was too vivid to have been a mere dream, those nocturnal chimeras that were even permitted to the infidel. His vision had been a message.

He understood what had been revealed to him. That warm and sunny place was the threshold to Paradise, the domain of the elect. The sea of blood represented his earthly mission, the blood that he would shed in the cause of Allah. The sword was his exalted weapon that would be returned to him in Paradise. Here on earth his weapons were less glorious, but their imperfect forms were sufficient to an imperfect world. But the sword meant that he was recognized as a warrior on the righteous path of jihad against the ranks of *takfir* and *kaffir*. It was he who would release the sea of blood, feeding its depths from springs of death.

There was also the storm cloud to be considered. There was danger loose. He knew with certainty that there were forces at work that meant to prevent his mission. The menace was not imminent; the storm had after all been a distant one. Still, there was no room for complacency. They needed to complete the mission before it could be compromised. What he could not know was how fast the storm was approaching. Had the vision offered further clues? He considered. The storm appeared out of a clear sky. This meant that an untroubling situation had altered. The storm front was far away. If the storm represented a threat, why was it not close at hand?

Al-Assad thought about this and ran through the possibilities. And then he knew. The distant danger. What element of their endeavor was far away? Ibrahim in Turkey, on his visit to al-Masri. He had talked to Ibrahim a few days ago and all had been well, but like the blue sky, the situation must have changed for the worst. If Ibrahim or al-Masri had been captured or compromised, he had to consider the implications. How much could they reveal under duress? Of course, if they had been martyred rather than captured, as bad as that would be, the risk of compromise would be greatly reduced. But no, he concluded, the storm in his vision had not diminished.

The danger was alive and would doubtless relentlessly move in the direction of Rosenheim. Under such circumstances, he had to plan. He unzipped the sleeping bag, stretched, and made his way to the improvised kitchen where he could consider what to do. He squinted at the illuminated dial of his wristwatch and saw that it was midnight.

Chapter 37

In Langley, it was six hours earlier than in Germany. At six p.m. in the Counter Terrorism Center, Caroline O'Kendell placed printed copies of the Ibrahim Baran interrogation cables on the desk in her office. She took an orange highlighter from the desk drawer and tapped it rhythmically on the desktop as she read Peters's reports. The interrogations were turning up useful information, she concluded. They had names now and a sense of the terrorists' plan, even if details remained lacking.

The arrangement between Robert Hirter and his Bavarian Kommissar seemed to be working well. Initial information from Baran's interrogation had been passed to them and was being acted upon. A search of warehouses in Rosenheim was underway.

On the negative side, the failed raid on al-Masri's Ankara apartment was a major disappointment. Capturing al-Masri would have been significant, given his position in the Islamist hierarchy. Al-Masri had outfoxed them, inflicted casualties, and gotten away. At least the young, first-tour CIA case officer wounded in the raid had sustained only superficial injuries and punctured eardrums, and he was being flown home for further treatment.

Caroline shuffled through the documents on her desk. She read Hirter's account of the interview with Kaltenberg's widow. Hirter had written he was troubled by Kaltenberg's chemist background. She shared that sentiment, but had nothing substantial to back up the feeling.

She again surveyed the cable recounting the conversation with Frau Bergdorfer. Caroline noted that the widow was certain her husband had been specially selected from the ranks of SS officers to lead the convoy. Caroline was inclined to pursue the chemical angle further. She reached for the secure telephone on her desk and punched in the extension for an office across the headquarters building.

"Technical services," a deep male voice rumbled on the other end.

"Hi. This is Caroline O'Kendell in CTC. I'd like to talk with somebody responsible for chemical detection. I want to see if you have an officer available to fly to Germany on short notice to check something out."

The other end of the line was silent for a moment before the bass voice resumed. "We probably do have somebody qualified for that. We can talk, Caroline, but what you've said sounds pretty vague. Remember, we have lots of competing calls to use our technical folks. Our question is always 'is it worth it?' So, you'll have to make the case."

"Right. How about this: determining whether there is a convergence of an active terrorist cell and the possession of a chemical weapon left behind in Europe after the war by the Nazis. A collision of two evil forces, one past, one current, combining to create a present threat."

There was again a pause on the other end. "That would pretty much work," the disembodied voice conceded evenly.

Chapter 38

Robert Hirter watched a red Deutsche Bahn passenger train hurtle by on tracks located a few feet from the loading dock of the warehouse. Hirter counted twelve cars. He watched the rattling mass of metal recede in the distance, on its way south. Turning back to the warehouse, he entered the cavernous space he had left moments ago. The light was poor, and Hirter squinted until his eyes adjusted. The place held the foul smell of industrial oil and wet cardboard mixed with cigarette smoke. A number of crates had been forced open and their contents spilled onto the stained concrete floor. Colorful plastic pellets in large cellophane bags intended for some extruder machine in a distant factory. Stacks of hubcaps emblazoned with the Opel automobile logo. Chinese-manufactured lawnmowers in long boxes.

The banal freight items of the industrialized world were on display, but nothing remotely sinister had been detected. The policemen with the crowbars appeared bored. Hirter saw Kommissar Waldbaer at the other end of the hall engaged in conversation with a blonde pony-tailed policewoman. The two were standing directly under a bare lightbulb suspended on a long cord and their features were angular and severe. Hirter decided to join them.

"Have everybody clear out, there's nothing here. Have your people take a coffee break, and then move to the Schenker warehouse down the tracks. It's huge, so inspecting it might eat up the rest of the day."

The policewoman glanced at Hirter as he joined them. "He's okay," Waldbaer said.

Hirter noted that the woman was petite for his image of a police-woman. She was pretty as well, though he noticed that she had a split lip and wondered why. The woman adjusted her black leather service jacket and pulled down on the visor of her white polizei cap, as if aware she was being scrutinized.

"Herr Kommissar, the problem is that we don't have a good idea of what to look for. Something big? A single object? How many crates, if the stuff is still in crates? Will this be tubes or centrifuges or what? I feel like we're flying blind."

"We are flying blind, but at least we are flying," Waldbaer breathed with a resigned grin.

Hirter cleared his throat and joined the chat. "Here's what I think. We're going after something old. We're looking for items that were stored over half a century ago. I think that the stuff looks like laboratory equipment, mixing vats, test tubes, vials. If you find that sort of thing, there's a good chance you're on to something. And there's a possibility that we might find some actual chemicals. Maybe in sealed drums. As to how much, something that would fill two truck beds at least. Right, Kommissar?"

Waldbaer ran his shoe over an indentation in the concrete floor. "I agree. Keep an eye out for chemicals, but God knows, there are lots of legitimate chemicals stored around here. One more thing, remind your people that it's possible we might get lucky and find the suspects along with the goods. Your people have the photos we provided. I ex-pect that they're armed, so make sure your uniforms are ready to use their weapons. We aren't dealing with teenage bike thieves."

The woman nodded and stole another look at Hirter, still un-sure of his role. "*Alles klar.* Don't worry, Herr Kommissar, if we find these gentlemen, my boys will know what to do. It's the finding part that's difficult, but we'll keep at it. If that stuff is anywhere near Rosenheim, we'll find it. It might just take a while." She snapped a salute to Waldbaer, nodded to Hirter, zipped her polished leather police jacket, and marched off.

"A while is precisely what we don't have," Waldbaer exclaimed to Hirter. "I can't escape the sensation that we're fighting time."

Chapter 39

Al-Assad had taken a bus to the outskirts of the city, killed time at a café to determine that he was not under surveillance, and had then taken another bus to Rosenheim center to place a call to Ibrahim. He would use a telephone booth near the train station. If he received no answer, or if anyone other than Ibrahim picked up the phone, he would know that the sacred vision referred with certainty to a problem in Ankara. Ibrahim knew the "under duress" parole and would employ it if he were in infidel hands. Al-Assad prayed that all was well, but prepared for the worst as he watched the suburban scenery slip by the grimy bus window.

As the vehicle lumbered to the train station, he noticed a collection of police cars in the parking lot of the Schenker warehouse. Strange, he thought, why would there be such activity at a freight storage facility? It hit him in a second. The bus rolled to a stop in front of the train terminal, and al-Assad exited along with the other travelers.

He did not go to the phone booth as planned, but walked to a newspaper kiosk that provided an unimpeded view of the warehouse farther down the avenue. He purchased the latest edition of *Spiegel* magazine, taking time to survey the parked police cars. Uniformed people were moving in and out, and he detected a policewoman with a long blonde ponytail spilling from her duty cap. Some of the policemen carried crowbars.

He knew that there was no need to make the call to Ibrahim, whose fate was now in Allah's compassionate hands. Al-Assad rolled the magazine under his arm, and strolled back toward the train station. He would return to the others. Their plans now required acceleration.

Chapter 40

The Schenker warehouse visit had, as Waldbaer expected, taken the rest of the afternoon to complete. Nothing had turned up. There had been a momentary surge of excitement when they had uncovered metal barrels containing blue powder, but it had been quickly determined to be purification material for swimming pools. Nothing else of interest developed, and Waldbaer dismissed the force as the sky provided its first suggestion of darkness. After the police cars rolled off, Hirter extended him an invitation for a beer at the nearby brewery.

They stood at a bistro table outside the brick façade of the century-old brew house, both sipping a slightly sweet Helles. Waldbaer permitted himself half a cigarette, finding this an acceptable compromise in his attempt to kill the habit entirely. He calculated that he was down to about ten cigarettes a week. Or perhaps fifteen. "Your health, Hirter; *Zum Wohl.*" They tapped their beer glasses together.

"What time tomorrow, Kommissar?" Hirter wiped foam from his lip with a sleeve.

"Eight. Now that we've checked the train station area we head to the outskirts where most of the other warehouses are located." He pulled a folded piece of paper from the pocket of his sports coat. "We meet at one forty-five Sterneckstrasse. There are several warehouses in the neighborhood, some active, some abandoned. We try them all."

Hirter nodded slowly, looking thoughtful.

"What are you thinking, Hirter?"

"About something you said. Abandoned warehouses. I hadn't thought about that. If you were not just storing stuff but mixing chemicals, what would you need? Not just a place to conceal equipment. You'd need working space. That's not something you find in an active warehouse being run by someone else. So you secretly set up shop in some abandoned warehouse that no one uses. That's what my instincts tell me."

"It makes sense. What do you suggest?"

"We prioritize our search. If you have a list that identifies specific warehouses as abandoned, we hit those first."

Waldbaer nodded. "Good. We'll do that." The detective consulted the slip of paper on the table in front of him, securing it against the slight breeze with his beerglass. "That means we start with the empty place at eighteen Kramerstrasse. We search there and then branch out until we've covered all the abandoned storage sites."

"We need to keep a low profile, Kommissar. The longer our search continues, the more likely it becomes that al-Assad and his friends get wind of it. They might figure that we've gotten our hands on their courier in Turkey. By the way, I received a secure call from my colleagues there a while ago. They're going to make Baran phone al-Assad and explain that he can't travel back to Germany yet. It's meant to assure al-Assad that everything in Turkey is okay."

Waldbaer's brow furrowed. "I don't know. Isn't that tricky? Could be that something in Baran's voice or intonation gives away that he's nervous. I'd be careful. That decision is with your colleagues though. All we can do is hope the ploy works."

Chapter 41

"We move to Munich in the morning," al-Assad instructed the other men, noting their expressions. Maintaining discipline would be important, and he knew he had to select his words with care. He spoke calmly to demonstrate that there was no reason to panic.

"Brothers, some things have changed, and we must react to the situation. When I went downtown earlier, I saw a large group of police searching a warehouse near the train station. I knew immediately that they were looking for us. How did I know? Because, brothers, I was graced with a vision last night and the vision provided a warning. I believe that our comrade Ibrahim has been captured or martyred in Turkey. Although Ibrahim doesn't know every detail of our plan, he knows much, and if the infidel has acquired that information, it could lead them here." Al-Assad glanced at his associates one face at a time, trying to read their reactions. *Good, they are concerned, as they should be, but there is no sign of hysteria.*

He continued, his tone controlled. "I think the police have only a general idea as to what we are doing. They know that we are using a warehouse, but not which one. We must conclude our work quickly and move out, taking only what we need for the mission. I'm going to get rid of my cell phone shortly. It's the only communications link that Ibrahim has to us and the phone is now surely being monitored. A cell phone is harder to trace than a landline, but is still vulnerable to technical attack. I'm going to throw the phone in the river. We work through the night, finish our project, and leave in the morning. We pack up our stuff in suitcases, take a bus to the Rosenheim outskirts, and take the *Interregio* train to Munich. We'll find accommodations there near the train station. That quarter of Munich is full of Turks and Arabs, so we'll blend in. All will go well, brothers. Do you know why I am confidant, despite these difficulties?"

His accomplices remained silent, awaiting an answer.

"Because we have been provided this warning. Do you think it was coincidence that I saw the police search downtown? I ask you, what would be the chances of such a thing? No, it was the hand of the Prophet that impelled me there, at exactly that time. The Messenger is watching over us. We will pass through these trials, which purify us for what we will soon accomplish."

The others nodded with animation.

Very good, al-Assad thought, they will follow my lead.

"All right, continue working until I return. Follow the written instructions. This is the final phase and we need to be careful. When we leave this place, we take the loaded canisters with us."

He turned and left the warehouse, exiting through a side door away from the street. He walked through an abandoned lot and headed toward the banks of the Inn River, two miles distant.

Chapter 42

Hirter had just entered the familiar lobby of the Alpenhof when his secure cell phone vibrated in his pocket. He found an unoccupied alcove and answered.

"Hi Robert," a soft, female voice said, the voice distorted slightly by the phone's encryption device. "This is Caroline O'Kendell. We met once or twice over on my side of the pond. Listen, I don't know if you're aware of it, but I'm sort of your partner over here on the case you're engaged in. I thought I'd try to reach you directly with some new information."

Hirter smiled to himself, but was not entirely sure why. "Caroline, I remember you, sure. It's nice to hear from you. I'm in a fairly private location so you can talk. The connection is decent, too."

He made out Caroline's slight laugh on the other end. "Secret technology gets better all the time. I remember using some of the old STU phones years ago and it was like conversing underwater."

"I hated those phones," he said, locating a lobby armchair and sinking into it.

"Robert, you'll see this eventually in a cable, but I wanted to alert you. The possibility that we might be dealing with a chemical attack has a lot of people excited. We've found someone who can fly over to Bavaria to assist. He knows chemical weapons and has field experience in Iraq and Afghanistan. His name is Allen Chalmers. He's getting a flight that reaches Salzburg via Frankfurt at ten tomorrow morning. I know its short notice, but we wanted to get someone there quickly in case the search turns something up. Can you square this with your Kommissar and pick Allen up at the airport?"

"Caroline, thanks for your help back there. I know how slow things can be at headquarters; you must be powering through the deskbound types. Sure, I can do a pickup at Salzburg tomorrow. I'll let Waldbaer know that we have an expert coming in. Can you give me a description of Chalmers?"

"Allen looks about forty. Six feet, average build. Glasses. Black man. Short hair, no mustache. For easy recognition, I'll ask him to wear a green tie."

Hirter chuckled. "No need for the green tie. I'll find him." Hirter thought for a second before continuing, listening to the background hiss of the encryption on the line. "You're running the case back there. Why don't you check out the scene here yourself for ground truth? Might make it easier to brief people at home on what it's like on this end. Even a few days would give you the picture, and you could make your own assessment of Waldbaer and whether we should stay with this arrangement or bring in German intelligence from Pullach."

He smiled at the feigned groan transmitted through the receiver. "You're killing me. Twist my arm to visit the Alps in the autumn. Mountain scenery, Oktoberfest, apple streudel. I wish it were that easy. But I can tell you right now that Randolph Stockbridge will say that my job is here and not to interfere with the field."

"Stockbridge. I've heard of him."

"He's a great guy, Robert, don't get me wrong. But he'd see my travel there as a junket — and he'd be at least partially right. So, I'll spare myself the embarrassment of raising it. But thanks for coming up with the idea."

Hirter mumbled something, weighing the odd disappointment he felt with the satisfaction he was deriving from the simple conversation. "Okay, your call, Caroline. The invitation is open if the opportunity arises. I'll keep our Vienna friends in the loop so there's no heartburn about coordination."

"Good. I'll tell Allen things are arranged for Salzburg. He'll be leaving soon for Dulles to catch his flight. Let's cross our fingers that something turns up in the search. The more I contemplate the information we have, the less I like it. And by the way, when this is all over and you're back in headquarters, I'll spring for a cup of coffee."

"I'll bring the apple streudel," he said, before ringing off.

Chapter 43

Al-Assad pushed through a brilliant yellow meadow of waist-high rapeseed, crossed through a narrow belt of birch trees, and found himself on a mossy bank of the river Inn. The river, heavy in natural chalk, flowed deep and light blue through the surrounding farmland. The water was very cold, he knew, much of it originating from snow-melt runoff from the mountains. Taking his time, he surveyed the opposite bank and found it deserted. He was alone. No fishermen or kayakers there to observe him. He tugged the cell phone from his pocket and was about to toss it into the driven swells when the device rang, nearly causing him to drop it. He listened to the phone's musical tune for a moment, unsure what to do. He decided to answer. The piece of plastic could no longer betray him.

"Hello," he said simply.

"Ah, Mohammed, it's good that I have reached you. Ibrahim here. I hope you are well. I'm calling to say that I will be delayed in my return. I have been ill, food I think. I can't travel yet. A few days and I'll be fine. My friend here is concerned about the wedding and asked that we delay it until I return, bringing his gifts for the bride."

Al-Assad felt cold sweat form on his forehead. Ibrahim had not employed the parole indicating that he was free from duress; al-Assad's fears were realized. There was nothing more to be said.

"Ibrahim, I wish you well, brother. Remain resolute and may the Prophet protect you." He detected what sounded like a choked sob on the other end of the line.

He prepared to launch the phone into the river when he picked

up sounds of commotion in the receiver. Another voice reverberated from the phone, gritty and angry, the pronunciation urban
Turkish.

"So, you've figured it out, you bastard? It doesn't matter. We'll get
you. Your crying, quivering little friend here has been very helpful.
You have no idea how cooperative he's been. He knows more than
you think. Not really cut out to be a martyr, I might add. You and all
of the fanatic deviants like you have defamed the name of Islam
around the world. You're no better than a common criminal."

Al-Assad heaved the cell phone into the river, watching as
the black shape performed a graceful pirouette in the air before
plunging into the swirling eddies of the Inn. He was breathing hard
and his limbs were shaking. He struggled to regain self-control, to
leash his anger. Who had spoken to him in this way? Some corrupt
Turkish official no doubt. Some apostate Moslem working for the
infidels.

With effort, al-Assad calmed himself and his anger slowly subsided. It didn't matter. There was no imminent danger from far away
Ankara. It was true that they held Ibrahim and had forced him to
talk, but Ibrahim did not know everything, and could not provide
the Turks with key information to disrupt the mission. Al-Assad had
employed solid security to protect the mission, and this had paid off.
The strike would proceed unhindered.

Breathing normally now, al-Assad did not linger by the foaming
ribbon of the Inn, and headed back toward the warehouse. No need
to tell the others of Ibrahim's conversation, he reasoned. It would
only upset them, and they were not as strong as he. They would proceed with the final phase before the attack.

"I can't say I'm happy with what you did, Ahmet," the American
told his Turkish counterpart. "We didn't need to let al-Assad know
that we're on his tail. No percentage in it."

Ahmet nodded almost imperceptibly, his dark Turkish features
revealing nothing. He adjusted the knot of his blue on orange striped
tie. "We revealed nothing. It was clear to me that our friend here,"

he gestured at Ibrahim, handcuffed to a stool near the speakerphone, "failed to convince. Probably didn't use some recognition code that he should have. Anyway, al-Assad knew that Ibrahim was lying. So, might as well play with the mouse before we kill it."

The American stared unhappily at his liaison partner. "Let's hope we kill it. Al-Assad and company aren't exactly in our grasp."

The squarely built Turk shrugged his shoulders, wrinkling the fabric of his brown suit. "I planted a seed. I suggested that Ibrahim knows more than al-Assad suspects. Not true, of course. But terrorists are paranoid. I'm hoping that he starts wondering whether we might have more information than he thought. That, in turn, could cause him to do something stupid. It wouldn't be the first time."

The American smiled. "I hope you're right. I would have kept my mouth shut, but the cat's out of the bag now. If you'll excuse me, I have to get back to my office and send an update to Langley. By the way, what do you think the chances are that al-Assad is still hanging onto that cell?"

"No chance at all, Peters. None at all. Your colleagues in Germany aren't going to catch this guy with something as simple as tracing a cell phone. It's going to take men on the ground, hard work, and luck."

Chapter 44

The Salzburg Airport radiated an unashamedly provincial look, betraying little in common with its larger cousins in Vienna, Munich, or Frankfurt. Robert Hirter was thankful for the airport's diminutive size. It would make it easier to locate Allen Chalmers.

Inside the terminal, Hirter noted there was a coffee shop and precious little else to distract the bored traveler. Hirter did not require distraction, however, as he noted from the television monitor that Chalmers's flight was on time and would touch down within minutes.

There were perhaps twenty passengers who passed into the arrival lobby, most in business attire. Chalmers, outfitted in blazer and tie with a raincoat over his shoulder, rolling a burgundy suitcase behind him, was the only black man. Hirter waved and caught the man's attention.

"I'm Robert Hirter," he said without elaboration, "Caroline gave me your information." The two shook hands, and Hirter pointed the way to the parking lot.

"Call me Allen. They call me Chemical Allen back home, like Chemical Ali in Iraq, but you can tire of that pretty fast. Where are we off to?"

"Hotel first, so you can freshen up. Then we'll introduce you to the police Kommissar running the case. Are you traveling under your real name or do you want to use an alias with the Germans?"

"No," Allen replied without hesitation, "Real name will do fine. I came out of the Directorate of Intelligence early in my career, which means I'm an overt employee, not undercover. Anyway, I'll follow your lead. Give me the dos and don'ts. As far as I understand from Caroline, I have only one reason to be here and that's to identify chemical equipment, chemicals, or trace elements." He spoke in a soft, well-modulated voice that Hirter found comfortable.

They exited the terminal, and Hirter led the way to the parking lot. "You mentioned Chemical Ali just now. Were you in Iraq, Allen?"

"Sure was. I went in with one of our weapons-of-mass-destruction teams after the invasion. We spent weeks driving around the desert in armored personnel carriers in hundred degree temperatures looking for chemical weapons caches. I must have visited a hundred Saddam-era military bases. We found some rusty ten-year-old mustard gas artillery shells, but that was all. It wasn't a very satisfying assignment. Unless you enjoy dysentery."

"I hope this turns out more to your liking. I'm not entirely sure what we're looking for, but I imagine that Caroline briefed you."

"She did. Let me summarize what I was told back home: we don't know what sort of chemical we're looking for, but we do anticipate locating chemical weapons production equipment. Don't worry, if we find suspicious-looking gear, I'll be able to ID it. If we locate chemicals, I have the kit with me to test for pretty much any chemical that could have weapons use. Something else to consider. It's true that a chemical weapon is easier to produce than a biological one and certainly easier than a nuclear one. Still, the level of ease is relative. To deploy a chemical weapon, a number of elements have to be right, such as the proper concentration of the chemical, an appropriate vessel for mixing a binary agent, and other factors. Target selection to inflict significant casualties. What I'm saying is that a terrorist group might want to employ a chemical agent, but that doesn't automatically mean that they can do it successfully."

As they approached the car and Hirter pulled the key from his jeans, he noticed a familiar shape standing near the vehicle, hands in pockets. Waldbaer. He had told the Kommissar that he would be doing an airport pickup in Salzburg, but hadn't expected the detective to meet him here.

"Kommissar Waldbaer, permit me to introduce a colleague from my organization, Mr. Allen Chalmers. Allen is a chemical weapons expert on loan to us."

Waldbaer's creased features eased into a smile and he extended his hand to the visitor. "*Gruess gott* and welcome to Europe. Your timing is impeccable." He turned his eyes to Hirter. "I think we've found it. An abandoned warehouse as you suggested. Some suspicious looking items. We're still looking around, but I think we won the lottery."

"When did this happen?" Hirter asked.

"About two hours ago. I came here directly to let you know."

Chalmers stared off at the craggy contours of the Unterberg Mountain, near the Austrian-German border. "Well, gentlemen, freshening up at the hotel can wait. Why don't we go directly to the warehouse and get to work. My curiosity is killing me." No one objected.

The first thing Hirter noticed as he followed Waldbaer's car was that the industrial park had a derelict look. A few small, dubious-looking businesses were evident, but most of the buildings seemed in various stages of disrepair, long wisps of grass growing through cracked sidewalks. Not far off, he noted a collection of police cars pulled up around a decrepit red brick structure. Yellow crime-scene tape staked out the building.

Inside, the yawning storerooms reverberated from the exertions of the dozen or so policemen. Some were opening wooden crates, others applying fingerprint dust to surfaces, concentrating on doors and windows. The place was loud with echoing voices and the static of walkie-talkies.

Waldbaer led the two Americans up a flight of stairs to the top floor of the warehouse. At the top, they entered a doorway, finding themselves in a cavernous space, lightbulbs dangling high above. Hirter noticed that there were cots and piles of blankets along one side of the room.

Waldbaer turned and addressed them. "Unfortunately, there was no one home when we came to call. As you can see, they were camping out in here, probably for some days judging from the food wrappings and empty water bottles. It seems that they left in a hurry; maybe they figured out that we were conducting warehouse searches. My suspicion is that they pulled out in the past day or two. We've put up checkpoints in the area and we have foot patrols going through the neighborhood, but, frankly, I think al-Assad and his band are far away by now."

Hirter moved on the balls of his feet. "Kommissar, let me ask you something. If you were al-Assad and you knew the police were on your trail, where would you go once you left here?"

Waldbaer thought a moment. "If I were al-Assad I'd hide in an urban area. I'd get to a big city and blend into the environment, exploit the anonymity, keep a low profile. He and his men have had to leave their homes, and they can't go back. They can't stay around Rosenheim either because they know we're on to them. If I were al-Assad, I'd take off for Hamburg or Frankfurt or Berlin, put some geography between themselves and here. Given their ethnicity, I'd choose a city with a mixed population, so as not to stand out. I'm sure that they've moved to a large city."

"Makes sense," Hirter replied.

"Our friends left something behind. I expect this will interest you." The detective shepherded the Americans toward the far end of the storage area, where there were a number of long tables, an array of metal equipment, and a collection of glass tubes and laboratory items.

"Bingo," Hirter said.

"I would have to agree with that sentiment," said a smiling Chalmers. "Gentlemen, I think I can be of utility to you at this point. Kommissar, do you mind if I conduct an inspection of that material?"

"Be my guest, Herr Chalmers." The chemist pulled a pair of white rubber gloves from his pocket and stretched them over his hands, retrieved a ballpoint pen and small notebook from his pocket, and began to survey the equipment. Hirter and Waldbaer watched, but said nothing.

Chalmers ran his hands over a large, gray cylindrical device and

pursed his lips. "This is called a distillation column. There's a man-
ufacturing plate attached here at the base. This piece of equipment
is older than it looks. It was produced in Berlin, Germany in nineteen thirty-eight by a company named Kuhn AG."

"Does that tell you anything?" Hirter ventured.

"Not much in itself, but I can research the company's history.
What's important is that this appears to be made of a nickel alloy."

"Why is that important?" Hirter queried, feeling like an untutored schoolboy in basic chemistry class.

"It's important because it suggests that the equipment was designed to be resistant to corrosion. In other words, this is specifically
constructed to handle highly corrosive ingredients." Chalmers continued examining the metal column, slowly tracing a gloved finger
down the side almost reverently.

It was Waldbaer who spoke next. "Corrosive material means
something like acid, a concentrated form of acid?"

Chalmers did not move his gaze from the equipment and replied
in almost a whisper. "In view of the other equipment here I'd imagine that this was designed to be used with an extremely corrosive
liquid, yes, but let me look further."

With some effort he unfastened four large clamps at the top of
the column and, standing on his toes, peered inside, and smiled
grimly. "This vessel is double walled. There's a gap between the walls
intended for air circulation. No doubt about it, this was built to handle extremely corrosive substances. The piping connecting the various pieces of equipment for chlorination is double-walled as well."

Hirter spoke up. "Can you tell what this stuff was used for?"

Chalmers looked up from the metal objects and fixed Hirter with
a stare. "I need to examine this equipment in more detail, of course.
But I can tell you without doubt that I'll be able to determine what
this equipment was designed to do. More important for our interests
is that if this gear was ever used in the past — recently or during the
war — I'll be able to find trace elements of the chemicals that were
introduced. That much I can guarantee."

It was Waldbaer's turn to smile. "That's excellent news, Herr

Chalmers. Please, conduct your examination in peace. Herr Hirter and I will wait outside. If you need anything, just ask."

"Fine. Before you go, Kommissar, pass me my attaché case. It's a suitcase laboratory. It will do the heavy lifting in identifying the substances that passed through this equipment. And, in case you're wondering, this won't take forever to figure out."

In front of the warehouse, the sun wrestled with broad banks of cloud, occasionally breaking through to illuminate the yellowing leaves of the chestnut trees bracing the street. Waldbaer permitted himself a cigarette. "I'm cutting down," he said almost apologetically to Hirter. "Well, Herr Hirter, Chalmers knows what he's doing, and he's convinced he can give us the answers we need. I applaud you for getting him here."

Hirter shrugged. "It wasn't my idea. A female officer back home thought of it. You're right though, this is a big step. Remember what Chalmers said in there about that column? Manufactured in Berlin in 1938. This has got to be the stuff in Sedlmeyer's story. That SS convoy wasn't carrying Goering's old masters or Nazi gold. It was transporting equipment for a weapon never employed by the Germans during the war. By the look of things, the equipment is still functional, unfortunately. Once Chalmers figures out exactly what it was used for, we'll be in a better position to deal with things."

"Gentlemen." Chalmers's dry voice was instantly recognizable. The chemist stood with his back to the warehouse, removing the rubber gloves from his manicured hands. "I've conducted sufficient testing to tell you what you need to know. The equipment represents an entire system for chemical weapons production, soup to nuts, including degassers, reactors, and glass-lined storage tanks. All of it first-class stuff, even though the most recent date of manufacture is 1941. The equipment permits the chlorination and fluorination steps in a fairly complex chemical process and there is air-handling equipment in there to boot. I also found a number of respirators and rubber lab suits in a pile against the wall. These boys knew what they were doing and were fully aware of the dangers."

"Dangers?" Waldbaer said, a note of concern seeping into his voice.

"Dangers," Chalmers repeated. "To cut to the chase, gentlemen, this equipment was designed to produce a nerve agent. A nerve agent, in turn, is designed to produce mass casualties. It is quickly lethal, and any exposure to it in its liquid or gaseous state while handling or producing it can kill."

Hirter frowned. "Do you know which nerve agent"?

"Yes. My suitcase lab confirmed it. This equipment was designed to produce Sarin. Sarin, by the way, was a German invention. My testing demonstrates that the stuff in there produced Sarin very recently. I measured a lot more than residual traces from the 1940s. The bottom line is the fellows who were working here produced a quantity of Sarin within the last few weeks, probably within the last few days. Whatever Sarin was produced is gone. In my view, we are almost certainly faced with a pending Sarin attack aimed at producing mass casualties. I also think the attack will happen soon."

Waldbaer looked at the chemist with a hint of skepticism. "How can you know that they intend to use it soon? That goes beyond chemical tests to guessing the intention of the terrorists, doesn't it?"

"Not really," Chalmers replied. "Sarin has a lot of qualities that make it a desirable nerve agent. But on the debit side, Sarin has a shelf-life problem and degrades over time. Storage is also problematic. Suffice it to say that immediately upon production, Sarin is at its optimal state as a weapon. It's the reverse of wine; it doesn't improve with age. If these people know what they are doing, and I expect that they do from what I've seen, they aren't going to let this stuff deteriorate before they employ it."

A high-pitched scream erupted behind them, followed by muffled shouts from inside the warehouse. Hirter, Waldbaer, and Chalmers ran toward the door. Before they reached the warehouse entrance, the gray door was flung open and the blonde policewoman with a ponytail staggered out and into the grass. Bending forward, she clutched her hands to her knees and vomited a brown stream into the weeds and then gasped for breath.

"Oh, God, please don't let it be the Sarin," Chalmers mumbled.

Waldbaer heard the imploration with quiet horror. He approached the retching woman and placed his hands on her leather-jacketed shoulders. "Were you near that equipment?" He took care to keep his voice calm.

The policewoman noisily sucked in a gulp of air and shook her head sideways. "Freezer," she said weakly, before unleashing another thick torrent into the tall grass.

"I don't understand," Waldbaer pleaded.

The woman regained her breath and seemed less convulsed, if pallid. "The freezer downstairs, in the back room. I was checking for chemicals. There's a corpse in there. Hacked up. He's decapitated, and the body has been cut into pieces like a pig at the butcher's. Damn it, I wasn't expecting something like that."

Gently, Waldbaer eased her upright and patted her back. "It's okay, stay here, get some fresh air. Better yet, go over to the van, there are bottles of mineral water in the back. We'll take it from here. Good work, finding what you did."

"Jesus," Chalmers exclaimed, his features also taking on a pasty cast. "Boys, this part is out of my league. If you don't mind, I'll watch after the young lady here."

Moments later Waldbaer and Hirter found themselves staring into the fishlike, lifeless eyes of a severed head. The eyes, like the rest of the body parts, were dusted with ice crystal. The body had been chopped into sections and the bottom of the freezer was a frozen black mass of coagulated blood. In addition to Waldbaer and Hirter, several policemen gathered around, taking in the grotesque sight.

"Get someone here with a camera," Waldbaer ordered with a tremor of anger in his voice. "Call the crime scene boys and have them get the coroner."

"I think I know who he is," a tall, gaunt policeman muttered from just behind Waldbaer.

"You know who this man is? Well, let's not keep it a secret."

"I used to do the night patrol at the train station. He slept on the benches in the lobby some nights. I rousted him a few times. He used to drink cheap schnapps by the liter, like a lot of those guys. I brought him into the station once or twice for making a nuisance of himself, the usual homeless alcoholic stuff. I think I know his name." The policeman removed his peaked service cap and stared at the ceiling for a moment, his brow furrowed. "Yeah. Niedermeyer. I never heard his first name, the other drunks called him Niedi. That's him, I'm certain of it."

"Bravo," Waldbaer replied. "At least we won't have to waste time trying to identify him."

Hirter shook his head in disbelief. "I don't get it. Why was he killed like this? What connection would a garden-variety drunk have to a terrorism case?"

Waldbaer put his hand on Hirter's shoulder. "That's easy. He had no connection to al-Assad and company at all, none. I can see what happened. Niedermeyer is homeless and wanders around finding a roof to put over his head every night. Sometimes it's the train station, but the police kick him out of there. He has other places where he gets some schnapps-induced sleep. Under a bridge one night, in some garage the next. And sometimes in an abandoned warehouse. He just picked the wrong night to nest here. He stumbled onto our chemical hobbyists or they stumbled onto him. They couldn't take a chance that he'd report them. He was done in here in the warehouse. What to do with the corpse? These guys don't have time to go wandering around with a body. The most logical thing to do is put him in this freezer. Problem: the freezer isn't large enough to take a corpse whole. Solution: chop it up and make it fit. That's how it happened, Herr Hirter."

"I'm impressed," Hirter said. "I guess that's why you're a Kommissar. Bad luck for this poor bastard."

"And bad luck for us. This makes at least two murders, and the terrorists still evade us. And now they have a chemical weapon. Bad luck for us again."

Waldbaer turned away from the corpse, having had enough of the scene, and what always struck him as the tawdry inelegance of murder. Hirter followed, feeling sullied and diminished by the sight of the dead man and desiring fresh air. They arrived at the main door and walked outside. The blonde policewoman was leaning against a van and gulping mineral water from a plastic bottle.

"You know, Kommissar, it's not all been bad luck. We were lucky in a positive way to find the equipment intact. Lucky to have had Chalmers on site to tell us what it means. The Turks were lucky in grabbing Ibrahim and getting him to talk. We shouldn't be too hard on ourselves."

"Only as hard as we need to be, Herr Hirter." Waldbaer glanced at his wristwatch. "We need more luck now, at least if Chalmers is right about the chemical shelf life. We don't know where al-Assad and his gang are located. If they're in a large city as I think they are, it could take time to root them out. Remember what Napoleon said, Hirter. 'Ask me for anything but time.' That's my worry — we don't have time on our side."

To this, Hirter could offer no consoling reply.

Chapter 45

The sounds of traffic drifted up from the urban street and seeped into the confined space of the hotel room. The noise was constantly present, sometimes more and sometimes less, but never absent. The hotel room itself had seen better days, but even in better days would have been regarded as pedestrian. The same could be said of the entire Rote Adler Hotel, from the musty dining room with its chipped white plates to the dim lobby lined with smudged paneling and plastic plants. Mohammed al-Assad and his associates inhabited rooms in the establishment because it provided anonymity. The hotel owner was a balding Egyptian in his seventies, and the staff consisted of Turks whose lack of energy was compensated by their complete disinterest in the comings and goings of guests. The hotel was precisely what al-Assad had been looking for as the launch site for the mission.

They were gathered in al-Assad's room on the fourth floor. They had checked in separately over the course of a day to avoid providing a profile as a group. Al-Assad passed around plastic bottles of iced tea that he had purchased down the street, across from the Munich main train station. Al-Assad sat on the narrow metal frame bed, Sayyid was slouched across from him in the room's sole chair, an orange and chrome creation that screamed 1970s. The others leaned against the faded green wallpaper without complaint. The circumstances were, after all, no worse than in the warehouse they had so recently evacuated.

"My brothers, we are safe. As I said, we are under divine protection. This hotel will be the last earthly roof over our heads before we meet in paradise, as a company of *shahid*. Only a few days more and our target will be ready, and we will be ready for our target. Fill the remaining hours with prayer. We will soon launch our attack against the *kaffir*. Although the infidels have captured Ibrahim and forced us to move more quickly than we might have liked, this has not compromised our plan." Al-Assad looked from face to face as he spoke, careful to make eye contact. "The most difficult phase was the production of the chemical. That production has been successful, thanks to you."

Al-Assad reached beneath the bed and pulled out a scuffed black suitcase. With a fluid motion, he unzipped it and removed a polished metal canister from underneath some folded shirts. He held the gleaming vessel securely in both hands. "This is our sword, brothers. This is our destiny, the reason we were born. There is one container for each of you; take them back to your rooms and hide them among your clothes in the dresser." He ran a hand down the smooth surface of the container. "These are one-liter vessels. They are fitted with a dispersing device. Be careful with these things, friends, they are sensitive. I need say no more."

Each man took a canister, cradling and examining it before setting the heavy cylinders softly on the worn gray carpeting covering the floor. There was a momentary silence punctuated only by the sounds from the street below.

"Mohammed, can you speak to us once again of paradise, of what awaits," Sayyid requested.

Al-Assad smiled with a flash of teeth and folded his hands on his knees. "Of course, Sayyid. I will begin by telling you that a sanctified place is even now being readied for us, to celebrate our arrival. Be sure of this — black-eyed virgins prepare to greet us, and their unblemished beauty is unsurpassed on this earth."

The weary faces in front of al-Assad smiled broadly, certain in the probity of what they were ready to do, and of the rewards that awaited them.

Chapter 46

Waldbaer recognized the crisp-as-paper voice immediately and held the telephone receiver close to his ear. "Frau Bergdorfer, what an unexpected pleasure. How can I be of assistance?"

The distant voice spoke with enunciated precision. "I expect you might be more interested in how I can help you, Herr Kommissar. I've been thinking about what you said, about trying to solve a recent murder. And as you noted, my husband is gone and is beyond harm. His past remains his past, that can't be changed. But perhaps a piece of the past can be of utility in the present. I don't mean to be cryptic, Kommissar, but if you are interested in driving to Freilassing I can provide you with something from long ago that might interest you."

"I'm on my way, Frau Bergdorfer; I'll be there within ninety minutes. *Auf wiederhören.*" True to his word, the detective hung up the desk phone, pulled himself from his leather chair, and, car keys in hand, prepared to journey into the past.

They stood again in the garden, wet now from a passing shower. Waldbaer had decided to travel to Freilassing alone, in the event that it made it easier for the old woman to impart whatever she had to tell. Waldbaer had a nagging sense that the widow had not quite revealed all that she knew about her husband's wartime activities. He hoped that was about to change.

The old woman smiled sadly and shook his hand, which the detective interpreted as not a bad augur. "Kommissar, I told you the truth when you were here last. I told you what I know of my husband's conversations about the war. But I failed to provide you with something not spoken but written."

With difficulty, Waldbaer retained his calm demeanor and said nothing, permitting her to continue.

"My husband left a *Tagesbuch*, a diary. There are entries from wartime. I decided to read through it after you left the last time, to see if there was anything about his last mission to Bavaria. There is nothing written during the war later than January nineteen forty-five, I'm afraid."

Waldbaer felt deflated, and could not conceal the rush of disappointment.

"Still, I did find some entries from nineteen forty-four that should interest you, Kommissar. You must be the judge, but I think some of the nineteen forty-four entries written in Dyernfurth-am-Oder might have a connection to the events of the following year. Much of it is too technical for me to follow, but perhaps it makes sense to you."

Frau Bergdorfer slipped a papery hand into the folds of her apron and removed two small books. The top book was bound in cracked brown leather. The word Tagesbuch was embossed on the surface, and underneath it the letters HK; initials for Horst Kaltenberg. The second book had a green fabric cover and was of more recent vintage.

The woman ran her hand slowly over the volumes and passed them into Waldbaer's palm. "I would like these returned when you've finished, Kommissar. You understand the sentiments of an old woman, I expect."

"Of course, Frau Bergdorfer, they'll be returned to you shortly. We'll copy them and get the originals back to you. This is your property, and I'm aware that you are providing it voluntarily. I thank you for that."

The woman nodded and folded her arms about her lean frame. "You might also find some of my husband's later entries interesting. From after the war, I mean. Those are in the second book. Horst didn't keep the diary regularly. But there are some entries from the nineteen eighties that you might profitably read, from his time as a chemical salesman."

Sympathetic but shrewd, Waldbaer assessed. As if reading his unspoken thoughts, the woman added in a clipped voice, "I am old enough to have learned, Herr Kommissar, not to pass judgment too quickly. To this day, I judge my late husband only on how he behaved to *me*. Why should it be otherwise? It would seem that he engaged in things that I do not understand, that I might have never done myself, but for all that I have not passed judgment. That much you will permit me, I hope."

Waldbaer took her hand in both of his in an old Teutonic gesture of respect that he had learned as a child. "Frau Bergdorfer, in my profession I'm forced to judge people all the time. It is, in a way, at the core of what a detective does for a living. Let me tell you this. Whatever judgment I might pass on your deceased husband, I judge *you* to be a person of honor. You have helped this investigation, and I expect it has cost you more than a little sorrow. I appreciate your helpfulness."

He left her there in the garden, surrounded by the fragile, fading flowers of autumn and by a meadow of memories from very long ago.

Waldbaer had ordered that three copies of the diary be made: one for the official file, one for his use, and one for Hirter's review. He and the American sat in the detective's office, Waldbaer in his desk chair and Hirter occupying a faded couch.

"Start at the entry for November ninth, nineteen forty-four. Read it aloud, Hirter, I find it a good method to give a text complete attention."

Hirter flipped through the sheets of paper until he arrived at the desired date. Kaltenberg had written in disciplined block letters, making it a simple task to read the text. Hirter cleared his throat and read the entry.

9 November, War Year 1944.

Today began directed assignment to the high-security facility at Dyernfurth-am-Oder. I had stated my preference for a

COLLISION OF EVIL 225

frontline assignment but was overruled by the Office of the *Reichsfuehrer-SS*. Nothing to be done. The ride from Berlin was depressing. It rained the entire way, and I expect sleet tonight once the temperature drops. The officer quarters here are adequate, but there is little coal for the stove in my room due to a general shortage. After depositing my kit in my quarters, I was escorted to the facility and found it unscathed by bombs. In fact, I was told by a lieutenant that this place has never been hit by Allied bombers. They must be unaware of what work goes on here; otherwise we would surely merit their attention.

Hirter looked up questioningly at his counterpart.
Waldbaer nodded. "Keep reading."
Hirter found his place in the text and resumed the narrative.

The production facility is now to come under direct SS control, as there have been too many accidents under the Army Weapons Office and a sense that the technicians are being sloppy. I don't know if this is the case, but we'll see. The equipment located in Building 144 is impressive, much of it lined with silver as an anti-corrosive. Production is dangerous work. When the production step is reached where the chemical agent is reacted with alcohol and degassed, there have been safety problems. As an alternative solution, we have experimented with a reaction using sulfur, which has advantages, but it's complicated and adds further production steps. Air handling and filtering is a critical element, and this is where the facility has suffered fatalities. There have been ten deaths so far. The last was a month ago, when a tear in a technician's protective clothing proved deadly. The poor fellow began experiencing breathing difficulty and he knew what that meant. His comrades tried to assist, but in his panic he fought them off, wide-eyed and screaming into his mask. The convulsions started shortly thereafter and there was nothing to be done, save the burying. These things have to stop; it is affecting morale. The present production design can be summed up graphically in the following way.

Hirter turned the page and saw a complicated sketch. He dropped the papers into his lap. "Kommissar, we should get Chalmers. The content will make a lot more sense to him than to me."

"Chalmers gets a copy," the detective replied. "But the point here, Hirter, is that Kaltenberg was involved in chemical weapons production, no doubt about it. And we know from Chalmers's tests that the agent involved is Sarin. Fact: Al-Assad and his friends have been using German equipment and technical knowledge from the facility at Dyernfurth."

Hirter considered. "We have the equipment now. Al-Assad can't produce any more of it, and he's probably more concerned about hiding from the police than anything else. We have them off balance."

"For the moment. But they produced the Sarin and doubtless have it with them."

Hirter frowned slightly. "I guess that's true. Do we have any clue as to the Sarin dispersion mechanism?"

Waldbaer repositioned himself in his oversized chair. "Keep reading." Hirter returned to the text, skipping past the illustration.

> The production of Sarin is not the sole reason that I was sent here. My superiors have made it clear that the Reich requires a means of chemical agent delivery other than artillery shells, the manner in which mustard gas was employed at the front in the first war. We are devising a delivery mechanism portable enough to be carried by a single soldier.
>
> The tactical requirement is for the gas to be used against Allied troops in enclosed spaces. Barracks, for example. Or a staff meeting of enemy officers in a house. A dispenser solution seems the most attractive for this purpose. I presume that we will need to marry the delivery device to a timing mechanism to activate distribution. To be militarily useful, our end product needs to be a Sarin container that can be infiltrated behind enemy lines by action groups and covertly deposited in enclosed spaces where troops are gathered. A timer is engaged and the

device activates at the assigned hour and minute, giving the German soldiers time to leave the area before the Sarin is spread.

The idea is to create panic behind the lines, bringing the Allied advance to a halt. This will require mass use of the devices, presumably hundreds of them. I find the idea compelling. Sarin in its gas form is odorless and invisible. Its presence is extremely hard to detect. Enemy forces will start dying and not know why. Employment of this weapon will not only cause significant casualties, the psychological impact should be tremendous, spreading horror through enemy ranks. Chaos could ensue.

Employing Sarin tactically can change Germany's strategic fortunes. If the relentless enemy advance can be halted, we will have time to get other weapons into the fight in quantity – jet aircraft and more accurate versions of von Braun's rockets. The fact that so much hinges on this Sarin weapon places enormous responsibilities on my shoulders. I get stomach cramps just thinking about it. I must not fail, whatever the difficulties.

Hirter lowered the pages to his lap and raised his eyes to the detective. "What a horror show. This Kaltenberg was a choice son of a bitch."

"Yes," Waldbaer replied, the single word unadorned.

Hirter drummed his fingers on the arm of his chair for a moment and raised his eyebrows. "Wait a minute. As chilling as it is to read this diary, there's something we shouldn't forget. Sarin was never used. As far as I'm aware there wasn't one instance of chemical weapons being employed in the Second World War, at least not in Europe. Am I right, Kommissar?"

Waldbaer pulled himself from his chair and strolled the office, hands thrust into his trouser pockets. "You're right, Hirter. The Nazis didn't use gas. Hitler never gave the order to use it. Hitler had been gassed on the Western Front in 1918. Maybe he retained an aversion to the weapon. Or maybe the Germans knew that if they employed gas, the allies would eventually do the same, wiping out any strategic advantage. Who knows? Based on the diary entries though, Kaltenberg seemed convinced that if he could solve the problem of a viable delivery system, Sarin would be employed. Desperate times produce desperate decisions, and things were not looking good for German fortunes in late 1944."

"Maybe Kaltenberg was overly optimistic about his ability to weaponize Sarin. What was it Clausewitz said? In wartime even the simplest task becomes difficult?" Hirter said.

"Let's read on," Waldbaer instructed.

The diary was not an uninterrupted chronology of nerve agent production. Waldbaer and Hirter flipped through pages dealing with Kaltenberg's comments on food shortages and the poor quality of wartime sausage. He noted the passage above Dyernfurth of allied bomber fleets on their way to pulverize German cities, and he wrote of the carnage wrought in Berlin, Chemnitz, and Frankfurt.

Some entries were more memorable.

> Two Wehrmacht deserters were discovered Tuesday as they passed through Dyernfurth. The field police asked me what to do with them. I had them hanged in the town square. We let their corpses swing for two days before burial. I had placards strung around their necks reading "I betrayed the Fatherland," in the hope that it will be a salutary message for other weak hearts contemplating desertion.

Eventually, the account of events at the chemical production site resumed. Hirter read aloud to Walbaer.

> Today a breakthrough. We have fabricated a nickel container and filled it with Sarin. A corrosion-resistant spray mechanism my team developed has been fitted to the top of the container, wired to a compact timing device manufactured in Essen. Although heavy for its size, the container can be carried by an infantryman. We set the timer for an hour delay and conducted a field test. It worked perfectly! When the timer engaged, the

sprayer activated and distributed the Sarin gas, propelling it several feet in all directions, a result of the rotating head that we
used. The dispenser heads are pointed upward, to counter the
effect of the particles descending to the ground too rapidly. I am
extremely pleased with these results. I had the test filmed and
have ordered the film dispatched to the Reichsfuehrer-SS for
viewing. With developments at the front being so grim, this break-
through came not a moment too soon.

"So, he did it after all," Waldbaer interrupted. "He worked
around the problems and found a functional delivery system for the
Sarin. The troubling thing for us, Hirter, is that more than likely,
al-Assad not only has Sarin gas, he has his smutty little hands on
the dispersal containers as well."

"And according to your instincts, al-Assad and his band are in an
urban area. Which means, if they have functioning nerve agent devices, all they have to do is set them off."

Waldbaer rubbed his forehead, just above the bridge of his nose.
"We have to find them soon. Even if we locate the group, can we
incapacitate them before they set the devices off?"

"In my view, Kommissar, this is a case where you can forget trying to take them alive. If we find them, kill them, just like that.
Come in guns blazing. The consequences of permitting them a few
seconds to react could prove disastrous."

The detective half-snorted a derisive laugh and shook his head
sideways. "My dear Hirter, Germany operates differently from the
States, I'm afraid. The police require special orders to kill without
warning. And that's something beyond my personal jurisdiction.
Something else — now that we've established not just the likelihood
but the *probability* of a mass-casualty plot, I have to notify higher authority, the political level. You can imagine if we have some sort of
Sarin incident and the politicians find out they weren't informed of
developments beforehand."

Hirter nodded in agreement. "You're right. Remember, though,

I'm here unofficially, and my people want to keep it that way."

"We'll find a way to handle that," the detective replied. "I'll brief my supervisor in Munich, and he can inform the minister-president of Bavaria, as a start. I guess we should go get Chalmers's view on the diary and what it tells us about the threat. He might see something that we don't."

Chapter 47

"Shave," Mohammed al-Assad said to his companions, some of them still chewing the last remnants of their meal. They looked at him quizzically, not comprehending his words. They were gathered in Sayyid's hotel room, and cardboard carryout trays, crumpled napkins, and plastic forks from a nearby Turkish restaurant littered the floor.

Al-Assad was seated on the narrow bed and he tugged at his full beard. "We need to shave off our beards. The time for the mission draws close, and we must alter our appearance. If the police know who we are, if they have driver's license photos, they envision us with beards. So, no facial hair. We need to blend in with the population. Do your work delicately, brothers, I don't want to see any nasty razor scars."

One of the men leaning against the stained wall wheezed a low laugh. "Mohammed, I think that you want us to look like the infidels."

Al-Assad fixed the man with an icy grin and crossed his arms in front of his chest. "That is exactly what I want, brother. When we leave this building for the last time, not long from now, I want us to look like the people who will be our victims. We will blend into them, however distasteful that might be for us. We will dress like them, comb our hair like them, and smile at them. And then we will kill them, these arrogant *kaffir*. Continue your prayers, friends, our time rapidly approaches."

Chapter 48

Chalmers, Hirter, and Waldbaer sat at an oval table on the back terrace of the Alpenhof. Chalmers was reading the copied pages of the diary and writing in a spiral notebook. Hirter and Waldbaer said little, sipping cappuccino from bright red mugs emblazoned with the hotel name. The table was situated directly in the late, deep yellow morning sunlight.

"Gentlemen, this is fascinating," Chalmers said. "It tells us a lot about the industrial production of chemical agents in Germany in the 1940s. The illustrations make it clear that they were also experimenting in Dyernfurth with Tabun, another nerve agent. They settled on Sarin as more transportable. I've heard of Dyernfurth-am-Oder previously, by the way. The Russians captured chemical equipment there at the end of the war, and shipped it to the Soviet Union on Stalin's orders. It became the genesis of the Russian chemical weapons program, which produced tons of stuff during the Cold War."

"That's great, Allen," Hirter said. "But we have to prevent an attack. What can you tell us that might assist our effort? The Kommissar believes the terrorists are in an urban area and that they could use the Sarin in, say, a city plaza or main street during rush hour."

Chalmers steepled his fingers and gazed off at the mountains framing the valley. "That's not the way Sarin works, not optimally. The problem with using a nerve agent as a weapon is that it dissipates fairly rapidly in wide-open spaces. I'm not saying that it wouldn't do any damage in a city square, but the level of lethality would be difficult to judge in advance. Effective deployment would depend on the strength and direction of the wind and other factors. Al-Assad and his mates did a professional job producing the Sarin so I assume that they've thought about how to use it effectively. I don't think they would gamble on hitting a city square and leaving the results to chance."

Hirter considered his colleague's comment. "So what kind of target would they settle on if an open space is problematic? If you were al-Assad, what target would you look for?"

Chalmers hesitated before answering. "If I were them, knowing how Sarin works and its limitations, I'd target an indoor space. Someplace that would confine the spread of the Sarin and ensure it remained concentrated. You'd want a place with a lot of people inside to ensure a large number of casualties. You know, something like a church or, God forbid, a concert hall or movie theater. A subway train or a bus would make excellent targets, as far as providing the right environment for the Sarin to stay concentrated."

"That's helpful," Waldbaer interjected. "Even knowing that much gives us a better grip on where al-Assad is likely to strike. It sounds like we can rule out a city plaza or an open-air sports stadium."

"That's right, in my view," Chalmers replied clinically. "You know, this stuff has actually been used by terrorists before."

Hirter raised his eyebrows and leaned forward over the tabletop. "In Japan. A cult was responsible. But you probably know the details better than I do, Allen. Fill us in."

Chalmers nodded. "Yes A crazy sect called Aum Shinrikyo managed to produce a crude sort of Sarin in a home laboratory in 1995, and get it aboard Tokyo subway trains during rush hour. The quality of the Sarin was nothing like the stuff that al-Assad has his hands on, but it was still deadly. The cult had a primitive dispersion device, which turned out not to be very effective."

"But there were casualties," Hirter said.

"Yes. The concentration was fairly high, but the agent didn't circulate well, and most of the particles stayed close to the floor. Still, twelve Japanese died. Hundreds of other passengers suffered ill effects severe enough to require hospitalization. If the cult had been able to produce a more effective dispersion device, fatalities would have been much higher. I think that in the case of al-Assad and his comrades, we can be sure that the Sarin will be dispersed much more effectively than in Tokyo. I think you should look for a venue that will permit them to kill hundreds of people, maybe several hundred. Somewhere crowded and enclosed. That's what they're looking for, I guarantee it."

Waldbaer blanched. "I guess I knew that, but it's still a shock to hear it put so directly. Thanks for your analysis, Herr Chalmers." The detective pushed his cappuccino aside and thought of cities.

Chapter 49

Dawn broke smoky orange and dusty over Ankara, as it did on so many days. As the sun rose, traffic gathered on the thoroughfares like herds of metal beasts. Peters hated tubercular congestion and left for work early to avoid a painful commute. The trip today had been uneventful, and Peters felt content as he parked his BMW sedan in front of the commercial office building where he worked. He and other CIA operations officers occupied a suite that bore the plaque of Robertson and Associates International Security Consulting (RAISC). The company was not legitimate and did not have real customers, but was covertly a fully owned proprietary of the U.S. intelligence community designed to provide plausible cover for operations in Turkey. As a cover company, RAISC functioned well, and the other business tenants of the building took it at face value.

Peters was the first one in the office and would have about an hour before his colleagues arrived. Today his first order of business was to update headquarters on the Ibrahim Baran case. He pulled index cards from his jacket, consulted them briefly, and began to compose.

JOINT INTERROGATION OF IBRAHIM BARAN (HEREAFTER SUBJECT) CONTINUES IN PRISON. SUBJECT EVIDENCES NO DISCERNABLE SIGNS OF DECEPTION. THIS OFFICER AND TURKISH LIAISON PARTNER AHMET SAYGUN HAVE ESTABLISHED RAPPORT WITH SUBJECT.

SUBJECT HAS BEEN COOPERATIVE AND PROVIDES OPERATIONALLY USEFUL DETAILS. ACCORDING TO SUBJECT, HE WAS RAD-

ICALIZED IN GERMANY WHERE HE WAS A GUEST WORKER FOR SEV-
ERAL YEARS. RADICALIZATION WAS VIA A SAUDI-TRAINED WAHABBI
CLERIC AT A MOSQUE HE ATTENDED FOR FRIDAY PRAYER. THE
CLERIC PERSUADED SUBJECT OF HIS DUTY TO ENGAGE IN VIOLENT
JIHAD AGAINST THE WEST. THE CLERIC INTRODUCED SUBJECT TO AL-
ASSAD, AND AL-ASSAD TRAVELED WITH SUBJECT TO PAKISTAN TO
MEET AL-QAEDA OPERATIVES. UPON RECRUITMENT, AL-ASSAD IN-
STRUCTED SUBJECT TO CEASE ATTENDING THE MOSQUE FOR SE-
CURITY REASONS AND MAINTAIN A LOW PROFILE.

AL-ASSAD EMERGES AS THE DRIVING FORCE IN THE CELL FROM
SUBJECT'S ACCOUNT. HE INTRODUCED SUBJECT TO OTHER CELL
MEMBERS AND ADVISED THAT THEY WOULD LAUNCH A SPECIAL JI-
HADIST MISSION AT THE APPROPRIATE TIME. UNTIL THAT TIME, CELL
MEMBERS WERE INSTRUCTED TO BLEND INTO THEIR ENVIROMENT
AND INTEGRATE INTO GERMAN SOCIETY. AL-ASSAD CALLED THE CELL
TOGETHER INFREQUENTLY FOR MEETINGS. HE USED PUBLIC TELE-
PHONES FOR COMMUNICATIONS AND EMPLOYED ORAL CODES.

SUBJECT CONTINUES TO INSIST THAT HE KNOWS LITTLE ABOUT
THE "SPECIAL MISSION," BUT BELIEVES IT INVOLVES MORE THAN
CONVENTIONAL EXPLOSIVE SUICIDE BELTS AS EMPLOYED IN THE AT-
TACK ON THE LONDON SUBWAY IN 2005. THIS SENSE IS BASED
ON THE APOCALYPTIC LANGUAGE AL-ASSAD USED WHEN REFER-
RING TO THE MISSION. FYI, SUBJECT BELIEVES THE OPERATION WILL
EMPLOY WEAPONS PROVIDED BY PEOPLE OUTSIDE THE CELL. DUR-
ING ONE CONVERSATION, AL-ASSAD COMMENTED THAT A "BUSI-
NESSMAN'S GIFT" PLAYED A ROLE IN THE PLANNED ATTACK (NO
FURTHER INFORMATION). SUBJECT CLAIMS TO BE UNAWARE OF THE
TARGET, A COMMENT THIS CASE OFFICER IS INCLINED TO BELIEVE,
AND A SENTIMENT SHARED BY THE TURKS.

Peters paused and consulted his notes, not wanting to miss a detail that might prove important later. No, he decided, he had covered the salient points. He rose to fetch a cup of coffee and noted a
billowing dust cloud blowing into the city from the parched ochre
hills beyond. He wondered what the weather was like in Germany.

Chapter 50

The twelve members of the *Sonderkrisengruppe*, Special Crisis Group, made their way into the spartan gray conference room of the old Reichstag building in the heart of Berlin. A view of the sky above the city was provided by the massive glass cupola over the main hall. The weather, a reflection of the temperament of the Crisis Group members, was somber, a thick cover of clouds spit a drizzle of rain at intervals.

Dr. Volker Rapp, fit and sleek at sixty-four, called the session to order by tapping his pen against the ebony conference table. Rapp, chairman of the group, was flanked by a male stenographer on one side and his corpulent deputy Maria Renate Schmeider on the other. Frau Schmeider did not take to Rapp, who she regarded as abrupt and abrasively dominating. Rapp returned the ill-willed sentiment, judging Schmeider politically untutored and sophomoric, but both had learned to deal with one another and assiduously maintained formal courtesy.

"Ladies and gentlemen, you have the executive summary of the Bavarian case in front of you. I presume you have familiarized yourself with the details." Heads nodded in agreement.

"So then, I propose that we reach concurrence on a plan of action." He smiled without warmth at his deputy, who returned the insincerity. "Permit me to outline the current state of affairs. We are dealing with a case of terrorism; the evidence seems incontrovertible. It appears that the terrorists involved have already killed at least two people, an American tourist and a German homeless man. We additionally know that one of the terrorists," Rapp glanced at the report on the table before him, "Ibrahim Baran is in custody in Turkey. He appears to be cooperating with the authorities there. It is suggested in the report that Baran is a go-between to an international jihadist terrorist and that his associates in Bavaria constitute a jihadist cell. The other cell members are on the loose somewhere in Germany; their location can only be guessed at. That's why we are here."

With a tug at the red-patterned silk scarf intended to conceal her multiplicity of chins, Maria Renate Schmeider intervened. "Doctor Rapp, considering Germany's interest in human rights, might we perhaps have grounds to be concerned about how Herr Baran is being treated by his Turkish interrogators? Information from him could have been obtained under duress, in violation of international conventions. Perhaps we should make official inquiries through our embassy in Turkey." A few others in the windowless room nodded in agreement.

Rapp kept his eyes directed at the table, hands folded in front of him. "Of course, Frau Schmeider, everyone here is concerned about human rights. To speak candidly however, the provenance of information obtained by the Turks is not the topic of our discussion. It seems to me that our task is difficult enough — trying to prevent a terrorist attack — without launching an inquiry into the police methods employed outside of German borders. As the Crisis Group has been called together to deal with a danger to German lives, I don't see the utility of a disputation about prisoner detention policies in Turkey. Would you prefer that we decline to receive the information provided by the Turks? Is that what you're suggesting?"

The heavy woman shifted in her chair, which groaned in rebuke at the strain. Her sausage fingers flittered about the scarf. "Doctor Rapp, I naturally want to get to the bottom of this conspiracy. Still, we aren't the Americans, running around the world justifying every dubious action by yelling 'war on terrorism.' Germany is a nation of laws, and we must ensure that our standards are maintained."

Rapp raised pale blue eyes and examined his deputy's bulk clinically. His face, devoid of smile or frown, radiated malign tranquility. "Very fine, Frau Schmeider. My question stands, however. Are you suggesting that we forego the information on this terrorist cell due to concerns about how the information is obtained? Yes or no, please."

The woman's digital nervousness increased, her hands inadvertently tightening the scarf into a more noose-like form around her substantial throat. "Doctor Rapp, I don't think the matter is that simple, but for the moment you might have a point. We can perhaps look at the Turkish interrogation methods later, at some less pressing time."

Without acknowledging her discommoded soliloquy, Rapp turned to the others. "Let's consider what we'll report to the chancellor. We've reviewed the facts. Now let's examine courses of action open to us. This case is currently in the hands of the Bavarian police. Are we in agreement with that or do we recommend that the lead be transferred to the Federal Interior Ministry? Since we appear to be looking at a planned mass-casualty attack, what should we advise the public, and when? Do we need to keep this out of the press, so as not to alert the terrorists? We have sufficient questions to occupy our time today, I'm afraid."

A ruddy-faced man in a brown tweed jacket raised his hand. "I understand that the Bavarian police are running this, but is there an individual responsible for the investigation?"

Rapp consulted the papers spread before him. "Yes. A Kommissar Franz Waldbaer has been leading the investigation since the beginning. Recall that this started out as a murder case. Waldbaer has presided over it moving from simple homicide to national threat. He apparently has been keeping his superiors well advised, from what I understand. Why do you ask?"

"Because I think continuity is important, provided things have been run professionally," the man in tweed said. "It sounds as if Waldbaer is capable enough. If we insist that the case be run by a federal body, it could complicate things and cost time, something we don't have. I say leave Waldbaer in charge and offer whatever assistance we can from a federal level."

Frau Schmeider signaled agreement. "Not only that, I don't think we have legal grounds to intrude at this point, and I agree that this kommissar seems to be doing a creditable job. I say leave well enough alone, for now at least." She glanced covertly at Rapp to see if his features would communicate disapproval. They did not.

"I think you're both right," Rapp replied dryly. "The last thing we need is to inject complications. Does anyone object strenuously to our recommending that the Bavarians remain in charge?"

No one did.

"Just one more thing," Schmeider ventured. "Although the Bavarian report is vague on this, it indicates that American intelligence is providing informal assistance. Are we comfortable with that? U.S. intelligence is hardly the most popular entity in Germany these days. If the Americans must play a role, shouldn't it be in formal coordination with the BND, German Federal Intelligence?"

Rapp nodded slightly. "The Bavarians do seem to be in touch with U.S. intelligence in an unofficial way. Again, the question should be, is the arrangement working? It seems to be. I don't see a reason to object, any more than I object to the Turks assistance. We can always ask for a formal arrangement later if that makes sense. Views?"

No one in the room raised objection and Frau Schmeider fell silent.

"All right," the chairman continued, "let's consider the public. So far, they know nothing about this terrorist conspiracy. Do we have an obligation to put out an advisory? Should the Interior minister hold a press conference? Consider things from this angle: the terrorists succeed tomorrow in setting off this Sarin in Frankfurt or Hamburg. People die. If our luck is bad, lots of people die. What do you suppose happens once it gets out that German authorities have been aware of the threat for weeks, and haven't provided a warning to the public? What kind of position does that place the chancellor in? There would be demands that half the government resign or face prosecution for gross negligence, or worse."

"Good point," said a group member's agitated voice from halfway down the table. "We should go public now, get the information out there. A press conference is best. The chancellor should make the announcement. And we probably need to provide information on the effects of Sarin."

Rapp examined his nails placidly. "On the other hand," he intoned, "informing the public can have negative consequences, too. Informing the public also informs the terrorists of what we know and what we don't know. To that extent, it provides them intelligence. A press conference could cause them to accelerate their plans and attack immediately. After which the press would condemn us as idiots for not having kept our operations secret. A textbook case of damned if you do, damned if you don't. Also, if we advise the public about a possible chemical attack, would this be useful or cause panic? How will the population react? We need to be careful here."

"So what do we recommend to the chancellor?" Frau Schmeider asked.

"We say that there is no perfect course of action, which is certainly the case." Rapp made a notation on his notepad. "Unless someone has a better idea, I suggest we advise that the interior minister, during the course of a routine press conference, note that international terrorism continues to be a threat to Germany and that we must be vigilant. That provides us some cover for later on, if needed. Perhaps the minister can say that the authorities are continually alert for terrorist plans. But nothing specific. I advise against mentioning chemical agents. If we raise the specter of a chemical attack, we need to be able to address countermeasures. Does anyone here know what has to be done against Sarin?"

No one responded.

"Just as I thought. I seem to recall that there is an antidote to nerve agents, but I can't say more than that. I'll make it a point to get that information confidentially from the Health Ministry when we leave. If there is an antidote, do we have stocks of it on hand? Can it be transported to the site of an attack? How effective is it?

God knows, there are more questions than answers. Once I get solid information, we can regroup. That's all for the moment."

The group vacated the conference room in a chorus of murmured conversation. A glance through the glass dome of the Reichstag revealed that the clouds, like the mood of the recently assembled, had not lifted.

Chapter 51

Waldbaer was surprised to receive the call informing him that he retained primacy in the investigation, and that he was free to request whatever resources he required to prevent al-Assad's attack.

His continued leadership of the investigation established, Waldbaer dialed the Hotel Alpenhof and summoned Hirter and Chalmers to join him in his office. "We need to finish going through Kaltenberg's diaries," he counseled Hirter, "and focus on hunting these guys."

"We're on our way," Hirter replied. "I was just in touch with my people and they're anxious to assist in any way they can. They want whatever new information we develop as fast as we can get it to them."

Hirter and Chalmers arrived at the detective's office in casual attire, with Hirter bearing a bag of warm chocolate croissants from a bakery along the way. "Not exactly what my doctor would recommend," Waldbaer mumbled as he bit into one of the concoctions with ill-concealed exuberance.

"How do you want to proceed?" Hirter inquired, savoring the soft dough of a croissant himself and combating the tension that coursed through him.

"We finished the first diary, the wartime one. Now we have the second, more recent diary to review. This is postwar stuff. I gave it a cursory glance, and it focuses on Kaltenberg's activities as a chemical salesman in the seventies and eighties. Most of what I read seemed of no importance — office politics in the firm where he worked, competition with other salesmen, and an accounting of various transactions. Dull stuff. Still, I don't want to miss anything useful."

"Right," Hirter interjected. "And I've brought along a debriefing report from Turkey." He passed two neatly folded sheets of paper to the detective. "What's interesting is that Baran says that al-Assad remarked that 'a businessman's gift' plays a role in the planned attack. A businessman: that has to be Kaltenberg in his postwar persona. What we don't know is how and why Kaltenberg's Sarin secrets got to a jihadist cell. It's a missing piece of the puzzle. Something happened between the nineteen-forties and today, but it remains concealed."

"I agree," Waldbaer said. "Let's read the second diary."

Forty minutes later Hirter stood up, one arm in the air like an orchestra conductor. "Here's something." He indicated the page to his companions and began to read.

Riyadh, Saudi Arabia
    Closed a deal for the provision of painkiller and disinfectants to the Riyadh hospital this afternoon; we make a solid profit under the conditions of the contract. A signed agreement will be sent to the Essen office tomorrow, champagne all around!

"What's so interesting about that?" Chalmers said, "Its boring business stuff. Probably the reason none of us here went into the private sector."

"That's just a prelude," Hirter corrected, with a dismissive wave of his hand. "Listen to this."

Following the closure of the pharmaceutical deal, I was invited to a buffet by Prince Hafiz, the Saudi royal who signed the contract. The prince is a small man whose form seems lost in his flowing robes. The prince is a capable businessman and shrewd with contracts. He engaged me in conversation, and in the course of our chat seized on a passing comment of mine that I had been an officer in the Waffen-SS during the war. Being

an Arab, the prince is, of course, no friend of the Jews. He was
very complimentary in his comments on the historic role of Germany in the thirties and forties, for which I thanked him.

Chalmers interrupted. "So, the Saudi guy is an anti-Semitic Nazi
fan. It must have been like homecoming week for Kaltenberg."

"It's the Arab view of the Israel issue," Walbaer shrugged. "Anybody who hates Jews can't be all bad, that sort of thinking. But
where's the relevance, Hirter?"

Hirter continued reading.

In view of the prince's enlightened attitude and his interest
in the history of the Reich, I elected to tell him of my final mission of the war.

Waldbaer and Chalmers sat up in their seats and Hirter smiled,
knowing that he had their attention.

The prince was silent as I recounted the journey from Berlin
to southern Germany and Austria. He was clearly taken by my
account of the foresight of the German leadership in trying to
preserve a weapon that might, someday under the right circumstances, serve Aryan interests. When I finished my account, I
could see that the prince was considering what I had said. He
asked what the status of the chemical equipment was today. I
told him the truth. The equipment, I said, was stored to survive
the passage of time and the cavern served to keep out the elements. Although Sarin degrades with time, the same is not true
of the equipment needed to produce it. I told him that, in my professional opinion, the equipment secreted away remains fully
operable and, in the right hands, could produce the portable devices that we successfully tested so long ago at Dyernfurth-am-
Oder.

The prince followed up with another question. He wanted to
know whether I still recalled the location of the cave where the

items are cached. I told him that the place is indelibly etched in my brain. It was odd, I must say, sitting in Riyadh, eating stuffed dates with this Saudi noble and revisiting things from long ago. The prince had a servant bring me a tall glass of Coca-Cola before excusing himself, noting that he had family business to attend to. As we shook hands, he said that he expected I would hear from him again. I count the prince a good contact who might be of utility in facilitating chemical transactions in the future. He is of commercial value in this strange, alien culture where personal connections count for so much.

Hirter dropped the sheets of paper on Waldbaer's desk. "Relevant?" he asked of the detective.

"I believe so, Herr Hirter. It sounds like the genesis of the terror act we're trying to stop lies in that conversation in Riyadh. This chat with a Saudi prince is the bridge between wartime events and today. It sounds as if Kaltenberg had lost interest in the chemical equipment until the prince inquired. If the inquisitive prince hadn't pursued the issue of Kaltenberg's wartime service, that Sarin equipment might still be holed up in the mountain cave today."

"Of course," Chalmers cautioned softly, "we still don't know how the Nazi production gear eventually got into the hands of al-Assad, do we?"

"True" Waldbaer replied. "Why don't you recite a bit more for your devoted readership, Herr Hirter?"

Hirter picked up the paper and scanned down a page. "The story is interrupted. The next entry, Kaltenberg is back in Germany; there's a discussion of purchasing raw material from a company in Hamburg. The entry after that describes a birthday party for his wife's brother in Munich."

Displaying a slight grimace, Hirter flipped through several pages. Waldbaer consumed the last bit of his croissant and guiltily wished that he had another.

"Here we go," Hirter said at last. "This entry is a few months later. Let's each read through it at our own pace." He provided his companions the page number, fell back into his chair and silently took in the words of what he regarded as

The German Businessman's Tale

I can now recount that an unexpected phone call I took at home in Freilassing last week has changed my life. I record it here for posterity to judge in some unseen future. Other than this account, the events of recent days are unrecorded. I will not share these developments even with my beloved wife; it could do her no good, and possibly cause her harm. But now to the phone call and the events that followed.

I was enjoying a fine, dry Austrian Gruener Veltliner white wine at seven in the evening when the phone rang out its shrill signal. I was confronted with a voice unknown to me.

"You are Mister Bergdorfer?" a heavily accented, bass voice inquired in English. I responded in the same tongue that I was indeed Bergdorfer and asked the identity of the caller.

"I'm a friend of the prince who hosted you a while ago," the deep voice replied. This introduction struck me as curious. I asked how I might be of service, hoping another sale was in the offing.

"I would like you to show me something. Something you mentioned to the prince; items of interest."

It took me a moment to understand that the caller was referring to the equipment that I had cached at war's end. The caller was speaking in a deliberately vague manner, as if the conversation might be overheard. How conspiratorial, I thought, but found myself responding yes, I could show the way to what I called "the goods."

"That's fine," the man said.

There was a pause in the conversation, and I asked why he wanted to see such old items.

"We can talk when we are together," the caller responded abruptly, a trace of annoyance coloring his voice.

The rest of the decidedly odd conversation was a matter of logistics. He would take a train to Freilassing; he provided a precise arrival time, indicating that he had consulted a schedule. Would I pick him up at the station? Yes, I replied, despite a certain discomfort. I described how I looked, so the stranger would recognize me. He stopped me in mid-sentence. "I know your appearance. The prince has well described you."

The meeting arrangement established, the caller hung up. As I returned to my wine and considered the call, I half-decided to ignore the appointment. I did not want to revisit the cave as it meant revisiting a past best left to slumber. A moment later I swept my doubts aside and concluded that an appointment made is an appointment kept. If the excursion satisfied the prince's curiosity, I might be rewarded with another pharmaceutical sale.

The next day broke wet and gray, laced with a cutting, damp April breeze. The snows were gone, but spring seemed hesitant to emerge in earnest, as if fearful it might be struck down by a resurgent Father Winter. I drove the short distance to the Freilassing train station, a prosaic structure that managed to seem run-down even after a fresh painting.

I entered the building and consulted the large clock in the lobby. It was as I was standing there that the caller's voice rumbled directly behind me. "Good morning, Mister Bergdorfer, good to see you." I turned to see a tall man with olive skin and a mane of thick hair, as jet black as the beard beneath. The foreigner had large brown eyes that dominated his face. His demeanor was serious, and I sensed that I was looking at an individual who did not routinely smile. He wore a waist-length black leather jacket and American jeans.

"Prince Hafiz conveys his regards," the man said.

Even after these initial words, I was a bit shocked to have

him standing there unexpectedly. "Your train arrived early?" I asked, confused.

"No, I took an earlier train."

"But, presuming you've come from Munich, that means you've been waiting here an hour. You should have called; I would have come earlier."

The stranger shrugged his broad shoulders. "It's of no importance." Only later did it occur to me that the prince's friend had intended all along to precede my arrival, to observe me and ensure that I arrived alone. I had been under surveillance by this mysterious visitor.

We chatted a bit in the bare station hall, in a stilted way, before I suggested that we start our journey. "It will take time," I noted, "not the drive but the walk that follows." The visitor nodded, pointed to the pair of expensive walking boots he was wearing and said, "I am prepared."

It occurred to me that I still did not know the name of the prince's friend, and I inquired as to how he would like to be addressed. His brow wrinkled for a second. "Call me Rashid," he replied. I suspected that Rashid was not his real name.

We drove from the train station, out of Freilassing, and into the countryside. I made a foray into small talk, but this proved unsuccessful, so I concentrated on driving the winding country road lined with linden trees. We headed toward Traunstein and the mass of the mountains beyond, majestically purple in the distance.

"When did you last visit the cave?" Rashid asked at one point, puncturing the prevailing silence.

"Long ago," I responded. "A decade or longer. Why should I return? The equipment is a footnote to history, an unacknowledged legacy. After the war was long over, I returned to the cavern once; nostalgia, I suppose. The place was undisturbed. The cave entrance was still concealed with forest debris, and large bushes had grown there in the intervening years, offering more cover still. Everything was as it had been. The crates were still sealed. I just gave the place a cursory look. Curiosity satisfied, I walked away and never ventured there again. Until today."

"Until today," Rashid repeated, and then returned to silence. Still, his question caused me to raise a query as well.

"Rashid, why is the prince interested in this matter? It's a vestige of the past. Dispatching you here to see old stuff from the war is a considerable effort."

Rashid did not reply for a moment, and I entertained the feeling that he did not like the question. He answered just when I thought he would ignore the query altogether. "The prince is avidly interested in history, it provides him enjoyment. Due to business obligations, he often cannot travel himself. I am his surrogate. I take pictures and give him written accounts that he enjoys reading. I don't mind this, it is my job."

"I see," I replied, apparently not convincing in my tone.

Rashid sighed, glanced out of the side window at the passing meadows, and continued. "I know you find it strange. I think the word in English is 'eccentric,' isn't it? Very well. Let's say that the prince is eccentric. That is his way. But he is a just master, and I try to fulfill his wishes without complaint." His gaze returned to the windshield, and he again became a cipher.

We continued the journey in pristine silence, until I parked the Mercedes by the side of a narrow country road in the valley beneath the precipice that we would be climbing.

My climbing days are behind me. I am still fit, but the ascent from the valley was trying. At first the climb was gradual, on a seldom trodden trace through abandoned meadows. The grade of ascent changed markedly once these open spaces were behind us. The way through the forest was steep, and my heart pounded from the exertion. My companion, as silent now as during the ride, did not appear to suffer from the exercise. We continued our ascent into mid-afternoon. The forest was thick with growth and the ground a tangle of fallen branches, forcing us to pick our way with caution. "I know where we are," I said to Rashid at one point, "it's not far."

He nodded his dark head at my words.

And then, shortly after the terrain leveled, we were at the entrance to the cavern. An eruption of dolomite stone rising from the soil formed a massive wall in front of us. With effort, I brushed aside some stubborn clinging vines, revealing the yawning entrance to the cave. Taking a flashlight from my pocket, we moved into the darkness. We proceeded gingerly, visibility imperfect in the play of moving light and shadow. After a few minutes maneuvering along the uneven walls of the cavern, we entered a large natural chamber, formed in prehistory. The flashlight played across the expanse. The pale beam illuminated stacks of wooden crates, coated with dust, but otherwise looking no different than they had in 1945. I could make out the stenciled cautions emblazoned on the crates. *Achtung! Vorsicht!* Attention! Be careful!

There was a flash and I recoiled, wartime training taking over. I recognized in a second that the flash was only Rashid taking a photograph. He held an expensive-looking camera in his hands and took a sequence of shots, the flash engaging with each advance of the film. He glanced at me for a moment, simply explaining, "For the prince."

He was finished in minutes and ran a hand over his beard, staring at the crates. "Are you sure these have not been disturbed? Are all of them here?"

The question struck me as odd. "This is everything." Nothing has been touched. I'm sure of it."

"I want to make certain," he announced. Before I could react, Rashid slipped a mean-looking knife from his leather jacket, bounded to one of the crates, and urged the blade between two wooden slates. There was a creak of resistance and the boards separated, revealing gray packing paper beneath. Rashid pushed this aside.

"What are you doing?" I asked with some alarm, unsure as to Rashid's intentions.

"Inspecting the goods, as the prince instructed," he said.

"Inspecting for what?"

Rashid busied himself widening the opening into the crate, carefully removing paper from the interior. "I want to make sure that the equipment is here. I need to be certain that it seems functional." It was in this moment evident to me that Rashid's — or the prince's — interests went beyond historical curiosity.

Rashid's hands revealed a gleaming metal surface. It looked to me to be one of the component chemical storage tanks. Then came another surprise.

"Is this nickel or silver lined?" Rashid asked me as his hands stroked the surface of the vessel. It was apparent that Rashid was no simple servant. He knew something about the anti-corrosive requirements of Sarin production equipment.

"Silver lining," I heard myself reply.

"Good," Rashid said. "Nothing seems damaged. No corrosion. Excellent." He replaced the slats as best he could.

It was now all clear to me. History did not concern Rashid or his prince. Their interests were in the present. Rashid had uncovered some lined tubing and was nodding approvingly at its condition.

"Rashid, I can see that you know what you're looking at. I've gone to some effort to take you here, which reflects the trust I've placed in you and the prince. I expect you'll speak frankly to me." I was aware that I was taking a chance. After all, Rashid was thirty years younger than I and in excellent condition. He was also wielding a knife and we were alone in a remote cavern. Rashid placed the knife on top of the crate, pushed his hands into his jacket, and stared at me.

"Mister Bergdorfer, you're right; I should be honest with you. But there had to be precautions. The prince is interested in history but more interested in political events, especially in the

Middle East, where we face a determined Zionist enemy. Israel has crushed Arab people underfoot and we need to level the playing field. Upon meeting you, the prince believed he had found a sympathetic soul who could help us in our defensive requirements. Do I make myself clear?"

He had made himself abundantly clear. "Yes, Rashid. The prince wants to remove this equipment to the Middle East to employ against the Israelis, right? You want to make sure that this isn't just corroded junk. Your inspection also ensures that I'm no charlatan. I understand."

"Good," he said, raising his thick eyebrows. "It's easier this way. When you left the Kingdom, the prince made inquiries. Through some sources we were able to determine your former identity. You were previously called Kaltenberg, Mister Bergdorfer, if I am not mistaken. We also confirmed your accomplishments with the SS and in chemistry. This made the prince increasingly interested in the story about the equipment. I am an employee of the prince, as I told you, but my profession, like yours, is chemistry. He selected me for this assignment to determine if the equipment remains functional."

"You want to bring these crates to Saudi Arabia and produce stocks of Sarin to use against Israel?"

"Things aren't that simple. We want the equipment, true. If we can ship it back to the Kingdom with no one knowing, fine. But that will require great care. If the European authorities ever found out, they would halt the shipment. As for attacking the Israelis, I don't know about that. I don't involve myself with politics."

"You realize that this equipment is not your property. It doesn't belong to you."

Rashid smiled coldly with a display of teeth; I thought of a shark. "You're right. The equipment is not ours. It is also not yours. It belongs to the former German government. Possibly the present German government constitutes the new legal owner, but I am, I fear, no lawyer. What to do? The prince has suggested the basis for an understanding, if you would care to hear it."

"Please continue," I said, curious as to what proposition would be forthcoming.

Rashid began walking the confines of the chamber, illuminated in the beam of the flashlight. "It's simple and reasonable. The prince is prepared to regard you as the rightful owner of the equipment. He would like to obtain it from you without fuss. The prince is willing to pay you for the equipment and for your surrendering all interest in it."

"Sounds reasonable so far," I replied, truthfully.

"Good. As for the compensation, the prince has given this much thought".

I waited, saying nothing, one hand on my walking stick and the other holding the flashlight.

"There is, of course, the simplest way — paying you an amount of money for the goods. That might not be wise, however, under the circumstances. A bank transfer to your account can be traced. Cash is also not optimal, especially if you were caught with undeclared income by the tax authorities. The prince proposes another possibility. He is aware that you own a portion of the firm you work for. The prince is prepared to use his influence in the Middle East to guarantee you sales there. You win commissions from your firm, stock value increases, and profits will be considerable. All will appear normal business. The prince is prepared to be generous. He can guarantee you sales of ten million marks annually for the next five years. I ask you to calculate your personal gain from such an arrangement."

"It's certainly an interesting proposition," I commented, not yet wanting to signal my willingness to accept the offer.

"There is one other thing," Rashid said at length. "You are proud of your race from Berlin, understandably so. But what did you accomplish? Those who were supposed to employ the equipment later never materialized. The mission was incomplete. Unfinished. You must feel that yourself. What Prince Hafiz offers you is fulfillment. The fruits of your labor will be turned over to those who appreciate your sacrifices. For a man like you, that should mean more than money. More than this I cannot offer you.

It was enough, of course. I heard his words like an epiphany. It occurred to me that I had been carrying emptiness with me all these years. Now I felt that burden lifting. I was delivering the equipment into the hands of history. I told Rashid that I accepted his offer. This entry is the only record I leave of this momentous transaction, the consequences of which, I expect, the world will one day learn.

Hirter replaced the papers on the desktop.

"We have our link," Waldbaer said.

"Most of it," agreed Hirter. "Kaltenberg passed nerve gas equipment to some anti-Semitic Arabs in exchange for money and his need to have a place in history. I'll ask my people to trace Prince Hafiz. He has to be the final figure leading to al-Assad."

"Fine," Waldbaer noted. "Now, let's go to Munich. I'm supposed to brief the Bavarian security coordinator on where we stand."

Chapter 52

Sayyid kept his eyes to the sidewalk as much as possible, not only to preserve his anonymity, but to avoid having to glance at the garish array of strip joints and pornographic video stores lining the streets near the Munich main train station. It had rained all day, and the wet evening pavement reflected the gaudy flashing lights advertising their carnal wares. It was Sayyid's turn to purchase food and bring it to his comrades in the hotel. He welcomed the opportunity to break up the suffocating boredom of sitting for hours in his room, long stretches of time interspersed only with briefer stays in the hotel coffee shop. He rejoiced in the fresh air, even if it was city air, its purity sullied, defiled even, by the readily discernable scent of hops emanating from the vents of the city's several breweries.

He had one stop to make before ordering kebab at the little Turkish carry-out. The stop was unauthorized, the one act that he had to conceal from his comrades. It is not a bad thing I am doing, Sayyid told himself, even though the others would not approve. It was just that Fatima, his wife, was so young and their parting had been so abrupt and final. He needed to assure her, to let her know one last time that all was well with him, so that she would understand later, after he had become *shahid*. Sayyid felt great affection for his wife and intended to include her in his company of the elect in paradise, along with the harem of dark-eyed virgins. It was a private matter, a last settling of his affairs.

What harm could a single phone call do? He made his way to a yellow telephone booth, entered its cramped space, and pulled the heavy metal-and-glass door shut behind him, dampening the traffic noise from the street. He slipped three euros into the stainless steel slot and dialed a familiar series of numbers.

Chapter 53

The wind picked up speed over the North Atlantic, turning the vast grey expanse of water into angry whitecaps. The waves were driven mercilessly toward the English coast, ultimately slamming with a hollow roar into the churning gravel at Dover beach. The wind did not stop at the water's edge but swept over grassy meadows and country lanes, urging pedestrians deeper into their rain macs. The gusts blasted over rolling countryside, punching the last, intransigent autumn leaves from surrendering branches. Eventually, the stream of air slammed into the Yorkshire region and clawed at the array of parabolic satellite dishes covering the verdant landscape of Malton Meadows Base, a sprawling communications monitoring facility jointly operated by the United States and a British counterpart, GCHQ — Government Communications Headquarters.

The field of antenna dishes in the Yorkshire countryside pulled in information from a series of high-range satellites concealed in the heavens above. The satellites picked up voice and data transmissions from several countries, including telephone calls. Some calls were intercepted due to the presence of key words, such as "Al-Qaeda" or "Shahid."

A number of antenna dishes were concealed within radomes: large white spherical units that looked like giant golf balls deposited on the terrain. It was one of these dishes with a diameter of over a hundred feet facing due east that down-linked telephone intercept data from Germany, despite the howling interference of the storm.

Spencer Pryce-Ashton, the lean GCHQ official in charge of the evening shift, walked the long corridor of Building 122 with a distinct military gait, carrying a yellow folder and a reel of audio tape. Even through the concrete walls of the bunker-like structure he could hear the ill-tempered assault of the wind. He smiled to himself, reflecting that he loved a good storm, a view common to inhabitants of the British Isles. He located the office he was looking for, and entered the open door past the nameplate that marked it as belonging to Mr. George Cienfuegos, U.S. Inter-Strategic Communications Bureau (ISCB).

Cienfuegos, a squat and broad middle-aged man, looked up from his word processor at his British colleague. He yawned into a pudgy hand and his features settled into a pleasant smile. "Spencer, what can I do for you on such a crappy night?"

The GCHQ officer smiled in return. "Don't disparage the weather, George, nothing to be done about it. If you'd bother to take a stroll outside you'd find it invigorating, I expect. Sadly, it's not the joys of Yorkshire weather that bring me here."

"To what do I owe the honor?" Cienfuegos asked, his voice taking on a more professional tone as he settled into his swivel chair.

"It's those telephone numbers in Germany that your Maryland betters alerted us to last week. We've had no hits to date, as you know. All the phone activity on those numbers has been entirely mundane. Until now."

Cienfuegos leaned forward, hands entwined on the government-issue desk in front of him. "Okay, Spencer, don't be a tease. What's up?"

"Quite. Well, it appears there was a phone call from a chap who seems to have been speaking to his wife. The caller referred to a 'holy mission' of some sort that he must fulfill. The female implores him to return home. The caller relates that she'll be proud of him 'once we have struck.' There's a bit more in this vein, the woman finally seems to accept that the chap isn't coming back, there's an exchange of 'Allah akhbar,' and he rings off. I imagine that your friends Stateside will want to give a listen."

Pryce-Ashton deposited the folder and reel of tape into Cienfuegos's hands. "Tape of the original conversation. I thought you might want to alert your bureau yourself to ensure this gets the proper attention. That should do it, George; I expect I can leave you to your business."

"Don't worry, Spencer, I'll send a cable to the fort and let them do their thing. By the way, where did this guy call from?"

"Munich. From a public phone, as one might expect."

Outside Building 122 the wind picked up as the storm rushed over the Yorkshire hills. Hundreds of miles away in Munich, Sayyid had returned to his charmless spaces in the Rote Adler Hotel after delivering warm Doener kebab to his comrades. He looked into the mirror above the stained sink and rubbed a hand over his beardless face. At least, he comforted himself, Fatima understood why he had vanished, and she would honor his martyr's death. Other than fulfilling the mission by unleashing the contents of the canister, there was nothing left to be done.

Chapter 54

"Munich is the source of the call," Caroline said, reading the transcript that had been forwarded to CIA from the ISCB.

Warren Stockbridge sat stern faced and attentive across the table from her. "Munich," he repeated.

"That's interesting," Caroline continued. "Munich isn't far from Rosenheim. Sixty miles or so. I'm surprised that al-Assad and company didn't put more geography between their new lair and the warehouse where they produced the Sarin. My guess was that they headed for Berlin, it's the capital and Germany's largest city. That struck me as the optimal place to conduct a terrorist attack. I was wrong."

Stockbridge smiled briefly. "Your logic is good. Berlin makes sense from a targeting perspective. Still, Munich is big enough. This intercept is watertight. The phone call was made to this Fatima, the wife of one of al-Assad's accomplices, Sayyid. The content refers to a pending suicide attack that Sayyid will be a part of. Most importantly, this call originated from a public phone in downtown Munich. Now for some supposition. I can't imagine that al-Assad or any terrorist employing good security would have sanctioned this call. I expect that Sayyid did it without authorization, which means that we got lucky. The Germans need to pull out all the stops in scouring Munich for this group."

Caroline nodded. "I'll place a secure call to Robert Hirter. He can pass the info to his police kommissar, and they can hit the Munich streets running."

Stockbridge adjusted his burgundy wool tie. "Caroline, it's not quite that easy, I'm afraid."

She stared at him blankly, awaiting clarification. "Here's our problem. The intercept people have declined permission for us to pass the communications intercept information to the Germans."

Caroline raised her eyebrows and slammed the palms of her hands audibly on the tabletop. "What? Have they gone crazy? This is a terrorism case for God's sake, it's actionable intelligence."

Stockbridge could not suppress a smile at the fervent display. He raised his long frame from the chair and strolled the beige carpeting of his office. "Stay cool, Caroline. Look at it from the Strategic Bureau prism. If they give the transcript to the Germans, they automatically make clear their ability to target the German phone network. German authorities would regard our intercept of their domestic communications as illegal and raise holy hell. Because we got the information via the UK, we would also have to get GCHQ to agree to pass the information to the Germans. A tad complicated, right?"

Caroline stood now as well, energized. "Great. Let me get this straight, because of bureaucratic complications we don't tell our people in Bavaria that al-Assad and his gang are in Munich? That's criminal."

Stockbridge clucked disapprovingly. "Caroline, I said stay cool; you are not cool. I didn't say that we would do nothing. What I said was that ISCB won't give the raw information to the Germans because it would compromise their collection method. Fair enough. What we need to do is disguise how the information was acquired, while ensuring that the Germans understand that Munich is the target."

"Oh," Caroline replied, her anger of a moment before dissipating. "That sounds okay in principle, but what do we ask Robert to tell the police?"

"I think we'll use a different messenger for this piece of information. Have Central Travel book you a flight to Munich. You can probably still get one from Dulles this evening. In the meantime, I'll work on a text suitable for passage to the Germans."

"You want me to fly to Germany? I thought you wanted me to honcho this case here? I'm not complaining, mind you."

Stockbridge shrugged his broad shoulders and stared out his office window at the treetops of Langley. "I expect you back soon. Spend a couple of days there. It shows the Germans that we're putting real effort into this case. Plus it lets you get an impression of how professional this kommissar is — or isn't. We need to assess him. If you think this Waldbaer isn't up to the task, let me know, and we can pull strings through our people in Berlin."

Caroline snapped a mock salute. "Will do, boss. Thanks for the vote of confidence."

Stockbridge narrowed his eyes theatrically. "Vote of confidence? Don't leap to conclusions. I want you to gain operational experience, Caroline. Field experience is what permits ops officers to mature. By the way, do you have an alias passport?"

"I do. Tourist passport in the name of Rebecca Skibiski, valid for five years."

"Rebecca Skibiski? Where does Cover Staff get these names?"

"From dead people I think."

Stockbridge uttered a sigh and ushered her to the door. "Use the alias. I don't want to identify you in true name to the Germans. Get your tickets, and I'll send you the liaison text shortly. Bon voyage."

Caroline walked to Central Travel, and booked a business class seat on a direct flight to Munich. Returning to her office, she decided to go through incoming cables one last time. Examining her electronic in-box, she focused on a message from the CIA installation in Riyadh, Saudi Arabia. The first line of text made it clear that the message provided background on Prince Abdullah Abu Hafiz, distantly linked by tribe to the ruling House of Saud and owner of Global Gulf Pharmaceutical Import-Export.

Caroline's eyes drank in the information that her colleagues in Riyadh had obtained through a unilateral Saudi contact. The CIA author of the message noted that the information could be passed to other intelligence services if not attributed to Riyadh. "This should get the attention of Robert and his German buddies."

Chapter 55

It occurred to Robert Hirter that he was spending lots of time meeting CIA employees in airports. Meeting Allen Chalmers at the diminutive and quiet Salzburg airport a few days ago, this morning preparing to greet Caroline in the more cosmopolitan expanse of Munich International, with its two main terminals and maze of levels, shops, and lounges.

Hirter heeded the signs, and made his way to the international arrivals gate. A glance at his wristwatch confirmed that he had ten minutes before the scheduled arrival of Caroline O'Kendell's flight, which had departed the States the previous evening. Hirter reached the arrivals area and found a place to stand. A large electronic board above the gate confirmed that the flight from Dulles had landed and was deplaning. A few minutes later the first passengers issued through the sensor-activated doors and Hirter spotted a slim, short-haired young woman in a stylish turtleneck and jeans.

"Caroline," he announced as she walked into the waiting area.

"No, sorry," the woman replied, the words disrupting his certainty as to her identity. "I'm Rebecca Skibiski. At least for the time that I'm over here. Hi Robert! Thanks for coming to get me." The attractive face flashed a very white smile.

He understood instantly; she was traveling in alias. He returned the smile. "Rebecca, welcome to Germany." He saw that she was pulling a suitcase. "I'll take that. We'll head to my car."

She nodded and let him pull her wheeled piece of luggage. Before he could say more, his visitor lightly placed a small hand conspiratorially on his arm. "Robert, we need to go straight to your detective friend. My hotel will have to wait." She glanced around at the clusters of people moving through the airport. "I guess we should wait until we're in your car. We can talk there."

Robert nodded, understanding a case officer's instinctive caution in conversation.

Caroline relaxed into the contour of the seat as Robert wheeled the VW Passat from the airport road onto the autobahn, heading to Munich. The engine issued a subdued hum as he accelerated, passing several trucks. The sky was cloudy, revealing no clue as to whether it would eventually rain or clear.

"The target is Munich," Caroline said with conviction. "And Munich is where al-Assad and his accomplices are right now."

Robert glanced at her in surprise. "Munich? I would have thought somewhere farther off. How sure are you?"

"Completely sure. Between us, ISCB passed us intercept material yesterday. That's why I'm here. It's time sensitive."

"And I thought it was your desire for schnitzel," Robert deadpanned, eliciting another smile from his passenger.

"That too. Really though, ISCB picked up a telephone call to the wife of one of the cell members. The call originated from a public phone in Munich. The caller is Sayyid Korad, his wife is named Fatima. Ibrahim in Ankara independently identified Sayyid as one of Assad's terrorist companions."

"Damn, Caroline, that information's exactly what we need. We can concentrate police resources in Munich. Waldbaer will love you."

"Well, things aren't that simple. I can tell *you* the truth about the source of the information, but we aren't authorized to tell the Germans about our intercept capability. The important thing is that we can alert them to Munich as the target for the attack."

Robert took in the information while concentrating on the fast-moving autobahn traffic around him. Robert pulled the VW into the right lane to let a red Porsche tear by.

"Okay," he replied. "I understand ISCB sensitivities; I've had to deal with it before. As long as we can let Waldbaer know the facts, we don't have a problem."

"There's more," the young woman added. "The transcript of the phone call makes it clear that Sayyid expects to be a martyr. That's why he called his wife. These guys are planning a suicide attack."

Robert exhaled. "That's not good news. You know — Caroline, I mean Rebecca — suicide attacks are hard to stop. They also have a high success rate. Any word on when the attack is supposed to happen?"

Caroline moved her head from side to side. "Nope, no date. But soon, that's clear from the way Sayyid spoke to his wife. He expects to die soon."

Hirter removed a cell phone from his shirt pocket and punched in a number. Waldbaer's voice answered. Hirter had earlier advised the detective that another CIA officer would be arriving, and Waldbaer had remarked that Langley seemed to be emptying out at the moment. "We need to meet immediately, Kommissar, there are new developments."

"Good news I hope," Waldbaer commented. "Let's meet in the Munich City Hall. I've been briefing some officials and they've given me a temporary office. Contact Chalmers and meet me in city hall, room 217. *Auf wiederhoeren.*" The detective rang off.

Hirter entered another number into the cell phone, contacted Allen Chalmers, and instructed him to get to the meeting place. As he did so, the automobile passed a yellow sign that announced the Munich city limits. In the distance, rising above the urban mass, the dark brick, twin onion-domed towers of the Munich cathedral loomed somberly in the diffused light.

The Munich City Hall seemed an improbable structure to host the pursuits of municipal administration. It looked like something transported to the city from Disneyland. The building was a massive construct of stone with an oversized central sally port leading to a cobblestone inner courtyard. The city hall was surmounted by high gables and faux-medieval crenellated towers. The tower high above the main gate had an opening in the façade revealing life-size carvings of brightly colored knights on horseback. At assigned times during the day, a mechanical device coaxed the knights into motion, accompanied by the peal of bells. Tourists gathered in Saint Mary's Square in front of the city hall to gape at these proceedings. Munich residents did their best to ignore them.

The interior of the building was more prosaic. Waldbaer had been given a musty and neglected-looking office to conduct his briefings of Bavarian officials. The detective now used the space to host Hirter, Chalmers, and the newly arrived woman who introduced herself as Rebecca Skibiski. Waldbaer held the memo the woman had given him. He read the English-language text. "So," Waldbaer said slowly, considering the paper in his hand, "you have a confidential human source who saw Sayyid Korad in Munich recently. Your source overheard Korad say that he intends to conduct a suicide attack here in the city. Remarkable. Your confidential informant is unfortunately no longer in the area and can't provide any further details. We can now concentrate our resources on Munich."

Waldbaer folded the piece of paper into a neat square and placed it in his loden jacket pocket. He walked the few steps to a dust-streaked window overlooking Saint Mary's plaza below. "Thanks for the information, Frau Skibiski."

"It's a sign of our cooperation, Kommissar. We want to stop an attack as much as you do. If we can help, we will." Caroline was seated on a long couch also occupied by Hirter. Chalmers was slumped into an upholstered chair opposite them.

Waldbaer continued to stare through the yellowed glass in front of him. "This is critical information, and I sincerely appreciate it, even though you haven't told the truth about how you acquired it."

The comment elicited silence for several moments. "Excuse me?" Caroline said softly at length.

"We needn't waste time on games. I understand that you've done what you have to do. There is no mysterious human agent, of course.

You don't really expect me to believe that you have someone in your pay who just happened to be wandering around Munich and also just happened to run into this Sayyid, who he just happens to know from somewhere in the past, do you?" Waldbaer laughed good-humoredly. He turned from the window to face his guests. "I understand your motives. I may be a Bavarian small-town detective, but I'm not as provincial as you might think. No, the information you've given me is from an intercepted telephone call."

Caroline looked at Waldbaer open-mouthed and searched for a riposte. The detective smiled at her. "The content of your memo is exactly the type of information one gets from a phone conversation. Sayyid called out from Munich, probably to his wife, right? He told her that he wouldn't be coming back, thus your notation on a suicide attack. That was stupid of him. I expect that his terrorist friends are unaware of what he's done. No matter, I'm glad you people monitored the call. Under German law I don't have the legal grounds to tap the phones of the 'suspected terrorists' relatives. This information is of great assistance and I understand your desire not to reveal your capabilities against German phones."

Caroline finally found her voice. "Kommissar, I appreciate your opinion, but you need to understand that I'm only authorized to pass you this memo."

Waldbaer retained his good humor and plunged his hands into his corduroy trouser pockets, rocking on his heels. "Of course, Frau Skibiski. We needn't speak of this again. What is important is Munich, that we concentrate our search here, not the entire Federal Republic. These guys aren't hiding out in high-income suburbs like Nymphenburg or Gruenwald. More than likely they're lying low in some multicultural, low-income area. Something near the East Train Station or the Main Train Station maybe. We have their photos, and we can sweep the area. It's convenient that we're already in Munich. This office just became our command post."

It was Hirter's turn to speak. "Kommissar, if you have the police bracket those parts of town, aren't the terrorists going to know we've tracked them to Munich? It could accelerate their attack plans."

Waldbaer dismissed the concern with a shake of his head. "Don't worry about that. We'll use plainclothes police for this job. We have photos, and should be able to ferret them out." A puzzled look gradually seeped into Waldbaer's features. "You know, Hirter, the attack is the puzzling part, now that you mention it. Why haven't they hit yet? What are they waiting for?" Waldbaer became animated and paced the room, old floorboards creaking beneath his heavy gait. "Think about it. What are they waiting for? Something doesn't add up. Al-Assad has the Sarin. Its ready to use and he knows it. What's more, from what Chalmers here says, the longer he waits the more likely the Sarin degrades in potency. Right?"

"That's correct, Kommissar," Chalmers answered.

"All right. We know that Munich is the target. Al-Assad is here, has been for a couple of days, but still no attack. Why? Another point: al-Assad and his team evacuated Rosenheim because they figured out we're searching for them. Another reason not to delay and risk detection before they can strike. Your people in Ankara called al-Assad on his cell phone and panicked him further, not well-advised in my opinion, but done is done. All of the evidence screams at us with one message — al-Assad should have already launched his attack. But he hasn't. The big question, ladies and gentlemen, is why not?"

Chalmers spoke up. "I agree. From a technical point of view, there's no reason to wait. They have a nerve agent and a dispersion device. They're in the target area. If I were al-Assad, I would have attacked by now."

Hirter snapped his fingers. "They haven't attacked because they're waiting for something. Maybe some anniversary date. You know, like blowing something up on eleven September. That would explain why they haven't hit yet. We know the strike is supposed to come soon. I can check with our terrorism experts to try to figure out what date might have significance."

Caroline took up a position in the center of the room between Waldbaer and Hirter. "Robert, I understand your point, but the fact is Islamist terrorists don't usually wait for anniversary dates. Once they're convinced that an attack plan is ready, they strike. They're decisive. Al-Qaeda tactical manuals captured in Afghanistan make that clear. Al-Assad is waiting on something. But not a date, I'm sure of it. There's some other reason, but I don't have a clue what it could be." She crossed her arms and looked up at the ceiling.

"Not a date," Waldbaer said. "But what then? If they're not waiting on a date maybe they're waiting on an event. Like the suicide bombing in Pakistan the other year against Bhutto during a campaign parade? Something like that? Or a major political meeting in Munich?"

"That makes sense," Caroline allowed. "Is there an international summit scheduled for Munich soon?"

Waldbaer frowned and shook his head with palpable frustration. "Not that I know of; certainly nothing imminent. I'm not aware of a pending state visit, like the queen or someone of importance. I expect that state visits and political gatherings aren't scheduled until after Oktoberfest. Otherwise, there's too much congestion, and too little attention given to politics."

Waldbaer had barely concluded his remark, when he felt queasiness spread in his stomach. "God, that's it. Oktoberfest! That's why they're in Munich. Why didn't we see it before? Oktoberfest begins Saturday. Today is Thursday. I bet they plan to hit it on opening day, no need to delay past that. Oktoberfest."

Hirter's eyes widened. "Oktoberfest? Why would anyone attack a beer festival for God's sake, what kind of targeting is that?"

"A host of reasons," Waldbaer whispered. "Masses of people in a concentrated place. The Oktoberfest is the largest fair in the world. An international crowd — not just Germans, but Americans, Australians, Japanese, British, people from everywhere. You want to hit an international target for global impact? Hit the Oktoberfest! People from all walks of life — professionals, workers, students, tourists, celebrities, off-duty soldiers. An exquisite target. Damn it, I should have seen this earlier."

Chalmers spoke, his voice controlled. "A question, if I may. I'm unfamiliar with Oktoberfest. Is it held in an open-air stadium? If so, we might be in luck. That's not the optimal environment for a nerve agent attack."

Waldbaer's eyes bored into the chemist's. "No, Herr Chalmers. The Oktoberfest is not held in a stadium. It's held on a field in the center of Munich not far from here. A series of giant tents are erected on this field. The festivities take place inside these tents."

"How large are the tents?" Chalmers queried.

"Each one holds thousands of people. They're full to capacity day and night. There must be six or seven main tents run by the Munich breweries lined up on a pedestrian boulevard. If I have my facts right, during its two week run last year's Oktoberfest attracted about six million visitors."

Chalmers looked somberly at the others. "Tents. That doesn't sound good. Tents could be a really fine environment for employing Sarin. A confined space is what Sarin requires to be effective. And if this confined space is packed with people, the lethality count is bound to be very high. Tell me, are the tents air-conditioned? Do they try to keep them cool?"

"There isn't air-conditioning at the Oktoberfest." Waldbaer clarified. "The tents can get pretty humid and warm from all of those partying, swaying, yelling, and singing bodies. Uncomfortably warm sometimes."

"That is unwelcome news," Chalmers said. "Humidity and dampness can work against Sarin dispersion, to be sure. But enough heat, a high enough temperature, counteracts the humidity. If the Oktoberfest is the target, it sounds to me like al-Assad knows what he's doing. If he succeeds in unleashing high-concentration Sarin in one of those tents, we could see mass casualties."

"Allen," Caroline interjected, "what makes you think they want to attack just one tent? If they have multiple canisters, I imagine they'll try to target several tents, to achieve maximum effect and panic."

"Agreed," Waldbaer added tersely. "You can continue discussing this, but I have things to do. I have to arrange for undercover police sweeps downtown. I have to alert the authorities to the target. This information is going all the way to the Chancellery in Berlin. And I'm still waiting on a decision on a shoot-first policy."

"A shoot-first policy?" Caroline inquired.

Waldbaer moved toward the door. "Under German law, Frau Skibiski, an armed police officer is obliged to first instruct a suspect to surrender or face being shot. Under the circumstances that might give enough time for one of these guys to set off a device. When we find these people, we need to take them down, immediately. That requires a legal decision. The administrative wheels are moving at my request, but I don't have approval yet."

There's something else you might need to consider, Kommissar," Chalmers said. "What if the Sarin is deployed, despite our best efforts? What's the plan? There is an antidote to Sarin, and it can be effective if administered in time. You might want to find out if the German armed forces possess stockpiles of atropine, Mark One injectors, that sort of thing. Depending on the circumstances of the attack, having those items on site could save lives."

"I understand that Berlin is working that angle already, Herr Chalmers, and I'll check on progress. Anything else I need to know before I go?"

"Actually, there is one last piece of information," Caroline replied. "Just to close the loop on how al-Assad got his hands on the production equipment. My organization checked into this Saudi prince Hafiz who arranged for his flunky Rashid to locate the equipment with Kaltenberg. As it turns out, Prince Hafiz had a track record of clandestine contact with al-Qaeda and Salafist groups, including the Taliban in Afghanistan. Hafiz covertly funded their activities from his businesses. According to our information, Hafiz was always urging his terrorist contacts to harness weapons technology. Kaltenberg's cache was exactly what he'd been looking for, and he clearly arranged to pass it to a terrorist cell."

"That ties up the chain of acquisition for the Sarin," Hirter commented.

Waldbaer placed a hand on the unpolished bronze doorknob and opened the office door a crack. "Frau Skibiski, you spoke of Prince Hafiz in the past tense. Why?"

Caroline fixed the detective with her bright, penetrating eyes. "I spoke of Hafiz in the past tense because he is past tense. Hafiz and three accomplices were killed by an explosion two years ago in the Yemeni desert. The press claims that the prince and his friends were struck by a Hellfire missile launched from a CIA Predator drone aircraft. But I wouldn't know anything about that."

"Of course not," Waldbaer smiled, disappearing into the long, linoleum-floored corridor of the city hall.

Chapter 56

Coffee cups and bottles of mineral water littered the long ebony table in the Crisis Group room of the Reichstag. Dr. Volker Rapp was unhappy with the information he was receiving from his eleven colleagues. A palpable tension held the room in its grip.

Rapp glanced at his wristwatch. "We've spent two hours trying to determine what's available in Germany to counter a Sarin attack at the Munich Oktoberfest. As far as I can figure from the conversation, we have crap for information."

Frau Schmeider, sitting beside Rapp, looked pained.

"Well," Rapp continued, "that won't do. Let's look at what we have. The *Bundeswehr* doesn't know how much atropine it has on hand. It has some in storage, but some percentage of the atropine might be beyond its effective shelf life. Additionally, some of the nerve agent antidote is on German soil, but held in NATO facilities, and the procedures for transferring the stuff to German authorities are hardly clear. Wonderful! Can uniformed military medics from the *Bundeswehr* be sent to Munich to administer the atropine? It would appear not, because that would transgress restrictions on domestic deployment of the armed forces. This means that we have to get the lawyers involved before we can involve the military. Which will, of course, take time, which is precisely what we don't have. As you are aware, I have to brief the chancellor today, and it's going to be damned hard to claim that we have an efficient response structure in place to handle an attack."

Rapp turned his attention to the huddled, red-smocked form of Frau Schmeider. "Am I being too pessimistic?"

Frau Schmeider, overwhelmed by the situation, had hoped to sit out the dreadful session in silence. Now that Rapp left her no choice but to participate, she shifted uncomfortably in her chair. "I expect that no one here is satisfied with our lack of preparation, Doctor Rapp. We should try to move to Munich whatever antidotes we have available. Given the situation, perhaps we need to do something drastic. Why not call off the Oktoberfest? If the Oktoberfest doesn't open tomorrow, there's no crowd; if there is no crowd there is no target. We should recommend that the Oktoberfest be cancelled." Her green, mascara-outlined eyes surrounded by puffy flesh searched the length of the table for sympathizers.

A representative from the Office for the Protection of the Constitution spoke up. He was a middle-aged man with a close-cropped red beard, and he spoke with a Rheinlander accent. "I don't think that would help. It's too late; this group is ready to strike. If we announce that the Oktoberfest is cancelled, they'll know why and they'll hit a different target. Maybe the train station. Maybe Munich Airport. We could cause them to shift the locus of the attack, but not the fact of the attack."

Rapp drummed his knuckles on the tabletop. "I agree. This plan is too far along for them to abandon. They have Sarin and they plan to use it. The only way to stop them is capture or killing by the police. If we cancel the Oktoberfest, these people might manage to leave Munich and attack a different city altogether — maybe the trade fair coming up in Düsseldorf next week or the economic forum in Hamburg. At least now we know where they plan to hit, and the police can take precautions. No, Frau Schmeider, not a good idea, I'm afraid."

The woman nodded almost imperceptibly and shrunk back in her chair like a deflating red ball.

No one else offered a comment. "All right," Rapp sighed. "I'll advise the chancellor that we'll stage in Munich whatever antidotes we have. We can't recommend stopping the festival or issuing a threat notice. That would only alter the venue of the attack and put us in a less-prepared position. This crisis will be resolved by police action and good intelligence, nothing else. Let's hope to God that this kommissar and the police get lucky."

As the others filtered from the room, Rapp organized his papers and placed them in his attaché case. He was the last to leave the chamber, and mentally started to prepare his briefing for the chancellor. In the Reichstag corridor he looked through the broad glass window at the rooftops of Berlin stretching across the flat landscape. The city was cowed and unanimated under a gray, drizzling cloud. It suited his frame of mind perfectly.

Chapter 57

On Friday morning at seven a.m., a force of four hundred plainclothes policemen began a circumspect sweep of downtown Munich,
concentrating on specific neighborhoods. Some of the law enforcement officers had been brought in from as far afield as Frankfurt and
sworn to secrecy as to the nature of their assignment. Most of the undercover force was male, but there was a smattering of women officers and, where possible, they were paired with a male counterpart
to appear as a "couple" innocuously strolling the streets. Some of the
surveillants roved in unmarked cars and others rode the blue and
white subway trains beneath the city. Most of the force was on foot,
however, and both Waldbaer and Hirter believed that they had the
best chance of spotting their targets on a sidewalk, in a park, or entering or exiting a hotel or other building.

Waldbaer had a battery of police transceivers set up in the city
hall office, and he and his American counterparts, along with four
uniformed Munich police officers, hung on the incoming reports.
The radios crackled regularly with patrols citing their positions and
routes. As the morning grudgingly gave way to afternoon, the most
commonly heard message was a simple "nothing to report."

Surely, Waldbaer reflected, they are out there somewhere.
Al-Assad had a mission to perform and he would do his best to succeed. He intended to die in Munich. Well, I intend for him to die
in Munich, too, Waldbaer thought. Still, he could not dispel a gnaw-
ing frustration as the negative patrol reports accumulated. He entertained a possibility that he would not express: a terrorist change

of plan? Perhaps al-Assad had learned of Sayyid's phone call to Rosenheim and moved to a secondary target.

Hirter listened to the radio reports as well and could see that Waldbaer was restive. He made small talk with Caroline and Chalmers, but found no relief in it. There was too much at stake to seek distractions. "Kommissar," he said at length, "everything is being done that can be done. You have a lot of people out there. If the terrorists are going to hit the Oktoberfest tomorrow, at some point they have to move into the open. It's a physical requirement that they hit the streets. And that's when they'll be vulnerable. I'm optimistic." He tried to sound encouraging, concealing his own uncertainties.

"Hirter, you don't need to cheerlead for me," the detective replied brusquely. "I know how this works. We have good coverage and a good plan. But that's not the same as having these guys dead or in custody. Not the same at all. So, you'll permit me to be less optimistic than you."

Hirter considered the situation for a moment. "I have an idea. Why don't we get out of here for an hour and ride the streets ourselves? We have our cell phones if something develops. It might do us good to take a break."

The detective snorted. "Good for my health or good for my nerves? Whatever. It's a sensible idea Hirter, let's go."

With a brief explanation to the others, they set off for Waldbaer's car parked behind city hall. Ten minutes later they were cruising slowly in heavy traffic near the *Karlstor* plaza, heading toward the *Hauptbahnhof*, the Munich Central Train Station. The two men checked the stream of pedestrians on the sidewalks lining both sides of the bustling street. The district was noisy and not prosperous, with small storefront shops hawking cell phones, jewelery, and electronic appliances of dubious origin, and selections of ethnic foods. The human tapestry passing on the sidewalks included Asian families, clusters of African blacks, Turks, and Middle Eastern Arabs.

"This is the type of area where they're hiding, I can feel it," Waldbaer half-whispered to his companion.

Hirter nodded without taking his eyes off the sidewalk traffic. "Eyes right, Kommissar, there are two of your undercover people, I believe."

The detective glanced as directed and saw two German males in nylon jackets and running shoes, eating pizza slices as they navigated the sidewalk, the appearance of boredom written on their features. The detective chuckled softly. "You're right, Hirter, I recognize them from my briefing. You have a good sense for the business."

"Like I said, Kommissar, when the bad guys move, your chances of seeing them are good."

The ride, the sense of movement, was improving Waldbaer's mood. Hirter had been wise to suggest it. "I suppose we have decent street coverage. You've heard most of this, but let me run through things one more time. First, we received the 'shoot first' permission last night from a special judge. Good. Second, we'll have people at all of the entrances to the Oktoberfest grounds tomorrow. We actually have the place staked out now in case al-Assad tries to pre-position before the official opening. Third, our plainclothesmen have taken over the duties of the private security guys who work the tents. That gives us another tier of coverage. Even if al-Assad and friends get on the Oktoberfest grounds, they still have to make it into the tents. Our people have been instructed to inspect backpacks, which should appear to be a normal security measure. In fact, they'll be looking for canisters that match the mock-up sketch Chalmers provided. If a suspect goes for a canister, we shoot to kill. Something else from Berlin — federal authorities are placing Sarin antidote near the Oktoberfest in case it's needed. The details are shaky, I gather, but at least something is being done. All in all, things could be worse."

"That's solid, Kommissar. As for the American side, Rebecca told me that our technical collection assets have been given this operation as a priority. Chalmers is plugged in with your emergency-response task force. Our hand of cards isn't all that bad."

"You know, Hirter, what these swine are planning isn't just about murder; you know that, don't you?"

Hirter looked over at the detective. "I know that. There's a limit to how many people they can kill, even with Sarin. What they're looking for is panic. Panic that reverberates and gets them publicity. And makes us look weak because we couldn't stop them."

"Right," the detective agreed. "Fear is the key. They want to kill as many people as they can and spread waves of fear to people they can't reach physically. They want to intimidate us with fear. God knows, they've found a good means to do it. My grandfather was a hunter. I remember an old Bavarian saying of his. 'Not the flesh of the prey only, but fear is the sustenance of wolves.' This is our pack of wolves, Hirter. Our pack of wolves."

"And we are baiting their trap, Kommissar," Hirter replied. "Your grandfather would understand that, too."

Waldbaer engaged his left blinker and turned onto Schillerstrasse before reaching the train station, an undistinguished edifice from the 1960s. Schillerstrasse hosted sporadic traffic, making it easier for the men to survey passing pedestrians. Waldbaer noticed a tall, young Nigerian in a bright blue shirt and a disheveled young German engaged in a drug transaction, but drove on. They drove past the nondescript entrance to the Rote Adler Hotel, the brightly lit, empty lobby of which received a passing glance from Hirter. The two men drove on, merging into the urban anonymity of Munich.

Chapter 58

At precisely the moment when the detective and the American drove in the street below, al-Assad had collected his compatriots in the confines of his hotel room. The mission was set for the next day. Al-Assad detected no nervousness from his associates. Only Sayyid seemed more reserved than usual, but al-Assad deemed that natural given the finality of their mission.

"We pay our bills at the front desk in the morning, one by one. We will not prepare for paradise while being indebted to anyone. We fast this evening to prepare ourselves. When we have accomplished our task, my friends, we will feast together with the Rightly-Guided Caliphs, served by the multitude of shy virgins who even now make ready our meal."

Al-Assad moved to the scarred plywood dresser and opened the top drawer. "Brothers, I have a few items, to ensure that we deceive any infidel forces that might be watching for us. We are more prepared than they."

He removed a plastic shopping bag from the drawer; it was emblazoned with the logo of the Schlecker discount drugstore chain. Reaching into the rustling plastic he retrieved two tubes that looked as if they might contain toothpaste. "It is good that we removed our beards. But there is more we can do to blend into the crowds tomorrow. Our hair, brothers. The infidel is looking for black-haired men. These gels are colored. This one is red and the other blond. Streak your hair with it. Trust me, it will make a difference."

Jawad, the shortest and most rotund of the group was hunched against the doorframe and snickered. "We'll look like those crazy ones here in Europe. What are they called? Goths? But it will certainly change our looks. You're right."

Sayyid's features creased into a frown. "Is this how we meet the Prophet? Is this how we will appear in paradise? With our hair painted like polytheist whores? How can we be proud of that? I don't think we should defile our bodies on this jihad. We should conduct our martyrdom proudly, not lower ourselves to the depths of the enemy. I don't want to do it. Shaving the beard I understand, but hair color goes too far. It's not how I want my family to remember me."

Al-Assad measured Sayyid's state of mind and weighed an appropriate response. He knew that he could not afford discontent at this stage. Should he demonstrate his primacy within the group, or would he be better counseled to act with flexibility? He silently implored the Prophet for guidance.

"I understand your sentiments, Sayyid," he spoke at last. "Of course you are uncomfortable. We all are. These are stratagems of war. They are permitted us. But I do not demand that you tint your hair, if you are uncomfortable with it, don't do it."

Sayyid's features lightened and he was clearly relieved. To ensure harmony, al-Assad returned to the dresser and retrieved another item, tossing it across the room at Sayyid, who, surprised, retrieved it clumsily. It was a navy baseball cap bearing the image of a Ferris wheel and a mug of beer. Underneath these icons was embossed the word Oktoberfest in bright orange.

"This should cause you less displeasure than hair dye, Sayyid," al-Assad intoned jovially to break the tension. "It's our alternate solution to have you looking like a happy tourist."

Al-Assad was pleased when the others laughed, including Sayyid. Crisis avoided, he concluded. "All right, friends, back to your rooms. We must prepare ourselves on this final night. Be back here at seven tomorrow morning. I will have some final instructions to ensure our success."

Outside, the teams of police surveillants continued their search for memorized faces and suspicious shadows, but detected nothing.

Chapter 59

An almost physical anticipation of festivity laced the Munich air as the Saturday dawn broke over the city. As night reluctantly withdrew its hand, surrendering its dominion in measured stages, the sky became fragile blue, contrasting with the solid brick towers of the Munich cathedral. Preparations for the Saturday events had been underway for weeks, and the waking inhabitants of the city were well aware of what would transpire. As every year, the opening of Oktoberfest had been heralded loudly and with promiscuous frequency on radio and television. The headlines of the Munich newspapers announced the pending celebration, providing street maps delineating the line of march for the brewery parade.

The parade, by long-established tradition, would wind a route through the narrow metropolitan streets and debouche onto the *Wies'n*, the meadow on which were encamped the long line of enormous beer tents, massive constructions of wood and canvas. The celebratory column of dray horses, flower-bedecked beer wagons, and brass bands would be followed at a short remove by the crowds, all intent on reaching the festival meadow and securing a place to sit and drink the specially brewed, strong and malty Oktoberfest beer.

The meadow was a meadow no more, of course, but a flat, paved plain in the center of the city, a physical pause in the crush of apartment buildings and businesses that constituted Munich in the twenty-first century. It had been a true meadow once, verdant and pastoral. Those days were long gone, however, the first Oktoberfest dating to 12 October 1810. In that year, the august occasion was a wedding celebration for now-forgotten royalty, the marriage of

Crown Prince Ludwig of Bavaria to Princess Theresa of Saxony. To win the acceptance of a suspicious populace for a non-Bavarian bride, the royal family had sponsored a festival and horse race on a pasture located at what were at the time the city limits. The celebration was a happy success and was subsequently repeated on an annual basis, supported by Munich's brewers.

The annual Oktoberfest moved through the centuries with few interruptions. The tents gradually became more capacious, the price of a liter of beer less reasonable, but a Munich time traveler from the nineteenth century would have recognized the Oktoberfest, nonetheless.

As every year, many participants in the revelry chose to shorten the path to the festival grounds by taking the Munich underground trains, the *U-Bahn*. Although the press of celebrants made the subterranean ride uncomfortable, the journey to the *Wies'n* was short and direct. From the underground platform, visitors had only to step onto stainless steel escalators and be lifted to the festivities above, deposited at busy stands selling pretzels, sausage, smoked fish, and souvenirs behind the boulevard of tents bearing the emblems of the Augustiner, Paulaner, Löwenbräu, and other municipal breweries. The sky promised to deliver the crisp, sunny weather that Munich residents associated with the Oktoberfest.

Two blocks from the festival grounds, on a narrow residential street carpeted with burnished bronze leaves, Waldbaer leaned against an unmarked police van. A squad of surveillance team leaders was gathered tightly about him. Hirter was present as well, but to keep the group small and inconspicuous, Caroline O'Kendell and Allen Chalmers had been instructed to join them later in the morning.

"Gentlemen, the chances of finding our targets yesterday was a long shot. Today is the day that counts. Today these guys can't conceal themselves. They have no choice but to move to the *Wies'n*. If we're alert, we'll get them. That's my unshakeable conviction." Waldbaer was conscious that he was sounding more optimistic than he privately felt. "Some of your teams are deployed along the parade route. Schneider, where have you stationed your boys?"

"In front of the Tannenbaum restaurant, Herr Kommissar. They have a perfect view there and can blend in with the onlookers," answered a tall, redheaded undercover officer in a checked shirt and brown lederhosen.

"Good. We cover the route to the festival ground. That said, ladies and gentlemen, I believe our best chance is on the *Wies'n* itself. I've ordered most of the teams to deploy there. I know we have to cope with an enormous number of people storming the place. We have to stay alert, but we can handle it. We have teams at the main entrances to the grounds and scattered along the boulevard in front of the tents. We have a separate cordon of officers at each tent, disguised as crowd control employees. Perfect cover. It gives them a reason to get eyes on everybody who tries to enter a tent and a chance to inspect backpacks. Remember, our targets have to be carrying canisters. Most likely, they'll be carrying backpacks to conceal the devices. Holz, what are the procedures if someone discovers a suspicious canister?"

A short, broad-shouldered officer spoke as if from a memorized text. "Immediately separate the backpack from the owner with force, alert other colleagues nearby, and apprehend the suspect."

Waldbaer nodded agreement. "And if the suspect resists apprehension or attempts to use the canister?"

"Shoot to kill. First shot to his center of mass, second shot to the cranium."

Waldbaer studied the sidewalk. He felt Hirter's eyes on him. "Right. Bam, bam, dead, if there is the slightest resistance. Now, let's be honest, it's one thing to say that. Doing it can be altogether different. Most of us here have never shot anyone. It would be natural to hesitate, understandable not to want to kill. Understandable but not justifiable. We can't take chances with Sarin. I will take personal responsibility for your actions. If you have a canister and a terrorist, you cannot hesitate. Is everything clear?"

A hushed murmur of agreement drifted down the street. Hirter took in the proceedings but had no real sense of how ready the undercover officers were to shoot without warning. He touched the compact nine-millimeter parabellum concealed under his shirt. He, at least, was ready to kill if required. But would he hesitate a second, perhaps providing a terrorist with a wink of time to wreak bloody havoc? It was something he could not know.

"Another thing," Waldbaer continued. "Atropine. Are you all comfortable with how to use it? You have your injectors? All you need to do is to administer or have a comrade administer one shot. Then we'll get you to the Ministry of Health doctors in this van." Waldbaer rapped the metal side of the vehicle lightly with his fist. "They're trained and ready for the Sarin threat. You just need to administer initial aid. Let's hope it doesn't come to that. Questions?"

Holz shot up a stubby hand. "Kommissar, we're wired, what's the communications protocol?"

Waldbaer glanced at the thick chestnut tree limbs above him and sighed. "Simple answer: with the noise level from those crowds, we're going to have trouble hearing clearly. It's a disadvantage we have to live with. Identify yourself and your location when you transmit. Speak slowly. Communicate discreetly. Remember, we're dealing with fanatics. I don't want them spotting an earpiece or microphone." The detective paused and thought for a moment. "This will work out. Not everything about it is optimal, but it will work out. Other questions?"

There were none.

"Okay. Go walk around. You have time before you need to move to the *Wies'n*. Good luck to all of you." The cluster broke up and the men shuffled slowly away, their movements betraying restrained tension.

Waldbaer turned to Hirter. "So, Hirter, what do you think?"

Hirter stretched his arms. "Kommissar, this is your show. You've done everything that can be done. It's like an espionage operation: the planning is everything. There comes a point where fate deals its hand. There's nothing more you can do."

"You believe we'll get them?"

Hirter considered. "They have to go to the *Wies'n* and try to get into the tents, you're right about that. I think we have a good chance of spotting them. Can we stop them before they do damage? I don't know. But there's nothing we can change at this stage. We stick with the program and hope for the best."

The detective displayed a weary smile. "You and your friends have been a big help, Hirter. We wouldn't have gotten this far without CIA assistance. However it goes, this will be a hell of a day. Times like this, I wish I had become a lawyer or a teacher."

"No you don't," Hirter replied, allowing his own smile.

Chapter 60

Television camera crews were setting up positions along the parade route as several blocks away, al-Assad's companions gathered in his musty hotel room for a final briefing. Al-Assad looked approvingly at the tinted colors in the men's hair and at the jaunty angle with which Sayyid wore his baseball cap. Al-Assad detected tension, his own, and that of his men. That was all right, he thought, given what would be accomplished over the next few hours. He stood at the window to address them one final time.

"Brothers, our attitude must be one of submission. Submission to Allah and the jihad. How fortunate we are to have been selected for today. Our names will be honored by coming generations of the *ummah* for what we accomplish here in the House of War. Are you ready?"

The men nodded in unison.

"Good. As we move into battle, there are a few final preparations. First, we leave the hotel not as a group but separately, at fifteen minute intervals starting an hour from now. I will be the first to go. Then Taamir, then Jawad, and finally Sayyid. All of us except Jawad go to the U-4 subway station at the end of the block and ride to the Oktoberfest. Jawad, to break up the pattern, I want you to walk to the *Wies'n* along the parade route. It's only a fifteen-minute stroll. All of you try to blend into the groups of people, feign being one of them. Remember, we are swimming in a sea of Oktoberfest visitors. I want you to look happy like the rest of the crowd. If the police are looking for us they expect to see earnest faces. Don't oblige them.

Now, I have a few items for you." Al-Assad gestured toward the bed and the objects atop the blanket.

"Plastic bags," murmured Sayyid, confused. Assad smiled broadly.

"Yes, plastic bags. One for each of you. They bear the Oktoberfest logo. These are bags you get when you buy a festival souvenir. These bags will arouse no suspicion. Thousands of people will be carrying them. We place the Sarin canisters into the bags. Next to the bags you will notice square cardboard containers. Those are what souvenir beer mugs are packaged in. I bought four mugs downtown and threw them away, just to get the containers. The canisters fit inside the containers snugly. We place the canisters into the cardboard boxes and the boxes into the plastic bags. The police will likely be expecting us to carry backpacks, but we are a step ahead of them. When you find a place inside the tents, choose the right moment, reach into the bag, open the carton and activate the device. The rest takes care of itself; you will have accomplished your mission."

Taamir spoke up, his soft voice sounding almost shy. "How long will it take? How long before we are martyred?"

Al-Assad nodded understanding. "Not long at all at that proximity and with these high concentrations. The symptoms will occur rapidly. Your nose will begin to run and you'll feel a headache. You will start to salivate and it will become hard to breathe. By that point, you'll feel dizzy and your limbs might start to twitch. It is over soon after that. Don't worry, our way will be made easy for us. Remember — get as deep into the crowd as possible. We want many to fall today. I have no more to tell you, brothers, except to state my respect at your fortitude. I will see you all again later today. But not on this earth."

He dispatched them to their rooms for the remaining hour before the sequence of departures would begin, his first of all. Al-Assad found that he did not feel nervous; felt only contentment. He went to the bed and reached down to retrieve his battered suitcase from underneath. Unzipping it, he extracted the metal canister secreted underneath some folded shirts. Al-Assad smiled, luxuriating in the feel of the object in has hands. He slipped the cylinder into the cardboard jacket emblazoned with the words *Original Oktoberfest Krug* and displaying a picture of the Munich cathedral. He nodded in satisfaction. The box was the image of innocence. He placed the container into the shopping bag and consulted his wristwatch. Soon. He turned toward Mecca, knelt on the hard hotel room floor, and began to pray.

Chapter 61

Caroline O'Kendell and Allen Chalmers were dressed in blue jeans and sweaters to blend with the crowd. They disembarked from a beige taxi directly at one of the Oktoberfest entrances. Caroline spotted Robert first, his tall frame easy to pick out as he stood in a relaxed pose underneath the twenty-foot-high, garlanded archway at the entrance to the *Wies'n*. She waved and Robert raised his hand in reply. She found him attractive in an understated way she decided, but pushed the thought aside with a nudge of professionalism.

A moment later the three CIA officers were huddled together.

"Time to party," Chalmers offered, with a glance at the brightly colored Oktoberfest structures stretching out before him. His eyes fixed on the imposing beer tents dominating the fairgrounds, the perfect environment for a mass-casualty Sarin attack.

Caroline crossed her arms around her lithe torso and shivered. "Munich will be associated with a new type of warfare — terrorist use of chemical weapons. The city will be twice-cursed. Remember the Munich Olympic massacre, back in the days of Mark Spitz? You can imagine what another terrorist attack will do for this city."

"You're right," Chalmers agreed. "But if they pull this off it will make the Olympic massacre fade into insignificance. Look at those tents. We could be talking about thousands of fatalities."

"Caroline, anything new?" Robert inquired.

She shook her head from side to side, her dark hair shimmering with the motion. "Nothing. I placed a secure call to headquarters, but there haven't been any intercepts. There's no more time, Robert, the parade has started. The tents will be opening soon."

292			JOHN J. LE BEAU

Robert smiled at her, aware of how pretty she was. "You're right, Caroline. Let's head toward the tents. The Kommissar has already ordered his men to their positions."

The parade of brewery wagons wound its way through the Munich streets, thronged with loud, mirthful crowds. Each garlanded wagon was laden with rows of oak kegs and drawn by a team of sturdy dray horses, their hooves clanging rhythmically against the pavement. Each steed was a paragon of equestrian finery, outfitted with silver or bronze accouterments, their formidable sides bedecked with the escutcheon of the brewery represented, a snarling, stylized lion for Löwenbräu, a hooded monk for Paulaner, a bishop's kreutzer for Augustiner. Unbeknownst to the laughing onlookers, stern-faced teams of surveillants silently monitored the faces and movements of those present, covertly searching for the earnest, bearded faces they had imprinted in their brains.

Chapter 62

Now, al-Assad concluded, glancing at his wristwatch. He studied the hotel room one last time, looking in the mirror at the blond streaks recently added to his hair. He went to the dresser and tugged a Walther pistol from the drawer and inserted it into his trousers. He doubted that he would need it, but it offered a reserve of protection. Pulling a blue windbreaker over a gray sweatshirt that read "Let's Party," he exited the room, took the stairs to the lobby, and paid his bill to a bored checkout clerk who didn't notice that al-Assad had no luggage with him, other than an Oktoberfest plastic bag.

A moment later he was on the street, boisterous with life. His trained eyes detected no sign of observation, and he merged with the stream of humanity heading toward the U-4 subway station a block away. He forced a vacuous smile and walked with an enthusiastic step that he truly felt, but for reasons far different than all of those around him. He felt like a shark invisible to the school of fish within which he swam. Staring ahead, he could see the U-bahn sign a few hundred yards in front of him. As he approached the stairs leading to the underground, al-Assad noticed two stationary men who seemed to be intently studying the stream of people passing them by. They could be policemen, he thought, or perhaps they were just waiting for a friend.

Taking no chances, al-Assad spotted a blonde woman in the crowd ahead of him and deftly moved to her side. As they approached the two suspicious men, al-Assad began talking to her as if they belonged together. "This will be even better than last year," he said to the slightly perplexed woman, "the weather's great and you can tell everybody is in a party mood." They swept past the two men and al-Assad drifted away from the blonde and moved with the human herd to the subway tracks, his grip tight around the plastic bag containing the Sarin. Al-Assad knew that a train would appear momentarily and he would be on his way to the Oktoberfest grounds, a few minutes ride away. He felt a rush of anticipation surge through his veins.

Fifteen minutes after al-Assad's scheduled departure, Taamir repeated the procedure of leaving his room and settling his account at the hotel desk. He, too, had left his luggage in the room and carried only the brightly colored plastic bag. Exiting the building, Taamir took the same route as al-Assad and merged with the torrent of pedestrians. Taamir's thick head of hair, now largely red, reflected the autumn sunlight. As al-Assad had instructed, he carefully arranged his features into a happy configuration.

A few moments later, and wholly unknown to Taamir, he was observed by one of two men standing near the entrance to the U-bahn station. The undercover policemen considered Taamir's features for a moment, but the lack of beard, broad grin, and red hair did not match the image in the officer's head.

Taamir continued on his way unmolested, cosseted by the crowd of revelers. Minutes later, as Taamir pushed himself into the jammed confines of a subway car, the diminutive form of Jawad left the hotel as well, but, staying above ground, walked a different route to his target.

Sayyid gazed at the plastic clock in his room and knew that the others had by now departed. He pulled himself from the bed, muttered a final *sura* from the Koran, and descended the creaking stairwell to the lobby. There were no customers at the front desk, only the balding, old clerk who worked the morning shift. "Checking out from room three twelve," Sayyid half-whispered, taking out his wallet. "I'll pay cash."

The clerk nodded, and entered strokes on the keyboard in front of him. The man hit another key and a printer groaned into brief life, spitting out a page that the clerk passed to Sayyid. "Where's your suitcase?" the man asked in a gravelly voice. Flustered by the unexpected question, Sayyid could only think to say, "I already took it out." He lifted his plastic bag into view. "This is the last of it." The clerk had already lost interest. Sayyid pushed the hundred euro notes across the counter. "Keep the change," he added, feeling more nervous and vulnerable than he had expected.

Bumping along the street with the endless crowd, Sayyid was halfway to the subway entrance when he discovered that he had left the baseball cap back in the hotel room. He cursed the oversight, knowing al-Assad would not be pleased. He considered returning to the hotel, but rejected the idea as it would entail another conversation with the clerk, perhaps being accompanied back to the room and then being discovered in a lie with his luggage lying on the unmade bed. No, Sayyid thought, better to go ahead without the cap. It was no big deal.

Markus Henkel touched his companion's elbow gently. "Straight ahead," he murmured, "edge of the sidewalk about thirty meters." His colleague Tobias Mauer shifted his eyes and focused on a dark-haired young man.

The observed man had a brooding look on his face not consonant with the occasion. The thick hair and low hairline matched at least one of the suspects — but no beard. As the man walked closer, jostled by the celebrating crowd, Mauer thought he could make out the outline of where a beard had recently been. Then again, the man was not wearing a backpack, only carrying a small plastic souvenir bag.

"What do you think, Tobias?" Henkel asked.

"Don't know, but let's stop him at least. Take a look into his bag, too."

The two men began a slow approach to intercept their target before he reached the subway entrance.

Sayyid saw the subway sign ahead and began to pray, the reality of his impending death affecting him more profoundly than he had anticipated. He tightened his grip on the plastic bag, nervous that the raucous crowd might dislodge it from his hand. The animated mass in front of him was now pouring into the yawning, shadowed maw of the subway entrance. But not all.

Curiously at first, Sayyid noticed that two men were moving against the crowd in his direction. He watched them carefully and quickly developed a sickening sensation that they were purposefully guiding on him. *I must be wrong,* he thought. *My nerves are causing me to imagine things.* He moved sideways to the opposite side of the street. As he did, he noticed that the two men altered their course as well.

With sudden, crystalline clarity, Sayyid knew that he had been discovered. He felt cold sweat erupt on his forehead and could think of nothing but to flee. He turned against the crowd and like a swimmer against the waves shoved his way through the phalanx of flesh. Elbowing those around him, he forced a path through the crowd.

"It's got to be one of them," Markus yelled at his partner as Sayyid bolted through the crowd. Both men simultaneously reached for the automatic pistols under their jackets, but realized they had no way of employing the weapons without inflicting innocent casualties.

"Shit," Markus shouted, "we have to get closer to him." They slammed two protesting teenage girls aside as they began their pursuit, keeping their target in sight.

"Shoot to kill," Tobias reminded his companion.

"Only if we get a clean shot." Pushing through the crowd, they began to make headway toward the dark-haired man.

Sayyid turned and saw with rising panic that the duo was gaining on him. He felt ill and wanted to vomit. Everything had gone unexpectedly, completely wrong in the span of a few seconds. He did not believe that he would reach the Oktoberfest grounds. He began to sob with the realization that he would not accomplish his sacred mission, would not be remembered as one of the *shahid* who had struck at the enemy.

He propelled himself forward, clutching in both hands the bag concealing the Sarin. As he darted down the street, he noticed that the Rote Adler, the hotel he had just vacated, was only fifty yards away. Lacking any other goal, Sayyid decided to reenter its familiar surroundings. He cleared the last group of festival goers and pushed into the revolving door opening onto the lobby.

"The hotel," Mauer yelled to his partner, his voice strained from running. Both men had their pistols drawn, safeties flicked off, and a round chambered as they closed on the unimpressive façade of the Rote Adler.

Mauer tore a police phone from his jacket pocket and hit the button that connected him with the task force in city hall. "Mauer here. We found one of them. He's trying to evade pursuit and is inside the Rote Adler Hotel. Send reinforcements."

Mauer was the first of the two through the finger-smeared revolving glass door.

Sayyid found the lobby empty save for the elderly desk clerk and one of the sluggish Turkish waiters from the restaurant who happened to be passing through the room. Both of them stared at the fear-stricken face of their former guest.

Sayyid knew that his pursuers would be upon him any minute. Barely thinking coherently, he plunged a shaking hand into the plastic bag and ripped the top from the cardboard container within. His hand found the activation plunger housed in the center of the dispersion mechanism. Sayyid pressed it down and heard the canister emit a soft hiss as the spray valve engaged. He heard the door behind him spin open and he turned. His mind had become a seething mess of confusion, torn by competing sensations of fear, anger, and self-loathing. He pulled the polished canister free of the bag and held the shining form close to his chest. His nose began to run.

Mauer entered the weakly lit lobby, weapon first. The cornered man stood in the middle of the room holding a metal object. The policeman spotted the two hotel employees and determined they were out of the line of fire.

The second policeman, Henkel, burst through the door just as his partner shouted at the suspect. "Police. Drop the cylinder. I won't ask twice."

Sayyid did nothing but stare balefully at the policeman and Mauer fired a round, the noise magnified enormously by the confines of the lobby.

The first bullet hit the target squarely in the chest, knocking him off his feet and sending him crashing backward. The canister pitched off to one side, hit hard, and rolled along the tile floor.

Sayyid had landed on his back, from which a dark liquid pool began to emanate. With a low moan, he tried to pull himself up. He had nearly achieved a sitting position when the second round, this from Henkel's pistol, punched a small hole into his forehead just below the hairline. The exit wound was substantially larger, tearing off the back of Sayyid's cranium in a shower of blood and brain tissue. The reverberation of the shots died away, and the lobby was again quiet. The clerk and the waiter had sought cover behind the reception counter and now slowly reemerged, gaping at the carnage.

Henkel and Mauer approached the prostrate form with their weapons still trained on the center of mass. They stared into dead brown eyes. The bullet hole in the victim's forehead emitted little blood.

The desk clerk and the waiter approached them with hesitating steps. "He just checked out of here a while ago. His name is in the registry," offered the clerk, eyes bulging and face flushed. The policemen nodded and urged him away from the corpse.

"At least he didn't have time to explode the device," Mauer advised his partner.

"Right, thank God," Henkel responded, moving to retrieve the canister from the spot where its rolling journey had ceased. As he approached it and reached out a hand his ears detected a faint sibilance. "Shit," he yelled, jumping back from the device. "Tobias, have them get everybody out of the hotel, it's doing something. Don't let them exit through the lobby for God's sake."

Mauer turned to instruct the elderly desk clerk to evacuate the building and noticed that the old man had a trail of mucous stretching from his nostrils to his chin. The clerk fixed the policeman with a vague look and weakly announced, "I don't feel well," before starting to twitch and pitching to the floor. Tobias grabbed the shaking, wheezing man by the arm and started pulling him toward the lobby door. He heard a crashing sound and looked up to see that the lanky waiter had also collapsed.

"Markus, we need to use our atropine," he yelled to his companion. Mauer watched helplessly as the clerk's brown eyes rolled back in his head and he began gasping for air like a fish yanked from a stream.

Mauer himself felt dizzy and pulled a small red tubular plastic container from his trouser pocket. Removing a cap at the top, he withdrew a hypodermic needle and prepared to plunge it into his thigh through the clothing. At precisely this instant, he noticed that his hands had begun to shake uncontrollably and his clenched fist opened involuntarily, the needle falling to the tiles. A blast of pain exploded behind his eyes, which refused to focus. He felt his muscles spasm and he went down hard, his legs denying him support. The convulsions intensified and his respiration became ragged and then failed altogether. A few feet away, his partner was already dead, lifeless eyes pointed at the hotel ceiling.

Green and white vehicles marked *Polizei* were arriving in front of the hotel, lights flashing. Uniformed officers disgorged from the fleet of Opels and Mercedes and cleared the area, setting up a cordon around the hotel. Inside the lobby, there was no movement at all.

Chapter 63

Waldbaer was easing himself from his unmarked car and preparing to join the others on the festival grounds when the radio banter took an ominous turn. He listened raptly to the initial call from officer Mauer alerting them to the pursuit of a suspect into the Rote Adler, which Waldbaer recalled was near the main train station; he had driven past it the previous night with Hirter. Waldbaer listened to the terse call-ins from cruisers reporting their progress to the hotel.

Minutes later, an officer reported from directly outside the hotel that, as seen through the front window, there were several bodies strewn across the lobby, all apparently lifeless. The officer also reported that a peculiar-looking object could be detected on the floor. "It looks like a stainless-steel thermos bottle. It has some attachment on top. It could be what we're looking for."

The voice of another officer intervened, announcing that hotel guests were being evacuated from the back of the building.

Waldbaer punched a button on the steering wheel of his car permitting him to transmit. "Make sure no one goes into that lobby, no one. Once you get a team there in protective suits, they enter unaccompanied. They know what to do. For God's sake, don't let on to the media what's happening. Tell them the cruisers are there due to a fire alarm. Everybody copy?" The radio crackled with affirmative responses. Tense but energetic, Waldbaer bounded from his vehicle and headed to the Oktoberfest entrance.

Chapter 64

Al-Assad rode the escalator from the underground station to the *Wies'n*. He held the bag containing the Sarin at his side, feigning a casual stance. The Germans surrounding him were irritatingly loud, but despite his annoyance, al-Assad fixed a grin on his face. He wondered how many of those around him would end up in the same tent as he and suffer the lethal consequences. His grin became more authentic.

Emerging into the sunlight, al-Assad squinted until he acclimatized to the prevailing brightness. He was propelled along by the force of the crowd, but managed to squeeze free and take up a position at a small roasted nut stand. Ordering a paper bag of almonds, he turned and observed the stream of humanity emerging from the U-bahn station he had just exited.

He wanted to ensure that Taamir, the next to leave the hotel after him, was safely on the festival grounds. Slowly consuming his purchase, al-Assad was relieved ten minutes later to see Taamir spill onto the *Wies'n*, the plastic bag with its deadly cargo inconspicuous by his side. Excellent, al-Assad concluded, things move as they should. Aware that Taamir would be going to the Augustiner tent, al-Assad popped the last almond into his mouth and began his journey to the Hofbräu tent, easing once again into the river of people flowing by.

Taamir moved at the pace of the crowd past souvenir stands and an establishment selling smoked fish. The main pedestrian street called the Wirtsbudenstrasse, where the beer tents were located, loomed ahead. Taamir considered the scene and concluded that it represented unalloyed decadence. There was no reason why those who chose to come to such a place should be permitted to live. The entire scene was an affront to the values that ordered Taamir's life. It would be a pleasure to engage the device secreted in the plastic bag gripped in his hand.

Entering the festival avenue, Taamir recalled the Oktoberfest map he had studied in the hotel. The Augustiner tent was located to his left. Navigating through the crowd, he maneuvered in that direction. A few minutes later he spotted the brewery tent, painted bright white and deep blue and bearing the golden emblem of a bishop's curling kreutzer.

Alert to potential danger, Taamir scanned the surroundings for any trace of police. He noted the line of sturdily built men at the entrance to the tent, monitoring the crowd that slowly snaked its way into the enormous beer hall. Through the bobbing figures ahead of him, he saw as well that these civilian security guards, intended mainly for crowd control, occasionally asked to inspect a person's backpack or handbag. This was not unexpected, and Taamir felt confident that his redhead appearance and souvenir bag would pass muster. Feeling tense nonetheless, he knew that if he were discovered, he would activate the device where he stood. Taamir moved forward resolutely.

"Sir, please open your bag" a baritone voice said in German. Taamir glanced to his right and saw the broad-shouldered bulk of a security guard sporting a crew-cut who was, in fact, an undercover special police officer.

Taamir smiled vacantly as if to suggest that he had already had a beer or two. "No problem," he replied. He held up the plastic souvenir bag and opened it for inspection.

The guard peered into the proffered bag through dark sunglasses. His eyes scanned the contents rapidly, taking in a couple of candy bars and a cardboard container decorated with a Munich scene. Before Taamir could react, the guard reached a large hand into the bag and flipped open the cardboard container, revealing a smooth, shining tubular surface. Not a beer stein, the policeman noted, it looked like a thermos. There was no end to the type of souvenirs they were selling, he thought to himself.

"Thanks sir," the guard intoned robotically, his eyes moving away from the red-haired man and again scanning the crowd.

Taamir passed through the tent entrance. He was inside. A scene unlike any he had previously experienced confronted him. Thousands of people were seated on benches at long wooden tables. A cacophony of voices produced a background roar, but even this was subdued by the amplified oompah music originating from a band seated on a dais at the center of the tent. Fleets of waitresses in dirndls moved at cruising speed through the tent, carrying their cargo of heavy glass beer mugs. Wandering vendors plied their wares of pretzels, salted radishes, and cigars. The air was gray-blue with smoke and redolent with spilt beer. Taamir took in the scene for a moment only and then made his way toward its epicenter, where he would be sure to kill the maximum number of people.

Not far away, Jawad entered the festival grounds through a different gate, arriving by foot rather than underground train. He was sure he had not been noticed and was careful to attach himself to groups of festival visitors to mask his profile. Moving at the pace of the crowd, he set out for the Löwenbräu tent. First the tent, he reminded himself, and then paradise.

Chapter 65

Waldbaer was troubled by the reports from the Rote Adler. Sarin casualties. One of the terrorists was dead, but there was no sign of the other three. They were presumably already on the *Wies'n*. More troubling, the dead terrorist had concealed his nerve agent weapon with some creativity, not in a backpack, as expected, but in a simple plastic souvenir bag, of which there were hundreds, if not thousands, on the festival grounds.

The device that the protective-suited specialists found in the hotel lobby was the same design described by Kaltenberg in his diary. It had been placed within a beer mug cardboard carton for concealment, something else that had not been anticipated. *Damn it*, Waldbaer thought, *the terrorists are ahead of the game and we're reacting.*

Waldbaer made contact with Hirter and the other two CIA officers near the main entrance, briefing them on the hotel attack.

"It could have been worse from the way it sounds, Kommissar," was Hirter's reply. "Now at least we know exactly what to look for. The other three are almost certainly using the same modus operandi."

Chalmers spoke. "The bad news is that we now know the nerve agent is viable and lethal. We also know that the dispersion device is functional. If there had been more people in the lobby when the device was activated, we'd have mass casualties already. If the remaining terrorists get inside the tents, it's hard to see how we can prevent a catastrophe a magnitude greater than what we already have."

"We can't waste time standing around," Waldbaer said. "Let's get moving." With that, they pushed into the swirling, eddying mass of people heading toward the large tents, the closest of which was the Augustiner.

"Plastic souvenir bags," Waldbaer rushed to explain to the undercover officers posted at the Augustiner entrance. "I know there are lots of those around, but that's what they're using. They probably have tossed touristy items inside for additional cover. Inside the plastic bag there will be a cardboard container for a souvenir beer stein. Instead of a beer stein, the container will house a metal cylinder. That's the Sarin device. It will look like a thermos bottle."

"Shit," said the tall, short-haired officer on Waldbaer's right. Waldbaer felt his stomach churn. "What is it," he snapped.

"There was a guy I let in a few minutes ago. He was carrying a souvenir bag, and I had him open it. There were chocolate bars inside and a cardboard beer stein container. I popped the container and saw what looked like a thermos inside. I thought it was just another souvenir. Hell, they sell everything here nowadays. Jesus, I'm sorry."

"No time for that," Waldbaer replied. "What did he look like?"

"Young, no beard, red hair. Now that I think about it, his complexion didn't match the hair; maybe he dyed it. He didn't look like one of our targets."

"He is," Waldbaer spat. "If he's already inside, we might be too late. Let's hope the hell not. You can recognize him?"

"I can recognize him," the tall officer said.

"Good. Let me call out an update to our comrades at the other tents. Then I'll explain what we do," Waldbaer said, pushing inside the tent with his phalanx of German officers and Americans.

Taamir had found it was difficult to find a place at one of the beer tables. The tent was rapidly filling to raucous capacity. It had taken several minutes of wandering the beer-slicked, wooden-planked aisles until he spotted a narrow sitting space on the edge of a group of Italian tourists. He smiled at them, and some of their glassy-eyed number nodded happily in return before returning to their loud conversation. He placed the plastic bag on the bench between his legs, concealed from onlookers by the tabletop.

A harried-looking, overweight waitress squeezed into a too-tight dirndl appeared before him. *"Ein bier?"* she shouted above the brass music.

He nodded and she disappeared into the maelstrom of the crowd. He would have no need to feign drinking a beer. It would be at least ten minutes before she returned, and that was time enough to activate the device.

Glancing about, he noticed that there were children in the tent, brought along by their parents. He refused to let himself be troubled by this. He was acting as a jihadi, and his actions had been sanctioned beforehand. His conscience was clear. He closed his eyes for a second and offered a brief prayer for his relatives. No need to wait, he concluded, and opened the bag wide, revealing the cardboard container within which the canister was secreted.

Another partygoer shoved into the remaining narrow bench space next to him with a muttered, "excuse me." Taamir didn't object. One more victim to the toll he would exact. He pulled open the cardboard lid of the cargo secured between his knees and saw the metal vessel and its activation button.

Taamir was suddenly aware that his left side felt oddly warm. At first he thought it was the press of people occupying the bench. The sensation rapidly escalated to pain, and he turned to the source of it and the newly arrived man next to him. He was puzzled to see that the man was regarding him clinically, the way one looked at an exotic animal in a zoo. Taamir felt a sharp burst of pain course through his side and opened his mouth in incomprehension.

The undercover officer twisted the blade of his service knife in the man's side. He felt corporeal resistance as the metal sliced through muscle and tissue. He withdrew the viscous blade and plunged it with force low to the abdomen, aware that he had already inflicted major damage. Amid the music and singing, no one noticed. A thick ebb of blood was pouring from the red-haired man's side onto the bench and floor. The point of discharge was low and not visible to others at the table, whose attention was entirely focused on the band.

Taamir could not make his fingers respond to his will. His arms twitched slightly as his eyes began to lose focus. The hard features of the man who was attacking him began to blur. He understood in a detached way that he was dying, which he had expected, but he had not achieved his goal, which was unanticipated. He could not understand why events had developed in this manner.

The officer twisted the blade again in his target's abdomen. He saw that the man's wide brown eyes were now glazed. Glancing down the crowded aisle, he found Waldbaer and nodded.

Waldbaer nodded back and beckoned with a move of his chin. The police officer withdrew the blade from the man next to him and dropped the slickened knife into a deep pocket of his leather jacket. With a quick, casual movement, the officer removed the jacket and placed it around the bleeding man's form, concealing the wounds. He secured a strong arm around his victim and lifted him to a standing position. One of the Italians glanced up.

The officer smiled disarmingly and shrugged. "Already drunk," he said, shaking his head. The Italian laughed knowingly and returned his attention to the Bavarian band. Unremarked, the undercover policeman half-dragged his open-mouthed victim into the aisle, toward Waldbaer.

"He's still alive," the officer advised the kommissar.

"Not for long from the looks of him," Waldbaer replied, hitching his own arm around the limp terrorist and helping his subordinate pull the man toward the tent entrance where Hirter and other undercover men waited. Other than an occasional, half-curious glance, their progress elicited no attention, not even the deep and spreading stain on Taamir's jeans.

Outside, they were quickly concealed by a group of undercover men and the CIA officers. A van had been brought up and Taamir, eyes rolled back in his head, was placed inside. "He's dead," a voice said matter-of-factly from within the vehicle.

Waldbaer nodded in acknowledgment and turned to the officer who had been in the tent. "You have the device?"

The officer lifted up the plastic bag. "In here. He never got to the canister. I cut him just as he got his hand inside the bag."

The officer looked away, taking in the Oktoberfest scene. He spoke to the kommissar in a lower voice. "I never killed anyone before."

Waldbaer clapped the officer lightly on the shoulder. "Remember this, you saved hundreds — maybe thousands — of people just now. You hear that singing and laughing back in that beer tent? That's going on because of you. If you hadn't gotten to that intending mass murderer in time, all we'd be hearing right now is screaming. Never forget that. I understand how you feel, but this guy lying in the van forfeited his right to life when he agreed to carry that canister."

Chalmers appeared by the police officer's side, asked for, and received the Sarin device. He removed it gingerly from the bag and cardboard container and examined it. "This is the design Kaltenberg perfected in nineteen forty-four. The device is simple, really, and built to be robust. The container is double-walled, and the button at the top activates the dispenser. The Sarin plays out until the container is empty. Kommissar, we need to put this thing inside a sealed metal container and transport it — carefully — to a controlled space for destruction."

"I'll arrange it," the detective said.

Hirter spoke up. "Kommissar, two more of these damned things are somewhere on the *Wies'n*. I hope our luck holds out, and your men spot the remaining attackers."

Waldbaer considered for a moment. "Did you notice anything unusual with the assailant? He dyed his hair. Not a bad way to alter a profile. I expect that his comrades have also dyed their hair to look more Western and have shaved their beards. Also note, this guy was

in the Augustiner tent. More than likely the two remaining assailants are targeting other beer tents. We check the remaining tents
one by one. That means Löwenbräu, Hippodrom, Bräurosl, Hacker,
Paulaner, and Hofbräu. We've reduced the threat, but that's not good
enough. Let's go."

They left the van with its cooling, open-eyed corpse behind and
forced their way into the milling crowd.

Jawad stared up at the twenty-foot-tall mechanical lion by the tent
entrance. Its features surrounded by a proud mane, the beast rubbed
its stomach with a clawed paw, waved its tail, and opened a sharp-
toothed maw to exclaim "Löwenbräu" in a stentorian roar before
lifting a mug of beer to slake its thirst.

Jawad watched the performance and laughed heartily.

"You are no match, my friend, for the lions of the Prophet." No
one took notice of him amidst the din, and Jawad, hair an improbable yellow, moved toward the entrance. A plastic souvenir bag
swung casually by his side.

Waldbaer and his phalanx pushed past flower-bedecked beer wagons, loitering throngs of partygoers, and tourists with minicams. The
Paulaner tent, surmounted by a tower emblazoned with the brewery
emblem, loomed ahead of them.

Waldbaer shouted into his police mobile phone, attempting to
drown out the background roar of the crowd. "Listen up. Here's your
new profile: subjects have probably dyed their hair to appear more
European. They aren't wearing beards. There are two subjects left
and they'll be traveling solo. Remember — look for souvenir bags.
Inspect anyone trying to enter a tent with a souvenir bag. Check for
a cardboard container holding what appears to be a metal thermos
or mug. If you find that, you've found our targets. That's all."

Chapter 66

Alfred Holzer pressed the receiver close to his ear, straining to make out Waldbaer's words over the noise. He glanced at his burly partner Jakob Spockmeyer, a few feet distant. Spockmeyer raised a thumb in the air indicating that he had copied the information as well. Both officers checked the flow of individuals passing into the Löwenbräu tent with renewed intensity. Holzer felt nervous and swept a hand over his bristling mustache. A trio of giggling teenage girls moved past him into the tent, and he suddenly found himself staring at a short, plump man in a denim shirt. The man had an olive complexion surmounted by an odd shade of blond hair. The man was nearly past him when Holzer detected the bright plastic bag.

"You there, stop," Holzer shouted at the man, who was just beyond arm's reach.

Jawad turned toward the voice and encountered an earnest, mustached Bavarian face. Security, he concluded instantly, then he slammed into the young girls in front of him, knocking one to the ground amid shocked shouts. He moved like a bipedal battering ram toward the interior of the tent, the towering policeman just behind him.

Things moved quickly, as if time had accelerated. Holzer was joined by his partner, and both men drew pistols from their jackets, muzzles aimed in the air.

"Stop!" Holzer roared one more time, but the plump shape continued to bull through the crowd.

"I can't get a clean shot; too many people," Holzer yelled.

"Christ," Spockmeyer shouted. "we've got to stop him, he's our target for sure."

In frustration both officers saw the plump man pull away and cross the threshold into the tent.

Holzer fired a round into the air and felt the recoil of the pistol push at his wrist. The report of the firearm unleashed a chorus of screams from the crowd.

"Make way," Holzer yelled hoarsely.

Concentrating on the small man with the bag, the police officer grabbed a middle-aged man in front of him by the shoulder and threw him aside, trying for a line of fire.

Jawad could sense that his pursuers were close and knew that he could not evade them for long, even in the protective press of the crowd. Although still near the entrance, he reasoned that he was at least inside the tent. He jammed his hand into the depths of the plastic bag and felt the cardboard within. He fumbled with the lid for a moment before tearing it off. He blindly located the activator button and slammed it down with his thumb. All the time he moved forward, deeper into the tent. Stripping away the bag, Jawad held the cylinder to his chest, continuing his plunge through the crowd, content that his every step spread invisible death a bit farther.

Holzer could make out a splash of denim amid the moving shapes in front of him. He aimed his pistol at the pitching image and pulled the trigger. The shot reverberated in the tent, intensifying the panic. Clusters of people dropped to the floor. The number of human obstructions suddenly reduced, both Holzer and Spockmeyer got off separate additional shots.

Jawad bucked forward as the first round ripped into his shoulder, tearing out a furrow of flesh and muscle along with denim fabric. He was swaying on his feet as the second and third bullets, spaced less than a second apart, exploded into the center of his back.

Jawad looked down, curious as a torrent of black blood spilled through the front of his shirt, above the waist. His stubby legs gave way and he fell to his knees. People were screaming and the band had ceased playing. He felt the onset of deep, throbbing pain, let his eyelids close, and welcomed the darkness, readying himself for his imminent appearance before the virgins. I will be taller in the next life, he thought.

People who had fallen to the floor were screaming and whimpering, but Holzer and Spockmeyer saw that their target was down and immobile. They could not see the canister.

"We need to get them out of here," Holzer yelled to his companion.

Spockmeyer yanked a police badge from his shirt and held it above his head; the metal glittering in the overhead lights. "Police! Everybody out of the tent. Stay orderly! Gather in front of the entrance and stay there until advised to leave. Move out."

The people closest to the officers lifted themselves from the floor, shaken, but moving as instructed, glancing uncertainly at the armed undercover men as they proceeded by.

Holzer produced a police phone from his jacket and held it to his mustached lips. "Kommisar, Holzer in the Löwenbräu tent. One suspect down, likely dead. We're evacuating the tent. We instructed the people to stay in front of the tent. They should be checked for symptoms. Don't know if the canister has been activated. We're searching for it now."

Waldbaer's voice crackled through the receiver. "Good. I'll get medical teams to the Löwenbräu. I'm not far away. Any officer who entered the tent, use your atropine now."

Holzer and Spockmeyer nodded to one another and applied the atropine syringes to their thighs, both of them wincing as they did so.

"Let's find that damned canister," Holzer instructed his partner.

A jarring crash in front of them drew their attention. A thin, middle-aged waitress had fallen to the ground yards away, a clutch of beer mugs rolling about her inanimate form, the frothing contents seeping into the floorboards.

"God," Holzer implored quietly, "don't let it be that crap at work." Running to the woman, the men noted that fluids were running from her nose and mouth and her limbs were twitching.

The woman's eyes were unfocused and she labored to draw in air.

Holzer pulled another atropine injector from his pocket and slammed it into the waitress's arm. A moment later her struggle for breath ceased, and Spockmeyer gripped her wrist. "No pulse," he mumbled to Holzer.

Nearby, a grey-haired, lederhosen-clad man vomited and moaned, staggering toward the tent entrance before collapsing in a quivering heap. The two officers noticed other people moving drunkenly, disorientation marking their features. More individuals fell to the ground. Some groaned, others emitted panicky whines. Still others, with red eyes or flowing nostrils, moved successfully out of the tent.

Holzer again grabbed his police phone. "We have casualties. Over a dozen," he said with a quiver in intonation. An auburn-haired woman fell a few feet distant; her male companion knelt by her side and tried to revive her.

"Carry her outside," Holzer instructed him. The man complied. His nose had started to emit a stream of bright blood, but he managed to carry the woman from the tent.

Waldbaer and the others had reached the Löwenbräu tent and watched as a wave of people poured from the structure. Behind the detective moved a line of ambulances, inching through the crowds along the chaotic runway, emergency lights flashing. People kept issuing from the tent, hundreds of them, not out of control, Waldbaer noted, but not far from panic at their sudden, mysterious affliction.

A guttural voice erupted through the receiver at the detective's ear and Waldbaer strained to catch the transmission. "Holzer here. We've located the canister. It's hissing, so it must still be active. We've moved the crowd away from it. What's the course of action under the circumstances?"

Waldbaer described the situation to Chalmers, who was watching the scene in front of the tent open-mouthed.

Chalmers considered for a moment before replying. "Kommissar, we have to improvise. If they can cover the Sarin device with a trash bag or something, that's a start. Have them see if there's a water container in the tent. If they can submerge the canister in water, that should reduce dispersion of the nerve agent or incapacitate the device."

Waldbaer repeated Chalmers's instructions and waited. He knew that it meant the officers inside the Löwenbräu tent would be directly exposed to Sarin at extremely close quarters.

"Holzer again. We can use one of the trash barrel liners here. We'll take the canister to the kitchen. They've got to have sinks there. We'll report back in a few minutes."

Waldbaer turned to Chalmers. Robert and Caroline were huddled with them, both feeling powerless to influence the events that had been set in motion. "Mr. Chalmers, an answer, please. The officers in there have injected atropine against the Sarin. Will that be sufficient to protect them while they dispose of the device?"

"I don't know," the chemist said. "I hope to God so, but there are too many unknowns at work. How concentrated is the Sarin in there? Did they employ the atropine injectors properly? Once they get that canister under water they need to leave immediately and let the doctors examine them."

Waldbaer nodded. "Right. Assuming they're able to make it out of the tent."

Holzer and Spockmeyer stepped over the corpse of an elderly man wearing a Boston College sweatshirt and lifted the black plastic liner from a metal trash barrel located next to a support beam.

"This will do the trick," Spockmeyer muttered. The two men emptied the bag of its pretzel remnants, empty cigarette packs, chicken bones, and grease-soaked paper plates. They carried the plastic to the corner of the tent where the Sarin container reposed, hissing audibly like an enraged goose. Both men held their breath and enveloped the gleaming device inside the trash bag, twisting shut the folds of plastic. The act concluded, Spockmeyer ran ahead of his partner to the kitchen at the back of the tent and located an industrial-sized stainless steel sink. He placed a black rubber stopper in the drain, twisted open a faucet, and let loose a cascade of cold water into the basin.

Holzer followed and dropped the Sarin container into the filling sink. It sank to the bottom, the hissing now silenced beneath the surface. Holzer activated his phone. "Holzer again. We're done. The device is immersed in water. We're coming out."

Both men moved hastily across the kitchen, heading for the tent entrance.

"Let's hope to hell that worked," Spockmeyer said to his colleague.

Ordered chaos prevailed outside the Löwenbräu tent as the two officers emerged. The mechanical lion continued its programmed pattern of activity, but no one noted its incongruous behavior. Walbaer slapped Holzer and Spockmeyer on their shoulders and ushered them to an ambulance and a waiting physician. A police cordon had been formed, isolating the tent and the people who had issued from it.

Hirter approached Waldbaer and spoke in a low voice. "What do we know about casualties?"

"Holzer estimates thirty to forty bodies inside. One of the medics said that at least three people have died outside. Some of the others being brought to hospitals have severe symptoms and could go either way. It looks like hundreds of others have symptoms of some sort, but most of them should recover with treatment. That's all I know. This will take time to sort out. We still have one more of these bastards on the loose. We're evacuating the other tents. With luck we can deny him a target."

Chapter 67

Al-Assad watched the scene outside the Löwenbräu tent with mixed emotions. Passing by the tent on the way to his own target, the Hofbräu tent, he had spontaneously decided that it made sense to wait a few minutes and ensure that Jawad attacked successfully. He loitered at a souvenir tee-shirt stand and was rewarded by a rising aural tide of commotion from the Löwenbräu structure. He could not suppress a smile as he contemplated the image of Jawad activating the Sarin in the crowded confines of the tent.

Al-Assad's momentary satisfaction was jarred by the unmistakable sound of gunfire. One round followed some seconds later by two more. Had Jawad been found out? Seconds later, people began streaming out from the tent's interior. Al-Assad detected that a number of them were stumbling, some falling to the ground incapacitated. Good, he thought, the Sarin has been discharged. Many infidels would certainly die. He hoped that Taamir and Sayyid had carried out their attacks as well.

Turning to continue his trek to the Hofbräu tent a few hundred yards distant, Al-Assad found his way blocked by a cordon of police. Worse, he saw in the distance that throngs of people were being ushered from Hofbräu and other beer tents. He cursed to himself and could not fathom how the authorities had reacted so quickly. He closed his eyes for clarity of thought. He saw again the gleaming sword of his jihad, floating above a burgundy tide of blood. He flashed his eyes open and knew that he had to change targets. He would still succeed in his mission. Physical speed would be required, but al-Assad knew that he was a strong runner. All would be well.

Al-Assad left the souvenir stand and walked deliberately toward the police line.

"Everyone stays here, those are our orders," a green-uniformed police officer was advising a confused-looking man in farmer's garb.

Al-Assad moved steadily toward the officer, carefully fixing a pleasant smile on his face as he approached. The officer glanced up at him just as al-Assad drew the Walther from his belt, took aim, and pulled the trigger. The policeman went down instantly with a low moan, his peaked cap in the dust at his side. Al-Assad fired another round and a second policeman crashed face forward.

Screaming erupted and the crowd surged in blind panic as al-Assad had expected.

The police cordon broke in confusion and al-Assad sprinted from the crowd, pistol in one hand and the plastic bag clutched in the other. The layout of the Oktoberfest imprinted securely on his brain, he headed for the amusement park section of the festival grounds, fixing on a large Ferris wheel revolving in the distance.

Waldbaer and the Americans squatted low and looked up as the two shots tore through the air nearby.

"I see him," Hirter yelled. He tore off after the sprinter.

Waldbaer drew himself to his feet with a huff and followed Hirter as best he could, Caroline and Chalmers by his side.

"Stay here," he rasped, and Chalmers obeyed.

The lithe woman remained in motion with the panting detective. "Not this time, Kommissar."

Waldbaer did not argue and pushed through the disrupted police line. "Follow me," he shouted and three uniformed officers picked up the chase.

Al-Assad quickly darted off of the main runway and onto a back alley behind the beer tents. The narrow way was devoid of people and al-Assad moved ahead unobstructed, keeping the Ferris wheel in sight. He was pleased that he had kept a fallback plan in reserve. Al-Assad reflected that his secondary target might even be better than his first. After all, what demonstrates a government's weakness more than its inability to protect its children?

Hirter watched the man with the firearm and plastic bag launch away from the main avenue. He made the same turn moments later, legs pistoning against the ground. He heard voices and knew that Waldbaer and others were following him. Hirter wondered if the target intended to leave the fairgrounds and disappear into the anonymity of Munich, hoping to strike another day. Or did this last remaining terrorist still have a target in mind? Hirter felt himself slowly, but perceptibly, close the intervening space separating them.

Waldbaer and Caroline watched the progress of both men. The detective held his service pistol above his head. He felt winded from the exertion of the run, and was frightened that he might not be able to keep up for long. "Halt or I'll shoot," he yelled with a sandpaper voice, hoping that the terrorist ahead of Hirter might react. He did.

Al-Assad had not focused on his pursuers until he heard the rasping command from behind him. *Filthy kaffir,* he thought as he stopped and turned, aiming his pistol. Hirter pitched to the ground to make a smaller target.

The terrorist's move had caught him by surprise.

Al-Assad ignored the man on the ground and fired at the rumpled shape in the near distance. Waldbaer's pistol barked at the same time. Caroline winced at the percussion as both rounds found their targets.

Waldbaer felt the impact of the bullet as it tore through his jacket and upper right arm, entering and exiting. His pistol tumbled to the ground, and Caroline retrieved it as it fell.

The blow to his hip pushed al-Assad sideways, and he felt an electric wave of pain travel up his side. He forced himself to remain standing and dropped neither the pistol nor the Sarin. Seeing that his bullet had disabled his attacker, al-Assad turned on his heel and, despite his throbbing wound, urged himself along toward his target.

Caroline watched as al-Assad lumbered off and turned her attention to Waldbaer's wound. She tucked the Walther into her waistband and yanked the scarf from her neck and wrapped it tightly around the detective's arm as a tourniquet.

"I know where he's going," Waldbaer gasped. "Damn it, there's a children's event by the Ferris wheel. He's after the kids."

The trio of uniformed policemen caught up with them and one of them called for an ambulance.

"Leave me here," Waldbaer growled. "Stop that bastard."

The officers and the female CIA operative broke into a run.

Hirter was on his feet. Keeping to the shadow of the tents as much as possible, he quietly gained on al-Assad who was now moving at a much reduced pace. The American saw his target dart around a smoked fish concession, heading for the the Ferris wheel. He could make out a crowd in the distance, gathered under a blue and white striped canopy. As he continued to close on the scene and on al-Assad, Hirter saw a gathering of children, several holding balloons. Al-Assad was limping directly toward them. Hirter forced himself to pick up speed, sucking in oxygen for his aching lungs.

Ten yards from the crowd of children cheering the antics of a clown on stilts, al-Assad heard a rhythm of pounding feet and labored breathing behind him. He turned and saw Hirter close enough to make out his features. Al-Assad recognized him as the man he had covertly observed weeks ago in the mountain meadow. *I should have killed him then*, he thought in self-reproach.

Al-Assad raised his pistol and fired, but Hirter dodged to the left and the round went wide. He took aim again, but the man crashed heavily into him before he could exert trigger pressure. On impact, al-Assad's pistol spun away.

Hirter slammed a fist directly at al-Assad's bleeding hip, evoking a shrill scream as a tide of pain coursed through his body. Al-Assad fought back with animal fury, splitting Hirter's lip and chipping a tooth. The two men rolled across the ground, while the children regarded the scene as another form of entertainment.

"Everybody get out of here," Hirter screamed, but there was no response from the young crowd.

Al-Assad scratched at Hirter's eyes, gouging a bleeding furrow in his cheek. Hirter grasped at al-Assad's wound. Al-Assad used the moment to reach into the plastic bag and tear the lid off of the cardboard container. Hirter slammed a fist repeatedly into al-Assad's ribs. Despite the onslaught of blows, al-Assad pulled the gleaming cylinder free of the bag.

"No," Hirter yelled through bloodied lips as he saw a grinning al-Assad depress the activation button. The device began to hiss and al-Assad raised his voice in a triumphal roar, oblivious now to Hirter's continuing assault.

"*Allah Akhbar,*" he chanted.

As he opened his mouth again to repeat the ancient invocation, Hirter grabbed al-Assad's head with both hands and slammed it down hard on top of the cylinder.

Al-Assad felt his teeth break as they impacted the metal device. He felt powerful and determined hands remorselessly force his mouth over the canister. He felt as well the cold spray as it coated his mouth, throat, and gums. He flailed blindly at Hirter, but his hands found no purchase. He tried to lift his head from the spraying vessel, but could not counteract the pressure Hirter applied. He was conscious that the man was whispering in his ear.

"This is for Charles, you piece of garbage. Drink in deeply."

This was not in the vision, al-Assad thought as his eyelids began to flutter uncontrollably along with his limbs. Blood ran from his nostrils and mouth, coating the slick sides of the Sarin cylinder. His heart was racing and he felt his bladder empty, soiling his twitching legs. *Not in the vision at all.* The mechanism atop the cylinder continued to efficiently spray its contents into al-Assad's throat and was carried deep into his lungs.

By the time Caroline O'Kendell and Waldbaer reached the scene, al-Assad was staring lifelessly at the ground, mouth still firmly fixed to the Sarin dispenser. Caroline turned her gaze to Hirter, whose face held a coldly contented look that was, she knew, in all aspects primordial. She knelt down at his side and, professional demeanor vanished, encircled him in her arms.

Chapter 68

Waldbaer's recovery was slow on all fronts. His physical recuperation took longer than expected. The shoulder wound became infected in a Munich hospital and required a series of operations. Eventually the damaged arm was repaired and functional.

Waldbaer's professional health was more complicated. The nerve gas attack on the Oktoberfest had been disrupted, it was true, but not entirely. When the final tally was taken, sixty-eight people had been killed and hundreds sickened. The two policemen shot by al-Assad had also died. Some newspapers applauded Waldbaer's performance, others criticized it. Politicians were equally split in their comments, and the Bavarian Interior Ministry conducted an official investigation. The Kommissar was fully exonerated in the ensuing report, but any chance of Waldbaer being promoted or assigned to a more prestigious location than Gamsdorf was buried by the controversy.

For his part, the detective did not seem to care a whit and went about his tasks with the same irritable attitude that he had always evidenced. Waldbaer had been invited to spend a week's vacation with Robert Hirter in Washington the next summer and had accepted. He told his beer drinking friends at the Alte Post that he intended to stop smoking within the year. He usually exclaimed this with a weary sigh as he reached without enthusiasm for a cigarette.

Robert Hirter, Allen Chalmers, and Caroline O'Kendell were presented with Exceptional Operational Performance awards by the director of the CIA's Clandestine Service. Their actions in working with foreign police to disrupt a major Islamist terror attack were re-garded as a textbook example of joint operations by the agency's Counter Terrorism Center. Robert Hirter and Caroline O'Kendell joined a Fairfax County tennis club together and, mutual acquain-tances believed, were on their way to building an association deeper in nature than friendship.

Ibrahim Baran grew slowly accustomed to imprisonment and found his universe of aspirations commensurately reduced. True to their word, his Turkish captors permitted him a respectable cell with a television, and gave him reading and exercise privileges. Just as im-portantly, Ibrahim's cooperative attitude bought him access to a bet-ter cut of prison food than normal inmates were accorded. He gained significant amounts of weight. He continued to read the Koran with absorption, but had decided that the requirements of jihad and *shahid* were not, after all, roles destined for him.

August Sedlmeyer continued to visit the dead in his dreams with nocturnal regularity. He knew that he was one of the last of his dev-astated generation, but was less proud of this distinction than weary. He still loved to see the outline of the Bavarian Alps at sunset, even if imperfectly through weakening eyes. Still, he felt increasingly out of place in a world of cell phones and satellite television, and an age that did not take much account of soldiers. It was time to leave and he waited for his exit, not with apprehension but with longing.

Abdul al-Masri crossed from Turkey into Iraq and eventually made his way to North Waziristan in the uncontrolled spaces of rugged, rural Pakistan. He heard the news reports about the Oktoberfest at-tack while en route to a gathering of Al-Qaeda principals near the Afghan border. The men, armed with AK-47s, stood around a small campfire behind an obscure village mosque.

Asked about the attack, al-Masri shrugged into his rough woolen cloak as he poked a long stick into the flames and stirred the em-bers. "It was not the success planned, brothers, true. We wanted to kill thousands, that was our holy ambition! We should not forget that the new weapon worked and can work again. Other weapons, too, await our use. It is a certainty. Be patient, brothers, the Prophet measures justice neither in days nor in years. There will come another time." The embers flared as a breeze eased over the village, driven from the harsh and wild mountains above. It was a terrain that a poet might characterize as inherently savage and eternally uncompromising. Al-Masri felt quite at home.

Afterword

This book is a work of fiction and none of the characters involved are real. Nonetheless, not everything in the novel is fantasy. The motivations attributed to the Islamist terrorists are based on fact, including the public statements of Islamist terrorist operatives, and the Al-Qaeda leadership of bin Laden and al-Zawahiri, among others. The transnational nature of Islamist terror networks and their cellular structure has also been established beyond doubt, and it is true that Germany has been targeted by Islamist operatives.

Sarin is a real nerve agent and was developed in Germany and eventually weaponized by that country — though never employed — during World War II. It is also part of the historical record that Sarin and other nerve agents were produced by Nazi chemists at a facility in the town of Dyernfurth-am-Oder, and that a number of German workers were killed at the site by contact with nerve agents. Sarin (which was for years also part of the binary chemical weapons arsenal of the United States) is, in fact, linked to Al-Qaeda. Films captured in Al-Qaeda camps following the U.S. invasion of Afghanistan in 2001 contain footage of Sarin being employed experimentally on a dog, with lethal result. The experiment clearly suggests Al-Qaeda's interest in employing Sarin as a weapon, both to inflict mass casualties and to instill fear of a weapon that cannot be seen or easily detected. The effects and symptoms of Sarin exposure as described in the story are factual, and there is a considerable body of professional literature on the chemical.

The Munich Oktoberfest is the largest public fair in the world and attracts around six million international visitors a year during its sixteen-day run. As described, beer from the six major Munich breweries is dispensed to the thirsty in a series of enormous tents. The Oktoberfest was the target of a terrorist bomb attack in 1980 that killed thirteen people and wounded hundreds. That attack was attributed to neo-Nazi elements.

Regarding the introductory episode of the novel, on July 17, 2003, a long-buried U.S. bomb from the Second World War exploded near the Salzburg train station (where the author was regularly underway during the period). Two of the technicians attempting to deactivate the bomb were killed and another seriously wounded. Could this entombed bomb have claimed the final casualties of World War II?